P9-AQE-841

THE
RISING TIDE

THE
RISING TIDE

SAM LLOYD

SCARLET
NEW YORK

THE RISING TIDE

Scarlet
An Imprint of Penzler Publishers
58 Warren Street
New York, N.Y. 10007

Copyright © 2021 by Sam Lloyd

First Published by Transworld Publishers, a
division of The Random House Group Limited.

First Scarlet edition

Interior design by Charles Perry

All rights reserved. No part of this book may be reproduced in whole or in part without written permission from the publisher, except by reviewers who may quote brief excerpts in connection with a review in a newspaper, magazine, or electronic publication; nor may any part of this book be reproduced, stored in a retrieval system, or transmitted in any form or by any means electronic, mechanical, photocopying, recording, or other, without written permission from the publisher.

Library of Congress Control Number: 2021922508

Cloth ISBN: 978-1-61316-271-2
eBook ISBN: 978-1-61316-272-9

10 9 8 7 6 5 4 3 2 1

Printed in the United States of America
Distributed by W. W. Norton & Company

Dedicated to James Shrouder
and a library of memories,
past and future,
amusing and terrifying.

'The true end of tragedy is to purify the passions.'
—Aristotle

This is going to be one of those letters you'll never read. Maybe because I'll burn it. Maybe because it'll go down with the boat.

I've given this a lot of thought. If there was another way, believe me I'd try. It's tough when two people have this much shared history. It's so hard to cause pain, even short-term pain. Even if it's the right thing to do.

The coming storm will be the most difficult you'll ever face. At points, I'm sure, it'll feel unbearable. You'll think it's too much, that you don't have the strength to cope. But I <u>know</u> you, Lucy. Your strength runs deep. You've survived tough times before and you'll survive this.

Pain can be purifying—do you remember telling me that? Suffering can be kathartic.

At first, you'll find this hard to forgive. But give it a year, maybe two, and you'll think differently. You'll look back and see I was right. That this was the best solution.

For all of us.

PART I

ONE

1

The news doesn't strike cleanly, like a guillotine's blade. There's no quick severing. Nothing so merciful. *This* news is a slovenly traveller, dragging its feet, gradually revealing its horrors. And it announces itself first with violence—the urgent hammering of fists on Lucy Locke's front door.

2

Lucy's in the study, hunched over Daniel's laptop. Breath whistles past her teeth as she frantically casts about. Onscreen is her husband's company balance sheet. Spread across the desk is a mess of bank statements, invoices and scribbled notes. Around her feet, cardboard folders spill over with receipts.

She's tempted to cram every scrap of paperwork into the fireplace and toss in a match, but that won't help them. If there's something here she's overlooked, it's vital she finds it.

Lucy's wet hair leaks cold water down her spine. The study is unheated and the bath towel around her torso offers little comfort. In the hall, the barometer mercury is plunging. No storm has yet broken. But gunmetal clouds, rolling in from the Atlantic, are pregnant with threat.

This doesn't feel like the end of the world. Not quite, not yet. In their nine years together, it isn't the first crisis they've weathered. She's saved him before. She knows she can save him again.

Lucy rocks back in the chair, tries to control her breathing. Glances around the grand old Georgian room.

On a side table stands a silver plastic photo frame, a relic from back when they were penniless. She's bought Daniel plenty of others since, but he's never replaced the original. In this house, items with little value gain it as they age: the scarred furniture, the chipped crockery, the art on the walls; all of it connects to a thousand different memories, priceless artefacts of the Locke family story.

The frame holds a photo of all four of them—Lucy and Daniel, Billie and Fin—taken six years ago on Penleith Beach. Fin's in a sand-crusted Babygro. Billie sits cross-legged beside him, an elfin twelve-year-old in a neoprene shorty. Daniel—in faded board shorts and nothing else—crouches over a foil barbecue. Summer sun has caramelized his skin. His eyes aren't on the steaks but the ocean, as if something out there has caught his attention.

Lucy, just into her thirties, wears the world's most contented grin. Her denim cut-offs and tie-fronted bikini top reveal flesh as smooth and supple as a seal's. Two belt-hoop stretchmarks on her abdomen are subtle evidence of her motherhood. Above them, her breasts are a far more obvious sign.

She's always teased Daniel about that, claiming they're the reason he keeps this photo close. And yet in truth she loves the image too. She can't remember who took it, but the photographer captured something of them Lucy has always felt, yet never managed to express.

When she realizes how tightly her jaw is clenched, she turns away. Too hard, suddenly, to contemplate her family.

Balanced on the desk is a stack of unopened post. Lucy begins to tear through it, alert for further shocks. The first three envelopes yield junk mail. The fourth is from an insurance company. She checks the date—flinches when she realizes how long it's been sitting here. When she scans the policy document, the muscles of her abdomen pull tight.

Lucy's gaze returns to the balance sheet, then the framed photograph where Daniel is looking out to sea. Only last night, in the darkness of their bedroom, she'd entwined herself around him and vowed they'd survive this. He'd muttered a reply, rolled on to his side. And Lucy, sensing his despondency, had felt her eyes fill with tears.

Beside that photo of their family is a time-battered Polaroid, creased and sun-faded. In it, eight-year-old Daniel, all elbows and knees, stands on the steps of Plymouth's Glenthorne Hostel for Boys. Lucy recognizes his expression. He was wearing it the day they met: a startled-prey wariness more suited to an animal than a human; a heart-rending fusion of fear and hope and longing.

That day, she'd felt a powerful compulsion to put her arms around him.

Whenever Lucy sees this photo—the earliest image of her husband that exists—she feels exactly the same way.

On the steps beside Daniel stands Nick, broader and taller despite their similar age. Whereas Daniel squints at the camera, Nick glowers. His arm is thrown protectively around his smaller friend. Lucy knows more than most how it's lingered there ever since.

Scowling, she rips open the remaining envelope. Realizes, too late, that the letter's addressed to Billie. Tossing it down, Lucy re-checks the balance sheet. She makes a fist, thumping the desk so hard its drawer rattles in its frame.

And then she hears a response, echoing along the hall. But it isn't another drawer rattling. It's the front door. Someone is pounding upon it.

3

Lucy blinks. Tilts her head. A cold pearl of water rolls down her neck. The sound of hammering ends as abruptly as it began. All she hears now is the tick of the wall clock.

A commotion at the window draws her attention. She turns in time to see a herring gull land on the frame. The bird is so large that it struggles to balance, flapping its wings for stability. It peers in at her with one pale eye. Then it taps its beak against the glass.

Her great-aunt Iris, since succumbing to dementia, has grown darkly superstitious of seagulls—doesn't like any part of them touching her house. Lucy glances away from this one to the clock. Just past two. Roughly an hour since high tide.

Did she imagine what she just heard? Nobody in this family uses the front door, nor anyone else who knows them well. Good friends and associates, in long-standing tradition, don't even announce their arrival; they wander in through the kitchen, reach for the biscuit barrel, whatever makes them feel at home.

The hammering resumes. Four emphatic bangs. With a cry, the herring gull flaps off the ledge. Lucy stands, gripping the bath towel to her chest. She moves to the study door.

Looks out.

Like the rest of this sprawling clifftop residence, the hall is grander in dimensions than repair. Duck-egg-blue walls—long in need of repainting—support a chipped yet finely stuccoed ceiling. On the parquet floor, a threadbare runner does little to deaden sound.

The house stood abandoned on Mortis Point for two decades before they bought it. Four years on, Lucy knows that even the pittance they paid was a ransom. Wild Ridge, as the place is named, is still salvageable, but they'll never afford the repairs. Certainly not now.

The front door is an immense mahogany slab. A transom window above it admits a rectangle of slate sky. The door itself features two panels of sand-blasted glass. As Lucy watches, a shadow moves across them. Proof, if any were needed, that the interruption wasn't illusory.

She calls up her mental map of Skentel, populating it with the people she loves most. Fin at Headlands Junior School, where she dropped him just before nine. Billie at college in Redlecker, further along the coast. Daniel in his workshop, on the backshore above Penleith Beach.

Lucy steps into the hall and pads along it. The hammering starts up again, so violently that the door shakes in its frame. From the force of the blows, and the size of the shadow, she assumes her visitor is a man. Could it be a creditor? A bailiff? One of Daniel's customers, intending to surprise him at home?

As she draws closer, the banging falls silent once more. Her fingers reach out, touch the brass latch. Hesitate there.

Something about this feels wrong. Portentous. To be avoided at all costs. Lucy's never been one to doubt her gut, but she can't ignore the intrusion. This is her home—until someone with authority says otherwise. No way she'll cower inside it.

Flipping up the latch, she hauls the door wide.

4

It's Bee.

Lucy's so surprised that she glances up the lane, expecting to spot an accomplice. Bizarre that someone so petite could create such a racket. Or cast such a deceptive shadow.

Dressed in black with bubblegum-pink hair, Bee peers up at her through lashes as extravagant as a giraffe's. What she lacks in height she compensates for in girth—wide hips, heavy shoulders, a pleasing roundness of belly. On her T-shirt is a rainbow unicorn with the legend: *I DON'T BELIEVE IN YOU EITHER*. Lucy's known her five years, ever since Bee walked into the Drift Net and demanded a job.

Bee jerks backwards when she sees Lucy's towel and wet hair. Her bangles ring like windchimes. 'Hey, Luce. Daniel in?'

Lucy's fingers fall from the latch. 'Bee?' Again, she glances along the lane. All she sees is Bee's electric scooter, leaning against a hedge. 'Who's running the Drift Net?'

'Eh? Oh, I left Tommo in charge.'

'Tommo? Is that— Do you trust him?'

Bee regards her strangely. 'Dude, he's my *boy*friend. Of course I trust him.'

Still, Tommo's a fresh catch, landed just six weeks ago. Lucy's only met him once, and hardly in the best of circumstances. 'Does he know how to—'

'I called you loads,' Bee says. 'Thought I'd better hop up. They found the *Lazy Susan*.'

That throws her for a second. She's never quite got used to the name of Daniel's boat. *Their* boat, she corrects. Although if ownership were awarded on maintenance effort, Daniel could probably claim it. Lucy may have scrubbed barnacles one or two seasons, diving beneath the hull in full scuba, but it's nothing to the effort Daniel's sunk in. Hard work and heartbreak's a price you don't see going all-in on a forty-year-old yacht. A saner couple might have learned from the experience of renovating Wild Ridge. Not them.

'They *found* her?' Lucy frowns. 'Who? Found her where?'

'Just drifting, I think. Somewhere out to sea. They're towing her in right now.' Bee cranes her neck, angling for a peek down the hall. 'So is Daniel here? I mean . . . shit, I know she's not *his* boat, especially.' She pulls out her vape and takes a hit, exhaling strawberry-scented smoke. Again, she glances past Lucy's shoulder into the house.

Lucy sidesteps, blocking her view. And feels instantly strange. But the study is visible from the front door. She doesn't want Bee to see what she's been doing. 'Are you saying someone stole her? From the dock?'

'I've no idea. Some guy came in, talking about what he heard. Coast-guard chatter, I think. Dunno much more than that, really, but I figured you guys should know.' She shifts her weight from one Doc Marten to the other. 'You . . . um . . . you good?'

Lucy feels another bead of water climb down her spine. The day feels like it's unravelling. 'Yeah, look. Thanks, Bee. I'd better throw on some clothes, find out what's happening.'

'You want me to come with?'

She shakes her head. 'Can you get back to the Drift Net? I'm sure Tommo's coping fine, but I'd feel better if you were there.'

Bee takes another hit of strawberries. 'Sure, dude. I'll skedaddle.' She pivots and trips down the path.

They found the Lazy Susan. *Just drifting, I think. Somewhere out to sea.*

Lucy glances behind her. Stalking along the hall to the study is a drag-gle of wet footprints. Seeing them makes her shiver.

By the front gate, Bee drags her scooter from the bush. She hops on the deck plate and hums away down the lane.

Lucy stands in the doorway, watching. Three herring gulls fly over the house from the west. She knows what it means, a trio of those birds. Clos-ing the door, she rushes back along the hall.

5

Plans change, and now Lucy's plans have changed too. She hurries to the living room at the back of the house. It's a cavernous space, dense with shadow. The rugs, bookcases and cracked-leather Chesterfields help anchor it. Dominating the far wall is a cast-iron mantel festooned with Gothic finials and pilasters. The air smells of woodsmoke, mixed with damp loam from the many houseplants Daniel grows. One corner's so dense with foliage it looks like it's been claimed by jungle.

Velvet drapes have been drawn across two huge windows bisected by stone mullions. Lucy crosses the room and yanks them apart. Light floods in. The view is astonishing.

Wild Ridge stands on the west-facing peninsula of Mortis Point, four hundred feet above the sea. The back lawn, flanked by cypresses and stone pines, recedes to a ring of natural terraces terminating in ver-tical cliff faces; beyond them, wild sea. Visible to the north is the crescent of sand forming Penleith Beach. Far below the peninsula's southern flank lies Skentel.

From here, Lucy has a bird's-eye view of the town. Its whitewashed buildings cluster around a steep cobbled street barely wide enough for a car. A curving stone breakwater protects its tiny harbour from the Atlantic.

This close to high tide, seawater slaps the quay. Unusually, most of the fishing boats are still tied up. The floating dock is cluttered with yachts. Smaller craft bob in the harbour, lashed to orange mooring buoys.

Lucy sees the lifeboat station, the Norman church and the Drift Net's sloped roof. Out beyond the breakwater, chugging into harbour, she spots a Tamar-class lifeboat. It's not the Skentel boat—this one must be from a station further along the coast. Towed behind it is the *Lazy Susan*.

Their navy-hulled yacht sits far too low in the water. Waves are breaking over the name painted on her bow. Two RNLI crew stand in the cockpit. The mainsail is furled, likewise the jib.

Something greasy hatches in Lucy's stomach. Snatching binoculars from the cocktail cabinet, she takes a closer look. One of the RNLI crew is Beth McKaylin, owner of the Penny Moon campsite. The other volunteer Lucy doesn't recognize. She snags the landline handset and calls Daniel.

Down on Penleith Beach, mobile reception isn't great. After a two-second delay the call goes to voicemail: *'Hi, you've reached Daniel Locke of Locke-Povey Marine . . .'*

Lucy waits for the beep. 'Hey, it's me. Something's up. Call me straight back when you get this.'

People are coming on to the waterfront, now. Someone points at the Drift Net. Someone else raises a finger towards Mortis Point.

They found the Lazy Susan. *Just drifting, I think. Somewhere out to sea.*

Lucy lowers the binoculars. If she leaves in the next few minutes, she'll beat the lifeboat to the quay. Upstairs, she throws on dungarees and boots. Back in the hall, she grabs her keys from the console table. In the black-spotted wall mirror, she catches her reflection. Her face betrays her disquiet, rust-flecked brown eyes showing too much white. The pallid light has bleached her skin. Her hair, hanging in wet blonde ringlets, offers barely any contrast. She looks like something washed up by the tide from a place deep down dark.

By the front door, she taps the barometer's glass housing. The mercury plummets further. No wonder most of the fishing fleet's still in harbour. Everyone's been warned of what's coming. The rapidly changing pressure suggests something even worse.

Outside, a salt wind hisses among the cypresses. Lucy climbs into her

Citroën and guns the engine. Her mobile phone's on the passenger seat where she left it. She taps the screen and it wakes: no messages; no calls; no reception. Tyres spitting stones, she reverses off the drive.

6

The lane takes her east. Little chance of meeting traffic on the peninsula. She drives as fast as she dares.

Reaching the coastal road, Lucy heads south. She doesn't take the Skentel turn-off, which leads down to the harbour via the cobbled main street. Instead she uses Smuggler's Tumble, a series of unpaved switchbacks dropping through pine forest to the shore. At the bottom she parks on the gravel circle where anglers sometimes leave their cars.

The air reeks of pine sap and seaweed. As Lucy emerges on to the shingle, a chill wind snatches at her clothes. This close, the ocean looks oily and dark. The swell is far higher than it seemed from Mortis Point. Breakers boom as they collapse into foam.

Crunching along the beach, Lucy checks her watch. Quarter past two. Only a few hours until the storm makes landfall. She thinks about trying Daniel again, but her phone is still flatlining. Reaching the breakwater's shoulder, she climbs the steps cut into its face.

A crowd has gathered on the quay. Even outside tourist season, lifeboat launches attract interest. All eyes are on the Tamar-class as it tows the stricken yacht through the entrance channel.

Lucy hurries along the breakwater, her eyes on the oncoming boats. She presses through the gathered onlookers, catching snatches of conversation.

'. . . *said they own the Drift Net* . . .'

'. . . *just in time, if you ask me* . . .'

'. . . *lucky it's still pretty calm* . . .'

Water spurts in a thick gush from the *Lazy Susan*'s bilge outlet. A salvage pump, presumably installed by the lifeboat crew, discharges seawater via a hose slung over the side.

Beth McKaylin stands at the bow rail. As the yacht closes with the breakwater, she tosses a dock line to a harbour official. More lines are thrown. On the lifeboat, a crewman detaches the towline.

'Lucy! Hey, Luce!'

She turns to see Matt Guinness edging through the crowd. Matt's an old classmate—an original resident of Skentel. Straggle-haired and balding, he lives with his mother in a fisherman's cottage overlooking the harbour. Judging from his polo shirt, he's currently working at the Goat Hotel on the high street.

'Been looking out for you,' he says, eyes bright with the prospect of sharing bad news. 'The *Lazy Susan*. Ain't that your latest fella's boat?'

No point clarifying she's been with Daniel nine years. 'Do you know what happened?'

Matt scratches the wisps of beard sprouting from his chin. Unlike his hair, his fingernails—long and curved like the claws of a burrowing mole—are scrupulously clean. When he grins, he reveals a lifetime of bad dentistry. 'Maybe *someone* didn't check their mooring lines.'

Lucy shakes her head. The harbour water churns white as the lifeboat's engines reverse thrust. 'You think she floated all the way round the breakwater without anyone noticing? Kind of unlikely, isn't it?'

'Maybe, maybe not. Weirder things have happened.'

'Bee said she was found drifting in open sea.'

Behind her a vehicle horn honks, followed by a brief squawk of siren. Matt's gaze settles on something over her shoulder. 'Uh-oh,' he says, grin widening. 'Looks like Hubby's got some explaining to do.'

Lucy turns to see a Land Rover Defender in coastguard livery nudging through the crowd. She's not going to get anything useful from Matt Guinness. Excusing herself, she pushes through the onlookers. She's tempted to follow the breakwater to where the *Lazy Susan* is being tied up, but the quickest way to find out what's happening is to track down her ex.

7

Skentel's lifeboat station sits high above the quay, on a coursed limestone base that juts from the cliffs of Mortis Point. Its slipway extends across the water, past the low-tide point. From the quay, a switchback metal staircase climbs sixty feet to the entrance deck. Lucy hurries up it.

She's halfway to the top when sound explodes overhead. A coastguard helicopter, nosecone and tail boom painted bright red, blasts over Mortis Point. It follows the shoreline south, anti-collision beacon flashing.

Thanks to Fin's collection of plastic kits, Lucy recognizes the model: a twin-engine AW189. It's a beast of a machine, eight tons in weight, bristling with search-and-rescue apparatus. The whistle of its turbines competes with the clatter-roar of its rotor blades.

Down in the harbour the Tamar-class lifeboat throttles up, heading back out to sea. On the quay, the crowd continues to build. Lucy sees activity along the breakwater and on the floating dock. Some of the boats are getting ready to cast off.

Her unease grows. She climbs higher. Around her, the protective cage sings and vibrates. When she reaches the next switchback, she notices a police patrol car parked beside the coastguard Land Rover.

At last she arrives at the RNLI boathouse's decked entranceway. Alec Paul, in T-shirt and salopettes, is standing outside the glass doors. Above his head, the sky has darkened to slate.

8

Alec's a bear: six foot three, shaggy brown beard, shoulders like oak barrels. He drops a meaty paw around Lucy's shoulders and guides her to the entrance.

'Jake said you'd come. Asked me to look out for you. He's been trying your mobile for the last hour.'

'I was at home. You recovered the *Lazy Susan*?'

Alec's brow clenches, as if he wasn't expecting the question. He looks over the railing. 'Those guys are from Appledore. Decided they couldn't leave her out there—not with what's coming. Too dangerous for other boats.'

'Is there much damage?'

His hand slides off her shoulder. He's full-on frowning now. 'I couldn't say.'

Lucy casts a glance at the yacht. 'She's sitting pretty low, but at least they've got the pumps going. This storm front—we're lucky the sea's still as calm as it is.'

'Yeah.' Alec takes her arms. 'Listen. Are you OK?'

Lucy thinks of the paperwork strewn across Daniel's desk; of everything they've built these last nine years; how, until only a few weeks ago, it felt like a fortress.

There's a sound in her ears like a far-off whistle. 'The police are here,' she says. 'I guess that means she was stolen.'

'Lucy, I'm not sure what you've heard. What *have* you heard?'

Something's crawling in her stomach now. Alec's wearing an expression she can't place. 'Bee said she was found drifting. Guy I know reckons she slipped her moorings but that can't be true. Someone must've stolen her. Someone must've sneaked—'

'She wasn't stolen.'

'—onboard and managed to hot-wire the engine or some—'

'Lucy, Daniel took her out.'

She flinches, shakes her head, as if a fly just swooped into her ear. *'Daniel?* But Daniel's at work. He left before I took Fin to school.'

'I'm sorry, I really am—but Daniel maydayed from the *Lazy Susan*.'

Lucy's throat clenches. It feels like someone's squeezing it. Her right hand finds her wedding band and twists it round her ring finger. She looks past Alec to the coastguard helicopter banking west, out to sea. Her gaze drops to the harbour, to the flotilla of small boats being readied; to the Tamar-class lifeboat, out beyond the breakwater, its propellers churning a white wake. Despite the gunmetal clouds, the falling pressure, the day still seems preternaturally calm.

The ringing in her ears intensifies. She weaves around Alec to the glass doors.

TWO

1

The entrance to Skentel's RNLI boathouse is dominated by its hand-painted service boards. They detail a century's span of notable rescues. Beyond them, a cavernous boat hall is ringed by two railed walkways. Right now, the roller-shutter door is up, exposing the giant steel slipway descending to the sea. In the nine years since Lucy's relationship with Jake Farrell ended, the place has changed hardly at all.

She finds Jake in the ops room, crouched over the VHF radio. A laptop shows graphics of the rapidly changing conditions. Jake straightens when he sees her. Since the split, he's never quite learned how to handle their encounters. He rolls his shoulders, rubbing his close-shaved scalp.

'Just tell me, Jake,' she asks. 'What happened? Where's Daniel?'

He motions Alec to replace him at the desk. 'Keep an ear out,' he says. 'Grab me if there's news.' Then he steers Lucy along the corridor to the changing room. 'Coastguard picked up a distress call from your husband, earlier.'

'And? Is he OK?'

'We don't know. We're in the—'

13

'You don't *know*?'

'Our lifeboat located your yacht, but the crew found no one onboard.'

Her ears roar, air rushing into a vacuum. 'So where's Daniel?'

'That's what we're trying—'

'He's still missing?'

'Right now, we're—'

'Have you heard from him *since*?'

Jake holds up his hands to silence her. 'Lucy, take a breath, OK? Listen to what I'm saying. Daniel put out a Mayday around twelve thirty. Twelve thirty-seven, to be exact. Said he was taking on water and needed assistance. We don't maintain a headset watch here. First we heard about it was a request from Milford coastguard, asking us to send a boat. Our DLA authorized the Tamar to launch. Crew went out twelve minutes later.

'Daniel stopped broadcasting before he sent his position, but the coastguard's direction finder picked up his transmission bearing. Still took us a while to find the *Lazy Susan*, even with that. Those currents are strong and she was just drifting, seven miles out, sails packed away like they'd never been used. Our offshore boat got a couple of crew onboard with a salvage pump, but they couldn't find hide nor hair of Daniel. When we relayed that, the coastguard bumped the priority. We left a crew member with the yacht and redeployed.

'You probably saw the helicopter. We've launched our inshore D-class to assist. Clovelly and Bude have sent their inshore vessels too. Plus Tamars from Appledore and Padstow. Good thing is, the weather's still holding. I don't know what it'll be like in a few hours, but right now we've a window. There's a small fleet heading out from Skentel. Fishing boats, yachts—pretty much the whole town is mobilizing.'

Daniel in the water. It's too distressing to take in. She shuts her mouth, opens it. *Focus, Lucy.* 'How long, exactly, since he made contact?'

'I didn't hear the broadcast. But he wasn't talking long.'

She looks at her watch. 'So—an hour forty-five?'

'There or thereabouts.'

Her throat tightens further. 'That water's *cold*, Jake.'

'Your boat has a life raft?'

'A Seago six-berth, bright yellow. Immersion suits too—enough for the whole family.'

He nods. 'We've got the very best people out searching.'

Lucy's gaze falls to Jake's sweater. She recognizes it—a cream rope-knit from a decade ago. The sleeve has a small repair, which she made during a brief spell of lunacy when mending his clothes seemed romantic. Already, her ties to reality feel frayed. For a moment, the sight of those clumsy stitches throws her completely. With effort, she swallows. 'Find him, Jake, please. Not just for me. He's Fin's dad.'

Again, her fingers reach for her wedding band. It's a cheap thing, really. Some kind of base metal. Every so often it goes green and she has to scrub it to restore the shine, but she's resisted Daniel's offers to buy a new one. As always, in this relationship, items with little value gain it as they age. Her wedding band may have cost a song, but it represents something priceless. She still remembers the moment he put it on her finger; that sense of a puzzle piece clicking into place; gears, somewhere in the universe, quietly meshing.

All at once, Lucy's back in her kitchen up on Mortis Point and time has rewound six hours. Fin sits at the breakfast table, bare legs swinging beneath it. He's working on a bowl of Frosties. Open beside him is his Match Attax folder.

'*Mummy*,' he says. He rabbit-wrinkles his nose until his glasses sit higher up his face. 'Eden Hazard has an *attack* of ninety-four, but a *defence* of forty-three. How can he be so good at *one* thing and so *terrible* at another?'

Since he learned to talk, Fin's injected melodrama into every sentence he's uttered. Just hearing him speak ignites Lucy's heart. She has no idea who Eden Hazard is. When she leans over Fin's shoulder, she sees what she thinks is a Real Madrid kit.

'Everyone's good at some things and bad at others,' she says, as Daniel enters the room. 'Take Daddy, for example.'

Daniel stops in the doorway, staring. His eyes are bloodshot. It looks like he's fighting a hangover on top of a poor night's sleep.

'Daddy's a genius at building boats and giving tickles,' she continues.

'He's not quite as clever at kissing his wife and son when he sees them at breakfast.'

Fin snorts with laughter. But Lucy's still looking at her husband and she knows her joke's fallen flat. When it works, this pantomime jollity can fool anyone. When it doesn't, it feels like everything in the world is collapsing.

Abruptly, Daniel jerks back to life. He bends over Fin's chair and plants a kiss on the boy's head. 'Love you, buddy.'

'You want some coffee?' Lucy asks.

'Thanks, no. Heading out early today.'

'You're leaving now?'

He glances through the window. Over Mortis Point, the sky's so dark with cloud it looks like dawn hasn't broken. 'Thought I'd go down while it's quiet. Get a few loose ends tied up.'

Her jaw tightens when she hears that. Because Daniel's task, later this morning, will bring him close to breaking. If only she could carry some of the weight. 'Better take a jacket. This storm won't wait much longer.'

His eyes are still on the clouds, as if he's searching them for something.

'Daniel?'

'Huh?'

Lucy raises an eyebrow, hoping to strike a more light-hearted tone in front of Fin. 'Kiss?'

No response. She waits, head tilted. More of the pantomime.

At the table, Fin puts down his spoon. He looks at each of his parents. '*Come* on, Daddy,' he says. 'Don't leave Mummy hanging.'

Daniel turns from the window and studies his son. Then he crosses the kitchen and kisses Lucy. His lips feel bloodless. Cold as the ocean.

She thinks about pulling him into a hug and repeating her vow from last night—that they'll survive the coming storm, that their love is a bulwark against all the bad weather heading their way. Instead, sensing his fragility, she rubs his arm. 'Listen, Goof,' she whispers. 'I swear this'll be OK.'

He nods and walks to the back door. 'Bye,' he says, and steps into the early-morning dark without looking back.

Cold air licks into the room, fading like smoke.

'Shall I tell you a *story*, Mummy? This one's *very* interesting. Yesterday, we had a *new* girl in our class. *Her* name was *Jessica*.'

Lucy stares at the back door. Outside, she hears the diesel clatter of Daniel's Volvo. *I love you*, she should have said. *None of this is your fault.*

'And do you know what *else*, Mummy? *Last* year we had a girl *leave* our class. And do you know what *her* name was? Do you *know*, Mummy?'

Lucy touches her lips where Daniel's mouth left its mark. Something in her chest quivers. Strange, how all her breath is in her throat.

'*Her* name was Jessica *too*. We swapped *one* Jessica for *another* Jessica. The *old* Jessica left, and a *new* Jessica took her place.'

The Volvo crunches over the driveway stones. Lucy imagines Daniel behind the wheel, still wearing that vacant look. It feels, recently, like Fin's anecdote happened to the man she loves. The old Daniel left and a new Daniel took his place. Only one person to blame for that, and it's not her husband.

'Do you know what *I* think, Mummy? *I* think they had to wait a whole year until they found someone with exactly the same name so Miss Clay didn't have to write out a new *locker* sticker. That's what *I* think, anyway, and that's what *I'm* going to say if anyone asks *me* about it.'

'If anyone asks you about what, Scout?'

That voice isn't Lucy's but Billie's. The girl bounds in, barefoot. As always, Lucy feels like she's viewing a younger reflection; her daughter shares the same brown eyes, upturned nose and square jaw. A neon-green T-shirt hangs off her shoulder. It exposes a strap of patterned bra and part of a dark tattoo. Her black gym shorts are cut to mid-thigh, bisecting another tattoo. A fabric band holds Billie's blonde bob off her face.

'Why'd you call me *Scout*?' Fin asks, stirring his Frosties.

'It's from a film.'

Lucy rolls her eyes. 'It's from a *book*.'

'Oops, I'm in trouble,' Billie tells her brother. 'Like that time you asked to dress up as Jack Sparrow for World Book Day.'

'Jack Sparrow's a *cool dude*,' Fin says. 'A *booty* pirate.'

Billie snorts with laughter. 'Where did you get *that* one from, little man? No, doesn't matter. My point was, Jack didn't come from a kid's book.'

Fin's gaze moves from his sister to the window. 'Did you know there's a *storm* coming, Billo?'

'Yup. I hear it's going to be a real monster.' She grabs her mascara bottle and plonks down opposite. 'What they call a threat to life.'

'*Threat* to *life*,' he repeats, testing the words on his tongue. Then he munches a spoonful of Frosties.

'After college, straight back home, OK?' Lucy tells Billie.

'Sure.'

'I mean it. Weather's due to hit late afternoon. I want you both here with me, baking or playing board games—'

'Or hiding under a table,' the girl interjects.

Lucy grins. 'Or playing board games under a table.'

'Or *baking* under a table, Mummy.'

'Great idea, Scout.'

The memory dissolves. Abruptly, Lucy's back inside the RNLI boathouse, shivering under Jake's gaze.

He frowns, touches her bare arm. 'Jesus, Luce, you're *freezing*.' From a peg, he grabs a yellow Helly Hansen crew jacket. He drapes it around her shoulders. She pushes her hands through the sleeves. 'You want a coffee to warm you up? Tea?'

Lucy thinks of those cold Atlantic waves. She shakes her head. 'I need to be out there. *Doing* something.'

'Should I phone someone for you?'

'Thanks, no. Look, I know you'll do a great job. Please, call me—the moment you have news.'

2

Outside, the sky is noticeably darker, the sea marbled with white water. At the rail enclosing the entrance deck, Lucy looks down at the quay. The harbour is emptying of boats. Fishing vessels and yachts are fanning out past Mortis Point.

The *Lazy Susan* bobs beside the breakwater, salvage pump still spitting. Beth McKaylin, the RNLI volunteer, is standing on the breakwater's inner wall. She's talking to the coastguard, the harbour master and two police officers.

Where are you, Daniel? Where did you go?

All morning Lucy's been trying to figure out how to save him. Is this his attempt to save her? To save their house, and Billie's and Fin's lives in Skentel? By vanishing into a storm and bequeathing them a pay-out?

She can't believe that. Won't believe it.

Because their house is just a house. And they can pick up their lives anywhere, but they can't be a family without him.

Tasting bile, Lucy hauls out her phone. She often gets a bar or two of reception on the quay. Right now, even that has gone. When she peers back over the rail, she notices Noemie Farrell outside the Drift Net, snug inside a grey woollen poncho. Lucy calls out to her friend.

At the bottom of the switchback steps they embrace. Then Noemie pulls back. 'My God. I've been trying to call. Where've you been?'

'I just finished talking to your brother.'

'*Jake?*' Noemie blows out a breath. 'Right, Jesus, so you know. I'm so sorry, Luce. It's ridiculous. I didn't believe it when I heard. When I couldn't get hold of you, I came straight down. You just know Daniel's going to be out there somewhere, floating around in that swanky life raft, embarrassed to hell about all the fuss. Probably why he hasn't shown up yet.'

Lucy's jaw muscles clench. It's good to see Noemie, but her forced jollity is awful.

'Did Jake have any update?' Noemie asks. 'I know a lot of the fishing boys just headed out.'

'No one's heard from Daniel since the distress call.'

'When was that?'

'Around half twelve, Jake said.'

The brief silence is loaded with meaning. Noemie's tight smile can't paper over it. 'He only bought the life raft recently, didn't he?'

'It's pretty much brand new.'

'Doesn't it have its own fresh-water system? Probably even churns out a decent latte.'

'Location light, thermal floor, ballast pockets, torch and signal mirror.' Lucy grimaces. Joining Noemie in this optimistic little deception feels like a mockery. Abruptly, she recalls something else from the Seago sales brochure. The realization is a knife sliding between her ribs.

'They'll find him,' Noemie says, turning her eyes to the sea. 'I know they will.'

Doubtless she also knows—just like Lucy and everyone else around here—how strong the currents are along this stretch of coast, how brutal the North Atlantic is in late winter. Skentel, after all, has a one-thousand-year tradition of losing its residents to the sea.

'I haven't seen him since Billie's party,' Noemie adds. 'How's he been?'

'Fine,' Lucy lies. 'Better. Much better, actually.'

'What about things with Nick? And the business generally? Did Daniel—'

'I need to speak to the coastguard,' Lucy says. 'Beth McKaylin, too.'

Noemie hesitates, nods. 'In that case I'd better tag along.'

They cross the quay and walk out along the breakwater. The *Lazy Susan* exhibits no signs of damage. Forty years old, with a fibreglass hull as tough as a Sherman tank, most of the essentials have long been replaced. Everything looks orderly and neat, just as it should.

As Lucy approaches, the group beside the yacht breaks off its discussion.

Beth McKaylin is first to speak, eyeing Lucy's borrowed RNLI jacket with obvious disapproval. 'You're bloody lucky we found her. Another ten minutes and she'd have been on the bottom.'

Among Skentel's natives, Beth's surliness is well known. But this is personal—the pair have history. Anger rises like a welt in Lucy's throat. 'I don't give a shit about the boat,' she says. 'Daniel's still out there.'

'Aye, and we'll find him, sure enough—if that's what he wants.'

Lucy stares, outraged. Chilling, how quickly everyone—from her best friend to Beth McKaylin—is groping towards a judgement. Only moments ago she'd wondered if Daniel's disappearance was deliberate herself. But not because he'd abandoned them. Quite the opposite.

Before she can defend her husband, one of the coastguard officials clears his throat. 'I'm Sean Rowland, station officer in Redlecker. I take it you're Daniel's partner?'

Rowland's hand, when she shakes it, is reassuringly coarse. 'Lucy Locke. I'm Daniel's wife.'

'This is your boat?'

'Both of ours, yes.'

He nods encouragingly. 'The direction finder calculated your husband's bearing, even though he didn't report it. That helped us plot the search area. Obviously, we've already found the yacht. He can't have drifted too far.'

'There's a storm coming.'

Rowland checks the sky. 'Just means we'll have to work faster to wrap this up. You only need to look around to see the effort going into finding him. Daniel's an experienced helmsman?'

'Very.'

A thought resurfaces. Lucy didn't want to confront it earlier. Now she has no choice. Because as well as the myriad features she listed to Noemie, the Seago life raft is equipped with three red hand flares and two parachute rockets. To Rowland, she asks, 'Has anyone out there seen a flare?'

'Nothing's been reported that I know.'

Lucy lets that sink in. A wave slaps the breakwater's outer wall; salt spray stings her cheeks. Only six weeks since the night she and Daniel sat up there, legs dangling, as snow fell on the ocean. Fur-lined parkas, champagne flutes borrowed from the Drift Net, a deluge of flakes so beautiful it rendered them both speechless.

She glances at the *Lazy Susan*, tries to silence the buzzing in her head. 'I'd better take a look down below. See if there's—'

'Probably best if you didn't.' The female police officer steps forward. She's taller than her colleague. Blonde hair, wide hips. 'Not just yet. We're still piecing together what happened.'

'But Daniel may have left a note. Something that'll—'

Beth McKaylin grunts. 'Why would anyone leave a note on a sinking boat?'

'Unless I'm *blind*, she hasn't sunk,' Lucy snaps. 'And there's all kinds of reasons he—'

'There was no note. The hatch was open when we found her. I went down and had a good nose about. Lot of wood needs drying out down there, but that's about all you'll find.'

The thought of Beth McKaylin poking around their private space makes Lucy's skin prickle. 'What about our life raft? Did you find that?'

Clear, from Beth's expression, that she never looked. Frustrated, Lucy turns to Rowland. 'Daniel keeps a six-berth Seago life raft onboard. Bright yellow, size of a small car when inflated, big flashing SOLAS light on top. We should find out whether it was launched, don't you think?'

'She's right,' Rowland says. 'Lifeboat crews need to know. The chopper, too.'

'Where's it usually stowed?' the officer asks.

Lucy points at the *Lazy Susan*'s cockpit. 'Either the port or starboard lockers. If you could just let me—'

'Wait here.'

The woman retreats along the breakwater, talking into her radio. A minute later she's back. From her utility belt she pulls two latex gloves and snaps them on. Then she steps on to the yacht, clambers into the cockpit and crouches in front of the port locker. 'It's padlocked. In fact, they both are.'

Lucy's stomach flops. No chance, in an emergency, that Daniel would have reattached a padlock, but she still has to check. 'Here.' She lobs her keys across the gap. 'The small silver one.'

Moments later the officer raises the locker's lid. 'Describe this thing.'

'Looks like a large suitcase. Cream-coloured, secured by black webbing. Should be clearly labelled.'

'Nothing like that in here.'

'Check the other one.'

The officer opens the starboard locker. 'OK, I've got rope, quite a lot of it. Fire extinguisher, barbecue, petrol can. Ah, hang on. Yep. Big cream suitcase, Seago branding. "Offshore life raft", it says.'

No air, suddenly, in Lucy's chest. Beside her, Sean Rowland can't hide his dismay. The police officer steps back on to the breakwater. 'I'm sorry, Mrs Locke. I'm sure that's not what you wanted to hear. This all must be very confusing.'

Lucy nods, even though it isn't. The facts couldn't be clearer. Daniel took the *Lazy Susan* out to sea. He radioed in a distress call. And now he's missing—in the North Atlantic at its coldest, without the Seago life raft that cost them so much money.

She touches her lips, remembering Daniel's bloodless kiss at breakfast; how she never pulled him into a hug. This morning, he'd been due to announce final redundancies at Locke-Povey Marine. Last night, considering it, he'd made himself physically sick.

'Does Mr Locke have a car?'

The cry of a herring gull pulls Lucy's gaze to the quay. Until now, she hadn't given Daniel's Volvo a thought. Did he go to his workshop, like he told her? Or did he drive straight to the harbour from the house? All the marked spaces along the quay are taken. The tiny car park at its southern end is obscured by the breakwater's shoulder. Could the Volvo be there? It wasn't at the bottom of Smuggler's Tumble. There are few other places around here to leave a car.

'Mrs Locke?'

She turns and finds the male police officer staring. 'A Volvo XC90. Dark grey.'

'The big SUV?'

Lucy nods.

'I'm PC Lamb,' he says. 'This is PC Noakes. As Mr Locke went missing offshore, the coastguard's coordinating search and rescue, but we'll still need some details. Is there somewhere we could go?'

Lucy glances at the *Lazy Susan*. She's tempted to leap aboard and scramble through the hatch, just to see the cabin for herself, but how batshit crazy would that look? She needs these people onside. Her role, right now, is Daniel's trustworthy onshore representative.

Her role is to be his wife.

THREE

1

The Drift Net stands in a prime position on Skentel's quay. Wide windows either side of its front doors offer a panoramic view. Right now, the glass is hazy with condensation, evidence both of the approaching weather front and the espresso machine running at full tilt inside.

Shopfront businesses open and close with depressing regularity in Skentel. City people, disillusioned with corporate life, arrive armed with romantic ideas masquerading as business plans. They see the town in summer, heaving with tourist wallets, and decide it's the perfect location for their craft brewery, organic juice bar or boutique record shop. A grand opening follows: trays of Prosecco and faces flushed with delight. And six months later—perhaps a year if a house has been remortgaged or an inheritance spent—the stock disappears, the front door is locked and the windows become advertising hoardings for whichever travelling circus is next to visit.

In general, only two types of business survive. Local staples like the pharmacy and post office, or high-season shops that make enough during the summer months to close up in winter.

From the start, Lucy wanted to appeal to tourists and locals alike. To succeed, her business would have to be a chameleon, changing its skin with the seasons: a hub for natives to patronize and visitors to discover.

After a difficult labour, with funding that often looked precarious, the Drift Net was born. The birth trauma was nothing to the uncertainty that followed. Never, in the first six months, did Lucy believe she'd survive another year. People insisted the concept wouldn't work. That she needed to narrow her focus, temper her optimism, downsize her ambition.

And yet, somehow, the Drift Net held on. Six years later, it's expanded greatly from its initial offering—a live-music venue that doubles as gallery space for local artists. She'd seen the model work in London. Against all expectations, she made it work even better down here. These days, the Drift Net attracts bands that would never normally venture this far west. Despite the big names, Lucy's always prioritized local-grown talent. As a result, she's curated a patronage of music lovers well beyond this stretch of coast.

During the day, the Drift Net transforms into an inexpensive eatery, offering food from a constantly evolving menu. There are speaking events, RNLI fundraisers and meet-ups for those struggling with loneliness or bereavement. Lucy's worked with charities to offer placements to adults with special needs and to ex-offenders trying to change direction. Skentel's various clubs and societies use the facilities free of charge.

Lucy's been praised regularly for its success. But all she did was plant the seed and tend the shoot. The Drift Net's flourishing has far more to do with heroes like Bee—who manages it during the day—and Tyler, who takes over after sunset. One thing everyone in the town knows beyond doubt: six years after opening, the idea of Skentel without its quayside venue is unthinkable.

As Lucy pushes open the door, a fug of warm air rolls over her. She smells fresh-baked pastries and ground coffee. It's a large space, low and wide, the light honeyed from so much wood. The bar top is a single slab of oak recovered from a decommissioned naval sloop. Fairy lights hang along it, illuminating the leather-topped stools beneath.

Of the Drift Net's twenty tables, over three quarters are full. Above the whirr of the coffee grinder and the steamy exhalations of the milk frother comes the urgent murmur of conversation.

It dies the moment Lucy walks in. Obvious that news of Daniel has spread. Customers glance away when she looks at them. Unsettling, how personal tragedy is feared as contagious. A shared look, a touch, and the bad luck rubs off.

The police presence is a catalyst: within moments the chatter is back, louder than before. Carefully, she manoeuvres through it. The station clock on the far wall marks the time: twenty to three. Two hours, now, since Daniel's distress call. Lucy's fear is shrapnel inside her head.

Bee is standing behind the bar beside Tommo, her new boyfriend. Despite her unicorn T-shirt and cartoony pink hair, she couldn't look more spooked. 'Luce,' she says. 'Dude. We just heard. When I came to the house I had no idea. I'm so sorry I—'

'Don't,' Lucy says. 'Seriously. You've no reason to apologize. Listen, I need to speak to the police. Can you keep the kitchen open? The more people we get through the door, the better we can spread the word.'

'Right,' Bee says. She turns to Tommo—late thirties, soft belly, T-shirt that says, *WHEN LIFE GIVES YOU LEMONS, GRAB SALT AND TEQUILA.* 'I need to steal you a little longer.'

He nods, an obedient puppy. To Lucy, he says, 'These things are sent to test us. Be strong and you'll get through it.'

In Tommo's expression Lucy sees something that steals her breath. She watches Bee loop an arm around his waist. Then she leads her group to a table and peels off her RNLI jacket.

PC Noakes takes out a notebook. 'Mr Locke's date of birth?'

'Thirteenth of January, 1979. He's forty-two.'

'Can you give me a description?'

'Five ten, average build.'

Lucy pauses, frowns. It's a pitiful amount of detail, but when she closes her eyes, she can't visualize *her* Daniel at all, just that lost little boy from the Polaroid. It frightens her so badly her eyes snap back open.

'Hair colour?'

'Black,' she replies, gasping. 'And he has blue eyes. Slush Puppie blue, you know? Like the drink.' She shakes her head. 'I'm sorry, I . . . I'm not making much sense.'

'Any distinguishing features? Birthmarks, that kind of thing?'

The question makes her flinch. No one's going to locate Daniel thanks to a birthmark, but they might use one to identify him. Seven miles of cold ocean lie between here and where he disappeared. And the plunging mercury is evidence that something truly awful is approaching.

'My husband has a scar along his right forearm,' she says. 'About four inches long. Fluke of an anchor once ripped it open.'

Lucy touches a point on her bare arm and traces the pattern. An image forms: Daniel lying dead on a hospital gurney, the scar on his forearm lightning white against the surrounding skin. It's such a shocking picture that her chin trembles, threatens to give.

Noakes finishes writing. 'Can you tell me the last time you saw Mr Locke?'

'Please,' she says. 'Not this "Mr and Mrs" stuff. His name's Daniel. You can call me Lucy. I last saw him around eight this morning.'

'Did he give you any indication where he was going?'

Again, Lucy casts her mind back: Daniel in the kitchen, staring through the window at the gunmetal clouds. 'He told me he was going to work.'

'And where's that?'

'Locke-Povey Marine, an outfitting company. His workshop's at the top of Penleith Beach.'

'He runs it? Owns it?'

'Runs and part-owns it. His business partner is'—*a crook, a cheat, a destroyer of all things good*—'Nick Povey. *Was* Nick Povey.'

'Was?'

'They went their separate ways.'

'Mr Povey's local to here?'

'Yes.'

'You've spoken to him?'

'Not this morning.'

'You have contact details?'

'Of course.'

Noakes starts scribbling again. 'Employees?'

'Twenty or so. Although not all of them will have been in. He's . . . They're . . . downsizing.'

'You know if any of them have seen Daniel today? Or spoken to him since he left the house?'

'No one's been answering the work phone. Customers usually go through to Daniel's mobile. It's a noisy place. They don't always pick up.'

'You haven't been down?'

'I only just found out. I came straight to the quay.'

'We'll get someone over there to talk to them. And to Mr Povey, too. Mrs Locke—Lucy—was Daniel . . . Has any aspect of his recent behaviour given you cause for concern?'

The cold kiss. The chilling goodbye. The sensation, all morning, that events are running out of control.

'Not at all.'

'I'm sorry to press you—but no indications of depression, anything like that?'

'Will it affect the search?'

PC Noakes tilts her head. 'I'm sorry?'

'I know how these things work. You start thinking this was deliberate—that he sailed out there because he didn't want to be found, and it lets you stand down the search, gives you a—'

'Mrs Locke—'

'—reason to call everyone back, when Daniel *is* out there, right now, depending on us to find him, depending on—'

'Mrs *Locke*—'

'It's *LUCY!*'

She rocks backwards, shocked by her loss of control. The two police officers study her as if she's just become a lot more interesting. Glancing around, she realizes that half the people inside the Drift Net are staring.

Let them. Never before has Daniel's reputation needed protection. And now, suddenly, it does; cupped hands around a stuttering flame.

'Lucy,' Sean Rowland says. 'The coastguard is coordinating search and rescue, not the police. No one's thinking of standing it down—we're only getting started. These officers are just doing their best to build up a picture of what might have happened.'

Lucy thinks of the Seago life raft, untouched in its locker. She takes a breath and blows it out. To PC Noakes, she says, 'I'm sorry. I just . . . It's hard to believe this is happening.'

Noakes nods, but her smile doesn't reach her eyes. 'It's fine. Believe me, we get it all the time.'

Lucy glances at the clock. 'School's finishing. I need to collect my son—arrange for someone to look after him. I'll be twenty minutes or so.'

'In that case let me take some contact details.'

Lucy recites her mobile, her landline and her email. She gives out Daniel's various contact numbers, as well as Nick's.

'Do you know your husband's vehicle registration?'

Lucy relays that too. Standing, she pulls on her borrowed jacket.

'Are you a volunteer?' PC Lamb asks.

She shakes her head. 'My ex is the lead coxswain.'

'Your ex-husband?'

'Ex-boyfriend.'

Beside her, Noemie rises. 'Hon, I'll tag along. You can leave Fin with me while this plays out.'

2

Before they leave the Drift Net, Lucy returns to the bar. Grabbing the landline handset, she dials Billie. The girl won't answer—she'll be halfway through her biology class—and yet when the pre-recorded message ends, Lucy hangs up without speaking. This isn't news to be learned over voicemail.

Instead, she tries Daniel again: *Hi, you've reached Daniel Locke of Locke-Povey Marine . . .*

Lucy remembers the day he recorded that message, and the near-fifty failed attempts that preceded it. He'd started while sitting on their bed, only managing to succeed by locking himself in the bathroom. Much of the failure had been down to her—pulling faces, tickling his feet, walking her fingers under his shorts. Finally victorious, he'd emerged from the bathroom and bowed, and she'd led him back to the bedroom for his reward.

The memory shrinks Lucy's stomach. *That* Daniel's been gone a while; she's been doing everything she can to bring him back. 'Hey, Goof,' she says. 'I don't know what's happening. But come home to me, OK? Nothing else matters.'

3

Outside, over the salt and seaweed, the wind carries a sharp tang of ozone. In the last half hour, conditions have worsened considerably. The ocean looks like a gargantuan black lung, expanding and contracting, steadily marshalling its power. Seven miles offshore, a swell that size will hide Daniel from all but the closest boats. While the coastguard helicopter should fare better, its flight time is restricted by the distance to its South Wales base.

To Daniel, out there all alone, that swell will feel enormous. With such a low vantage point, he won't even see land. She imagines him battling those waves in a simple immersion suit. Or, even worse, with no buoyancy or insulation at all.

There's a third option, of course: empty ocean; a liquid graveyard.

Lucy stops dead. When she blinks, the world seems different, as if she's come alive in a different reality.

'Luce?'

'What if—'

'Don't,' Noemie says.

'I lied earlier. Things haven't been fine. Recently, they've been even worse. All this stuff with his business, and with Nick. Daniel's always needed to be in control—and now he isn't, and everything he built has fallen apart, and I haven't even known how to *help* him. I just have this horrible—'

'Luce, *no*. Just don't, OK? Save your energies for Fin.'

4

Noemie offers to drive, but Lucy can't be a passenger. On Fin's booster seat she sees Snig, the comfort blanket he's had from birth. It's a tattered thing of white cotton, stretched out of shape from so many repairs. To her son, it's an artefact of near-mythical power. Climbing behind the wheel, Lucy wonders what she's going to tell him.

Halfway up Smuggler's Tumble, rain starts crackling off the windscreen. At the top, rounding the last switchback, they emerge on to the exposed coastal road. With no trees to deflect it, the wind is formidable. Westwards, white breakers rib the sea all the way to the horizon. Waves are bursting against the shattered stacks beyond Mortis Point.

She'd always thought that nothing bad could happen to Daniel while she loved him this deeply; that her love could protect him like it protects Billie and Fin. But recently her love *hasn't* been enough, even though it's been just as strong. It hasn't protected any of them.

Why has nobody seen a light? The *Lazy Susan*'s parachute rockets discharge their flares nine hundred feet above the sea. Lucy knows how bright they are because Nick detonated one from their garden last year. The whole peninsula glowed red. Why didn't Daniel launch the Seago life raft? She can think of no explanation that's bearable. And the one that's most likely is the one that terrifies her most of all: that Daniel, in his desperation, decided he was more valuable to his family dead.

FOUR

1

Three o'clock. Nearly two and a half hours since the distress call. In the playground, waiting with other parents, Lucy paces back and forth. Beside her, Noemie looks like she's craving a cigarette.

Headlands Junior School sits along the coastal road between Skentel and Redlecker. It's a low-rise modern building, the classrooms opening directly on to the playground.

A volley of rain pings off the tarmac. Overhead, the sky is a steel sheet. Lucy's phone buzzes, then chimes. As she hauls it from her pocket, it chimes again. Three bars of reception, suddenly. Sixteen missed calls. The voicemail prompt appears and the phone begins to ring. Lucy raises it to her ear.

Come on, Daniel. Give me a clue. Something, anything. Help me figure this out.

Deep inside the school, a handbell starts ringing. Classroom doors fly open. Teachers emerge smiling, ready to pair parents with kids. Lucy spots Miss Clay, Fin's teacher, in one of her trademark outfits: today, a tartan shorts suit matched with Day-Glo orange tights.

'*You have five new messages. Message one, received today, 9.56 a.m.*'

The voice changes. '*Hey, Lucy, Graham Covenant from Covenant Logistics, just following up on that chat we—*'

With a stab of her finger, Lucy erases him.

Miss Clay summons Ellie Russell to the door, sweeping the playground for Ellie's mum.

'*Message two, received today, 10.04 a.m.*' Again, the voice changes. '*Hey, Lucy, Graham Covenant again. Didn't want you to miss out on—*'

Swearing, Lucy consigns him to the ether. Kids are streaming out steadily now. The air fills with screams and shouts.

'*Message three, received today, 11.26 a.m.*'

'*Hi, Lucy . . .*'

That voice belongs to Ed, Billie's boyfriend. From his words, it seems they're having problems again. Lucy can barely tune in. She saves the message, skips ahead. At the door to Fin's classroom, Miss Clay spots her and waves.

'*Message four, received today, 12.17 p.m.*'

Crackles on the line. Clicks and whistles.

'*. . . Lucy . . .*'

2

It's him. It's Daniel.

And yet something in his voice—dark, *alien*—isn't Daniel at all. In an instant, Lucy knows she's utterly unprepared for how bad this might get.

Around her, the playground darkens. The sound of children's voices fades. Time slows, then stops completely. Parents and offspring become graveyard statues welded to a tarmac sea. Colour seeps from their skin, their clothes. Lucy feels no wind in her hair, no speckling of rain on her cheeks. Her heart doesn't beat. The blood in her veins doesn't flow.

The phone is clamped so tightly to her ear that the hiss and burr of static fill her head. She concentrates hard, as if by deciphering those electronic shrieks she can divine Daniel's location, his intent. She hears wind, or what sounds like it. A chaotic symphony of whistles and chirrups, as if the broadcast is reaching her from deep space.

Lucy feels sure the connection is about to drop entirely. And then, with a buzzing that makes her wince, the clarity on the line is restored and she hears something else, something she didn't expect, another voice, fainter than the first, one that she recognizes as clearly as her own: *'Daddy, no—'*

3

The world opens beneath her feet. Lucy feels herself falling.

Around her, time pulls another trick. Because now it's *her* reality skidding to a halt, while everything else stirs back to life. Colour pours into those it abandoned. Movement returns to those it left.

Lucy's knees strike the tarmac, twin gunshots of pain. Sounds of delight rush into the playground. Screams and laughter and high-pitched chatter. 'Fin?' she asks, dumbfounded. But this is a recording, not a live connection. Her son can't answer from three hours in the past. And yet she can't help calling his name. *'Fin!'*

A scream follows that burns her throat.

In the playground, kids stop their games. Shocked parents pivot towards her.

The static in Lucy's ear dies, replaced by the measured tones of the voicemail assistant: *'To hear the message again, press one. To save it, press—'*

Noemie crouches at her side. 'Hon, what is it? What's happened?'

But all Lucy's attention is on Fin's teacher.

Miss Clay is walking across the playground, a riot of orange legs and yellow tartan. 'Mrs Locke?' she calls.

Lucy shakes her head, but she can't deny her identity. Nor the news she knows is coming.

'Are you here for Fin? Did his dad not tell you?'

Fighting her dizziness, she forces herself upright. Her stomach grips so hard she thinks she might be sick. 'Where is he?'

Miss Clay takes a step back. 'Mr Locke came by mid-morning. Said Fin had a dentist's appointment you'd forgotten about. He signed him out and off they went. That's OK, isn't it? I mean, you guys, I didn't . . .'

'Daniel took *Fin*?' Noemie asks. 'When the fuck did *that* happen?'

Miss Clay winces as if she's been slapped. 'Mid-morning, as I said. Around eleven. He signed the register. There was nothing'—her larynx slides up and down—'*untoward*.'

Lucy sways on her feet. She exhales explosively, sucks down a lungful of air. *Where did you go, Daniel? What could have happened to make you take Fin out of school? Why didn't you let me know?*

In her ear, the voicemail assistant is still chattering. She kills the connection. When the keypad appears, she dials 999. Her breath is coming harder now.

Daddy, no—

She thinks of the waves smashing the rocks beyond Mortis Point; the escalating violence of the sea. She recalls the trio of herring gulls flying over her house, and what her aunt used to say about those birds travelling in threes—a warning of death soon to come.

The old Daniel left and a new Daniel took his place.

On the phone she sees a message: *CALLING*. But it takes an age to connect.

How foolish of her to live here, on the periphery where land meets sea, where mobile reception is poor and you can't summon help the very instant you need it. Why did she ever return to a place with so much cold water, where fathers and sons can disappear with such ease?

Another voice, now: 'Which emergency service do you require?'

Lucy asks for them all.

I know it's frightening, this swift descent into chaos. Like standing on the deck of a yacht that's starting to break up. Everything is in motion. Nothing is solid. Suddenly, there's no sanctuary from the deep.

Taking Fin—undoubtedly—is the part you'll find hardest to grasp. But this is a tragedy written entirely for your benefit. Without Fin, it couldn't exist.

You remember that philosopher you used to talk about? Not Plato, but his student, Aristotle? How he believed tragedy was the most valuable of the dramatic arts? I know you think I never listened, but I did.

Tragedy makes us feel pity and fear. And through the experience we are healed. Aristotle even had a word for it, didn't he? Katharsis.

The longer I thought about it, the more it made sense. These last few weeks, I started to consider something else: How much purer the experience if the tragedy were real?

Everything that happens from this point is deliberate. But it's more than just a severing, Lucy. It's a purification. A renewal.

We both know you need it.

FIVE

1

DI Abraham Rose travels to Skentel beneath a sky preparing to release a monstrosity. The journey from Barnstaple usually takes forty minutes. With DS Cooper driving a pool car under blue lights, they make it in less than half that.

Strange, but blasting through traffic with siren wailing, Abraham feels a moment of peace. He knows it won't last. Still, for a few minutes yet he can find sanctuary inside the chaos and welcome the opportunity to be tested. He'll fall short of expectations. Everyone falls short. But falling short is not the point.

Westwards, a black wall is moving in from the Atlantic, so stark and implacable that the words of the Saviour describing the End Times ring in his head: *And there will be signs in sun and moon and stars, and on the earth distress of nations in perplexity because of the roaring of the sea and the waves, people fainting with fear and with foreboding of what is coming on the world. For the powers of the heavens will be shaken.*

Abraham is used to seeing portents in the world around him. Rarely do they offer much succour. As he studies the approaching weather front, he imagines a host of black stallions charging towards him, and thinks of another passage in Luke's Gospel: *People were eating, drinking, marrying and being given in marriage up to the day Noah entered the ark. Then the flood came and destroyed them all.*

'Jesus Christ,' Cooper says. 'Will you look at that shelf cloud?'

Abraham flinches at the blasphemy. In his thirty-year career, he's never reconciled himself to his fellow officers' faithlessness. One would have thought, surrounded by crime and misery, they'd have far greater reverence for the Word.

One would have thought.

'Shelf cloud?' He ducks his head for a better look. 'What's that?'

Cooper wrenches the steering wheel. They overtake an articulated lorry carrying farming equipment and swerve back into their lane.

'A type of arcus cloud,' the DS says, changing up a gear. 'You get a shelf cloud like that along the gust front of a major weather system. What you're seeing is the cool air sliding under the— *JESUS!*'

Ahead, a red Nissan pulls out of a side road, directly into their path. Its driver sees the approaching blue lights and locks his brakes. Cooper flicks the wheel. The car rocks wildly, veering into the opposite lane with no loss of momentum.

Cooper throws a daggered look at the Nissan's driver as they pass. 'Sliding under the warmer air hugging the coast,' he continues. 'The warm air rises and its moisture condenses.'

'Quite a sight,' Abraham mutters, releasing his grip on the door rest.

The road, now, is flanked by tall hedgerows. Cooper hugs the white line as they round a blind bend. 'In the most extreme cases,' he says, 'you'll see vortices along the leading edge. Gustnadoes, they're called.'

'I didn't realize you were so interested in weather.'

In truth, Abraham hadn't realized Cooper was interested in much at all. There's a wife somewhere, he believes. Has he seen a photo on Cooper's desk, confirming that? About the only thing he knows for sure is that the man never seems to eat his meals at a table or use a knife and fork.

If he had his time again, he'd make far more effort with those around him. Too late now.

Abraham shifts his weight, hunting for a more comfortable position.

The bar beneath the passenger seat is broken. As a result, his six-foot-four-inch frame is squeezed into a space more suited to a dwarf. Seatbelt or not, if Cooper hits another vehicle, Abraham's face is going through the windscreen.

He distracts himself by recalling what he knows about the situation they're racing to meet. Just under three hours ago, the coastguard picked up a distress call from Daniel Locke, skipper of the *Lazy Susan*. Locke went off air before relaying his position, but rescuers approximated the signal. A lifeboat located the vessel, but not Daniel.

Along this part of the coast, a sad but unexceptional tragedy. Then, thirty minutes ago, Locke's wife called 999. Arriving at her son's school for pick-up, she'd learned that her husband had collected the boy hours earlier.

It's the kind of case few investigating officers relish and from which there are likely no good outcomes.

The boy, Fin Locke, is seven years old. Hazel eyes, mouse-brown hair, 110 centimetres tall. He wears thick plastic glasses with characters from *The Avengers* along the side and was dressed in his Headlands Junior School uniform. Abraham hasn't seen a picture, but he knows when he does it'll snap his heart in two.

So far, that's all he has on the boy. Pulling out his notebook, he reviews what he scribbled down about the father.

Daniel Locke. Forty-two years old. Blue eyes, black hair. Five foot ten, average build, a four-inch scar on his right forearm. Last recorded sighting around 8 a.m., when his wife says he left the house. He told her he was heading to Locke-Povey Marine, an outfitting company he co-owns. Right now, no one there is answering the phone. A patrol car has been dispatched to check the place out, but with so few officers assigned to this stretch of coast, even the simplest of tasks takes time. Meanwhile, a uniformed patrol in Skentel is searching for Locke's car.

Abraham looks up from his notes. Westwards, above the treeline, that wall of black stallions charges closer.

Shelf cloud, he thinks.

The gust front of a major weather system.

Abraham hasn't yet glimpsed the ocean. The coastguard chatter suggests that conditions are rapidly deteriorating. He wonders how long the search can continue. And he wonders, more than anything, what Daniel Locke did to his son.

There are no more vehicles in front of them. Nothing but empty road and sky. Cooper switches off the siren. They blast along the carriageway, blue light bouncing off the road signs. Finally, through a break in the trees, Abraham spies the sea.

Anyone dismissing the recent weather warnings as hyperbole can't dismiss them now. From coast to horizon a destructive force has mustered that's frightening to behold. The muscles tighten in Abraham's neck, his chest. If ever there was a sight to confirm God's power over His creation, this is it. Troubling that he doesn't find himself more awed. How cruel—that at the point in his life when he needs his faith most, he can *feel* it ebbing away.

While the sky has marshalled black stallions, the sea commands white chargers; rank upon rank of them chase towards the land. The rocky stacks beyond the peninsula known as Mortis Point are being smashed. And yet in the instant before trees yet again block his view, he sees something remarkable: a flotilla of yachts and fishing vessels spreading out from Skentel's harbour.

'I don't envy them,' Cooper mutters. 'Not one jot.'

Abraham can't agree. If finding the boy is his ordained task, he has far more chance at sea. Of course, he has to find the father too, but it's the boy he wants to save.

Glancing back at his notes, he spots something there that disturbs him: his initials, inked in shaky capitals, sheltering beneath a dome. He's been scrawling this motif everywhere recently. Hurriedly, he scratches it out.

Abraham feels a familiar pain spreading out across his back, sharpening when he breathes. He clenches his teeth against it, taking short sips of air. His pills are in his jacket pocket. He's already swallowed more than he should. He can't take more without Cooper seeing.

Flipping down the sun visor, he examines himself in the mirror. Like his overlarge frame, every one of his features is supersized: lumpen nose, thick ears, Neanderthal brow. Beneath it his eyes are a strange combination: fierce and sad and dull. A forty-year smoking habit has wrinkled the skin around them.

Sometimes he thinks he was chiselled at speed from the roughest clay to hand. A priest once suggested something similar: that God, knowing the importance of Abraham's future works, deployed His servant in haste. Abraham might have taken comfort in that, had he thought it true.

He's grateful, at least, that his face betrays few signs of his disease. Nothing, so far, to alert anyone he's terminal.

Abraham coughs, too suddenly to catch it. Mustard-coloured sputum spatters against the mirror, along with a pink mist of blood. He grimaces, glancing at Cooper. Thankfully, the DS hasn't noticed.

The car slows. Abraham tips forward in his seat. He wipes the mirror with his sleeve, flips up the visor and sees a white sign ahead: *HEAD-LANDS JUNIOR SCHOOL.* Beyond it, a low-rise modern building stands beside a sports field. Cooper swings the car through the front gates.

2

At a service window inside the reception area, Abraham shows his warrant card. A receptionist buzzes him through.

The school's head, Marjorie Knox, greets him on the other side. She's immaculately coiffured and dangerously obese, in a floral-print dress so bright it hurts his eyes. Her make-up-caked face shines with perspiration. Her hand, when Abraham shakes it, is flaccid and wet.

Knox leads him along a carpeted corridor. She spends far longer talking about the school's security measures than the missing boy. Abraham spends far longer looking at the children's artworks than listening. On the walls he sees crayoned depictions of Noah's Ark, Jonah, Moses parting the Red Sea.

The art pleases him. Marjorie Knox does not.

'Is Headlands a faith school?' he asks.

'A Church of England primary. We're affiliated to St Peter's.' Knox's bosom heaves, as if the short walk has tired her. 'As I was saying, we take our safeguarding responsibilities very seriously. But we had no reason to believe anything was amiss. Mr and Mrs Locke aren't separated. There's no history of abuse of which we're aware. I'd go so far as to say that the school has acted in full—'

' "For by your words you will be acquitted," ' Abraham says. ' "And by your words you will be condemned." '

Marjorie Knox's eyes bulge a little at that.

'Matthew twelve, verse thirty-seven,' he adds.

Her head retreats into her neck, creating a necklace of double chins. 'Indeed.'

'Do you have CCTV here? In the car park or inside the school? I didn't notice any cameras in reception.'

'We've never had any reason to believe it necessary. We have very stringent security arrangements. As I said, our safeguarding—'

'Is exemplary, yes. And you're one hundred per cent certain Fin Locke's father collected him?'

'Of course.'

'I don't need to point out there's going to be a lot of attention on this school.'

'I realize that. Which is why—'

'Which is why I want to make sure you're *personally* certain—and I mean stake-your-career-on-it certain—that it was the *father* who collected the boy and not some imposter.'

Knox blinks. Her chins bob as her throat contracts. 'I didn't *personally* sign Fin out. Our receptionist oversaw that, along with his teacher.'

'And your receptionist knows Mr Locke personally?'

'Well, I don't—'

'Does Fin's teacher know Mr Locke personally?'

'I'm quite—'

'I presume they're both still here?'

Knox gasps for air. 'My first priority, when I learned of this whole rigmarole, was to ensure everyone remained on-site. If you wish, I can introduce you to the relevant parties right now.'

Rigmarole, Abraham thinks. *Fuss and bother. A complicated and unnecessary inconvenience.*

Knox's breath is musky and sweet, and yet under it he detects the whiff of something rotten. Suddenly, he has a very real sense of Satan's presence stalking the halls of this school. Disturbing and inexplicable—how his faith in God can be crumbling while his fear of the devil remains strong. That pain is back, worse than before. Claws inside his chest. He makes two fists, straightens.

'Detective?' Knox asks. 'Would you like to see them?'

When he turns towards Marjorie Knox he sees, in her throat, the jump of her pulse. He stares with horrified fascination. Above him, the hum of the strip lighting intensifies into an angry buzzing.

Abraham's gaze settles on an olive-wood cross fixed to the opposite wall. Abruptly, he finds he can breathe again.

Detective? Would you like to see them?

He glances at Cooper, who returns him an odd look. 'Please.'

3

In the staffroom he meets Fin's teacher, Sarah Clay, and the school receptionist. They satisfy him on something Marjorie Knox could not: that it *was* Daniel Locke who arrived mid-morning and took the boy away.

The receptionist walked to Fin's class with the message. Sarah Clay handed the boy over to his father. She's met Locke senior five times previously. Yes, she'd stake her life on it being him. No, she recalls nothing unusual in his behaviour.

When Abraham asks her to describe the boy, Clay's eyes fill with tears. 'Eccentric,' she says. 'Funny. Interested in just about everything. I never like to say I have a favourite, but if I did, it would be Fin.' She glances at Marjorie Knox. 'He has faced some issues with bullying lately. Being so small, he's an easy target.'

'Issues we *promptly* stamped out, Sarah.'

When Abraham bares his teeth, Knox's head shrinks into her neck like a tortoise retreating into its shell.

'I've gone over and over it,' Clay says. 'Tried to think of something I should have noticed. Fin's mum—imagine. Have you spoken to her?'

It's Abraham's next task.

4

The head's office is thick with perfume and dusty radiator heat. A female PC leans against a desk. Two other women stand by the window. With Marjorie Knox beside him, Abraham feels acutely outnumbered. Beyond pitiful, to reach his age and still feel so uncomfortable around the opposite sex.

It's easy enough to identify Fin's mother. Dressed in an oversized RNLI jacket, she looks like she's either woken from a coma or is about to fall into one. Abraham knows that expression well enough. Here, though, it's a little different. There's something—in the angle of her jaw, or perhaps the square of her shoulders—that sets her apart. She looks like a warrior readying for battle.

As she returns his stare, he feels himself being measured. The scrutiny straightens his spine, until he remembers how most people recoil from his size. Lucy Locke doesn't, though. She steps forward until she's as close as Marjorie Knox.

How to address her? If *Locke* is the surname she took in marriage, it comes from a man who may have drowned her son.

'Lucy,' he begins. 'I'm—'

'By my reckoning we've got about two hours,' she says. 'That's until it gets dark or this storm hits or both. Things get more difficult, then. They kept me here waiting when I could be out *there*, searching. I've talked to the coastguard, the police at the quay, these officers, now you. So this better be good. And it better be quick.'

He feels the anger boiling off her, the frustration. He hopes it'll sustain her a good while, because he knows what replaces it won't help. 'Lucy, I'm aware you've given a statement and I don't want to duplicate any work. It probably seems like we have all the facts, but these situations rarely—'

'I last saw my husband, Daniel Locke, just before eight this morning at home,' she says. 'Home is Wild Ridge, the big house up on Mortis Point. He said he was going to his workshop, Locke-Povey Marine, behind Penleith Beach. I don't know if he ever made it, but they're saying he arrived here around eleven. He took our son, Fin Locke, seven years old, I have plenty of pictures. He told the staff Fin had a dentist's appointment we'd forgotten about—which we hadn't, because no appointment existed, and I've phoned the dentists to double-check, and the two of them never showed up. Three hours ago Daniel broadcast a Mayday from our yacht, the *Lazy Susan*. The boat's been found but my son and my husband are still missing. They never launched the life raft. No one spotted a flare. I know how it looks—what everyone's thinking—but Daniel's a good man, the best there is. He wouldn't have put Fin in danger unless he had no choice.

'I've given your colleagues every possible contact method. Is there *any-thing* else you need to know before I get out there on the water?'

She pauses, takes a breath, twists something between her fingers. At first, Abraham thinks it's a rag. Then he realizes it's a child's comfort blanket. There's no sadder sight.

Beside him, Marjorie Knox mouth-breathes her rotten musk. 'Oh dear,' she says. 'This is all *very* distressing.'

'There's lots I need to know,' he tells Lucy Locke. 'But I appreciate you don't want to be here and'—a glance at Knox—'I certainly can't blame you. We can talk on the way to Skentel.'

5

Abraham takes the passenger seat. Cooper drives. Lucy Locke sits in the back and Noemie Farrell follows in Lucy's car.

The shelf cloud he saw earlier has crept across half the sky. Strange shapes cavort and flicker inside it: gulls or guillemots, driven to confusion by the changing conditions. Watching them, Abraham can't help recalling the fifth angel from Revelation and the star that fell from heaven: *He*

opened the bottomless pit; and there arose a smoke out of the pit, as the smoke of
a great furnace; and the sun and the air were darkened by reason of the smoke of
the pit. And there came out of the smoke locusts upon the earth.

Cooper glances at him from the driver's seat. For a moment, Abraham thinks: Does he feel it too? This sense of something awful approaching?

On the warm air spewing from the car's heaters, he can smell the closing storm. He turns in his seat and watches Lucy scrolling through her phone. 'How long have you and Daniel been together?'

'Nine years. Married after two.' She looks up, red-eyed. 'I love him—even more now than I did then. He loves me too. Not every couple can say that after nearly a decade, but we can.'

Listening, Abraham wonders what it must be like: to find such deep and enduring love with another human being; to be granted such a gift. He thinks of his keepsake box at home and feels, for a moment, as hollow as a reed. And then he considers what Lucy Locke's husband may have done to her children; and the evil that men do. 'You've lived here all your life?'

She blinks, rubs her face. 'What?'

'Have you always lived here? In Skentel, I mean.'

Lucy shakes her head. She glances back down at the phone. 'I went away. For a while. Then I came back.'

'You have a picture of Fin I could see?'

Lucy winces from her son's name as if it's a blade. Moments later, she reverses her grip on the phone. Abraham leans closer. Suddenly there's no air in his chest.

Angel, he thinks.

Fin's face is unforgettable, his features just wonky enough to melt a heart. His glasses create a cartoonish effect, magnifying his eyes and making them seem far too close together. He doesn't smile, he *beams*—a wattage bright enough to light a cave, all pink gums and baby teeth and gaps for adult ones to fill. His nose is a wrinkled button. His ears stick out so far he'll be teased about them mercilessly when he's older. Never has Abraham seen a picture of someone so naively radiating love.

Three hours ago, Fin Locke was sitting in class. Then a knock at the door spirited him away.

Abraham's fingers twitch. *God, I praise you for your compassionate heart. Give me the relentlessness of the good shepherd who goes after wandering sheep and never gives up.*

'He's a lamb,' he says. The words stick in his mouth like paste. 'We'll find him. We'll find them both.'

Lucy's eyes lock on his. He knows the commitment he just made is a lifebuoy, something for her to clutch while she struggles to stay afloat.

'You want to see a video?'

He's seen the photo. He doesn't need to see a video. But Lucy's need to share matters more. Abraham nods. While she returns her attention to the phone, he glances out the window: marching trees, glimpses of dark ocean; white breakers and black sky.

The boats have fanned out further since his school visit.

Bless them. God bless them.

Whatever that means.

'Here,' Lucy says, holding out the phone.

Onscreen, a kitchen heaves into view. He sees a rectory table. Behind it, tall windows offer a panorama of sea and sky. *Wild Ridge*, he thinks. *The big house up on Mortis Point.* What a place for a kid to grow up.

Lucy must be filming. Abraham hears her stifled giggle. He can't imagine the current version of her making that sound—the day's events have created a doppelgänger.

Fin enters shot, holding a sheaf of papers. The boy walks stiffly, glasses off-kilter on his nose. He's wearing a shirt and purple waistcoat. At his throat is a velvet bow tie, comically large. He sits at the table and imperiously shuffles his papers. A flicker of annoyance crosses his face. '*Mummy*, you're *meant* to *introduce* me.'

Another barely suppressed giggle from Lucy. 'I am pleased to introduce Master Fin Gordon Locke. Weaver of words, teller of fine tales, storyteller extraordinaire.'

She waits.

Fin waits. Then he shakes himself. Not a subtle flinching but a struck-by-lightning full-body twitch. 'Oh,' he says. '*Me*.' With an extended forefinger he precisely readjusts his glasses. Blinking owlishly, he peers at the camera.

Every mannerism, every little tic, seems designed to elicit laughter. Abraham wonders if the boy knows he's funny or is utterly unaware.

'The *Bogwort*,' Fin says. 'A *story* by Fin Gordon Locke, aged seven and a half. Weaver of *words*, teller of *tales*, storyteller ex . . . extra . . . extra what?'

'Extraordinaire,' Lucy says.

'One of those.' He clears his throat. Then he does it again, louder. The bow tie jiggles. One wing flops down.

Abraham grins. His stomach tightens. Hard not to laugh. Harder not to cry.

'*Once*,' Fin says, 'there was a hunchbacked old man called *Bogwort*. He had *silver* hair, *orange* eyes and long green ears like *trumpets*. Bogwort was *very* grumpy, because *he* believed everyone thought he was *ugly*, even though they *didn't*.

'Bogwort was *lonely*, too. What was so, *so* sad is that he *could* have had lots of friends if he hadn't made people *nervous* of him, and *frightened* of him too. But I don't want you to worry *too* much about that, because *this* isn't going to be one of those *sad* stories at all but one to cheer you *up*, cos you'll see that *actually* in the end some *nice* things happened to Bogwort. Because he *deserved* it. And that's what people *get* if they're good.'

The bow tie, hanging by its clip, falls off completely.

'Dagummit,' Fin mutters.

Old Lucy howls with laughter. New Lucy closes her eyes in pain.

'Can you think of any reason Daniel might have taken Fin from school and sailed him so far out, knowing what's coming?'

She shivers. 'I can only think he was trying to protect Fin from something.'

'Like what?'

'That's what I keep asking myself.' Lucy's face crumples. 'But I just don't know.'

Cooper slows the car, turning off the coastal road towards Skentel.

'Fin's an only child?'

'I have a daughter, too. Billie.'

'Older or younger?'

'She's eighteen.'

'You must have had her young.'

'A year older than she is now.'

Really young, Abraham thinks. 'Is she working? College? In between?'

'Billie's doing A levels over in Redlecker. Hopes to study marine biology.'

Abraham nods. For a while, he thinks about what he just heard. The longer he thinks, the colder he feels. He glances out of the window again, working out how to phrase his next question. But when he turns back to Lucy, her phone is already clamped to her ear.

'Billie, it's coming up to four. Can you call me, please, the minute your lecture ends.' She hangs up, dials another number. 'Holly, hi, it's Lucy, Billie's mum. Please can you call me back—soon as you get this message.' She scrolls through the phone for another contact. She's trembling now; her jaw, her fingers.

'Which college?' Abraham asks.

'Arthur Radley in Redlecker. She has a biology lesson. Due to finish any moment.'

'Keep trying her friends,' he says. 'I'll call the sixth form.'

Lucy makes a sound like a wounded thing.

SIX

Lucy's in her kitchen, throwing chopped onions into a pan. It's Billie's eighteenth birthday and the party starts in a few hours.

Propped on the counter is Fin's iPad. Onscreen is the recipe Lucy's been following—but what she's really concentrating on is the conversation in the next room.

'But what if they *can't?*' Fin moans. 'What if someone put a *spell* on me?'

'Scout,' Billie says gently. 'No one can do magic. Which means no one can put a spell on you.'

Fin pauses, sniffs. '*Santa* can do magic.'

'I'm not talking about Santa. I'm talking about the kids in your school.'

Fin starts crying again. 'But they can't *see* me, Billo. *Any* of them. Whatever I try, nothing *helps.*'

'Is this why you've been eating so many carrots?'

'And satsumas. But *that* didn't work either. What happens if it gets *worse?* What happens if I start getting invisible to *you?*' His voice cracks. 'Or to Mummy and Daddy? What if it ends up just *me?*'

Lucy puts down her knife. Wednesday afternoon, Fin came home complaining that no one in Magenta Class could see him. A few days later, and it's swept through the whole school. Worse, Lucy suspects it's been going on longer than he admits—that Fin, after trying to deal with it alone, only confided in her as a last resort. She's seeing Marjorie Knox on Tuesday morning, the earliest the head teacher said she was available. That angered Lucy even more.

'It's never going to happen,' Billie says. 'And I mean *never*, OK, Fin? I'm serious. I don't even want you thinking that. Right, so tell me. Which kid started this horseshit?'

'*Billie!*'

'Sorry.'

'You'll go *blind*.'

'Which kid, Fin?'

'Nobody started it. It just happened.'

'OK, let's backtrack. Who was the first kid who couldn't see you?'

Fin's silent a while. 'Eliot.'

'Eliot's in your class?'

'He sits next to new Jessica.'

'Is Eliot your friend?'

'He's my *arch-enemy*.'

'Is he the one who tore a page out of your *Hulk* comic?'

No answer to that. Just soft sounds of misery.

'It's OK, Scout,' Billie says. 'It doesn't matter if you need to cry. So— we're talking about the same kid?' She pauses for his answer. 'Right. And who was the second person not to see you?' Another pause. 'New Jessica, who sits next to Eliot? You know what? I think we're getting somewhere.'

Beside Lucy, the onions start to sizzle. As Daniel comes in from the garden, she touches a finger to her lips.

'You think my *arch-enemy* started this?'

'It's possible. Either way, what's important is how you deal with it.'

'You mean how I make them *see* me again?'

'They *can* see you, Fin. This invisibility thing is complete rubbish.'

'But why would they be mean? Why would a *whole school* be so mean?'

51

'Because sometimes, little guy . . . sometimes people just don't think. And when people don't think hard before they act, they can end up being part of something hurtful without ever really meaning to. Kind of like they're half asleep.'

Daniel touches Lucy's shoulder. She leans into him, welcoming his closeness.

'So what do I *do*, Billo?'

'Shall I tell you a story? Something nobody in this family knows? You remember when I was fifteen, that time I cut off all my hair? You were only four, so you might not. Thing is, Scout, it wasn't me. Three girls from school grabbed me on the way home and went at me with their scissors.

'I'd been getting grief for a while—all kinds of nasty stuff. I'd thought, if I kept my head down, they'd eventually leave me alone.'

Lucy remembers the hair-cutting incident. And her sharp words to Billie at the time. Guilt rolls over her like a wave.

'So what *happened*?'

'That night, I snuck down to Penleith Beach. I sat on the sand and cried my eyes out. Afterwards, I swore a vow—that from then on, I wouldn't back down. I'd take control of my life. Whatever the cost, I wouldn't give anyone power over me again.

'Next day in class, the trouble started even before our teacher arrived for the register. Kerrie Bray, behind me, was one of the girls who cut my hair. She made a few comments and then she punched me between the shoulder blades.'

'*Uh-oh*,' Fin whispers. 'What happened?'

'I warned her that if she touched me a second time she'd regret it. The whole class erupted. Honestly, Fin, it was like a zoo. I don't think anyone had ever stood up to Kerrie before. I'm pretty sure she realized if she backed down, she'd lose all the status she'd built up. She waited until my back was turned. Then she cracked me over the head with her phone.'

'*Coward!*' her brother hisses.

'I thought I was going to pass out but I didn't. I got to my feet and punched her right in the mouth—harder than I'd ever hit anyone in my life.'

Billie blows out her breath. 'You don't realize how much it hurts your knuckles until you try it. That punch split both Kerrie's lips across her teeth. She looked at me, at the blood dripping all over her desk, at all the other kids watching, and then she fled. Straight to the nurse's office to get patched up. Obviously, I had a week of detentions. But Kerrie Bray never bothered me again.'

'So, you think I should bust Eliot in the *chops*?'

'*No!* Jeez, Fin—I don't think you should do that at all.' Billie hesitates, lowers her voice. 'Not unless you really have to. The point of the story is that people only gain power over you if you let them.'

Silence, for a while, from Fin. Then: 'I'm frightened to go back.'

'I know you are, Scout.'

'What if they do something else?'

Lucy hears her daughter thinking.

'You remember the phone Commissioner Gordon uses to call Batman whenever he's in trouble?'

'The Batphone?'

'The Batphone, right. I think you need one of those, programmed with my number. And then, whenever you've got a problem, you can call me and I'll come running.'

'Like Batgirl?'

'Exactly like Batgirl.'

'But Mummy and Daddy say I can't *have* a phone. Not till I'm eleven.'

'No, Scout. They said they wouldn't *buy* you a phone until you're eleven. But I can. And it's my eighteenth, which means—*ker-ching*—I'm in the money.'

Daniel puts his head close to Lucy's ear. 'She's a good kid.'

'The best.'

He smiles, kisses her forehead. 'You don't even realize, do you?'

'Realize what?'

'How much of it's down to you.'

Lucy thinks of her life before she returned to Skentel. Of how bad things were in London, around the time of Billie's birth. Of how much worse they grew in Spain. And in the Portuguese beach town where she ended up. 'More luck than judgement,' she tells him. 'Sometimes I feel I owe Billie everything.'

Then you'd better find her. Hadn't you?

Appalled, Lucy jerks her head away. And suddenly she's no longer in her kitchen but in a police car, and Daniel and Fin are missing and she can't get hold of her daughter and she doesn't know why this is happening but she has to figure it out, and fast.

A thought breaks through the chaos in her head: the voicemail from Billie's boyfriend, Ed. Earlier, standing in the playground, she'd barely listened to his message. Lucy tunes out the detective, talking on his phone, and dials her voicemail.

As she waits for the call to connect she thinks of Bee, standing outside Wild Ridge in her rainbow unicorn T-shirt: *They found the* Lazy Susan. *Just drifting, I think. Somewhere out to sea.*

She recalls the three herring gulls flying over the house; and Matt Guinness, down in Skentel's harbour, his greasy hair and grin: *Uh-oh. Looks like Hubby's got some explaining to do.*

The voicemail assistant is in her ear: *'Message one, saved . . .'*

Lucy closes her eyes, shuts out everything else.

'Hi, Lucy.' Ed's voice. *'When you see Billie later, can you say I'm sorry. Not sure what I've done, but just say sorry anyway and I'll figure it out when I see her. Oh . . . also . . . don't tell her I don't know what I'm sorry for, if you know what I mean. She was meant to meet me before chemistry and she didn't even call, which means something's definitely up. Everything's been a bit messy since the whole Sea Shepherd thing but I thought . . . uh . . . Never mind, sorry. I'm rambling now. I'll catch you soon.'*

Lucy's world is collapsing—the members of her family vanishing one by one. She finds Ed's number and dials. *'Hi, this is Ed Shoemaker—'*

When she hangs up, her phone starts ringing.

'Lucy? It's Holly Cheung. Did you call?'

'Have you seen Billie today?'

'She never showed.'

Hard not to shout. Hard not to scream. More pillars of her world crash down. 'Have you heard from her at all? Phone? WhatsApp? Anything?'

'No. Which is weird, actually. Is everything OK? I've been in lectures most of the day. Was just about to shout her.'

'I need you to do me a favour, Holly. I need you to call everyone who might've seen Billie or heard from her. And I need you to call me straight back, soon as you find out anything.'

'Sure.' Unease, now, in the girl's voice. 'Has something happened?'

'I can't find them,' Lucy says. 'Daniel, Billie, Fin.'

'You can't *find* them?'

'Our boat was found drifting, no one onboard. I think they were all on it.'

'You're . . . Jesus, *what?*' Static on the line. Holly's ragged breathing. 'OK, I'll start phoning, right now. See if anyone else has heard from her. Have you spoken to Ed?'

'His phone's going straight to voicemail.'

'He might be in rehearsals. I'll see if I can track him down.' A pause. 'There's a storm coming. Meant to be a big one. What the hell were they thinking?'

No answer to that. Lucy cuts the connection. Next, she calls Bee at the Drift Net.

'Luce? Dude, we heard from Noemie about Fin. There are people and boats coming in from all over. Is there any update?'

'He's . . . I think Billie went with them.'

'*Billie?*' In the background, Lucy hears raised voices, the hiss of the steamer. 'Oh God, Luce. I don't know what to say. I just don't. You want me to pass it on?'

'They need to know. Everyone needs to know. We're looking for three people, now, not two. My whole family.'

Those last three words she speaks in bewilderment.

Her whole family. Out there in the water.

'I'll send Tommo up to the lifeboat station so Jake knows, too.'

Lucy thanks her and hangs up. Her eyes are gritty. She's having trouble focusing. Daniel sailing out there alone she could just about understand. But what possible reason could he have for taking Billie and Fin? And why not let her know?

In the passenger seat, the detective is on his phone. 'More people down here,' he says. 'Might've taken the stepdaughter too. And find out what's happening with this Locke-Povey Marine.' He turns in his seat when he realizes she's listening.

Their eyes meet. Lucy knows what he's thinking.

Victim.

But she isn't. No way. This doesn't end with an empty boat.

DI Abraham Rose lowers his phone. 'We don't know for certain that Billie went with Daniel, but it's safer to assume that she did. I'm going to need a full description. Photos, contact details, the works.'

He reaches out, placing a huge hand over her own. Lucy flinches away. She doesn't want his compassion. Empathy, from this gravel-voiced detective, means something *truly* awful has happened. She won't believe that. Her children are alive. Her husband too. Missing, yes. In terrible danger, possibly. But alive.

In his expression she sees something she doesn't understand.

'You're not alone in this,' he says. 'I'll be with you. Every step.'

Lucy stares, unable to break eye contact.

'Until we find them,' he adds.

Her throat clenches. Boa-constrictor tight.

SEVEN

1

Even in the most acute distress, Lucy Locke couldn't bear his touch. Abraham shouldn't be surprised by that. He knows he's a uniquely unattractive man. What *does* surprise him is his hurt. It's a cut he wasn't expecting; the opening of a wound he thought long healed. Perhaps it stings more because of who dealt it—a woman whose world, until an hour ago, had seemed so obviously steeped in love.

He can't forget Lucy's words when asked how long she'd been with Daniel: *Nine years. Married after two. I love him—even more now than I did then. He loves me too. Not every couple can say that after nearly a decade, but we can.*

Miraculous that she could be so steadfast in light of what's happened. Or perhaps it isn't. Perhaps love obscures as much as it reveals. How on earth would he know? Certainly, no woman has made, or ever will make, such proclamations about Abraham Rose.

There'd been a chance, once.

In his head, his mother's voice from that time: *God ordained your path. And that girl wasn't it.*

Beside him, Cooper curses, braking to a stop. Lifting his head, Abraham sees why. Some idiot has tried to drive an outside-broadcast truck down to the harbour. The vehicle, equipped with an enormous satellite dish, is nearly as wide as Skentel's cobbled high street. Cooper thumps the horn in frustration.

Abraham throws open his passenger door. A gust of wind tries to slam it shut. He glances over his shoulder at Lucy Locke. 'This isn't clearing any time soon. Come on. It'll be faster to walk.' To Cooper, he adds, 'Find a place to park. Then meet me on the quay.'

When he extracts himself from the passenger seat, cold rain strikes his face. He smells seaweed and tastes salt. On the roofs of the whitewashed buildings, herring gulls have formed miserable colonies. Lucy casts them a dark look.

Together they hurry down the street. When they get to the TV truck, Abraham sees the problem. Squeezing along the kerb to muscle its way through, the vehicle's burst a front tyre. Its driver is loosening wheel nuts with a wrench. A woman in a purple cashmere coat stands over him, drawing on a cigarette as if it's oxygen.

Journo, Abraham thinks. When his nostrils catch her smoke, his lungs tighten with craving. No advantage in berating her or the driver. Already, this has morphed into something far worse than anyone expected. The last thing he needs is a pissed-off hack. Lucy studies the woman as she passes. She must know her personal torment is about to become a news item. And yet Abraham sees something unexpected in her expression. Not just horror but calculation.

Chin tilted, the journalist returns Lucy's stare. Abraham wonders if she realizes that this is the wife, the mother. But then he sees what she sees: a young woman in an RNLI jacket hurrying down to the quay. A story, but not the one she thinks.

He slides past the TV truck and there it is below him: the sea. Abraham's breath catches. The waves—huge, muscled slabs of grey water—look like they're rising and falling in slow motion. In the harbour, the remaining boats clank and lurch on the swell. One, in particular, takes his interest: a navy forty-footer moored to the breakwater wall. A police officer, pelted by spray, stands guard beside it.

He thinks of that motif he found earlier—his initials inked in shaky capitals beneath a protective dome—and grimaces.

Overhead, the storm's vanguard has moved in. Abraham feels like he's witnessing the arrival of an extinction event. No longer does he glimpse shapes flickering inside the clouds. Earlier, he'd assumed they were gulls or guillemots. Now, he could almost imagine they were windborne devils making landfall.

Of everything he sees before him, what robs his breath most is that fleet of tiny boats dispersing across a turbulent sea: Skentel's residents setting out on the water, hunting for two of their own.

Three of their own, Abraham thinks. And wonders, should they find Daniel Locke, what they'll do to him.

2

The Drift Net is a fug of warm air and raised voices. Abraham smells good coffee. His lungs scream for a cigarette.

At a nearby table, three men in salopettes cluster around a nautical chart. By the window, two coastguard officials scowl at the incoming weather. Fishermen in stained bib overalls queue to get their flasks filled at the bar. At other tables, sailors pull on wet-weather gear. This place has the feel of a coastal militia preparing for an invading aggressor.

Abraham watches Lucy weave through the crowd to the bar. So focused are the volunteers on their plans that her presence hardly registers. Digging out his phone, he heads to a quieter corner. So many things he needs to do. What began as a standard coastguard search and rescue has evolved into something far more complex. Daniel Locke had no good reason to take Fin out of school. The teacher and receptionist saw nothing to suggest he was acting under duress, nor that he was fearful for his son's safety. And while there's no firm evidence he took the boy on the boat, Fin Locke is still missing. Now Billie Locke, too.

I love him, Lucy had said of her husband. *He loves me too.*

But not enough, it seems, to tell her where he was going, or what he was planning to do.

Abraham needs to speak to the control room back in Barnstaple. He also needs to call Middlemoor, the force HQ. He wants a forensics team examining the *Lazy Susan*; a cell-tower analysis of Billie and Daniel Locke's phones. And he needs to find Daniel's car.

The coastguard is running the offshore search, but Abraham intends to flood the accessible areas of coastline with police officers. If, by God's grace, Fin or Billie have washed up alive, they'll be half frozen. Unthinkable to survive the sea, merely to die of hypothermia on some deserted beach. He's still compiling his to-do list when Lucy Locke climbs on to an empty table and calls loudly for silence.

EIGHT

1

Last time Lucy was in the Drift Net, she was trying to find Daniel. Seventy minutes later, she's lost her whole family.

However deeply she tries to breathe, she can't seem to fill her lungs. She's still holding Snig, Fin's security blanket. Just now, in the police car, she pressed it to her face and inhaled. She'd hoped it would strengthen her. But Snig's almondy smell—*Fin's* smell—nearly stopped her heart.

Bee is waiting behind the bar. Her eyes, under her bubble-gum-pink hair, are huge. She looks like she's standing too close to a car crash and can't tear herself away.

'Listen,' Lucy tells her. 'I don't know what's happened. I don't know how this ends. But I need to be out there looking, for as long as I possibly can. You've got to keep this place running, Bee, OK? It has to be a hub—somewhere people can come for information, somewhere those who've been searching can recharge. Close the tills. Don't charge for anything. I want everyone talking about Billie and Fin, about Daniel. We have to make them famous until they're found.'

Bee glances at her boyfriend. 'We've got this, Luce, I swear it. We'll make this place an HQ. Tommo's a pretty good artist. He can run up some posters, put them on the windows.'

'Count on it,' Tommo says. 'We can print off some flyers, too. I'm just sorry this is happening. I'm guessing he knew this storm was coming. You have any idea why he'd sail those kids straight into it?'

'Daniel wouldn't have risked their safety without good reason.'

Tommo nods, but he looks unconvinced. And the more Lucy repeats her mantra—Daniel the caring father, Daniel the responsible parent—the more desperate it sounds.

Please, Daniel.

Give me a sign. Something. Anything.

Bee squeezes Lucy's arm. 'Dude, I'm not sure what else to say. But I know in my heart this'll end well.'

Lucy's eyes fall to her friend's T-shirt, its rainbow unicorn and accompanying legend: *I DON'T BELIEVE IN YOU EITHER.* She turns from the bar, surveys the crowd. She knows what she has to do, but that doesn't make it any easier. All her life, she's had a terror of public speaking. Considering the situation, she'd expected her phobia to melt away. Instead, her terror has magnified. It's a vacuum in her throat. A fizz of acid in her blood.

As she goes to the only empty table, the bell above the front entrance jangles. A blast of cold air rolls in. She can't look, can't acknowledge that her audience has just grown larger. She thinks of the TV truck jammed in the high street—the sharp-looking woman in purple cashmere who could only have been a reporter.

Lucy pulls a chair from the table.

Where are you, Daniel? Why haven't you confided in me?

She climbs on to the chair. Blood rushes from her head. The room seesaws. She twists Snig in her fists. From the chair she steps on to the table.

Heads are turning now. The chatter is starting to die. Lucy's mouth is drier than ashes. In the far corner, she notices DI Abraham Rose. The crag-faced detective looks out of place here, a crusader knight forced into an ill-fitting suit. His eyes, as he watches her, are unfathomable.

Lucy's stomach grips. She thinks of her children and again it's a mistake. Her eyes burn. The room fragments. She hears herself clearing her throat.

A memory comes to her from six weeks ago—a fortnight before Billie's eighteenth. She's in her bathroom at home, searching the cabinets for Benylin as Fin's coughing echoes along the hall.

All his life he's been prone to chest infections, throat infections, anything going around. She'd always imagined her boy would be an athlete and outdoor adventurer, just like her. But the adventures Fin likes best are those he keeps on his bookcase or captures in his telescope. Even his football-card collection doesn't stem from an interest in sport but from a desire to befriend other boys.

So many times Lucy's tried to toughen him physically: surfing, canoeing, canyoning. Fin's tackled everything she's thrown at him without a word of protest, but none of it has improved his resilience. She loves her star-gazing, card-sorting little bookworm even more fiercely as a result.

Lucy finds the Benylin bottle and closes the bathroom cabinet. Back in Fin's room, she spoons red medicine into his mouth and kisses his forehead.

'Shall I tell you about *Bogwort*, Mummy?'

'About what?'

'My *story*,' Fin says. '*You* remember. So Mummy, Bogwort is a *fairy*-tale character. Which means he either has to be a *baddie* or a *goodie*. What happens is, Bogwort lives in a castle with a king and queen. And they have a princess they love very much.'

He pauses for a fit of coughing. 'But what nobody knows is that *Bogwort* doesn't *like* the princess very much so he kidnaps her. He takes her off to a tower he's built in the middle of *nowhere*. The king and queen are *very* sad. They get all the heroes in the kingdom to look for their missing daughter and hunt down the person that took her.'

Fin beams, his lips sticky with cough mixture. 'But of course, *none* of them know that the person who *took* her is right there in the *palace*. Right there *living* with them.'

Lucy smiles, ruffles his hair.

'*CREEPY!*' Fin shouts, through red teeth.

'That's a great story, little man.'

'I've hardly got *started*. You just wait for what comes *next*.'

She kisses him and retreats to the hall. Downstairs, in the dining room, she finds Daniel and Nick. The air is thick with Nick's cigar smoke. The table is crowded with playing cards, whisky tumblers and far more cash than she'd like to see. Most of it's stacked in front of Nick. Daniel's on his feet, patting his pockets for his keys. When he sees her, he flashes a smile. 'I promised I'd run Billie back from the Goat. Save a cab fare.'

'I'll go.'

Lightly, Daniel touches her arm. 'You've been on your feet all day. Just don't let this guy drink all the Talisker while I'm gone.'

Nick chuckles. 'Just don't empty every cashpoint in Skentel while you're out. I don't want to confiscate any more of your filthy lucre.'

Once Daniel's gone, Lucy raises the sash window. Frigid night air pours in.

'Jesus, Lucy-Lou. You're gonna freeze my balls off.'

She picks up a coaster and slides it under Nick's drink, wiping the wet spot with her sleeve. 'You smoke outside or with the window open. I've told you enough times. Fin's asthmatic, remember?'

He lifts a hand in apology and stubs out the cigar. 'You wanna drink?'

Lucy stares at him. The big, tough kid from the Polaroid grew into an unusually brutish man. Unlike Daniel, the legacy of Nick's early upbringing is much more apparent. There's a street-kid intensity to his gaze. Subjected to it, Lucy feels all her shortcomings on display.

Fetching a tumbler from the cabinet, she sits opposite. Nick pours her a measure of Talisker and arranges his money into one large stash. 'Is my boy Danny going to be in trouble?'

'Not with me. We trust each other's decisions, always have. You know that. At least, you should.'

Nick's eyes glimmer as he contemplates her. Lucy's skin contracts into goosebumps. When he takes a swallow of whisky, she matches him, wondering if her reaction is due to his scrutiny or the cold night air.

'We all live with our choices,' Nick says. 'Nine years ago, when you guys first met, it should've been me stranded in that lay-by outside Skentel. Daniel only offered to do the trip at the last minute.' He turns the whisky glass in his hands. 'You ever think about that, Lucy-Lou? How things might've been different?'

She knocks back her drink. 'A butterfly can beat its wings in Peking—'

'—and in Central Park you get rain instead of sunshine.'

Nick holds her eye longer than the length of their laughter.

Leaving him to his winnings, Lucy retreats to the kitchen and loads the dishwasher. When she straightens, she realizes that Nick has followed from the dining room and is watching her from the doorway. Suddenly, she's far too conscious of what she's wearing—grey stretch shorts and a black halter—and just how much it reveals. 'Are you hungry?' she asks.

'Half starved.'

'You want something?'

Nick runs his tongue around his teeth. 'I guess it depends what's on offer.'

For a moment, Lucy's knees give. Only in the act of rebalancing does she come back to herself fully, no longer in the kitchen of her home on Mortis Point but on a table inside the Drift Net before this crowd of expectant faces.

No Daniel, no Billie, no Fin.

Her entire family, out there in that heaving sea.

'Some of you know me,' she says, fighting the tremor in her voice. 'Most of you don't. What you might know is that my husband, Daniel Locke, sailed out from Skentel this morning and hasn't come back. Our son, Fin'—here, her voice cracks and she briefly closes her eyes—'was with him. It seems now that our daughter, Billie, was with them too.'

A murmur passes through the crowd. Lucy tries not to guess the thoughts of those watching. 'I know there's a storm coming. But I also know my family's still out there. Daniel won't have let Billie or Fin drown. He'll have found a way to keep them safe. If you're thinking of joining the search, I want to thank you. But I also . . . I need to be out there too. Will someone please take me?'

Another outbreak of muttering—this one far more uncomfortable and prolonged. No one wants to meet her gaze. She understands why. Who'd relish having her onboard? Who'd risk the prospect of—

'I'll take you.'

Lucy's eyes move to the front entrance. When she sees who's standing there her chest swells. Jake Farrell is wearing yellow salopettes under a Helly Hansen RNLI jacket. The expression on his face is unfathomable.

2

His boat, *Huntsman's Daughter*, is a twenty-eight-foot cruiser. Thirty years of sun and saltwater have inflicted damage Jake can't afford to repair. Her hull is an ugly mess of stains and gelcoat patches. Right now, Lucy only really cares that she floats.

The swell, even inside the harbour, is the most violent she's ever seen. Jake goes first, walking along the segmented dock as it caterpillars up and down.

The stone breakwater obstructs Lucy's view of the sea, but she hears the booming of the waves as they strike. She sees the white spray exploding upwards. Wind, sharp and spiteful, tears at her clothes. She thinks of Daniel and her children. *Out there.* Clenching her teeth, she follows Jake.

3

It takes a few minutes to ready *Huntsman's Daughter.* Jake pulls off sail covers and unlocks the hatch. Lucy waits on the dock, ready to cast off. The engine starts on its third attempt. She slips the moorings and tosses him the lines. Then she vaults into the cockpit.

Nine years since she last came aboard. All that's changed is the disrepair. If there's a boat in Skentel less suited to these conditions, she can't think of one. Jake throttles up. *Huntsman's Daughter* vibrates beneath their feet. Water churns white behind the stern.

'Get down below,' he shouts. 'Grab some life jackets. Safety lines, too. No lie—this is going to be rough.'

Lucy squeezes past, finding handholds where she can. The yacht's pitch and roll is ferocious and they haven't even left harbour. Below-decks, the cabin spins her back a decade. To her left is the gimballed stove, familiar mugs and utensils swinging from hooks above it. To her right she sees the chart table, the VHF radio and Garmin GPS. In front are the bench seats that transform into single beds. A collapsible table between them is stacked with gear. At the far end she sees a closed concertina door. Behind it is the cramped bow cabin where, on weekend trips, they used to sleep.

So many memories flood back that they knock her off-kilter: Billie, seven years old, swaddled in a blanket while Lucy cooks dinner on the tiny stove; Jake, crouched in four inches of bilgewater, trying to replace an O-ring; the three of them camped out on deck, sipping hot chocolate as a full moon rises over the water; nights of stealthy passion in the bow cabin, her hand over Jake's mouth to keep him from crying out.

The chart table still bears a few faint marks from Billie's colouring pencils. A woollen pompom the girl once made crowns a brass barometer on the bulkhead. Hard to look at it. Hard to look at any of this.

The boat heaves up through the water. Planting her feet, Lucy switches on the VHF radio and GPS. Moving to the galley table, she rifles through the piled gear. She finds salopettes—incredibly, the same pair she wore on cold-weather days ten years ago—and quickly pulls them on. Then she grabs life jackets and safety lines and climbs back up the ladder.

To port, the *Lazy Susan* rises and falls against the inner breakwater wall. If Jake's boat triggers memories, it's nothing to this close-up view of the family yacht. This is the boat Fin calls his Water Home; the boat Billie first learned to skipper; the boat whose anchor once tore open Daniel's arm. They've sailed her to Orkney, to Nazaré, through Norway's Geirangerfjord and Nærøyfjord. On her deck, and inside her cabin, they've lived their best days.

Lucy strains her eyes, hunting for any clues to what happened. A row of paper men hangs along the main cabin window. Each wears a different crayoned expression: happy, sad, angry, surprised, scared. Lucy cut them out a few months ago. Fin drew the faces.

Her chest feels like it's being crushed. She tears her gaze away—studies the furled sails, the hull. Nothing seems different. Nothing looks amiss. And yet the yacht *exudes* malevolence. The clanking halyards and empty cockpit stir the bile in Lucy's stomach.

As they approach the pier head towards open sea, Jake swings the wheel. *Huntsman's Daughter* begins her turn. 'Hold tight!' he yells.

Lucy struggles into her vest and clips on her safety line. A heavy wave surges through the entrance channel. The bow rears up. Then they crash down the wave's trough. Lucy takes a faceful of saltwater cold enough to make her gasp. When she looks up, she sees something horrifying.

4

Before her, wind and sea and sky have conspired to create a panorama of devastation. She feels like she's gazing across a landscape of snow-ravaged mountains—except *these* mountains are moving, sliding, smashing. The snow on their peaks foams. It bursts and rolls.

Off to starboard, waves sacrifice themselves upon the shattered altar of Mortis Point. Plumes of spray climb heavenward, whipped into spume by tearing wind. Overhead, chariot-wheel clouds scythe towards the land.

Never has Lucy seen such terrible conditions. Hardly possible that she's sailing into them—*inconceivable* that Daniel ventured out here with Billie and Fin. But although the spectacle is terrible to witness, it's nothing to what Lucy sees spread out across the water: scores of yachts and fishing vessels, all with their bows pointed shoreward.

'What're they *doing*?' she cries. Her question is lost in the detonation of another wave against the hull. It pitches them up and tosses them back down. Lucy feels the impact through her knees. She turns to Jake for answers. Watches him throttle up, pushing the engine as hard as he dares. There's so much pressure in her chest it feels like she's beneath the sea rather than above it. 'Why are they turning *back*?'

Huntsman's Daughter punches through another massive wave. All around them, marbled water fizzes white.

'Take the wheel,' Jake shouts. 'I'll get on the radio.'

Lucy switches positions. He disappears below. She keeps the yacht pointed west, aiming for a gap between the boats returning to harbour. Waves are breaking in all directions. A large one hits from port, swamping the deck. Cold water bursts over her, pouring down the inside of her jacket.

Moments later, *Huntsman's Daughter* plunges down the back of another monster. Its trough is so deep she can't see the oncoming flotilla. When she glances past the stern, even the breakwater has disappeared.

At last, the yacht rises out of its trench. Lucy sees the boats again. Most are shallow-draught fishing vessels, a few day cruisers among them. She wants to get on the horn, urge them to turn around. But the cruisers aren't designed for these conditions. Even the fishing boats have dangerously pushed their luck. As one of them passes to starboard, its skipper shakes his head at her.

Jake emerges from below and seals the hatch. 'Coastguard's reporting waves up to twenty feet past the Point. Winds of forty knots and forecast to get far worse.' He looks past her to the boats struggling back to Skentel, grimacing as another wave bursts across the bow. 'You can't blame them.'

She doesn't. But of all the days her family could go missing at sea, why this one?

'Not everyone's coming in,' Jake adds. 'I spoke to a few skippers still in the search area. Good guys. They'll keep looking, long as they possibly can.'

Which means—which *has* to mean—that no one's been found.

Lucy's stomach spasms. She tenses, feels it spasm again. Surrendering the wheel, she leans over the rail and vomits. For a moment she hangs there, staring into the sea. The water's so turbulent it looks carbonated. Oxygen fizzes in the energy released from colliding waves.

Wiping her mouth, she turns back to Jake. 'Where're we headed?'

'Coastguard plotted a search pattern using SARIS. They took a start position from where our lifeboat found the *Lazy Susan*. Tidal drift's carrying north-easterly and wind's still from the west. They've got a pretty solid grid mapped out. Trouble is, seas like these, people get lost in the troughs. Easier from the sky, but up there they've got their own problems. On the water you have to be up close with the waves falling right, just to stand a chance.'

He sets his jaw. 'Sorry. I know that's not easy to hear. At least we still have light.'

But even that is dying.

'I'm going to run up some sail,' Jake tells her. 'I need you to take the wheel again.' He nods at the deck-mounted ball compass. 'Keep her pointed at three hundred. Watch out for rogue waves. Some of these are easily big enough to flip us.'

Bracing her feet, Lucy steadies the wheel. All around her she sees foaming water, jagged white peaks. While Jake prepares to unfurl and reef the mainsail, she lets herself cry—huge, wracking sobs that spiral away on the wind. A few minutes of that and she can concentrate again, on their bearing and the waves and the dipping and lifting bow. Clenching her teeth, she pushes out a thought: *Where are you? Please show me.* Perhaps, if she focuses hard enough, her family will find a way to answer.

Rain, sharp as needles, stings her face. To starboard, water pulls away from the boat as a giant wave begins to build. Lucy spins the wheel, turning *Huntsman's Daughter* to face it. She doesn't react fast enough. When the wave breaks across the deck, water surges into cockpit, lifting her off her feet. The yacht rolls wildly. She's so frightened of being swept away that she forgets for a moment that she's tethered. Water floods her salopettes and soaks her dungarees—so shockingly cold that it flushes Lucy's head of thoughts.

Jake clambers back into the cockpit. With the mainsail uncovered, he starts winching. Bit by bit the canvas rises, spooling out from the boom. The wind is wailing now, a banshee lament. Lucy turns the wheel. The sail flaps once and fills.

Jake puts his hand on her shoulder. She wants to lean into him, resists. She wants to close her eyes, wrap her arms around his neck and imagine this all away. Instead, she sets her gaze on the sea.

NINE

1

Ten minutes after *Huntsman's Daughter* casts off, officers locate Daniel Locke's Volvo. Abraham Rose gets the call in the Drift Net, while he's talking to coastguard officials.

When he steps outside, a fist of wind punches him backwards. The harbour looks like the inside of a washing machine—a sudsy froth churned up by the huge swell. Rain blows from one direction, then another. Within seconds, he's soaked through.

He finds Locke's Volvo at the back of the quayside car park. A female police officer stands beside it, chin tucked against the storm. Abraham flashes his card. 'You touch anything?'

'No, sir.'

He peers through the driver's window. Inside, the car's spotless—not a mote of dust or streak of dried mud. On the passenger seat is a Spider-Man booster seat. A canvas tote bag lies on the back seat.

Pulling on a latex glove, Abraham tries the door. It pops open with a clunk. The female officer shoots him a doleful look. Even in Skentel, people lock their cars—unless they're not coming back. When the door swings open, the glint of glass catches his eye. He sees, in the door pocket, a bottle of Talisker single malt. Half of the whisky's been consumed.

Abraham pulls out his mobile. He dials Billie Locke's number, ducking his head inside the car. The first two attempts fail. On the third, the call connects. On the Volvo's back seat, blue light glows through the tote bag's fabric. There's a waspy vibration. In his ear he hears the girl's voice: *'Hey, you've reached the auditions for Billie's favourite voicemail message. Don't screw it up!'*

Abraham hangs up, his gaze returning to the whisky bottle. Immediately, his phone shrills. He straightens so abruptly he whacks his head on the Volvo's roof.

'I'm in that hobby shop on the quay,' Cooper says. 'A few doors down from the Drift Net. They have CCTV.'

'Daniel Locke?'

'We're getting to it. Guy here's a bit . . . well, you'll see.'

'I'll be right there.'

Abraham pockets his phone. He stares at the tote bag; at the Spider-Man booster seat; at the bottle of Talisker stuffed into the door pocket. Individual beats in an unfolding family tragedy. He thinks of the mother, venturing out across that hostile sea. Abraham doesn't know much about Lucy Locke, but he does know one thing: however these last hours before darkness play out, her old life is over. A good chance it'll never be rebuilt.

Exhaustion washes over him. He bares his teeth against it. He has a job to do here; people to help. His illness can damn well wait.

Abraham peers across the Volvo's roof to the gap in the breakwater. The first fishing trawler is returning. Black smoke chugs from its stacks as it surfs in. For a moment he fears it'll smash straight into the quay. But its engine, churning the harbour water in full reverse, drags it back. Two oilskin-clad volunteers on the quay catch tossed lines.

To the officer guarding the Volvo, he says, 'Don't let anyone touch it.' Blotting rain from his eyes, he gives her a closer look. 'Are you warm enough?'

She offers him a bleak smile. 'I'll survive.'

Crossing the car park, head bowed against driving rain, Abraham calls Barnstaple. He should be back there already, running things from the newly established incident room. But events are moving so fast that by the time he returns this could be over.

A forensics team is inbound, tasked with the Volvo and the family yacht. In addition, Abraham requests a police search adviser from Middlemoor. The coastguard is leading the offshore search and rescue, but survivors could wash up anywhere along this stretch of coast.

It's now 4.17 p.m. The distress call came in at 12.37. The *Lazy Susan* was located thirty-six minutes later. If Daniel Locke and those kids are still out there, they've been in the water over three hours.

A wave—the largest yet—booms against the breakwater wall. A geyser of white water climbs sixty feet. Raising his shoulders, Abraham strides along the quay.

2

When he enters the shop, he understands Cooper's warning. The proprietor—pot-bellied with a luxuriant grey ponytail—is dressed like an extra from *The Lord of the Rings*: riding boots, tan leather trousers, unbleached linen smock. His left forearm sports an archery bracer. One side of his face looks like it's in painful retreat from an enormous white-headed boil growing in the crevice of his nose and cheek. The shop itself is piled high with games, comics and science-fiction merchandise. There are action figures, replica movie weapons, a full-sized Dalek. One corner is stuffed with blank canvasses, easels, paintbrushes and oils.

'Greetings, traveller,' says the man, from the stockroom doorway. When he fails to raise a smile, he glances at Cooper, behind him. 'I hazard we're met by another forthright officer of the law.'

Cooper throws Abraham a flat-eyed look. 'Sir, this is Wayland Rawlings. He owns the place.'

'Or perhaps it owns me,' the man replies, eyes twinkling. 'Such is the dichotomy of commercial enterprise.'

'DI Rose,' Abraham says. 'Where's the CCTV?'

'Ah. You refer, of course, to our Orwellian older sibling.'

'What?'

'Big Brother,' Rawlings explains. 'Pray, do follow me.'

In the stockroom, a desk supports two widescreen monitors. An expensive-looking PC rig stands on the floor.

'I've already shown your venerable colleague,' Rawlings says. 'But I've rewound the footage so you can experience it first-hand.'

The left-hand monitor displays four frozen images in high-definition colour: an external shot of the quay, two interior shop views and a fourth of the stockroom. The time-stamp reads 11.19 a.m.

'This set-up didn't come cheap.'

'Nor do our vendibles. We do what we can to protect them.'

'There's demand for this stuff in Skentel?'

'Oh, we don't sell much over the counter these days. Except, perhaps, for the art materials. We're based here purely because of my romantic attachment to the sea. Most of our wares we hawk on that remarkable invention of Tim Berners-Lee.'

'The internet,' Cooper says, as if Abraham were ninety years old.

'The information superhighway,' Rawlings adds.

'Show me the tape.'

The man bends over his keyboard. Onscreen, the water in the harbour begins to move. Boats bob up and down. A herring gull lands on metal railings. Then, travelling not much faster than walking speed, a silver Volvo XC90 passes the shopfront. The number plate is clearly visible. It's Daniel Locke's car.

'Go back,' Abraham says. 'Pause it.'

Rawlings does something with the mouse. The car reverses and freezes outside the shop.

'Can you full-screen it?'

Four times larger, the image is far clearer. Abraham sucks air through his teeth. Privacy glass obscures the Volvo's back seat. Daniel, behind the wheel, is only partly visible. But the passenger-seat occupant is easily identifiable. Raised by his booster, Fin Locke stares up at his father.

The boy looks frightened.

Abraham's scalp goes cold. There's something horrific about the image—something unutterably bleak. He thinks of the video he saw en route to Skentel—the boy describing the story he was writing.

This isn't going to be one of those sad stories at all but one to cheer you up, cos you'll see that actually in the end some nice things happened.

Not much chance, looking at this, that some nice things happened to Fin Locke. Abraham feels like he's watching two dead people.

'How far back did you go?'

'Eleven a.m.,' Cooper says. 'Just before they left the school.'

'This is the first sighting?'

'Yes.'

'Keep playing it,' Abraham tells Rawlings. 'Triple speed.'

'We already checked,' the man says. 'This is the only time the car drives past.'

'Just do it. Triple speed.'

They watch in silence. Boats bob so fast in Skentel's harbour they look as if they're bouncing on the water. People zip past the windows. The shelf cloud rolls in from the Atlantic, gobbling up the sky.

'There,' Abraham says. 'Back up. Now play it again, half speed.'

Rawlings works the mouse. All three men lean closer. Top left, the *Lazy Susan* appears, crawling past the inner breakwater wall.

'Pause it,' Abraham says. They stare at the frozen image.

The boat is much further away than the Volvo was, but the resolution is crisp enough to show some detail. Daniel Locke stands in the cockpit, hands on the wheel. Watching him, just visible above the hatch, is his son.

'We're going to need this footage,' Abraham tells Rawlings. He nods at the monitor. 'I didn't see you on camera. You weren't here when it happened?'

'I was availing myself of coffee in the establishment a few doors down. Owned by the poor lady whose family you see before you.'

'You know her?'

'*Know* her? Sir, I attend her art class every Wednesday afternoon at the Drift Net. Thanks to Lucy Locke and her enthusiastic students, I've added an entirely new range of stock.' He indicates the artists' materials in one corner. '*Flies* off the shelf, that little lot. The lady deserves a medal for her services to the good folk of this community. And to some of the coarser folk, too.'

'The coarser folk?'

'Oh, ignore me.' Rawlings dabs his brow. 'I tend to overdramatize, sometimes reflected in my choice of words. Boredom, mainly. Or an excessive craving for stimulation.'

Abraham nods at the screen. 'Is *that* stimulating enough for you?'

The man's face crumples. Then he steadies himself. 'I'm sure our brave lifeboat volunteers will bring them back safe and sound.'

'You know the husband? Daniel Locke?'

'*Him.*'

Abraham blinks. 'Meaning?'

'We *all* know *him.*' Rawlings picks up a tasselled cushion from the desk chair.

Inside Abraham's lungs, something foul is mobilizing. Beside the desk stands a huge blank canvas. He imagines, for a moment, the horror if he coughed. 'Sir, do you have any information about Daniel Locke you think is relevant to this investigation?'

The man hugs the cushion to his belly. 'So you're *investigating* him, then?'

'We're trying to find that family. If you know something about Daniel Locke you believe is important, you can help us enormously by sharing it.'

Rawlings sighs. 'I don't have anything specific. But some people—one just gets a feeling, doesn't one?'

Abraham is starting to get a very strong feeling about Wayland Rawlings—so strong he can taste it, like bad coffee, in his mouth. He can't stand gossips and troublemakers. And he dislikes Rawlings' treatment of the Locke family's misfortune as vicarious entertainment; the very worst kind of road-accident gawper. He hands the man a card. 'We'll need the computer. First, I want you to email the footage to this address.'

'A moment's work, my liege.'

'If you need to contact me directly, you can use the details on that card.'

Rawlings looks at the screen. 'Those poor children,' he laments. 'I wonder what that beast did to them.'

3

Outside, the wind is unyielding. Abraham feels like he's walking into an opposing magnetic force. Rain needles his face. Debris tumbles along the quay: leaves; stones; carrier bags; three rattling beer cans.

The search adviser from Middlemoor will be here in an hour. His comms team wants to schedule a press conference back in Barnstaple, but most of the available media is rushing towards Skentel. Forensics should arrive soon, too. In the meantime, Abraham wants a closer look at the Lockes' boat.

'What the hell does *vendibles* mean, do you think?' Cooper asks.

'Why don't you look it up?'

Abraham's phone buzzes. It's the contact centre in Exeter. He winces— already, it feels like the established lines of communication are blurring.

'I have a call for you from the SMC,' says a voice.

'The who?'

'The coastguard's Search and Rescue Mission Coordinator. Seems like they found something.'

TEN

1

Towers of white water, whichever way Lucy looks.

Each slope *Huntsman's Daughter* climbs is the one she thinks will flip them. Each trough they plunge down is the one she knows will swallow them. Her terror is a living thing, a bird beating wings inside her chest. Every minute that passes is a minute her husband and children haven't been found; a minute they remain in the water in this cold and hellish sea.

Standing in the cockpit, Lucy feels like she's made of glass, so brittle that the slightest hammer tap could shatter her. All she wants—*all* she wants—is to be reunited with her family, to pluck them, hearts beating and lungs heaving, from the clutches of this malicious sea. She needs to kiss Fin's hair, breathe his almondy smell, hug Billie tight enough to make her groan, look into Daniel's eyes and tell him how much she loves him, even though a part of her is angry with him—*furious*—for sailing her children into this and leaving her all alone.

What rational explanation could there be for his actions? Only one that Lucy can imagine: Daniel feared for Billie and Fin's safety on land and chose to bring them out here instead. But what could they have been fleeing? Certainly nothing that makes any sense. And why, in any case, not take her with them? Or, at the very least, find some way of making contact?

Daddy, no—

Lucy cringes from her son's words.

So far, the prospect of not finding her family has been inconceivable. Now, the possibility grows so real it takes physical form, a presence coalescing in the boat. Even worse is a voice, half caught on the wind. She knows it wants her to listen, and she knows she has to resist. Because the secret it hopes to share, the truth it wants her to face, is simply too shattering to accept.

Daniel, she thinks. *Daniel, tell me you kept them safe. Tell me you're protecting them, you're keeping them alive. Tell me you're safe too.*

As *Huntsman's Daughter* climbs another wave, Lucy spins back to the study, the balance sheet, the paperwork; her husband's cold kiss and lost expression.

That voice sings its horrors on the wind.

Another image comes: Fin, in the water, blue-lipped in a maelstrom. Her boy without his glasses, unable to see.

Lucy covers her ears and screams. Beside her, Jake takes the wheel. He keeps the yacht on its course as the ocean thrashes beneath them. A clout of water bursts across the deck. It foams and hisses in the cockpit before draining out through the scuppers. Jake turns to starboard just in time to avoid another wave hitting them broadside, this one so solid it surely would have driven them under.

She thinks of Billie, exploding with ideas, with sheer unadulterated *life*. Earlier this year the girl joined Sea Shepherd, the marine conservation charity. In July, she's sailing to the Danish Faroe Islands for Operation Bloody Fjords. There, she'll attempt to disrupt the annual *grindadráp*—an all-summer-long slaughter of pilot whales in the bays around the archipelago.

Lucy remembers the photographs Billie showed her: laughing men wading in a blood-red sea; whales hooked by their blowholes and dragged on to beaches to be butchered; rows of shining carcasses—calves and pregnant mothers among them.

'They banned us from their waters,' Billie told her. 'So we can't stop them driving the pods ashore. But this year there's something different planned.'

Lucy knew that meant direct action. Knew, too, that it would likely end in violence. Daniel lobbied the girl hard to change her mind. Ed joined him. If it had been a sudden preoccupation, Lucy might have added her voice. But Billie didn't just grow up by the sea, she grew up *in* it; enamoured of its wildlife, committed to its protection. Her heroes form a *Who's Who* of marine conservation.

Again, Lucy senses that voice calling out across the waves. She casts a furtive look at Jake—worried, irrationally, that it'll get inside his head and use him as its mouthpiece. Because if it does, what then?

The cold eats into her bones. She can't feel her fingers, nor the binoculars Jake passed her to scan the sea. She should go below and strip off her soaked dungarees, but they can't afford to lose her eyes on deck.

Lifting the binoculars, she scours the water for a sign. The *Lazy Susan's* immersion suits are deep red. Sealed at the extremities and triple insulated, they form a completely waterproof barrier. Worn correctly, they'll delay hypothermia for hours.

That voice presses close.

Lucy clenches her teeth against it.

2

At six knots, it takes over an hour to reach the edge of the search pattern plotted by SARIS. This far out, in these conditions, there's no sight of land. Despite Jake's assurances, Lucy sees no evidence of a rescue operation. No sign, whatsoever, of humanity.

Beyond *Huntsman's Daughter's* bow, the world has emptied of colour.

Overhead, the sky resembles an ash cloud, boiling and rolling, driving the rain before it.

The weather worsens. The sea comes at them from all angles. Wind slices a full metre of water from each wave's crest. They hit with the power of a cannon salvo, rocking the boat, filling the cockpit, repeatedly knocking Lucy off her feet.

She knows she's risking Jake's life. Knows, too, that he'll search these waters for as long as she asks—that he'll accept whatever danger that brings. It's selfish to the point of monstrous, but she needs to be out here and Jake is her only means. However barbaric it may be, in a trade for the lives of her family, she'd willingly sacrifice him as collateral. It's a deal with the Devil to make her teeth squeal, to make one part of her soul recoil from the other. But she can't deny the reality: there's *nothing* she won't do to bring her husband and children home.

That voice returns, poisoning her with questions. This time it doesn't quit. It beats in her ears, thumps in her chest. Suddenly—impossibly—she senses that Jake hears it too, because she *sees* it in his eyes when she looks at him, and she's just about to cry out and prevent him from acknowledging it when she realizes it isn't what she thought but something quite different: the whistle of turbines, the violent chopping of rotor blades, the sound, unmistakeable, of a hovering coastguard helicopter.

3

Lucy searches the clouds, hunting for a breach. That pulse of rotors ebbs and swells. One moment it seems to be fading, the next it sounds like it's directly overhead. She casts about, frustrated. For precious seconds the wind roars so intensely it drowns out everything. And then—

'*There!*'

At first, Lucy can't see the helicopter, just its flashing anti-collision beacon. It floats behind a maroon ring of cloud, a vast cataracted eye.

She can't fill her lungs. Despite the falling air pressure, it feels like she's being crushed. Because a helicopter, hovering all the way out here, means *some*thing, even if she doesn't know what.

Jake turns the wheel, marginally adjusting their course. *Huntsman's Daughter* plunges down another wave. Everything is lost in a blinding eruption of spray. Then, ahead of them, a curtain of cloud parts. And there, hanging like a huge mechanical jewel, utterly implausible in size and shape, is the AgustaWestland Lucy saw hours earlier.

Its body is frozen in place, defiant of wind and rain. If ever there was an example of humanity's arrogance in the face of nature's savagery, this is surely it.

The downdraught has created a white sinkhole upon the sea, its surface flayed open to reveal the pale ribs of water beneath. Winched from the eye of that sinkhole by the helicopter's steel umbilical come two drenched humans.

A buzzing, now, in Lucy's head. Her jaw tightens. Every muscle in her body locks in place. She wants to cry out her family's names but they form a logjam in her throat.

Please, she begs.

Please be here. Please be alive.

Jake seizes her wrist. 'Watch out for other boats!' he shouts. 'They could be close. We won't spot them easily.'

In this sea, a collision would likely be fatal. Despite the danger, Lucy can't do anything but stare at those steadily ascending figures. In the red light of the helicopter's anti-collision beacon, water pours off them like blood.

Lucy sees no movement of their limbs, no signs of life. Both wear red immersion suits so similar it's impossible to make any distinction. One of them, in a visored orange helmet, is clearly the winchman. The other figure's face is obscured.

It can't be Fin. Far too big to be her boy. But whether it's Daniel or Billie or someone else entirely, Lucy cannot tell. So disjointed are her thoughts that for a while she forgets what she clutches to her chest.

Her paralysis shatters. Gasping, she lifts the binoculars, but before she can seek out her target, those figures reach the top of the winch. Lucy looks over the lenses just as the pair are pulled inside.

She's panting now. Crying, too. Has she just seen a miracle? Or the very worst of endings? If the rescued figure is Billie, what of Fin? If the heart of that sinkhole released one child, could it conceivably be persuaded to release two?

She tears her gaze from the helicopter. The sea looks vengeful now, furious with its loss—a battlefield of ragged water rising all around. A wild thought strikes. Lucy's free hand closes on her tether. Perhaps, if she casts herself into the water, she can trade her life for theirs.

But the sea doesn't want her fealty. It isn't sentient. Nothing beneath these waves, nor anything in this wind and rain, gives a damn for Daniel or Billie or Fin. Never has she believed in an omniscient creator. Never has she prayed to one. She might feel a compulsion now, but that's all the more reason to resist. To plead for mercy from a God she's previously denied would surely bring more trouble than good.

Overhead, the helicopter's nosecone dips. The whistle of its turbines rises in pitch. It sounds, suddenly, like it's struggling to stay aloft. Only a hundred feet of turbulent air separate it from the waves. If those rotor blades clip the water, it'll flip and sink like a rock. Instead—slowly at first, quickly gathering speed—it flies over *Huntsman's Daughter*, heading east.

Lucy watches it depart. Then she twists back to Jake. 'What happened?' she shouts. 'Who *was* that? Who did they save?'

But Jake can't answer her questions. The look he gives her is bleak.

'Listen to me.' His words are almost lost in an explosion of saltwater across the bow. 'It's getting worse out here. We can't stay much longer. I'll get on the radio, see what I can find out. But you've *got* to focus, Lucy. If one of these waves broadsides us . . .'

Jake doesn't have to finish his sentence. She knows what's at stake. 'I've got this,' she tells him. 'I swear it.'

'Keep us on this bearing. Stay *vigilant*. I'll be as quick as I can.'

They swap places. Lucy takes the wheel. Jake waits for the shattering impact of another wave to dissipate, water pouring off the deck in white torrents. Then he opens the hatch and dives through.

Eastwards, the AgustaWestland vanishes inside a cloudbank. For a handful of seconds its anti-collision beacon is visible as a bloody smear inside the grey. Then that, too, disappears.

Finally, it's just Lucy. No evidence of humanity. Just a patched fibreglass hull separating her from this savage and godless sea. A wind gust tilts them violently to starboard. She spins the wheel, too late to stop a wave broadsiding the boat. Water surges over the gunwales, so colossal in weight that she feels like she's been struck by a car. Her feet lift from the deck. She crashes into the pushpit with an impact that makes her scream. The water keeps pressing. Only the safety line stands between her and the sea, but a few inches of nylon can't resist such an all-consuming force. She feels the webbing vibrating, knows it's going to snap, knows she'll be driven into the water like a nail beneath a hammer. With the helicopter gone, with Jake belowdecks, she stands no chance of rescue.

When her scream runs out of breath, she seals her lips tight. The water keeps coming, so hard against her head that her eardrums feel as if they're perforating. Her jaw is knocked open. Seawater presses into her throat. The deck bucks beneath her, tossing her to port.

Suddenly there's air where before there was only water. An instant later Lucy slams against the wheel. Something snaps in her left side. A rib, she thinks. Possibly two. When she tries to breathe it's agony.

The hatch opens. Jake staggers up the ladder. He takes one look and mouths an expletive. After scanning the sea for danger, he puts the boat on autopilot. He's at her side moments later, cradling her head. 'Are you hurt?'

She wants to reply, wants to assure him she's OK. But her teeth are clattering uncontrollably. She can't think, let alone speak.

'I couldn't get the coastguard,' he tells her. 'There's too much activity on channel sixteen. But I raised another boat.'

He breathes deep. Lucy braces herself for what's coming. She wants to cover her ears so she doesn't hear. Cover his mouth so he can't speak.

But then Jake does something unexpected. He flashes a white-toothed grin. 'That coastguard chopper. It *found* them, Lucy. Billie, Daniel, Fin—I can't quite believe it but it did. They're alive, all three. Your family are all alive.'

4

The storm fades. No fury, no violence, no cold.

The deck turns statuesque beneath her, as if the boat has beached itself on sand. The roar of wind departs. The agony in her side dissipates.

Lucy searches Jake's eyes for any sign of a lie. Because she *cannot* let herself believe this, should it be untrue. If any of her family are still out here, she won't abandon them, whatever the outcome or cost.

But Jake's eyes harbour no deception, and when she gives herself a few seconds to think, she realizes there's no reason they would. He's dedicated his life, after all, to rescuing people from the sea.

Lucy recalls the red-suited figures rising into the helicopter. She thinks of Billie and in a beat she's nineteen again, screaming her lungs out inside London's University College Hospital. Never in her life did she expect pain like it, nor the existential jolt that follows when a wet and mewling mass is lowered to her chest.

'Billie,' she murmurs, knowing it's a girl, trying to work out how she feels about this unplanned upheaval of her future.

'There's a young man asking for you,' the Jamaican nurse tells her. 'Says his name's Lucian, handsome as all Creation. Is he this pretty little gift's father?'

Lucy shakes her head. Lucian's just her ride home.

In truth, she has no idea of Billie's provenance. Her first semester at the Slade School of Art was far wilder than she ever intended. Skipping back along the timeline, she can count at least seven candidate fathers. All that effort to get there, and then her oldest demon raised its head, culminating in this strange, unworldly creature at her breast.

Lucy doesn't need a therapist to explain her promiscuity. Her first six years of childhood were as difficult as Daniel's or Nick's. Lucy's parents—both substance abusers—offered her zero affection or interest. By the time social services removed her, she was surviving on scraps scavenged from takeout trays. Although her nightmare ended when her great-aunt won custody, it still left scars.

Never, in the years following her deliverance, could she refuse anyone prepared to show her warmth. As she moved into her teenage years, the consequences were entirely predictable.

Even Lucian, handsome as all Creation, had wanted to be more than just a ride home. When their friendship soured, Lucy decided to escape London for good. Fleeing with Billie to the Continent, she found stability, for a few years, at a commune in Spain's Tabernas Desert.

But the relationship Lucy embarked on in the badlands brought consequences even more disastrous. Relocating to Portugal, another upheaval, she hit her darkest period. Finally, terrified of how her nomadic lifestyle was affecting Billie, she returned to Skentel. Remarkable, really, that through it all the girl still thrived.

And how Billie *has* thrived, more so with each passing year. Lucy hasn't always agreed with her choices, but she's always admired her motivation. Seldom has Billie turned down a fight she's believed worth having—particularly on issues of animal welfare or conservation. A steady drift towards direct action led to her recent sign-up with Sea Shepherd.

Lucy clenches her teeth. She tries to imagine her daughter now—alive and shivering in a coastguard helicopter.

And Fin.

When she thinks of her boy—when she recalls his bare legs swinging beneath the breakfast table and Avengers glasses hanging askew from his nose—she moans like an animal impaled. Because even relief *this* transformative can't expunge completely the horror of recent hours.

If the helicopter rescued all three members of her family, they must surely have still been together. Which means the figure on the winch must have been Daniel. Doubtless he'd have sent Billie and Fin up first.

Lucy's not quite ready to think about her husband yet. Instead she turns her mind to Jake—this man she once loved, and who clearly loves her still. Back when they were together, she couldn't content herself with a hero. And now here he is, risking himself for her, for her children and the man she chose instead.

She recalls her earlier betrayal. How, in a trade for her family, she'd willingly sacrifice him. She's shamed even more by that thought now—repulsed by it—even though it's still true.

While she doesn't believe in God, she does believe in equilibrium, in a universe that balances good with bad. And suddenly she's terrified she *has* sacrificed Jake. Has consigned him to some future catastrophe.

She presses her fingers to his cheeks. Leaning forwards, she kisses him, hard and deep. Tries to push some of her lifeforce into him and counter her earlier treachery.

On his lips she tastes the sea and a place in the past almost tangible.

Jake's grey eyes flare. For a moment he relaxes into her. She senses his sadness, then; his desolation. It's a door left open, an unhealed wound. Another beat and he's pulling away, breathing deep, searching her face for answers. 'Lucy,' he begins.

She shakes her head, realizing her mistake. How naive—to shove against the universe and not expect a response. Chastened, Lucy kisses his cheek. Jake recognizes the change. His eyes register the tiniest flicker of pain.

'We've got to get back,' she says, as salt spray bursts over them.

'Can you stand?'

'I think.'

'You're still attached?'

Lucy gives her leash a tug, nods. Words are hard, now. Emotion plugs her throat. Beyond the bow, another huge wave is building. She looks up at Jake, sees his safety line hanging loose from his waist, thinks again of that devil-deal she struck and her awkward attempt to revoke it.

Lucy grabs his carabiner, locks him down. 'Careful,' she tells him. 'On the way back in. We aren't safe yet.'

The wave hits. *Huntsman's Daughter* barrels out of it, buoyant as a cork. The air fills with confetti-like shrapnel. Incredible, that in the depths of this maelstrom she can suddenly find beauty.

Overhead, the last light is dying. No chance they'll make it back before full dark. Already, the easternmost clouds have turned to soot.

But Billie and Fin are alive, Lucy thinks, even though she knows, without doubt, that this is far from the end.

Daniel's alive.

Soon, she'll have to consider what comes next.

5

As night draws its shutters across the sky, a leeward wind pushes them home. The sea throws cathedrals of black water heavenward. *Huntsman's Daughter* steers a perilous path between them. The boat's white mast light and her red and green navigation lights cast diamonds and precious stones into the spray.

Lucy wants to go belowdecks and get an update on her family, but the conditions are too intense for one person to handle alone. Jake follows an easterly bearing, shouting instructions while Lucy keeps her eye on the raging water, constantly repositioning her tether.

She's so cold and wet that everything takes three times longer than it should. The only thing to slip past her numbness is pain. Pain when she slams a shin against a moulding. Pain when the blisters on her winch hand tear open. Pain when seawater bites raw flesh. Pain in her back, in her neck. Pain, most of all, from her broken ribs. But far worse than the physical pain is the commotion inside her head.

That coastguard chopper. It found them, Lucy. Billie, Daniel, Fin—I can't quite believe it but it did. They're alive, all three. Your family are all alive.

Jake's words allowed her to breathe again, but only barely. Because so many questions now demand answers. She has no clue how long they were in the water, nor their condition when rescued. Secondary drowning could kill them in the helicopter. Hypothermia might stop their hearts dead back on land.

Monstrous thoughts shouldn't be given food to take on flesh. Deliberately, Lucy steers her mind away. But one thing she can't outrun is that quietly insistent voice. Now, it overtakes her, relentless with its questions.

What was Daniel doing out here with Billie and Fin?

Why did he lie about where he was going?

Why did he take Fin out of school?

Worse, there are two voices now, where earlier there was only one. That second voice, she discovers, is far darker, far more insistent. And it doesn't ask questions. It accuses.

You know, Lucy.

You know EXACTLY what he was doing.

No. She won't have it. She loves Daniel. She trusts him with her life.

And Billie's life? asks that first voice. *Fin's?*

Lucy finds herself nodding through her tears. She knows her husband more intimately than anyone.

But sometimes the damage in a person runs deeper than anyone imagines. You're not the only one carrying scars, Lucy. You, Nick, Daniel—you all reacted differently to broadly the same trauma. You went on your demeaning little love quest. Nick's covetousness, over the years, grew into something monstrous.

And Daniel . . . Daniel's reaction to childhood trauma was perhaps the most intense of all. His desire for control—his compulsion to create order from chaos, to micromanage the smallest details of his existence—veers close to the pathological.

And what did Daniel just lose, Lucy?

He lost control.

She thinks of the balance sheet on his laptop, the paperwork spread across his desk; of what happened between her and Nick a few weeks ago; of how much Daniel had been hurting.

'Bullshit,' she hisses. 'It doesn't make sense. He loves them. He loves *me.*'

Around her, the sea reacts with scorn and fury. For almost an hour they're forced to turn from shore and point directly into the storm. When the boat surfs down a wave, it picks up so much speed it risks ploughing beneath the next. They deploy a sea anchor from the bow—an underwater chute that slows them in the water. It barely helps. Lucy loses count of breaking waves so immense they hardly seem scalable. She fears constantly for a snapped rudder or keel. Without them, they'll have no way of keeping the bow aligned. A broadside from one of these monsters will bury *Huntsman's Daughter* and likely drown them both.

Only once, off to port, does Lucy spot any sign of humanity—the red portlight of another boat travelling east at speed. She wonders if it's the Tamar-class lifeboat returning to Skentel. Within moments it disappears into the darkness.

Around six thirty, they reel in the sea anchor and come about. By now, the pain in Lucy's side is so intense she can only take small sips of air. Cold has settled like mercury in her bones.

Jake guides them east. The coastline emerges—a bank of purest black on which Skentel is a cluster of twinkling lights. Never has Lucy been more grateful to spot land. Never has she felt so frustrated that she doesn't already stand upon it.

The distance shrinks. The source of each light grows clear. She sees the sulphur-yellow gas lamps outside the Goat Hotel; the brightly lit windows of homes higher up the slope; further south, the multicoloured lanterns of the Penny Moon campsite swinging on their cables.

Winking on and off along the beaches and bays are scores of other lights. They confuse her at first, until she realizes they must be the torch beams of shoreline searchers returning to Skentel.

The breakwater wall obscures much of the town's quay, but Lucy sees the lifeboat station perched above it, bathed by cold white spotlights. The Norman church of St Peter's is similarly floodlit. No lights shine from Mortis Point. Up there, the darkness surrounding her home feels prescient.

Entering Skentel's harbour is perilous. Accurate positioning is everything. Waves break heaviest in shallow water. With their bow pointed shorewards, they risk being swamped from the stern. They'll need to surf in on a wave, but if they go too early it'll break right on top of them. Go too late and it'll roll beneath their hull, leaving them at the mercy of the next one.

As Jake lines up their approach, the gap in the breakwater reveals itself. There, shining more brightly than she's ever seen it, is Skentel's quay. Golden light blazes from the Drift Net's windows. On the flagstones outside stand an ambulance and two police cars, emergency lights strobing. Silhouetted along the waterfront is a packed row of onlookers.

Lucy's grateful for their interest, but she cringes at the prospect of facing them. The coastguard helicopter will have flown to the North Devon District Hospital in Barnstaple. All she wants is to put her arms around her children and sleep. She's been on this boat too long. The hospital's still forty minutes away by car.

'Get ready!' Jake shouts, opening the throttle.

She twists around, sees a wall of rising black glass. Already, the crest is high above them, spray blowing off it like smoke. The stern lifts. *Huntsman's Daughter* begins to accelerate.

And then Lucy sees that Jake's judged it all wrong, that he's gone far too early. They rise faster, sliding up the wave's face until their bow is almost vertical beneath them. Lucy slams against the hatchway. The air is punched from her lungs. Her ribs feel like they've sheared off inside her but she can't scream, can't even draw breath to try. The lights of the quay dance like fireflies. Lucy's head lolls forwards. Her face cracks against the bulkhead.

With the wave about to break, *Huntsman's Daughter* rockets down its face. Lucy sees they'll either be flipped into folding surf or catapulted into the stone quay.

And then it does break. The lights on the quay go dark. Her world is enveloped in sound. Water in her nose, in her mouth. A huge pressure on her spine, forcing her against the bulkhead. The yacht gathers more speed, shaking like a locomotive on warped rails. She feels it rolling to starboard. Closes her eyes for the impact.

The water's so cold, the pressure so intense, that Lucy can no longer think. Beneath her, *Huntsman's Daughter* twists back to port. The bow rises, the thunder recedes. A deluge of black water fizzes from the deck— and suddenly they're surfing, arrow-straight, towards the jewelled lights of the quay.

Jake spins the wheel to starboard. The boat turns hard, slipping around the pier head into the harbour's calmer waters. For the first time in hours, Lucy can plant her feet securely, can hear something other than wind and crashing sea.

She glances at Jake. Smiles through her tears. Despite her betrayal, she didn't kill him—her hands are clean of the act, if not the thought.

'Can you take over?' he asks, tipping out the mooring buoys. 'I'll jump on the radio. See if I can get an update.'

Lucy just wants to hug the bulkhead until they're safely tied up, but she unfolds her frozen limbs and shuffles across the cockpit as he opens the hatch.

A slot's been reserved for *Huntsman's Daughter* on the floating dock.

Already, people are waiting there to help. She reverses thrust as the yacht swings around, throwing the stern line to an outstretched pair of hands. Someone leaps on to the bow and tosses a line to more volunteers. The boat bumps the dock. Lucy barely has enough energy to climb on to the side deck, but she manages, just about, teeth clenched from the effort.

Hands reach for her. She's lifted off the yacht. 'Jake,' she mutters, glancing over her shoulder. Wrong to leave him without a word of thanks. But the hands pulling her to the quay are irresistible.

Something white shines in her eyes. Only as Lucy draws closer does she identify it: the light of a television camera trained on her face. A smudge of purple reveals the journalist from the high street.

Faces begin to resolve. Lucy sees people she knows, people she doesn't. In their expressions she finds no joy, no satisfaction that the sea has been beaten. Perhaps, like her, they've reached the end of their strength.

Despite her exhaustion, her brain can't quit. It dredges up another of Daniel's stories: how in Ireland, centuries ago, survivors of shipwrecks were thought to bring bad luck. All too often they were murdered on the beaches where they washed up, by locals fearful of the sea's vengeance.

But that can't be the thinking behind these haunted faces. The pain in Lucy's side is joined by another in her gut. A twisting premonition that this nightmare is continuing to build.

She glances at the lifeboat station. The Tamar-class is back in its cradle. Did all its volunteers return safely? She thinks of Craig Clements, Jake's relief coxswain. Volunteers like Alec Paul and Patrick O'Hare. People with loved ones of their own.

But when Lucy examines these faces crowding close, she knows this is something different. Suddenly, she can't control her breathing. Earlier, she couldn't draw air into her lungs. Now, she can't expel it.

Her diaphragm spasms. There's a sound in her throat—*uh-uh-uh-uh*— she can't stop. When her feet touch the quay, the crowd draws back—as if she's dangerous somehow, contagious. She hears the clacking of heels on flagstones.

From jagged silhouette, Noemie materializes. Lucy sees her friend's eyes. The sound in her throat climbs in pitch.

Jake's voice, behind her: 'Lucy! Lucy, wait up!'

She turns, sees him leap to the dock. His eyes hold the same horror she glimpsed in Noemie's.

Lucy is caught between them: her friend; her old lover. Her lungs can maintain the pressure no longer. She hears herself scream, just once, a fleeting pressure-whistle of sound.

Noemie hurries forward, arms outstretched.

'No,' Lucy moans. Whatever her friend is offering, she doesn't want it. The white light of the TV camera swells—as if it's gorging on her fear, growing fat.

Noemie's arms are around her. Others are touching her too. No longer is she to be reviled, it seems, but comforted.

Here comes that scream again. Her mouth can't contain it. There's a buzzing inside her head. A jar of honey bees has been tipped into her skull. The light from the TV camera merges with those on the quay: white and gold, green and red, a riot of carnival colour.

'Lucy, I'm sorry,' Jake shouts. 'Lucy, wait—'

But he can't reach her. She's at the centre of a tightly packed circle. Light and sound, people and faces, questions, questions, and that voice, deep inside her head.

'It's not too late,' her friend tells her. 'Oh, my darling, it's not.'

'Please,' Lucy whispers. 'Please tell me what's happening.'

Noemie puts her ear to Lucy's mouth and talks.

ELEVEN

1

An hour before sunset, with rain falling in sheets, Cooper collects Abraham from the quay. The DS doesn't ask questions as they drive up Skentel's tiny high street. Abraham's grateful—he needs a little space to think.

The heaters pump out hot air, but they struggle to thaw Abraham's bones. For the last hour he's been on the quay, examining Daniel Locke's car and the family yacht. He's talked to Skentel's harbour master, the coastguard officials and the forensics team from Barnstaple.

It's clear, from the CCTV footage, that Daniel Locke took his son—and possibly his stepdaughter—and sailed into a maelstrom. Other than what happened next, the only remaining question is why. Abraham's lucky to have the yacht—since examining it, he has no doubt that a crime's been committed. He needs to speak to the mother again, and others who know the family well. When Lucy Locke returns, he'll stick a family liaison officer on her so tightly they'll have to sleep in the same bed.

Ahead, the TV truck that was blocking the high street has disappeared. Cooper takes them up to the coast road. Overhead, clouds churn like grey rags stirred by a paddle. Wind flings salvos of rain at the windows. At the top of the slope, its ferocity intensifies fivefold. Abraham fears for the boats still at sea; and, indeed, the coastguard helicopter.

He's skimming through his updated notes when he stumbles across another motif: his initials and now his date of birth, sheltering beneath a dome. It swells large in his vision. He has no memory of inking it.

'I found out what *vendibles* means,' Cooper says.

Abraham grunts, slamming shut his notebook. His hand closes around the pill bottle in his pocket.

'Do you want to know?'

'Not particularly. Did you speak to Beckett about the financial investigation?'

'It's being passed up the line. And vendibles,' Cooper continues, 'means—'

'Goods,' Abraham says. He looks out of the passenger window at the waves exploding against Mortis Point. 'Items you can sell.'

The DS pouts. 'You said earlier you had no idea.' Then he brightens. 'Did you know it was Middle English?'

'Probably derived from the Latin *vendibilis*.'

Abraham's about to say more when his ears fill with noise. He ducks down in his seat as a helicopter in coastguard livery blasts over them, red light winking.

Cooper blasphemes, nearly swerving off the road. The helicopter banks and heads east. 'G-CILP,' the DS says, reading the letters along the side. 'That's them. Not hanging around, are they?'

Within moments the craft is a speck. Abraham grimaces as his knees collide with the dash. 'Come on,' he says. 'Let's blue-light it.'

2

They reach North Devon District Hospital as the last light is fading. Earlier, Abraham dispatched two officers to meet the helicopter on the pad. He finds one of them in the accident-and-emergency waiting area.

'Daniel Locke,' Abraham asks. 'What can you tell me?'

'He was wearing an immersion suit when they fished him out,' the officer replies. 'Definitely saved his life, but he was still in a bad way. Core temperature down to twenty-eight degrees. They've been using a dialysis machine to warm his blood, which seems to have stabilized him. He's not awake yet, but they don't seem too concerned.'

'What are the medical staff saying?'

'You know what they're like. Confidentiality and all that. Most of what I just told you we picked up from listening in. Can you believe they prioritized this guy? Over patients who didn't try to kill their kids?'

Abraham knows why the hospital staff would have done it. But it doesn't make it any easier for most people to understand. 'Our healthcare practitioner is en route. If these doctors won't talk to us, they can talk to her—get an understanding of how long Locke might take to recover and how quickly we can bring him in. Once the press gets wind, this place will be a zoo. In the meantime'—he glances around—'is there a place to get coffee?'

'Let's hope so.'

'Do you want one?'

'You're a lifesaver, sir.'

*

TWELVE

Lucy on the hospital bed, a nurse to hold her hand. Every other face a stranger.

Sharp smells in her nose. Agony like a hall of screams. And then Billie, Billie, Billie: a wet mass on her chest, emotions so tangled their beginnings can't be grasped.

Then—a different hospital, a different bed. And this time Daniel's there, telling her just how much he loves her. Pain, worse than before. And when soft new life is placed in her arms, she can't believe how much smaller it is this time, and even more precious for its fragility. 'Fin,' she whispers, and finds herself back on the quay. Noemie's arms are around her, and she's cold, so cold, so utterly lacking in strength.

Jake's voice, behind her. For a moment she wonders if he's a memory too. When his hand touches her shoulder, she knows without question he's real, that he's about to confirm what Noemie just explained.

'A live situation,' he says, 'things get muddled. Messages get relayed, one boat to another, and before you know it it's Chinese whispers. That's no excuse—I should've confirmed with another vessel before I shared. I'm so very sorry, Lucy. They found Daniel but not the kids.'

She unravels, then; a flower shedding petals. Noemie can't hold her up, and Jake reacts too late to save her. Her knees strike the flagstones. Pain comes, a dagger in her side. The crowd presses close. Hands reach out, as if she's the centrepiece of a religious ceremony, no longer a contagion but a relic in some pagan ritual beside the sea.

They found Daniel but not the kids.

Lucy's breath comes in snatches. She has no strength but she has to stand.

Because she can't be here—

> *They found Daniel*
>
> > —on the quay—
> >
> > *but not the kids.*

> > > —while

Billie and Fin are still missing.

Her lungs fill and she screams again. Not the sharp steam-whistle from before. This is a cry of separation from somewhere deep. She pushes up with her hands. Gets a foot beneath her. Straightens.

Missing.

Missing. *Missing.*

Lucy stands, almost. Then she trips forwards, cheekbone slamming the flagstones. Her brain reverberates in her skull. The crowd *ooohs*. More hands reach out. The world goes dark, reduced to muddy voices.

'—*sus, she's frozen.*'

'*Soaked through.*'

'—*her to the ambulance now!*'

'—*of the way, please. Stand back, everyone.*'

Up, suddenly. A feeling of weightlessness.

'No,' she moans, then yells. She has to get back on Jake's boat. Has to get back out there, beyond the breakwater.

They found Daniel but not the kids.

That can't be. It just can't.

She twists her head, opens her eyes, tries to make sense of the fractured images she sees.

There's a sign. The Drift Net. Golden windows of light. A few seconds more and Lucy's on the quay no longer. She's in a cramped room full of warning signs and tubes and machines. A woman crouches opposite. Green uniform, blonde hair.

'OK, love. Looks like you've banged your head. We'll fix that in a jiffy, but first let's get you out of these wet clothes.'

'Billie,' Lucy manages, as the woman unzips the RNLI jacket.

'I know, love. It's Lucy, isn't it? Do you mind if I call you Lucy?'

Lucy shakes her head. As if she could care a damn for what anyone called her. Something trickles down her forehead and into her eye. She blinks, tries to wipe it, but her arms are stuck inside the jacket sleeves. 'Fin,' she mutters. Important, even if she can't form sentences, to make this woman understand. She focuses on the uniform. Sees an embroidered name badge: *JOHANNA*.

Her jacket comes off. The top half of her dungarees. Her T-shirt follows, then her bra. A blanket is round her shoulders and it's such a simple comfort she can't stop herself from weeping.

Johanna pauses, strokes her shoulder. 'I know, love. I know. Let's lie you down, get your boots undone, these salopettes off.'

'Ambulance,' Lucy says. 'My daughter. My son.'

Johanna nods, easing her on to the stretcher. 'That's it, there we go. Haven't had a sea like this in years, have we? Waves up to ten metres off the Point.'

'My children are in the water.'

Beneath them, an engine turns over. Lucy realizes what's happening. She tries to struggle up.

Johanna needs the strength of two fingers to press her back down. 'Lucy, you're very cold and we need to warm you up. And we really need to treat that head wound.'

'Back to the boat.'

'I'm afraid not, lovey. You're coming with us to the hospital.'

'Ribs.'

'Ribs?'

'Broken, I think.'

The ambulance door swings open. Cold wind corkscrews in.

A face appears that she doesn't recognize—another green uniform. 'We all set?'

'She's going to be OK,' Johanna says. 'Let's go.'

Commotion behind the second paramedic. Lucy sees Noemie and Bee, Tommo and Jake. A white light shines in, dazzling her.

'Jesus, man, back *off!*' Jake shouts. The light is shoved aside.

'North Devon District?' Noemie asks.

Johanna nods.

'We'll follow by car.'

Lucy focuses on Jake. 'Don't let them stop looking. Please, Jake. Don't let them stop.'

He stares at her, stricken. And then the door is closing. She gets a last glimpse of the sea. It's Armageddon out there. The end of everything she knows.

Lucy blinks, struggles to keep her eyes open.

Two warning blips from the siren. Movement, beneath her. And now they're underway.

That white borehole in the sea, slowly closing.

Darkness. Horror.

Death-like sleep.

THIRTEEN

Daniel Locke is moved from the emergency department to ICU and from there, hours later, to a side room on Lundy Ward, up on the third floor.

DI Abraham Rose is notified while he's nursing his third coffee, scrolling through photos of Billie Locke harvested from social media. Minutes later he's staring at the hospital bed.

Lucy Locke's downstairs. From the sound of it, frozen half to death. Crazy-brave to have ventured into that sea. But Abraham heard her plea inside the Drift Net. He saw her raw desperation. However bad her physical condition, it'll be nothing to the trauma inside her head.

Silent, he watches the consultant examine Daniel Locke. Dr Hara Annapurna is a striking-looking woman: steel hair, thin lips, cheekbones like glass prisms beneath the skin. As she bends over the bed, Abraham shifts his attention to her patient.

Right now, only Daniel Locke's head is visible. The rest of him is wrapped inside a Bair Hugger—a ribbed inflatable connected to a warm-air pump. The dialysis machine used to heat his blood has gone. In its place, a simple gravity drip administers warmed saline. A mask delivers oxygen. Various leads snake out of the Bair Hugger to a vital-signs monitor.

Even now, returned from near-death, Locke looks younger than his forty-two years: sharp features, black hair, white teeth—the kind of face used to flog sports cars, watches or expensive designer suits.

His eyes are closed. No hint of movement beneath the lids.

Annapurna writes something on a clipboard and hands it to the nurse. When she turns back to Abraham, his diaphragm spasms. He swallows, fearing the onset of a coughing fit. 'Doctor?' he asks. 'A word?'

A single once-over is all Annapurna needs to figure out his connection. 'It'll have to be brief.'

'Of course. You're aware of the background. Neither child's been found. There's a chance Daniel Locke has information that could save them. I need to know whether he'll recover. And if so, when I can speak to him.'

'He's lucky to have survived, certainly,' Annapurna says. 'But he's also incredibly resilient. Under the circumstances, I have no objection to you questioning him whenever he wakes.'

'How long before he's discharged?'

She purses her lips.

'Between me and you.'

'In a presentation like this, I'd always keep the patient in overnight. Barring any complications, considering his good physical condition, I wouldn't expect a longer stay.' She pauses. 'I understand his wife is downstairs.'

'That's what I heard. And in not much better shape.'

Annapurna shakes her head. 'It's all very sad. Was there anything else?'

'No. Thank you. You've been a great help.'

She tilts her head. 'Are you OK? You look a little . . . wrung out.'

His heart jumps. It's the first time anyone's noticed anything wrong from his physical appearance alone. 'I'm fine.'

'Just remember to get some sleep.'

The small kindness makes him awkward. He can't look at her again.

Once the consultant leaves, Abraham returns his gaze to Daniel Locke. It's quiet in here, just the two of them. Peaceful. None of the chaos Lucy Locke is facing in the emergency department. None of the crowding.

Through the double-glazed windows, he hears barely a murmur from the storm raging outside.

Locke's eyes remain still beneath their lids.

Abraham turns to the monitor. He notes the numbers: heart rate, blood pressure, oxygen saturation and temperature.

' "He's lucky to have survived, certainly," ' he says, repeating Annapurna's words. Approaching the bed, he peers at Locke's face, then retreats. 'She struck me as a competent physician. But in that particular respect I'd say her judgement's questionable, wouldn't you? I'm Detective Inspector Rose.'

One corner of the room houses a tea and coffee station. There's a kettle, a mug tree, a box filled with supplies. Abraham lifts the kettle from its base and shakes it. Empty.

'My job—officially—is to find out what happened on that yacht. And the fates of the two you took with you. You might imagine it an impossible task, what with the *Lazy Susan* at the bottom of the ocean.' He returns the kettle to its base. 'But the thing is, Daniel, she isn't.'

No response from the man on the bed. No flicker of awareness behind his eyes. Abraham glances at the vital-signs monitor. Then he returns his attention to the bed.

'Maybe you made that distress call just a tad too early. Or maybe you didn't realize that the coastguard can pinpoint a VHF broadcast even if you don't report your position. Another ten minutes and that yacht *would* have been on the bottom. But those lifeboat volunteers—they're a resourceful bunch. They found her just in time.'

Slowly, deliberately, Abraham approaches the bed. 'I took a look around. You did a pretty good job of scuttling her—smashed off the seacocks completely. Fortunately, the lifeboat team screwed in a couple of marine plugs, rigged up a salvage pump and towed her back to Skentel.'

The hum of the Bair Hugger's pump is the only sound. Abraham conjures a memory: the *Lazy Susan*'s drenched cabin; the red polyurethane TruPlugs wedged into the hull. It's a forensic examiner's nightmare: an entire crime scene flushed through with seawater. But he *can* prove, at least, that the damage was deliberate.

'I told you I'm a police officer,' Abraham says. 'And I'll bet you've made a long list of assumptions about me as a result. What you don't know, Daniel, is that I care very little, these days, for the proper application of the law.'

God, I praise you for your compassionate heart. Give me the relentlessness of the good shepherd who goes after wandering sheep and never gives up.

He leans over the bed until only a few inches separate them. 'I follow what you might call a higher authority.'

Watching Daniel Locke's face, Abraham asks himself if it's still true. *Does* he still follow that higher authority? Or have the last pillars of his faith finally collapsed? When this foul and filthy disease claims him, is there really anything waiting except worms and cold earth?

He waits, holding his breath.

Daniel Locke opens his eyes.

FOURTEEN

1

Lucy Locke spends her first three hours at the hospital on the ambulance gurney that brought her. Gone are the clothes she was wearing on Jake's boat. Nobody can tell her what happened to them. Nor what happened to her children. Nor anything much at all.

She shivers, naked, under two grey blankets. Other than her wedding band, all she has left is Snig. It's cold and wet and torn, robbed by seawater of her boy's scent.

The emergency department rings with the sounds of squealing doors, trilling phones, beeping monitors, people talking, people shouting, people weeping. For a while Lucy plugs her ears with her fingers, but then all she hears is the ocean, and that is infinitely worse. Each thought is a spike inside her head, a sliver of broken glass.

When a passing nurse drops a medical gown on to the gurney, Lucy struggles up. The blankets provide scant privacy as she dresses. Teeth clenched against the pain in her side, she ties Snig around her arm and steps on to the floor. The emergency room tilts. Sound distorts, deepening to a bass thump. The faces of patients and hospital staff liquefy. She staggers, thinks she's going down. Grabs the gurney and straightens.

Daniel.

He's here. In this hospital.

She has to find him.

2

Lucy moves, glacier-slow, through people operating in fast-forward. They zip past in all directions, leaving tracers in their wake. Sound that slowed to a bass thump now climbs to a tinny screech. She has to concentrate so hard to stay upright that the chaos in her head recedes. All her focus is on balance, on breathing, on distilling meaning from the swirl of clashing colours.

No one pays her any attention. No one tries to interfere. Somehow, she finds the reception area and joins a queue of miserable people seeking treatment. She hopes Daniel didn't have to face this. That he had more luck getting help.

Daniel.

Thinking of him is a mistake. Because then she thinks of Billie and Fin and the ocean; and waves tall as houses and the cold, the deadly cold.

Her mouth falls open. She turns her mind back to the simpler tasks of breathing and balancing. And then, somehow, she's at the front of the queue, straining her eyes to resolve the shape that sits before her.

Breathe, she tells herself.

Slow in, slow out.

The shape is a woman. Grey hair and cardigan, lips a thin line.

'I'm looking for my husband,' Lucy says. 'Daniel Locke.'

Her words elongate and ping back, as if they're attached by elastic. Suddenly, everything resolves. She sees the receptionist clearly. Sees how she flinches from Daniel's name. As if it's a knife. Or a sharp loosed stone.

The woman taps her keyboard. 'That's the . . . He's the one who . . .'

'Daniel,' Lucy says. 'His name's Daniel.'

The woman's lips shrink further. 'Looks like they transferred him to Lundy Ward. A room of his own.'

'He's alive.'

'No one told you?'

She shakes her head. 'Lundy Ward?'

'Follow the signs. Third floor.'

Lucy turns, nearly collides with the person behind her. Mutters an apology and stumbles away. Follows a corridor to a staircase. Limps up it to ICU. Lundy Ward is opposite. She passes a police officer stationed outside a door. Looks for a ward sister, anyone who can help.

'Mrs Locke?'

Lucy wheels around. Waits for the corridor to settle.

'I'm Sergeant Hurst. We thought you were downstairs.'

'Where is he?'

'Did they let you—'

'Where's Daniel?'

Hurst's expression flattens. 'Wait here,' he tells her. 'I'll see if you can go in.'

FIFTEEN

1

His face inches from Daniel Locke's, Abraham says, 'I see I have your attention. That's good.'

Locke's blue eyes are startling in their intensity, cold and savagely beautiful.

Wolf, Abraham thinks. And knows he'll have to tread carefully. 'In future, I'd advise against feigning sleep while hooked up to a vital-signs monitor. You might fool the doctors, but they're not the ones asking difficult questions. What happened to the children, Daniel? Where are Billie and Fin?'

Locke's eyes flare like struck match-heads. Beside him, the monitor records another spike in heart rate and respiration.

'Were either of them alive when you last saw them?'

The man's jaw begins to work, as if he's trying to lubricate his tongue.

Abraham reaches down and lifts away the mask. 'You reek of booze. Was that to give you courage? I don't know if you intended to kill yourself out there. If so, you're out of luck. Your window is long gone. When I leave, there'll be an officer in here at all times. Later, when we take you to the police station, you'll be placed on suicide watch. Whatever you did, whatever crime you committed, I'll uncover it. As I said before—and you need to listen very carefully, because I guarantee you haven't come across anyone like me before—*I follow a higher authority.*'

Hearing that, Locke bares his teeth.

In truth, even in custody it's difficult to keep determined prisoners from killing themselves. But Abraham is going to learn what happened to those kids. And Daniel Locke, one way or another, is going to help him.

He feels a cough coming, this one a real blood-burster. He's half tempted to let it fly, showering Locke with diseased lung. Instead, he buries his mouth in the crook of his elbow. The pain is bad, but it passes. When Abraham returns his gaze to the bed, he finds Locke staring.

'I have a message,' the man hisses. Again, his eyes flare. 'A message for that *bitch.*'

2

Beside the bed, the vital-signs monitor beeps in warning. Abraham doesn't break eye contact. He notices the Bair Hugger start to shake. Daniel Locke, wrapped inside it, is panting for breath.

Abraham leans closer. He doesn't expect violence—not here, not now—but should it happen, he's ready. He hears raised voices in the corridor. His gaze flickers to the door. 'What's your message?'

Those blue eyes aren't just cold. They're *frozen.* Chips of turquoise and azurite veined with arctic ice. Abraham recalls something a doctor once told him, about a cold and lifeless sailor pulled from the sea: *You're not dead until you're warm and dead.* So it had proved with that sailor. Thirty minutes without a pulse. Then the medical team warmed his core and shocked him back to life.

Such is the world Abraham now inhabits. But although the dialysis machine reheated Daniel Locke's blood, there's no warmth apparent in his face.

'Tell her,' Locke whispers, lips drawn back over his teeth. 'Tell her she deserves every fucking thing she gets.'

Eyes clenched shut, he starts to sob. His back arches. The tendons in his neck bulge. A sound emerges from his throat—as raw as if it were torn out by a hook.

The door bangs open. Abraham rears back. He's so thrown by Locke's words that it takes him a moment to focus. In the corridor he sees Sergeant Hurst, arms around a mad thing. It writhes and screams, all hair and claws and bared teeth.

With a lurch, Abraham realizes the mad thing is Lucy Locke. Gone is the woman he met before. In her place is a creature half crazed with grief or hysteria or both. Draggled snakes of hair hang about her face. Her eyes look like they've taken a blast of pepper spray. Her hands and feet are blue. She's wearing a hospital gown, badly tied. Around her arm is the torn scrap of cloth she'd been holding at the school.

I love him. He loves me too. Not every couple can say that after nearly a decade, but we can.

Lucy finally twists free. She grabs the door post, drags herself into the room. 'Daniel!' she screams. '*Daniel!*'

Squeals of rubber from the corridor. Annapurna appears, alongside two nurses. In an instant, the room's occupants grow from two to seven.

All sorts of alarms are triggering on the monitor. Inside the Bair Hugger, Daniel Locke starts to thrash. Annapurna rushes forwards, shouting at the nurses to restrain him. But Locke doesn't look like he's having a fit, more as if he's freaking out.

'What's happening?' Lucy wails. 'Where's Billie? Where's Fin? *Daniel, TELL ME!*'

Those last words she screams so fiercely that Abraham's ears ring with them. As Lucy approaches the bed, Daniel Locke's struggles intensify. Abraham grabs his shoulders and pins him down. Annapurna arrives at his side with a syringe. Locke begins to buck. His strength is unbelievable. He wrenches his arms free of the Bair Hugger, grabs Abraham's wrists.

Lucy Locke is screaming again. Abraham bellows at Hurst to remove her. And then, somehow, Annapurna's needle is in, and half a minute later, Daniel Locke's animal fury fades and his struggles cease.

'*Tell* me,' Lucy sobs. Her voice sounds as broken as her husband's. She stares in horrified disbelief.

I have a message. A message for that bitch.

Hurst has his arms around her now. When she sags, he holds her up. '*Please*,' she croaks. 'Where are they? This wasn't meant to *happen*.'

Tell her she deserves every fucking thing she gets.

Despite Abraham's earlier provocation, designed to elicit a reaction, he'd been keeping an open mind on Daniel Locke. The man's outburst has changed everything.

Abraham is a detective inspector but he's something more than that. He's God's blunt-edged tool, formed at speed from the roughest clay to hand. Inelegant, uncivilized, but crudely effective.

His strength may be failing. His faith, too. Little chance, now, that Lucy's children are still alive, but he's going to find out what happened to them, regardless of the consequences to himself.

I'm angry, Lucy, I'll admit it. Angry and sad and emotional. I like things to be perfect, and on that boat they nearly were. When things don't go as planned, I get upset.

I never intended to go to the hospital. I certainly didn't intend to see you. There's a saying soldiers have—that no plan survives contact with the enemy. But I still can't believe what happened out there in that sea.

For a while, just now, I almost lost heart. It's so hard to see your pain. Even harder to be the cause. And yet I know what I'm doing is important. I'm committed to this. It's too late to turn back.

I thought I knew you, and I didn't. The person I met—the person who stole my heart all those years ago—isn't real. She's an invention, a sham, a character from one of Billie's plays.

The thing is, Lucy, you hurt people. You might not realize it, but you do. You slide through life, charming everyone, touching lives and sharing the Lucy magic. And that's fine for those who don't get too close, who don't meet the reality beneath the facade. But those of us who do get too close discover what a dark magic you wield, one that leaves nothing but misery in its wake.

I have you to credit for the cure. Remember all our drunken conversations about philosophy? Everything you taught me about Aristotle? About his theory, particularly, of dramatic tragedy?

Tragedy transports us from happiness to misery. And, at the end of it, we are cleansed.

That's what I've created for you, Lucy. Do you see? I've removed it from the theatre and made it real. Not a single tragic event but a sequence of them, each more devastating than the last.

I'll change you from the hurtful creature you were. I'll purify you, make you beautiful.

And, once it's over, I'll disappear a free man, just as cleansed for the experience.

I can sense my heartbeat slowing. I can feel my breathing start to settle. This takes a different shape now. But it isn't over. This is a tragedy written entirely for your benefit.

Katharsis. Purification through suffering.

Time for the second act.

SIXTEEN

1

A police officer helps Lucy Locke downstairs. She can't process what just happened. Can't make sense of what she just saw: Daniel, thrashing to get free, a look in his eyes she's never seen; the consultant, plunging a needle into him; the detective, pinning him to the bed.

As Lucy arrives back in the emergency department, she hears her name being called. Across the floor, she sees faces she recognizes: Noemie, Tommo, Bee. Her relief is so great that she nearly collapses.

Noemie reaches her first, sweeping her into an embrace. 'Luce. Oh my God, Lucy.'

'Ribs,' she croaks. 'Think they're broken.'

Noemie releases her, steps back. 'Hon, you're *barefoot*. And you're *freezing*. Has anyone seen you? Have you been examined?'

'Not yet, I—'

'Not *yet*?' Noemie swings towards the police officer. 'You know we've been sat out here *three hours*, right? And not a single person to tell us what's going on?' When he begins to respond, she dismisses him. 'Forget it, we'll sort this ourselves. Tommo, hunt down some blankets. Bee, sit with her while I get some answers. Medieval, that's what this is. Chris*sakes*.'

Bee drapes her jacket around Lucy's shoulders and leads her to a seat. Lucy's so overcome she starts crying. 'I didn't find them,' she says. 'I don't know where they are.'

'Dude. Listen to me. We're here, OK? It's messed up, but we're here and we love you. We're going to get you through this. You've a whole team now.'

'I don't know who I just saw. Daniel was . . . He . . .'

'You saw Daniel?'

'I don't . . . He was like a *stranger*.'

Noemie returns with the registrar. Tommo comes back with some blankets.

Events speed up after that. Lucy's taken to radiology for chest X-rays. Afterwards, a doctor confirms two broken ribs. Fresh clothes are found, painkillers prescribed. Soon she's on the back seat of Tommo's car, sandwiched between Noemie and Bee.

Rain hammers the roof. Scenes from a war zone roll past the windows. Lucy sees downed trees, flooded streets, blown-out shopfronts and pavements strewn with glass. But it's not just the devastation that has rendered the landscape unrecognizable. This is a world that has taken her children and replaced her husband with an imposter. It resembles nothing of the place she knew.

Snig lies quarter-folded in her lap. Lucy smooths it obsessively, pressing out every wrinkle. She rests her head on Noemie's shoulder, closing her eyes tight. And then she's not in the car at all. She's at home, up on Mortis Point, and it's the night of Billie's eighteenth, when everything started to change.

2

Four weeks. Different world. Different life.

Barely a month since Christmas and the house is resplendent once more. Everywhere, tealights in glass holders cast golden reflections. Perfume laces the air, mingling with the scents of winter wreaths and fresh-cut flowers. In the living room, where ivory church candles flicker inside hurricane lamps, a huge fire burns.

Outside, the clouds have parted to reveal a rash of platinum stars. Frost sparkles on the back lawn. Later, if the clear skies hold, everyone on the peninsula will be treated to a supermoon total eclipse.

Only when they started sending invites did Lucy realize just how many people Billie knows. Only when the acceptances flooded in did she realize just how much the girl is loved: friends are coming from Billie's old school, her college in Redlecker, her youth theatre group, people she's met through part-time jobs in Skentel, through clubs or societies from years back and via her various volunteer networks: environmental charities, animal sanctuaries and even the regular Penleith Beach clean-up group.

But Lucy doesn't stop there. Invites go out to all her own friends and Daniel's, to the Drift Net's regulars, the artists who've exhibited and the musicians who've played there, to those in Skentel's business community, to its lifeboat volunteers and fishing crews. Daniel invites the staff of Locke-Povey Marine and many of its long-term customers. By the time they're finished, it seems like half the town is coming.

This is a celebration not just of Billie reaching eighteen but of every hurdle climbed along the way. The early years weren't easy, particularly during Lucy's darker travails around Europe. Even back in Skentel, their fortunes took a while to improve. Lucy worked such long hours, for such low pay, that she hardly saw her daughter at all.

Now, standing at the kitchen counter in her gold slip dress, arranging vegetable crudités on a board, she's determined to make this night unforgettable.

Beside her, Billie taps a watermelon with a manicured finger. 'You think it's worked?'

'Of course it's worked.'

'It certainly *smells* of vodka.'

'Then it's worked.'

Billie grins. 'I bet it tastes gross.'

'Please don't feel obligated to try any.'

'Are you shitting me?'

'Such a *delightful* turn of phrase,' Lucy replies, digging her with an elbow. 'It makes you sound all grown-up and edgy.'

'That's because I *am* all grown-up and edgy. Don't I look it?'

She looks more than edgy. She looks downright dangerous: black leather jacket, rockabilly dress in red polka-dot, blonde hair twisted up inside a fifties-style headscarf. Billie's eyelashes are extravagantly curled, her lips the same letterbox shade as the dress. She's a blazing sun, radiating heat.

The back door swings wide. New arrivals spill into the kitchen. Lucy beams, greeting the guests with kisses and hugs. Prosecco corks detonate. Beer-bottle caps fly. Alcohol fizzes and froths.

Ed appears, scrubbed and scented. Billie wraps herself around him and they disappear to the living room. Daniel comes in from outside, apron smudged with charcoal. The frozen evening hasn't stopped him barbecuing. Later, there'll be enough pulled pork to feed everyone for a week.

Usually, the gold slip dress stops him dead; likewise, the Guerlain scent clinging to Lucy's skin. Right now, though, it barely registers. 'Have you seen Nick?' he asks.

She shakes her head, noticing a pinch to his eyebrows that wasn't there an hour ago. 'Everything OK?'

'Sure. Weird conversation is all.'

Draining her gin and tonic, Lucy watches him rifle through the cutlery drawer. Unsettling, how his momentary lack of interest instantly ignites her old insecurities.

Growing up, she couldn't resist any attention thrown in her direction. Sad little Lucy—unable to distinguish between those who genuinely liked her and those who just wanted sex. Later, her teenage promiscuity evolved into a serial monogamy that left a litany of casualties in its wake.

And then, nine years ago, she stopped in a lay-by outside Skentel and everything changed. Although—considering her sudden uneasiness—not *quite* everything.

Daniel finds what he needs in the drawer. He looks up. This time, he properly notices her. The tension ebbs from his expression. When he grins, it lifts her heart. 'Bloody hell, Luce. You outshine every living thing on the Point.'

'In a houseful of eighteen-year-olds, I doubt it,' she snorts.

But Lucy flushes with pleasure at his words; and at the knowledge, despite her fleeting insecurity, that seven years of marriage have eroded nothing of their love—that it suffuses the walls of this grand old residence and fortifies everyone it touches.

Coming close, Daniel kisses her. His lips are warm against her mouth. 'You smell even better than you look.'

'I'm not sure that's quite the compliment you intended, Goof.'

'Well, I'm an engineer, not a poet.'

'*You* smell like a Cub Scout on summer camp,' she tells him.

'Barbecue smoke and pig's blood.'

'Woof.'

Daniel chuckles and returns to the garden. Lucy grins and pours herself another drink.

3

The moon rises. The temperature outside plummets.

Bee arrives. Lucy meets Tommo for the first time. He's fascinated with her art collection. When he asks about the history of each piece, she's delighted to oblige him. Bee holds his hand throughout, beaming like a lottery winner.

Nick shows up an hour later. He brings a tiny wrapped box for Billie. Inside is a set of keys on a dolphin-shaped fob. Outside, a brand-new Vespa scooter stands on the driveway. A giant teddy bear sits astride it.

'It's electric,' he tells her. 'So once you've done your training, you can ride it around guilt-free.'

'Oh my God, Uncle Nick!' Billie cries. 'You can't . . . It's too much!'

'What else am I going to spend my money on?' he laughs. 'Go on. Enjoy the damned thing.'

Billie embraces him. 'Thank you,' she says, kissing his cheek.

Lucy stares at the scooter, bemused. Nick's displays of largesse are nothing new. Still, this is unusual even by his standards. Back inside, she tops up her drink and escapes to the study for five minutes' respite. By the window she stands in darkness, watching the rising moon, listening to the party begin to hum under its own steam. Behind her the door opens, sound and light spilling in. It closes before she looks round.

'Busted,' says a voice.

Lucy hears Nick cross the floor. When she turns, all she sees is his silhouette, and the two bright points of his eyes.

'Just a quick time-out,' she tells him. 'Getting old, that's the problem.'

'Not you, Lucy-Lou. All that gym work—you'll stay young for ever. Look at you in that dress.'

Lucy sips her drink. Ice clinks against her teeth. 'So, Mr Povey. Who're *you* hiding from?'

Nick grunts. 'Daniel didn't tell me he was inviting industry people.'

'He didn't?'

'Like a damned marine engineering convention out there.'

'And enough single women to form a football team.'

'None my type, though.'

Lucy laughs. 'You don't *have* a type.'

Nick pulls a paper wrapper from his pocket. Into a triangle of moonlight on the desk he tips a pile of white powder. Pulling out a credit card, he begins to grind and chop. Lucy watches, feeling a pinch of irritation. Rude not to ask permission. But everyone's had a few drinks—she can forgive him. Not that Nick would care either way.

'I hope you approve of the gift,' he says.

'Pretty extravagant. Even by your standards.'

'I think you're meant to say generous.'

'OK, generous, then. But it's still a fortune on a present. Tell me you're not dying of something inoperable.'

'Affirmative. Although I do have to tell—'

The door swings open. Bee and Tommo appear. Nick straightens, angling his body to hide the coke. Instinctively, Lucy retreats a step.

'Oh,' Bee says, stopping short. She screws up her face, peering from Nick to Lucy. Her T-shirt is a wall of orange text: *DRINK LIKE*

DWARVES, SMOKE LIKE WIZARDS, SING LIKE ELVES AND PARTY LIKE HOBBITS. Tommo's T-shirt features a Wookiee behind a pair of turntables, beneath the words: *CHEWIE, DROP THE BASS.*

'Sorry, dude,' Bee says. 'We didn't . . . I mean, we were just trying to find an empty . . .'

Her words fizzle out. She hiccups.

Everyone grins.

'Come on,' Tommo tells her. 'Let's find you some more hobbits.' He mouths an apology and guides Bee out.

'Well,' Lucy says, once they've gone. 'That was awkward.'

'Nah. Everyone's just enjoying themselves.'

Nick goes to the door. He shuts and locks it. The darkness resettles. But it's thicker, now, more claustrophobic. Back at the desk, he forms the coke into two fat lines and snorts one with a rolled-up twenty. Then he offers Lucy the note.

She rolls her eyes. 'I don't think so, party boy.'

Nick moves to the right, placing himself between her and the door. 'Go on,' he tells her. 'Just a cheeky one. Promise I won't tell.'

This close, she can smell him. Not barbecue smoke and pig's blood, like Daniel, but an aftershave almost as unpleasant. She wonders if his arrival in the study was entirely coincidental.

Lucy's tempted to step around him, but there's no guarantee he won't block her again. *Arsehole*, she thinks. And feels the darkness press closer. She just wants to get out of here, now; wants to get back to Billie and Daniel and the party. But she knows how petty and vindictive Nick can be; a confrontation just isn't worth it. 'Hold my drink,' she says, snatching up the twenty.

'That's my girl.'

Lucy bends over the desk. It's a far bigger line than she realized. Holding one nostril closed, she snorts half of it. Years since she did anything like this. The buzz hits almost immediately.

She blinks, shakes her head. 'What am I doing, Nick?'

'Having fun. Go on—finish it up.'

This time, when she bends over, he slides his hand up the inside of her dress. His fingers almost reach her underwear before she manages to jerk away. A glazed pot, made by Fin for Daniel, scoots across the desk. It hits the floor and shatters.

'What the *fuck*, Nick?' Lucy hisses. 'What was *that?*'

'Ah, shit. Shit, Luce, I'm sorry. I just . . .'

They stare at each other in the darkness. Lucy feels her heart pounding. She can't figure out if it's the coke or something else. She feels dirty, outraged; overwhelmed with guilt. Billie's eighteenth and here she is, locked in the study with the lights off, snorting coke with her husband's lecherous friend. Did she do anything to encourage him? To suggest she might welcome it? Why the hell didn't she leave when Bee and Tommo showed up?

'Please,' Nick says. 'Let's pretend this never happened. I don't know what I was thinking. I don't know what I'd do if Daniel found out.'

The emotion in his voice is so raw that Lucy decides, right there, to respect his wish. Arsehole he may be, but his lifelong friendship with Daniel is more important than a single error of judgement.

On impulse, she bends back to the desk and snorts up the remaining coke. Best that no evidence remains of this sordid little encounter. Pinching her nostrils, she hands Nick back his twenty. The drug hits her system before she reaches the study door. She's energized, now, jittery as fuck. Her fingers fumble for the key.

Lucy steps into the hall just as Daniel emerges from the kitchen. The frown he's wearing deepens when he sees her. His gaze flickers to the darkened study. Lucy's heart beats faster. Her cocaine rush blossoms into panic.

'Have you seen Nick?' Daniel asks.

Lucy runs her tongue across her teeth. She knows Nick's still in the study, knows Daniel must have heard the door unlocking. Her skin feels far too hot. The colours in the hall seem far too bright.

And then Billie appears, racing out of the living room. 'Mum, it's about to start!' she shouts. She takes Lucy's hand and pulls her along the hall.

Outside, the view from Mortis Point is of a world made ethereal by night. Even though Lucy's stood here a thousand times before, the sight robs her of breath. Overhead, the moon appears close enough to touch. Its light daubs the sea with a procession of milk smiles.

Bee and Tommo stand nearby, sharing a cigarette. More guests spill from the house, many carrying blankets. Billie snags one and drapes it around them. Noemie appears, followed by Ed, who wraps his arms around Billie.

'Look,' someone says, lifting a finger to the sky. 'It's *happening.*'

Across the lawn, two hundred faces tilt heavenward. Sure enough, a crescent-shaped slice of the full moon has turned pink. As Lucy watches, that blush of colour begins to spread. It looks like blood filling a cheek, or poison starting to discolour flesh. There's a murmur of appreciation from her guests.

Cocaine fizzes in Lucy's arteries. How strange, she thinks, to be riding on a planet interposing itself between sun and moon. Within a few minutes, all three bodies are aligned. The moon turns red; and with it, her stomach drains of blood.

Up there, the mountains and craters of the lunar surface look like they've mutated, the familiar shadows transformed. Down in Skentel, a dog starts barking. Two others join it. An owl hoots from one of the stone pines.

'Spooky shit,' Tommo mutters.

Lucy can't watch any longer. Instead, she studies her guests. She sees awe, curiosity, unease. And, by the kitchen door, she sees Daniel.

His eyes are narrowed, his mouth a tight line. She recognizes that look from the photo of them on Penleith Beach—everyone laughing except her husband, staring out to sea. Before she can catch his eye, he retreats inside.

Lucy's chill deepens. She untangles herself from Billie and heads to the French windows. All the while she feels that enormous blood-red orb hanging overhead. She doesn't believe in fairies or demons, in folk tales or religion, but she can't shift the feeling that the eclipse is a portent; a sign of bad things heading her way.

At the cocktail cabinet in the living room, she chugs down a glass of soda water. From another part of the house, she hears raised voices. She goes to the living-room door, steps into the hall.

The front door is ajar. The voices are coming from outside. One of them is Daniel's. He's not shouting, but the emotion in his voice is clear—beyond mere anger; this is cold rage. Lucy walks to the door.

On the front drive, Daniel is breathing through his teeth. Blood shines on his knuckles. Nick stands a few feet away, the front of his shirt torn, a bruise swelling beneath his eye.

'Daniel?' Lucy asks, emerging from the house. 'What's going on?'

He turns on her, teeth bared. For a moment she barely recognizes him. 'You know what I just found out?'

She steps back, shaken. 'Whatever you're angry about, it's Billie's—'

'Tell her,' Daniel snarls, wheeling towards Nick. 'Tell her what you just told me.'

4

Lucy comes back to herself fully in the rear of Tommo's car. Five seconds of confusion, a frantic scrabbling for memory. Then her back arches. Her lower legs corkscrew in the footwell.

Noemie touches her arm and it's too much. Lucy bucks, twists. It takes the strength of both her friends to hold her down. Tommo casts anxious looks behind him. 'You want me to pull over?'

'Let's just get her home,' Noemie says. 'Coast road up to Mortis Point.'

'No,' Lucy shouts, struggling up. 'Not home, not yet.'

'Where else do you want to be?'

'The beach,' she says. 'Penleith Beach.'

'The *beach*? Hon, I don't think that's a great idea.'

'Please, I just need to—'

'Luce, you just had a—'

'*PLEASE!*'

Pain drills her side. It feels like her ribs have snapped into spearheads. 'Please,' she gasps. 'Not to the house. Listen to me, please listen. I can't go there, not yet. Penleith Beach—I just need to stand there a while. I just . . . I just need to say . . .'

Lucy can't finish the sentence. Can't do anything except take shallow sips of air.

Tommo looks round for guidance.

Noemie nods.

5

Penleith Beach lies north of Skentel, separated by the peninsula of Mortis Point. They reach it via a sandy track off the coast road. At the bottom, a tall dune blocks their view of the sea.

'If you follow it along,' Bee says, 'you'll reach a point where you can drive directly on to the sand.' Tommo does as he's instructed. Finally, the beach reveals itself.

This is the place where Fin learned to swim; where Billie learned her love of the ocean; where Daniel set up his business. It's the beach from the photo on his desk, the light golden and the sea a turquoise calm.

It doesn't look like that now.

If the town they left behind was a war zone, this is a hostile planet. From north to south, the Atlantic rolls oil-black behemoths towards the shore. Each new wave blows streamers of smoke-like spray into the night. By the time they break, they're of such colossal size they appear to collapse in slow motion. Every explosion of surf produces a shockwave that Lucy feels in her chest.

The beach itself is a graveyard. Flotsam and jetsam litter the sand all the way to the backshore. Boulders the size of family cars have crashed on to the southern flank from what looks like a partial collapse of Mortis Point's north face.

'Can we get closer to the water?' Lucy asks.

Penleith's hard-packed sand is drivable all the way to the surf. As the car crosses the beach, its headlights pick out the junk the sea has washed up. Driftwood is piled in huge stacks. Broken netting and plastic packaging lie everywhere. Among it, Lucy sees sun-faded navigation buoys, smashed lobster pots, barnacle-encrusted ropes, a rusted bicycle, scores of dead fish. When they draw closer to the sea, she spots what looks like the backbone of a sperm whale. Seaweed flutters like rags from its individual vertebrae.

'Remember that container ship back in '97, the *Tokio Express*?' Tommo asks. 'Lost half its cargo off Land's End. Five million pieces of Lego went overboard.'

Everyone in Skentel knows about the *Tokio Express*. Twenty years later, the plastic bricks are still washing up. Fin has a small stack in his room.

Fin.

Lucy closes her eyes.

Shallow breath in. Shallow breath out.

The sea is closer now. Breakers glitter in the headlights. Twenty yards from the waterline, Tommo stops the car. When he kills the engine, the booming of the breakers intensifies. Two thousand miles of wild ocean separate them from the next land mass.

Wind buffets the car, rocking it on its springs.

'I need to get out,' Lucy says.

Her friends trade silent looks. 'OK,' Noemie replies. 'But just for a little while, OK?'

Such is the wind's power that they have to force open the doors. Outside, they huddle on the wet sand. Hardly imaginable, staring at that sea, that Lucy was out there a few hours ago. Utterly unimaginable that Daniel sailed Billie and Fin into it.

A tangle of netting skids across the beach. Lucy watches it pass. Then she raises her voice above the wind. 'We had so many good times down here. I always told them this was my favourite place on Earth. Now look at it.'

Noemie rubs her shoulder. Lucy steps away, breaking contact. She can't bear to be touched. 'They're not gone,' she says. 'Billie and Fin. I'd feel it. If they weren't here any more, I'd know.'

Hard to swallow. Hard to acknowledge her friends' silence and its meaning.

'That happens, doesn't it?' she asks Bee. 'Some kind of mother's instinct?'

'I think only you know what you know.'

'I *do* know. They're alive. I can tell.'

Lucy walks forwards. Ahead of her, the surf looks like foaming milk. She strips off Bee's jacket. Before anyone can stop her, she charges into the water. The shock of it's so sharp it's like wading through broken glass.

Noemie cries out. Another breaker detonates. Suddenly, Lucy's submerged to her waist. The returning water pulls her off her feet. Quickly, she gathers speed, sliding feet first towards an open maw of sea.

Noemie's screaming now. Bee, too. Frantic sounds, lost to a fizzing of white water.

Ahead, a monster wave is building. Geysers of spray twist off its crest. Lucy floats in marbled surf, too stunned to take a breath. The wave breaks over her. The world goes black. She's rolled, blasted backwards, bounced along the bottom.

Opening her arms, she makes claws of her fingers, drags them through hard sand. But the water's too powerful. She can't make an anchor. The water switches direction and she's sliding even faster out to sea.

Up on the surface, another wave breaks. The pressure in her ears is huge. Air bubbles from Lucy's mouth. She kicks her legs, ignoring the agony from her broken ribs. Reaching out, she tries to swim. Her head knocks against something hard. Her hand manages to snag it.

Then an arm is around her back. Her face is out of the water. She hears voices—Noemie's and Tommo's and Bee's. She sees them waist-deep in water. Shouting, they drag her through the surf. Another wave is forming, this one even larger than the last. There's no way they'll outrun it, or prevent the rip from carrying them out.

6

But somehow they do.

Gasping, panting, Lucy's friends pull her up the beach. Once they're out of danger, they collapse on to the sand.

Noemie coughs up seawater. Bee dry-heaves. Tommo stares in disbelief.

'I'm sorry,' Lucy moans. 'I just had to remind myself. I just had to see what it was like.'

They help her into the car. Tommo starts the engine, putting the heaters on full blast.

'It's not that cold,' Lucy whispers. 'Not really. Back in the hospital, I heard people talking. About Billie and Fin. One to three hours, they said. In water that cold, one to three. And for smaller children, like Fin . . .'

She swallows. 'Daniel was wearing an immersion suit, a really good one. We bought them for the kids, too. That one-to-three hours thing is for someone without any protection. Immersion suits like ours, they'll protect you at least twice as long. At *least*. The distress call came in around lunchtime. Which means they've been in the water . . .' She shakes her head. 'Can you believe I don't even know what time it is?'

'It's just gone midnight,' Tommo says.

Lucy shivers, shudders. Feels cold water leak down her spine.

'What happened?' Bee asks softly. 'At the hospital. What did he say when you saw him?'

Lucy leans her head against the rest. She recalls her husband, wrapped in that heated inflatable; the detective using all his strength to pin him down. She knows her arrival triggered Daniel's reaction, but she can't explain it. She can't explain any of this. 'They're not gone,' she says again. 'Billie and Fin. They're alive.'

Tommo flicks on the headlights. The sea reveals itself, a wide-open wound. They turn in a circle and retreat across the sand. Back on the coastal road, they head towards Mortis Point. Twice along the peninsula's twisting lane they have to stop and clear debris. When they pull on to the drive at Wild Ridge, the headlamps illuminate a figure crouched on the front step.

SEVENTEEN

1

With Daniel Locke sedated and officers posted outside his room, Abraham has no reason to remain at the hospital. Before he leaves, he calls Mike Kowalski, his deputy SIO.

'It's starting to feel like you're avoiding us,' Mike says.

'What's going on with the family liaison officer?'

'Trying to find someone with capacity. Is Lucy Locke still at the hospital?'

'Waiting on X-rays.'

'*She's* injured now?'

'She recruited her ex to sail her out to the search area. Lucky to have made it back.'

'Jesus. What can you say?'

Tell her she deserves every fucking thing she gets.

'What's the latest from the coastguard?' Abraham asks.

'This storm's breaking all records. We've got harbours up and down the coast in lockdown. Even the RNLI are having trouble.'

'What about the helicopter?'

'Last I heard, it was flying back to St Athan to refuel. They'll make a call later on whether they can send it back out. I'm not hopeful. Crew wants to go but it isn't their shout.'

'She showed me a video,' Abraham says. 'Of the boy.'

'The seven-year-old?'

'Fin Locke. I never saw . . .'

In Abraham's nearly thirty years on the force, Mike Kowalski is the closest he's come to a friend. They don't go drinking because Abraham doesn't drink, but they've formed a bond of sorts. It's OK if, for a moment, he cannot speak.

He doesn't know why that clip of Fin Locke affected him so deeply. Right now, he can't recall the boy's exact words as he narrated his story to the camera, but he remembers the gist: a lonely old hunchback who could have found companionship if only he hadn't driven people away. In a way, the character seemed too well observed to be a seven-year-old's creation. But Abraham has no experience of children and never will.

He thinks of Lucy's agony when she realized her daughter was also missing. How she'd flinched from his touch as he tried to comfort her. He hadn't expected that to hurt quite so much as it did.

You're not alone in this, he'd told her. *I'll be with you. Every step. Until we find them.*

Cheap words. Because he hasn't been with her. Not when she ventured on to that sea. Nor when she returned, broken, to be ignored by medical staff far more focused on Daniel Locke. 'How many people do we have searching the coastline?'

'As many as we could muster,' Kowalski says. 'Thirty or so officers, around one hundred civilians. But they've done all they can tonight. Conditions are so atrocious there's a good chance they'd miss any signs. We'll send them out again at first light. Hopefully, the worst of it will have passed by then. There's been so much flooding inland we've had to divert some of the search-and-rescue effort to deal with it.'

Abraham recalls his conversation with coastguard rescue officers in Skentel. Cold water, they'd told him, lowers body temperature thirty times faster than cold air. At this time of year, the sea off this coast is nudging nine degrees. Daniel Locke was recovered after five hours, half dead despite his immersion suit. Another six hours have ticked by since then. If those kids are still in the water, they're already dead. His greatest hope is that they've washed up somewhere south of Mortis Point. It's the slimmest of possible chances—and depends on them having left the boat much further south than where the Mayday was broadcast. Otherwise, SARIS plots their likely drift taking them north-east towards the Bristol Channel. Even if they *have* washed up along this stretch of coast, what chance have two frozen and exhausted kids of surviving the night?

'What's the latest forecast?' he asks.

'Next couple of hours, these winds should ease off a little. Rain, too. Can't come soon enough, if you ask me. We've got two dead from an RTA outside Redlecker. And a falling tree in Soundsett hit a parked car with a couple of horny teenagers inside. Messy as hell, that one. Punched the driver's head through his ribcage while he was groping his girlfriend's tits. I'll leave you with the image.'

Abraham hangs up. As he approaches the hospital's entrance doors, a purple shape peels off the wall and begins to flank him. He doesn't need to look to know who he's going to find.

She reeks of perfume and cigarettes. If the devil has a smell, doubtless this is it. 'Detective Inspector Rose?'

Breezy and assured. No accent he can detect.

Abraham doesn't break stride. 'If you block Skentel's high street with that truck again, you're going to be unpopular with the locals.'

'I *am* the locals. One of them, at least. And I told Max not to drive down that street. A blind man could see we'd get stuck. You look like you've had the day from hell. Can I buy you a coffee?'

'Thank you, no.'

'Is Daniel Locke out of danger?'

'There'll be a press conference in the morning.'

'Did he kill those kids?'

'You can ask all your questions in the morning.'

The front doors roll open, ejecting him into a maelstrom. Wind is driving rain horizontally across the car park. Black rivers of water are streaming down the tarmac to the entrance. Abraham pauses beneath the overhang. When the doors close behind him, he remembers that Cooper drove off in the pool car.

He hears the click of a piezo lighter. The roar of a tiny gas jet. Cigarette smoke sails past his face, whipped to shreds by wind.

'You need a lift?'

Abraham turns, sees the same sharp jaw he remembers from Skentel's high street, the same no-nonsense hair. But her eyes are wiser than he expected, more thoughtful. Suddenly, it's harder to pin upon her all the stereotypes of her profession.

She holds his stare, sucking so hard on her cigarette that her cheeks invert. 'Want one?'

When she offers the packet, Abraham shakes his head. As she goes to put it away he reaches out, then snatches back his hand.

She grins. It transforms her face. The packet dances back and forth. 'Hold your breath, folks. What's he going to choose?'

It's a small moment, but it disarms him. He takes a cigarette, lighting it in the blue flame of her burner. The first pull hits his lungs like a wall. The second is softer. He feels a little tension seep from his shoulders.

'Bad boy,' she says. 'Naughty, naughty. Emma Douglas, by the way—in case you didn't know me from my *numerous* Press Gazette awards.'

Her self-effacing style doesn't fool him, but he still feels himself thawing. He's had enough misery today. They stand side by side, wind snatching at their clothes. Abraham watches the rain.

'It's got a name, you know,' Emma says.

'What has?'

'This storm. Used to be just the Yanks who did that. 1953, they started naming hurricanes. Women's names only, for the first twenty-five years. Our Met Office started playing copycat in 2015. You know what we called our first one?'

He shakes his head.

'Abigail. Doesn't sound much like a storm, does it?'

'What are they calling this one?'

'Delilah.'

He glances over. 'Really?'

' "Why-why-why, Delilah?" ' Emma sings.

She has a nice voice.

'Judges, sixteen,' Abraham replies.

'You whada-what?'

'You've heard of Samson?'

Emma cocks an eyebrow. 'Nazarite hardman with big hair. Armed himself with a donkey's jawbone and laid out an entire army of Philistines. Delilah was his lover. She found out his secret, got a servant to shear off the mane. Then his enemies slung him in a Gaza prison and made him grind grain for a living.'

'Until his hair grew back.'

'At which point, he knocked down the walls of their temple, killing himself and everyone in it. Mic drop,' she adds, miming something that Abraham doesn't understand. 'They always said there'd be benefits to a convent-school education.'

'Samson's my middle name,' he tells her, and immediately wishes he hadn't.

Emma's laugh is deep-throated and genuine. 'Fuck off.'

'It's the truth.'

'How fucking tall are you, anyway?'

'Six four.'

'You want that lift?'

'I shouldn't.'

'Oh, *pffsh*. You think you'll get an Uber in this?' She takes a last drag and bounces her cigarette off the no-smoking sign. 'Come on, Samson. Quick march.'

2

Emma walks away without a forward glance. Within moments, her hair is plastered to her scalp.

Abraham knows he's being played, he *knows*. And yet her conversation's so diverting he craves more. Corporate Comms might not like him accepting a lift, but he's deflected Emma's questions about Daniel Locke. He breathes deep, stepping out from the overhang.

Emma's car is a small hatchback. Inside, Abraham slides back the passenger seat as far as it'll go.

She pulls on her seatbelt, blots her face of rain. 'Police station? Pub? Curry house? Kebab shop? Home? Not necessarily in that order.'

Abraham frowns. He knows she's joking, but he doesn't know how to respond.

Emma starts the engine, flicks on the wipers and gets a good blast of air going. 'Relax, Samson. The pubs are shut, the curry houses too. And you don't strike me as the kind of guy to chow down on a lamb doner.'

'You know the station?'

'Nasty-looking grey building beside the river?'

'That's the one.'

'If the Taw bursts its banks, you'll be the first lot carried away.'

They pull out of the car park and head up to the roundabout, rain tattooing the roof. None of the streetlights are working. The North Road is a graveyard of fallen trees. Emma switches on her full beams. 'I know you don't want to talk about the case.'

'Correct.'

'But purely from a human perspective . . .' She winces, shakes her head. 'Ugh, that was shit. Listen to yourself, Emma. Have some self-respect.'

'You swear a lot.'

She flicks her head towards him. It's too dark to see her eyes. 'I fucking try.'

Abraham frowns, says nothing.

Emma steers around a wheelie bin beached in the centre of the road. 'You think you'll find those kids?'

'I've *got* to find them.'

'You think you'll find them alive?'

'I pray that I will.'

The emotion in his voice must be noticeable because he hears Emma draw breath. For a while they drive in silence, the storm raging around them.

'If they're not . . .' She hesitates, and he knows she's choosing her words. 'If they're not, and you *don't* find them, will you be able to get a murder conviction?' Another long pause, during which the rain drums down. 'I've seen the CCTV footage. In case you were wondering.'

It takes all his self-control not to react.

'Well?' she asks.

'You know I can't talk about it.'

'Proving something like that, without bodies. It's hard, isn't it? Even with the CCTV. Because that footage doesn't show *intent.*'

Abraham glances out of the passenger window. They're passing through the centre of Barnstaple. A huge oak has crashed down, blocking a side road. A fire engine, blue lights strobing, is parked nearby. Three firemen are working on the tree with chainsaws.

Eyes on the road, Emma asks, 'Did the Lockes have personal accident insurance covering them for this sort of thing?'

Eve, he thinks. And immediately castigates himself. She's doing her job, same as him. Likely she's just fishing, but that felt like more than a random question.

The car rolls to a stop. 'Here you go, Samson.'

3

He picks up his car and leaves without visiting the incident room. Some of his contemporaries will view it as negligent, no doubt, but Abraham follows a higher authority.

Ever since he glimpsed that black wall moving in from the Atlantic, he's sensed the approach of something transformative. It's not just the storm. Not just the slow-motion destruction of Lucy Locke. Nor the look of wolfish cunning in Daniel Locke's eyes.

At the school, Abraham had sensed a tangible evil stalking the halls. At the hospital, too, he'd felt the same thing. His own reckoning, he knows, is gathering speed. Perhaps he's being given one last opportunity for redemption before it arrives.

It takes him half an hour to travel the eighteen miles home. The house stands inside the boundaries of Exmoor National Park, nestled in a dell out of sight of the nearest road. No streetlights, no neighbours. Tonight, not even any stars. Inside, he's greeted by the smell of mothballs and dust, the steady tock of a grandfather clock. Abraham pulls off his wet shoes and climbs the stairs.

For years, there were two of them in this house. These days it's just him. In the master bedroom, he sits on his mother's bed and smooths the eiderdown. Her side table, once cluttered with framed photographs, is empty save a film of dust.

Abraham looks around: at her hatbox crowning the wardrobe; at the faded Caravaggio print on the far wall. Fishing out his mobile, he dials a stored number. On the fourteenth ring, a sleepy voice answers.

'It's Abraham Rose,' he tells the night manager. 'I just wondered if by any chance she's still up.'

Silence precedes a sigh. 'Mr Rose, it's two a.m. Your mother went to bed hours ago. I can't wake her. Even if I did, she wouldn't know who—'

'You're right,' Abraham says quickly. 'Sorry. I hadn't realized it was so late.' He hangs up before he can embarrass himself further. Glancing at the side table, he sees a familiar motif now traced in the dust: his initials and date of birth, sheltering beneath a dome. Scrubbing it out, he retreats to his own room.

It's a small space, austere. Bottle-green walls, floorboards dark as ship's timber. A wooden cross hangs above the single bed.

On the dresser is his keepsake box. Going over, Abraham raises the lid. Most of its contents were added by his mother: a lock of his hair in a tiny, yellowed envelope; a coin and a stamp from his birth year; a photo of him on his father's lap; a medal from his first sports day. Unfortunate, really, that he failed to make more memories. About the only thing he's added is a warrant card from thirty years ago.

Except, of course, for the letter.

Years since he last read it; the handwriting alone is enough to lighten his stomach. With trembling hands he unfolds the paper.

Dearest Abe,

I hope this letter reaches you safely. Father Cuomo promised he'd post it to the priest in your new town. (He respected your mother's wishes, by the way, and hasn't told me where you've both gone—just that it was far away.)

I've promised myself I'll try to reach you this way only once. I hope you'll write back with a correspondence address. I hope, more than anything, that you'll think hard about whose interests your mother's really serving. One day she'll be gone, Abe, and then what will you have?

There—I've said it. I'm sorry if I've hurt you, but I couldn't hold it in any longer. I miss singing with you in the choir. I miss our talks after church. Please write back, if you feel you can.

All my love and God bless,
Sarah

Abraham returns the letter to the box and shuts the lid. In his head, he hears his mother's voice: *God ordained your path. And that girl wasn't it.*

Doubtless she'd been right—their relocation to Exmoor and the severing of that fragile beginning a necessary sacrifice. He's God's blunt-edged tool, after all, formed at speed from the roughest clay to hand. At least, that's what he once believed.

What a lonely path it's been.

Abraham strips down to his underwear, folding his clothes in a pile. In the brown-spotted wall mirror, he examines his frame.

He's deteriorating fast. No denying it. His muscles hang withered and loose. His reserves of fat have almost entirely shrunk away. On his arms and belly, a rash of liver spots looks like a star map printed on white skin.

Dropping to his knees, Abraham clasps his hands together. He prays for Billie and Fin Locke. He pleads for forgiveness, for guidance, for strength and stronger faith.

When he opens his eyes twenty minutes later, he feels more frightened and alone than he ever thought possible.

EIGHTEEN

1

The figure on Lucy's front step is wearing full waterproofs: black jacket and storm hood, orange overtrousers and boots.

'Who *is* that?' Noemie mutters.

Lucy stares through the windscreen as the wipers scrub off rain. Her exhaustion is so acute it's hard to focus. The figure's too big to be Billie. For a moment she thinks it's Daniel, until she remembers he's at the hospital.

Rain drives down harder, overwhelming the wipers. Noemie and Bee crack their doors and climb out.

'You know who that is?' Tommo asks, frowning.

'About to find out,' Lucy says, sliding across the seat. 'You'd better come in and dry off.'

2

She follows her friends to the front porch. In the instant before Tommo kills the headlights, the figure stands and lifts its head.

Jake Farrell looks more ragged than Lucy's ever seen him. Studying his face, she's forced to confront her earlier betrayal—her willingness to trade his life for her family, should the chance arise. She'd kissed him, too. However well intentioned, it was a terrible abuse of his friendship.

'Your phone,' he says, handing it over. 'You left it in the boat.'

'Oh, Jake. You didn't have to come all the way out here this late.'

He pauses, uncomfortable. 'I needed to update you on a few things.'

Noemie delves into her bag and brings out Lucy's keys. 'Let's get inside,' she says. 'And out of these wet clothes.'

They assemble in the kitchen. Noemie disappears upstairs, returning with towels and dry clothes. One by one, they slip away to change into the oddments she turned up.

In the living room, Jake builds a fire. 'Reason I came,' he tells Lucy. 'This storm's got every emergency service stretched to breaking. I figured they might not be keeping you as dialled in as they'd like. If it was me, I'd want to know.'

He grimaces. 'We had to suspend the search. Only until morning, but right now the conditions are simply too dangerous. It's a once-in-a-lifetime event. Once in a century, even. We couldn't send the Skentel boat back out. The stations in Padstow and Appledore recalled theirs too. And the shoreline search has been stood down till first light. It's just too difficult to see anything. I'm sorry, Lucy. I think . . .' His grimace deepens. 'It's brutal, I know it is. I never imagined having to tell you this. But I think you need to prepare yourself.'

Silence, as Jake's words sink in. A log pops in the grate, sending up a shower of sparks.

Lucy listens to the breath entering and leaving her chest. It's like wind in a crypt. Not something belonging to the living. She stands, goes to the window. With the lights off, her view of the violence beyond the glass is panoramic: black trees bent sideways by wind; black sea veined with white.

Far beneath the house, the pounding of waves against Mortis Point sounds like incoming mortar fire. 'Their immersion suits,' she says. 'Their suits will keep them safe until morning.'

Lucy can't look at her friends. She keeps her gaze on the storm.

'Hon,' Noemie says softly. 'You have to tell us. What happened when you saw him at the hospital? What did Daniel say?'

She closes her eyes—thinks again of how he thrashed and fought when he saw her. How the detective had to hold him down.

She recalls Billie's party, how all their problems seem to flow from that night. Suddenly she's transported. Not to the darkened study and her crass encounter with Nick. Instead, she's back outside, watching blood drip from her husband's knuckles as he glares at his lifelong friend.

'Tell her,' Daniel growls. 'Tell her what you just told me.'

Opposite, Nick tries to repair his ripped shirt. When he sees it's useless, he scowls. 'In my position, you'd have done exactly the same thing.'

Daniel's lips curl back. Lucy sees what's about to happen. She wraps herself around his arm.

'You weren't even going to tell me,' he hisses. Horrified, she opens her mouth to respond. And realizes he's still addressing Nick. 'You only came because you thought the party was just family, no industry people. A happy little interlude to salve your conscience before you made your break.'

'Daniel?' Lucy asks. 'What's happening?'

'He sold out, that's what. Some broker offered him a boatload of money to sell his stake, and he took it. What he didn't know—or didn't bother to find out—was that it was a set-up. Turns out the buyer was actually Hartland, proud new owner of his fifty per cent share.'

Lucy stares in disbelief. For years, Locke-Povey Marine has fought a bloody competitive battle against the far larger Hartland International. Despite the strong opposition, they've grown their market share through a combination of Daniel's creative genius and Nick's aggressive selling.

'But he can't sell his shares just like that,' Lucy says. 'You've got pre-emption rights, surely?'

'Jesus, Luce. Our partnership agreement was some worthless thing we printed off the internet years ago. There aren't any protections. We didn't need belt and braces when it was just the two of us. And now the word is out. Hartland will exercise their shareholder rights, put a stranglehold on the entire business. I've had customers sidling up all evening, telling me they'll have to transfer.'

Listening, Lucy can't even begin to process the implications. Daniel survived a childhood more brutal than most people could imagine. At ten years old, he couldn't read or write. Even now, he has difficulty with his spelling. And yet somehow, thanks to a love of numbers and an insatiable appetite for learning, he dragged himself up. He taught himself physics, engineering and CAD. He set up a business from nothing, expanding it year by year. And while Nick can take some credit for its success, Daniel was always the driving force.

Never has she fully trusted her husband's childhood friend. Too often, the arm around Daniel's shoulder—so visible in that Polaroid snap of them—has felt superficial; less like genuine guardianship and more the protection of an investment. She's never been able to say anything. Nick's loyalty might be questionable; Daniel's, by contrast, is iron-clad.

How will this affect him? The collapse of everything he's built. Daniel's need for control doesn't extend to those around him, but it rules every other aspect of his life: from his focus on the most inconsequential elements of his design work to his insistence on the very best life-saving equipment for the *Lazy Susan*.

How will it affect *them*? There's a hefty business loan secured on the house. They could even lose Wild Ridge.

Her temples throb. The cocaine at the back of her numbed throat is making her gag. Billie appears in the doorway, flanked by Tommo and Bee. Lucy shakes her head, but nobody retreats.

'You had the chance, six months ago, to sell,' Nick says. 'Twice, they've offered to buy us out. I told you then it was a good idea. But that's the trouble with you, Daniel. You hold on to things far longer than you should.'

He looks at Lucy, and she braces herself. But when he speaks, his accusations are for Daniel alone. 'Something happened to you,' he says. 'You used to listen. These days you don't.'

Daniel lunges forward. Lucy drags him back. '*That's* your justification? Because I don't *listen*? That's your reason for selling me out?'

Nick's face tightens. He turns and crosses the drive to the lane.

'This is why you bought the scooter, isn't it?' Daniel shouts. 'So we wouldn't think too badly of you when we found out. You're a joke, Nick. The way your mind works—it's actually fucking sad.'

'Hon?' Noemie asks.

Lucy flinches, comes backs to herself; no longer at Billie's party but sitting on the sofa in front of four anxious faces.

Outside, another mortar round strikes the peninsula. It feels like the entire coast is under attack.

NINETEEN

1

Abraham Rose arrives back at the station just before 6 a.m. Over seventeen hours have now passed since Daniel Locke's distress call. The operation resuming after sunrise is no longer a search and rescue. It's a hunt for bodies.

His first conversation is with Mike Kowalski. 'Where are we with Lucy Locke's family liaison officer?'

'Jesse Arnold's going out to see her this morning. I know it's shit, but that's the reality.'

'It's not your fault. Still, we should have had someone with her last night. What's the latest at the hospital?'

'Locke is up and dressed. Drinking a cup of tea, last time I heard. Word is, they're likely to release him later.'

'I need to be there before that happens.'

'We're going to arrest him?'

'I want to get him in an interview room and see what he has to say.'

'You're not the only one.'

'You know what he said to me at the hospital? *"Tell that bitch she deserves every fucking thing she gets.*" And when his wife turned up, he lost it completely.'

'What's your gut feel?'

'There's something going on between that couple. I just don't know what.'

His night shift complete, Kowalski departs for his bed. At 7 a.m., Abraham summons his team. It's a pitifully reduced crew. He assigns tasks: call logs from Daniel and Billie Locke's phones; a check of every business in Skentel that might have CCTV; ANPR data for Daniel's Volvo. He also wants officers visiting the twenty or so addresses along the coastal road between Skentel and Redlecker. Possible that someone might have seen something.

So far, none of the employees at Locke-Povey Marine have been interviewed. The dispatched patrol car was redirected to another incident and never made it back. No point getting angry about that—immediate threats to life take precedence. In the last twenty-four hours there's been a deluge.

He has to find those kids. Because, without bodies, what has he got? Daniel Locke took his son out of school, that's beyond dispute. CCTV proves he took Fin on the boat. Circumstantial evidence suggests Billie Locke joined them.

Enough for an arrest warrant, but a charge? Even if the bodies of Fin and Billie are recovered, proving that Daniel Locke caused their deaths *intentionally* will be a huge challenge. Right now, all Abraham has is the *Lazy Susan's* smashed seacocks—the valves controlling seawater flow in and out of the boat.

At eight, he calls Patrick Beckett in the South West Criminal Finance team. Yesterday, he briefed Beckett to dig up everything he could find on Daniel Locke. Predictably, Beckett hasn't had time to start.

At eight thirty, he liaises with the media office in Middlemoor. At nine, on the steps outside the station, he holds his first press conference. The suggestion of foul play has swollen the attendant press pack. Journalists hold out digital recorders. Abraham counts six different camera teams.

Despite the crisp morning, sweat is beading on his brow. He hopes no one sees what Dr Annapurna noticed yesterday: death, beginning to cast its shadow. As he speaks, he tries to ignore the purple coat in his periph-eral vision. Instead, he concentrates on his message, on making sure that everyone watching understands the severity of what's happened.

Yesterday lunchtime, Daniel Locke sailed out of Skentel with his sev-en-year-old son. It's believed Locke's eighteen-year-old stepdaughter went with them. A lifeboat crew recovered the empty boat. Daniel was winched from the sea five hours later. Fin and Billie are still missing. The search, suspended overnight, has resumed this morning.

He doesn't mention the *Lazy Susan*'s smashed seacocks but he does make it clear his officers are still piecing together what happened. He ends with a plea for relevant CCTV or dashcam footage.

'Is this still a search-and-rescue operation?' someone asks. 'Do you hope to recover the children alive?'

Abraham thinks of Lucy Locke. 'Yes,' he lies. 'Very much so.'

'Will Daniel Locke make a full recovery?'

'I can't comment.'

'Are you going to arrest him?'

That question comes from Emma Douglas. It forces him to confront her. 'At this time,' he says, 'our efforts are focused squarely on recovering Fin and Billie Locke.'

Emma opens her mouth for another question. He pre-empts her, rais-ing his hands. 'That's it for now. Thanks for coming out. Please take care on the roads during the storm clear-up.'

Abraham turns his back. Emma asks her question anyway. 'Did Dan-iel Locke kill his children for money, or was there some other reason?'

2

Abraham doesn't recognize the officer stationed outside Daniel Locke's room. He introduces himself and shows his warrant card. 'Been here long?'

'About four hours, sir.'

'Had any breakfast?'

'Not yet.'

'Moment you get a chance, make sure you do. And sit down while you have it—none of this eating on the go. The hospital's given Locke the all-clear?'

'Just now.'

Abraham glances at Cooper and the uniformed officers he brought along. 'Let's do this.'

3

Seventeen hours since he last saw Daniel Locke. Amazing, the difference. Gone is the Bair Hugger, the saline drip and the vital-signs monitor. Locke sits in an easy chair by the window, wearing hospital-issue clothes. His gaze is fixed on his lap, leg jigging to a silent beat. In one hand he holds a writing pad, in the other a sharpened pencil. His skin looks flushed, almost like he has sunburn. He doesn't acknowledge his visitors with a look. The leg jig speeds up a notch. Then it stills.

'Daniel Locke,' Abraham says. 'I'm arresting you on suspicion of the murders of Fin and Billie Locke.' He follows with the standard script.

When he's finished, Locke raises his head. His eyes are frightening, their mineral-blue colouring fierce and unyielding—as if they've absorbed all the violence of last night's storm. They're also wet with unshed tears.

'Took you long enough,' he says.

Abraham lets the retort settle. Locke tears the top sheet from his pad. He scrunches it into a ball and drops it into the plastic-lined bin beside his chair. Then, slowly, he stands. Anticipating trouble, the uniformed officers give him space. They're carrying tasers, PAVA spray and collapsible batons—but they won't need any of it, because Locke slides the pad and pencil into his pocket and holds out his wrists, ready to be cuffed.

'This is a hospital, Daniel. Lots of vulnerable people. Unless you've a particular desire for trouble, I'll not add to their burden by parading you past them in handcuffs.'

Locke rolls his shoulders. 'No trouble from me.'

'I'll have to take that pencil.'

'Uh-huh.'

Their eyes meet.

Nobody moves.

Finally, his gaze drifting to the window, Locke raises his hands above his head. Abraham extracts the pencil from the man's joggers. In his peripheral vision, he sees Cooper bend to the waste bin and retrieve the plastic liner.

Outside, Locke searches the sky. Then he examines Abraham. 'Fin,' he says. 'My son. Did you recover him?'

'Get in the car.'

4

Five minutes later they're at the station. Locke is taken to the custody suite and allocated a cell.

Before the interview, Abraham catches up with his team. Although they have a basic timeline for yesterday's events, huge gaps remain. At least the Locke-Povey Marine employees have now been questioned. Yesterday morning, Daniel Locke arrived at the workshop just after eight, driving off again between ten thirty and eleven. Staff at Headlands Junior School place him there at eleven, so the latest he could have left the workshop is ten minutes prior. CCTV footage shows him on Skentel's quay a quarter of an hour after leaving the school. Five minutes after that, he sailed out of the harbour.

No other evidence ties him to a particular place at a particular time. No ANPR cameras cover the coastal route between Skentel and Redlecker. Phone data has been received for Locke's mobile, but the dearth of local cell towers means it's virtually useless. His phone only pinged one tower, which means no triangulation and no assisted GPS positioning. Besides, based on the timings, it's clear he was never more than fifteen minutes from all four locations. He made three calls yesterday, all to Lucy's phone—the last one two minutes after the coastguard logged his distress call. Abraham listened to the message. Fin Locke's voice—'*Daddy, no*'—is clearly audible.

Billie's movements have been harder to pin down. Lucy says her daughter was still at home when she took Fin to school at eight thirty. What the girl did afterwards is unclear. She used her phone a few times yesterday morning. But, just like Daniel Locke's, it only pinged one tower. Most of the activity comprised WhatsApp messages to various groups.

Did Locke return home for his stepdaughter before collecting Fin from school? There's certainly enough of a window. And it would explain why her phone was found in his car.

Billie's friends have been interviewed, but no one's offered much insight. She was popular, passionate, in love with the sea and its wildlife. Her relationship with her stepdad seemed strong. Her text messages and emails show nothing odd.

While the CCTV can't place her on the boat, there's no reason to think she was anywhere else. Which means Billie, tragically, has probably shared Fin's fate.

The shore-based search recommenced at first light. So far, there's no news. Now that the worst weather has passed, a second fleet has left Skentel, supported by lifeboat crews from stations up and down the coast. The coastguard's SARIS system has plotted a revised search plan, but its area is far larger than yesterday's and the storm's intensity has greatly reduced its reliability. Even if Billie or Fin *are* recovered, there's zero chance they'll be found alive.

It's beyond heartbreaking. For Lucy Locke. For the whole of Skentel.

He breaks up the meeting and summons Cooper. 'What was written on that notepaper you retrieved from the bin?'

'Just his wife's name, over and over, scratched through with a pencil.'

Abraham grimaces, thinking of the motif he keeps finding. Then he leads Cooper to the interview room, where Daniel Locke is waiting.

TWENTY

1

Lucy wakes to pain.

For a few merciful seconds, physical pain is all there is. Pain in her chest, in her side. Pain in her knees, in her hands and feet; in her neck and her throat and her cheeks.

She's face up on her bed, still dressed in last night's clothes. Through the window she sees bouldered sky. Atlantic wind is wailing up Mortis Point's west face and corkscrewing over the summit, battering the house like an advancing shield wall.

Dark things swarm at the edges of Lucy's perception. Then, sudden and shocking—cold clarity. Her brain, filling up. Memories that make no sense, falling over her like frames plucked from a cine reel.

Bee at the front door. The *Lazy Susan* sitting low in the water. The playground at Headlands School. Miss Clay. The detective.

And then . . . and then . . .

The coastguard helicopter, the white borehole in the sea. Daniel, screaming at her from his hospital bed. Jake, in her living room, firelight reflecting in his eyes: *We had to suspend the search. I'm sorry, Lucy. But I think you need to prepare yourself.*

Her back arches. A sound of agony rolls from her throat. She grabs fistfuls of bedclothes, hauls herself up. Beside her, Noemie blinks into wakefulness.

Lucy stares at her friend, watches the same slow dawning. Rolling away from her, she steps on to the floor. Her body is a big-band rhythm section of cracking and clicking. She limps to her wardrobe, knees squealing in their sockets. When she halts before it, the room takes a moment to catch up.

'Lucy,' Noemie mutters. 'Oh God, Lucy.'

Opening the wardrobe, she snags a hoodie from its hanger and pulls it on. Behind her, Noemie says, 'I'll make coffee.'

'No time.'

'No time for what?'

'Got to get going.'

'Get going where?'

'Got to find Billie and Fin.'

Noemie screws up her face. 'Hon, after what you went through yesterday, I—'

Lucy doesn't hear the rest. She's already left the room.

2

Downstairs, she shrugs on her parka and hobbles to the living room. Embers glow in the grate from last night's fire. She goes to the velvet drapes, rips them open.

Cold half-light pours in. Lucy narrows her eyes against it.

That sky. That sea.

The tide has rolled in overnight. Northwards, Penleith Beach has shrunk to a narrow strip of sand. Flotsam tumbles in the surf. Water swells around the rocks dislodged from Mortis Point.

South of the peninsula, Skentel looks like it's been hit by an aerial bombardment. At least three buildings are roofless. Perhaps a quarter of the trees lining its slope have been flattened. A telephone pole has come down near the church. Debris litters the streets: broken satellite dishes, splintered fence panels, bits of shrubbery, rubble. In the harbour, a yacht is floating keel-up.

With the cloud cover so thick, it could be any time of the morning. Lucy's internal clock tells her it's a little before dawn. She grabs her binoculars, training them on the stretches of coastline she can see.

Jake's words from last night echo in her head: *The shoreline search has been stood down till first light. It's just too difficult to see anything.*

Lucy sees no searchers out looking. A few miles offshore, a tiny orange boat is ploughing a white wake. The Tamar-class lifeboat? Or the inshore D-class? Panning south with the binoculars, she seeks out the RNLI boathouse. From here she can't tell whether its steel cradle is occupied. Lights are blazing inside. At least someone there is busy.

Lucy stuffs the binoculars into her pocket. Back in the hall, she meets Noemie coming down the stairs.

'You have a plan,' her friend says. 'That's good. I want to help.'

'Then you'd better keep up,' Lucy tells her. 'Because we don't have much time.' In the kitchen, she checks the wall clock: quarter to seven. 'One thing I know without doubt: Daniel will have done everything he can to keep them alive. I know what people think. But he's not the kind of man to . . .'

Tightness in her throat. She can't finish the sentence. From a cupboard she finds a box of paracetamol and swallows two pills. At the sink, she fills a tumbler with water and knocks it back.

Her keys are on the counter.

'Car,' Lucy says, drawing up short. She reached the hospital by ambulance. Tommo drove her home.

'Shit,' Noemie replies. 'It's still down in Skentel.'

'That's OK, we'll ride.'

Back in the cloakroom, she grabs two crash helmets. Outside, she raises the garage door, revealing Daniel's old Triumph.

The bike wakes on Lucy's first kick of the starter. Once Noemie's climbed on, they peel out of the garage.

3

The lane off the peninsula is clogged with snapped branches and fallen saplings. When they reach the coastal road, it's even worse.

Although Lucy saw Penleith Beach from the house, she still wants to check it out. At the turn-off, she steers the Triumph down the track. Sand coats everything—the trees are rusty with it. Each gust of wind raises a blizzard of tiny grains; they hiss off Lucy's crash helmet, crackle against her visor.

She climbs the backshore dune, grabbing handfuls of marram grass to pull herself up. The sea is a dirty wash of grey. Violent still, and dark.

Near the rocks of Mortis Point, a trio of seals are watching her. Immediately, she thinks of Billie. Not general recollections but a specific one: the girl in her bedroom two days ago, hunched over her Chromebook. When Lucy walks in with clean laundry, Billie turns away too slowly to hide her tears.

A video is playing onscreen. The scene is a shallow bay. Grinning men stand waist-deep in water, armed with hooks and knives. A huge pod of dolphins is swimming towards them, fleeing a flotilla of small boats. Pretty soon the animals run out of deep water. That's when they discover death wading among them.

The men select their prizes from whatever comes close. They lunge at the panicking animals, stabbing with knives and hooks. Their killing method, once the first strikes are delivered, is to saw the dolphins open behind their heads. It's not quick, but it's messy—blood *gushes* into the water. And yet, strangely, it appears to be fun. The more the men kill, the more they want to kill. They grow competitive with each other, less careful with their knives. Injured dolphins thrash to bloody exhaustion. Others are only partially hacked open before being abandoned. Mothers swim in circles, trying to shield their calves, but the young are easiest to catch and quickest to kill. Afterwards, the mothers go more quietly.

The *grindadráp*, Lucy realizes. She's heard all the counter-arguments. Now she's seen the reality.

On the bed, Billie wipes her face clean. 'White-sided dolphins. They're social animals, live to their mid-twenties. The mothers nurse their calves for up to a year. They stay together up to five years after that. Jesus, there's so much *blood*. I'm not sure I can do it, Mum. I'm not sure I'm strong enough.'

'You're eighteen,' Lucy says. 'Nobody's going to think less of you if you change your mind.'

But Billie's already shaking her head. '*I'd* think less of me. I've been talking about this for years. It's my chance to *do* something—to finally make a difference.'

'You can make a difference in lots of ways.'

Billie looks at the screen. 'I can't be one of those people who help from afar. I just can't. I'm not knocking them. But that's not who I am.'

Now, as then, Lucy knows the truth of those words. 'Keep her safe,' she tells the trio of seals. As one, they wink out of sight beneath the water.

4

From Penleith Beach they ride to Redlecker. They stop at every headland where there's a track, visit every beach they can't see from higher ground. Overnight, this entire coast has been ravaged. Hard to imagine, witnessing the destruction, that wind and rain alone could be culpable.

On their way back to Skentel they encounter the first search parties: groups in all-weather gear, some with dogs, swarming the inlets and coves.

If the storm washed up Billie and Fin alive, they might well have crawled to higher ground. Protected from the worst weather by their immersion suits, they could have kept each other alive by huddling close. The road dissolves as Lucy pictures that. She slows the bike until she can see again.

Her last stop is Smuggler's Tumble. Its forested switchbacks have taken a pounding overnight, but already someone's been out with a chainsaw. The gravel parking circle is clogged with cars. Among the civilian vehicles she spots a coastguard Land Rover and a police patrol car.

A thirty-strong group of volunteers stands on the path, listening to a coastguard official. As Lucy climbs off the bike, a few glance over. When she removes the crash helmet, a murmur passes through the crowd. She notices a range of expressions, not all of them sympathetic.

It angers her for a moment, that. Bewilders her. And then she decides it's OK. What's important is that they're here for Billie and Fin.

Nobody moves or says a word. Lucy realizes they're expecting her to speak. She hadn't prepared for this, is hardly in the right mind for it. But she can't let the opportunity pass.

Walking closer, she starts to recognize faces: Luke Creese, the pastor from St Peter's; Gordon and Jane Watson, the couple from the local pharmacy; Ravinder Turkmish, owner of the Bayleaf, and three of his serving staff.

Her head rings with Jake's words from last night. *I think you need to prepare yourself.*

Fuck that.

'I'm so grateful to see you all here,' Lucy begins. The wind whips away her words. She tries again, forcing a strength into her voice she doesn't feel. 'I know Billie and Fin will be grateful too. And Daniel.'

A few snatched looks at that. Lucy ignores them, but it's a warning to switch tack. 'This is still a search and rescue. I know how that sounds, after yesterday's storm. But Billie and Fin would've been in their immersion suits. Daniel would've made sure . . .'

She can't breathe.

It takes a few moments to fill her chest. Jane Watson, she notices, has tears running down her cheeks. Hard to look at that.

'The immersion suits will have kept them warm. Even so, if they've washed up ashore, we need to find them quickly. Billie's a gym nut, as strong as anyone here. But Fin . . .' This time, as she says her son's name, it feels like an arrow has punched through her sternum. 'Fin's seven.'

Wind, in the trees. Thirty sets of eyes, all watching.

'Some of you know I own the Drift Net. When you're hungry, come down and we'll feed you. When you're cold, come inside and we'll warm you up. But please—*please*—keep looking. The next twelve hours . . .'

She doesn't need to say it. Everyone knows how that sentence ends. 'I know you won't give up. I know you'll do everything it takes. In the meantime, I just wanted to say thank you. From me, from my whole family.'

In the ensuing silence, it doesn't feel right just to turn away. There's an awkwardness, suddenly. A sense of something missing.

Then Gordon Watson puts his hands together and starts clapping. Moments later, the staff of the Bayleaf join in. The applause builds gently, steadily. Witnessing it, Lucy notices something important. The handful of hard looks from earlier have softened.

Noemie's hand slips around her arm. Together, they walk back to the Triumph. Lucy swings her leg over the seat, grimacing at the spike of pain from her ribs. Glancing up, she sees Matt Guinness, her old classmate, approaching the bike.

Matt's shaved off the wispy beard since she last saw him, but he still hasn't washed his hair. A greasy snake of it hangs over one shoulder of his lime-green cagoule. 'Luce. Hey, listen. I just wanted to say—I'm sorry for yesterday, at the quay. I was kind of a dick.' He wipes his nose on his cagoule and offers his hand. 'At the time, I just thought it was some dumb shit—your hubby not checking his mooring lines.'

Matt's fingernails are like a mole's claws, long and curved and sleek. The last thing Lucy wants is to touch him, but he's here, at least, first thing on a Saturday morning. Another pair of eyes in the hunt.

'Thanks for being here,' she says, shaking his hand. Lucy pulls on her crash helmet and fastens it. Noemie climbs on to the pillion seat.

'No worries,' Matt tells her. 'We're Skentel natives, you and me. Like I told my mum, it's the least I can do to come out. Last thing any of us expected was your hubby going full psycho. We'll find them kids, Luce, if it's any comfort. Whether it's today or next week, I just know they'll wash up.'

Lucy stares, appalled. She wipes her hand on her jeans, starts the Triumph. With a blip of the throttle, she gets out of there.

5

She's unprepared for what she finds outside the Drift Net. Filling the window left of the door is a giant image of Fin. It's a colour composite, made from multiple A4 sheets. Beneath, in stark black letters, is her son's name and date of birth. The right-hand window displays an identically sized image of Billie.

Confronted by her children, Lucy starts to shake. She sits on the bike, feet planted, unable to do anything but stare at those larger-than-life-sized pieces of her heart.

Fin's laughing, Billie too. But their eyes plead for life with an intensity that's almost physical. A cavity opens inside Lucy's chest.

'Christ, I should have warned you,' Noemie says, climbing off the bike. 'Bee said she was going to get down here early with Tommo, turn this place into a hub, like you asked.'

Lucy moves her head from left to right.

Fin, then Billie.

She swallows. 'It's fine. It's good, actually. More than that—it's exactly what we need. It's . . . I just didn't . . .'

'I know, hon. None of this is easy. For the foreseeable, you'll need to be one hard-as-nails bitch.'

Inside, the Drift Net is rammed. Everyone Lucy wanted to see is here: fishing crews, yachting folk, local business owners, coastguard volunteers and uniformed police officers. Conversation is urgent and loud.

Near the bar, eight tables have been dragged together. A huge coastal map has been tacked to it, divided by purple felt-tip into eight sections coded A to H. Matching lists have been fixed to a nearby wall. Each contains rows of names and telephone numbers.

Behind the tables stands Sean Rowland, the coastguard station officer from Redlecker. With a green pen he's cross-hatching a section of map. Watching him is Bill Shetland, Skentel's harbour master, and a female police officer.

The conversation fades as Lucy's presence registers. On her way to the bar, a hand squeezes her shoulder. Someone else touches her arm. She cringes—doesn't want their sympathy, certainly not their pity.

But something strange happens as she moves through the crowd: the touches and embraces and pledges of support soak in, begin to fill her up. By the time she reaches the bar, the cavity in her chest has refilled.

Bee is standing with Tommo at the till. Her pink hair's the brightest thing in the room. She's wearing another black T-shirt: *ATOMS MAKE US ALL MATTER*. Tommo's T-shirt reads: *EVERYTHING HAS BEAUTY BUT NOT EVERYONE SEES IT.*

'You're here, that's good,' Bee says. 'They need to see a figurehead.'

'You did all this? You put it all together?'

'Not just me. Tommo helped. And let me tell you—we're just getting started. We'll find them, there's no way we won't. That guy Sean is organizing the shoreline searches. A lot of the boats have already gone back out. I saw Jake earlier. Coastguard asked him to send the Tamar to the new search area they plotted. He's got the inshore boat patrolling the coast. From what the radio nerds are telling me, there's even a navy frigate out there looking. Plus all sorts of craft in the Bristol Channel.'

Bee pauses. Her gaze flickers from Lucy to her boyfriend.

'What is it?' Lucy asks.

'We're getting lots of questions about Daniel,' Tommo says quietly. 'A few nasty rumours starting to fly. There are one or two journalists milling about. We're just telling you so you're armed. Have you spoken to him?'

'Hospital visiting's from two. I thought I'd come down here first, get things organized. Not that it seems I needed to. You're both doing an amazing job. I'm going to run off some extra photos. Make sure there's no danger of running out.'

'You want some help?' Bee asks.

Lucy shakes her head. 'You've got your hands full here. Remember— the tills stay closed. We feed these people, get the word out. We make Billie and Fin famous until they're found.'

Excusing herself, she goes to her office. It's a cramped, windowless space. A shelving rack bows with the weight of box folders, drinks promos and other detritus. On the desk is her iMac. A screensaver worm crawls across it.

Lucy sits, sweeping a sprawl of paperwork to the floor. She waves the computer mouse, types in her password. The screen changes: an image of Billie. It's the same one from the front window, pasted into a photo editor. Lucy flinches as if stung.

She resizes the image, adds the one of Fin. Then she opens Safari. It takes a while to find images of the *Lazy Susan*'s immersion suits. She drops the best ones into the photo editor below her children's photographs. A few mouse-clicks and the printer begins to spit pages.

While the job completes, Lucy opens her Gmail and finds ninety-two new messages. She scrolls through them: marketing circulars, supplier invoices, newsletter notifications, messages from friends, messages from journalists; and there, incongruous among them, an email from Daniel.

6

Claws on her shoulders. Hooks in her skin. Lucy turns, half expecting to find something crouched behind her chair, but the office and passage are empty. Leaning backwards, she flicks the door closed and returns her attention to the screen.

>> Daniel (Not Work)　　　　Over and Out　　　　03 Mar

Lucy can hear the roar of her blood, a sound like white noise. Only yesterday she'd watched a shadow beat its fists against her front door. At the time she'd hesitated. Something about the intrusion had felt wrong, portentous. To be avoided at all costs.

She feels the same way now.

And yet she cannot ignore this.

Over and Out.

No way Daniel took Billie and Fin into that storm without good reason. No way he'd do them harm. *She* knows that, even if no one else does.

Over and Out.

Her finger hovers over the mouse.

03 March. Yesterday's date.

Over and Out.

Oh God, oh God, oh God.

Click.

TWENTY-ONE

1

It's a small, unwelcoming space. White walls, fluorescent strip lighting, a table, recording equipment, three chairs.

Abraham takes the seat opposite Daniel Locke; Cooper settles beside him. He switches on the recorder, introduces those present, notes the time and location. Then he confirms that Locke understands he's being interviewed under caution.

'I also need to ask if you want a solicitor, Daniel. Or if you're content to speak to us without one.'

Those cobalt-blue eyes, tinged now with red, are as unnerving as they were yesterday. 'I don't need a solicitor.'

Abraham's pulse accelerates a little at that. 'OK,' he says, keeping his expression neutral. 'Obviously, you can change your mind at any time.'

Silence, from across the table.

'Yesterday morning, at eleven a.m., did you visit Headlands Junior School in Skentel?'

'Yes.'

'While you were there, did you pick up your son, Fin Locke, and leave with him in your car?'

'Yes.'

'Why did you do that, Daniel?'

'I want to talk to Lucy.'

'There'll be time to speak to—'

Locke clenches his teeth. 'I want to talk to her now.'

'Daniel, we're interviewing you under caution because you've been arrested. You're not going to be talking to your wife or anyone else—with the exception of a solicitor—until we've either charged or released you. I'll ask again: do you want a solicitor?'

'I want to see Lucy.'

'And I told you that's not going to happen.'

'Then I want to make a phone call.'

'You can make a phone call later, when we're done.'

'I have a right to—'

'You have a right to let someone know of your whereabouts. But the duty sergeant can make contact on your behalf. I hate to destroy myths, but you don't get a phone call.'

Daniel Locke scowls. His gaze pivots to the camera.

'Do you want us to let someone know where you are?'

Locke's gaze moves from the camera to the door.

'Daniel?'

'I want you to tell Lucy.'

'The custody sergeant will let her know. Why did you pick up your son from school yesterday morning?'

'No comment.'

'Did you tell the school receptionist that Fin had a dental appointment?'

'No comment.'

'You wrote in the school logbook that you were signing Fin out for a dental appointment. Do you recall doing that?'

'No comment.'

'We have the log, Daniel.'

The man leans back, folds his arms.

'Did Fin have a dental appointment yesterday?'

'I can keep saying no comment all day.'

'And I can keep asking questions. All night, too, if required. We can spend the next twenty-four hours playing ping-pong in this nasty little room if you like, but you know the answers to these questions and you know we know the answers too. We have multiple witnesses, CCTV. There's really no point prolonging this. So, after you left the school, did you drive Fin to Skentel's harbour?'

Locke rolls his neck, stares at the ceiling. 'I'm assuming you know I did.'

'It would be really useful if you could answer the question.'

'Yes,' he says, through clenched teeth.

'Did you park your Volvo XC90'—Abraham pauses to read out the number plate—'in the car park beside Skentel's quay?'

'Yes.'

'Do you own a yacht called the *Lazy Susan*?'

'Last time I checked.'

'Please could you—'

'It's my yacht.'

'And where's the yacht usually moored?'

'Skentel harbour.'

'Was it there yesterday?'

'Yes.'

'After parking the car, did you take Fin aboard the *Lazy Susan*?'

Locke licks his lips. He closes his eyes, opens them. 'Yes.'

'Thank you. I'm grateful for your honesty. You'll find it stands you in good stead. Did you take your stepdaughter, Billie Locke, with you on the boat?'

Daniel Locke laughs, a savage expulsion of breath. He shakes his head, sucks down air, blows it out through his cheeks. Then he looks up and nods.

Abraham feels something shift inside his chest. 'For the tape, please.'

'Yes.'

2

Cold, suddenly, inside this windowless room.

'Where are they now, Daniel?'

At the question, Locke goes so still it appears he's not breathing. Abraham feels like he's watching a predator frozen before the strike. Only the table separates them. He'd like nothing better than to catch an attempted assault on camera.

Finally, Locke laces his fingers together. 'I drowned them,' he says. 'I drowned them both.'

Abraham feels an itching in his knuckles, his eyes. He thinks of everything he's learned about Billie Locke, her passion and her activism; her yearning for a better world. He thinks of Fin, the little storyteller. Even now, his recollection of those curvy chimp ears and lopsided glasses makes him want to smile. But he can't smile because then he'd roar, and then he might do something inside this room that would destroy any chance of justice. So he swallows down his rage, waits until he's sure his voice is steady, then asks, 'How did you drown them?'

Daniel Locke sighs, as if he's savouring the heat inside a sauna. 'I tied them up and put them in the water. And when they . . . when they were gone, I jumped in after.'

They're difficult words to hear. To counter them, Abraham conjures a fragment of Psalm seven: *See how wicked people think up evil; they plan trouble and practise deception. But in the traps they set for others, they themselves get caught.* 'Why did you drown them?'

'You remember what I said? At the hospital?'

Abraham consults his notes. 'In the hospital, yesterday, you said to me, "I have a message. A message for that bitch. Tell her she deserves every fucking thing she gets." Is that what you're referring to?'

'I'm not going to say it twice.'

'I'm not asking you to repeat it. Just whether that's what you're referring to.'

'That was it.'

'And that's your reason for drowning Fin and Billie Locke? Your son and your stepdaughter?'

Daniel lifts his chin. He stares again at the ceiling-mounted video camera. 'Is this going to be on the news?'

'You want to be famous? Is that it?'

'You know what? I want a solicitor. That's what I want. This conversation is over. I want a solicitor and I want to speak to my wife.'

It's a waiting game now.

I'm far, far calmer than I was. I never appreciated, at the start, how deeply this would affect me. How emotional I would find it. How traumatic.

The police will believe what they hear, or they won't. It doesn't really matter. What matters is you, Lucy. Your purification and renewal—the erasure of the hurtful creature you were; the creation of something beautiful.

I know you'll be splashing about, desperately trying to keep your head above the water. What lies have you told yourself? How long will you avoid the truth?

No one I've met has more talent for self-deception. But the longer you maintain hope, the harder this will be. What you've faced so far is just the start.

You've bewitched this town, Lucy. I see that. You're loved by everyone in it. But soon you'll see how easily perceptions can sour. Especially once the lesser-known points of Lucy Locke trivia come to light.

Because you're not innocent, are you? You're not the virtuous, home-baking, child-raising, life-affirming, Skentel-businesswoman-of-the-year creative soul you make out.

You deceive. And you cheat. You thought I didn't know but I do.

Have you received my email yet? I have to apologize for its tone. My emotions were running pretty high. Lately, my head hasn't been as clear as I'd like.

Just remember; this isn't bitterness, or sour grapes. This is a tragedy written entirely for your benefit. An opportunity for redemption, should you wish to take it.

TWENTY-TWO

1

Sitting at her desk, staring at the subject line of Daniel's email—*Over and Out*—Lucy falls into a memory.

Saturday night, a week ago. She should be at home, helping Billie with her college work. Instead, she's standing in darkness, halfway up Skentel's wooded slope. The hood of her sweatshirt is raised against the rain. Water has soaked through it, matting her hair to her scalp.

Through the trees, she sees glimmering lights.

Lucy glances over her shoulder to the darkened lane at her back. No way she can risk being seen. Shivering, she starts walking.

The house is a world away from the whitewashed buildings on Skentel's main street. It's ultra-modern in design: all glass, aluminium and silvered wood.

The front door—a single glazed panel—is flanked by two topiary trees in black planters. Lucy presses the ringer. Moments later, light spills into the hall. Nick Povey appears, holding a whisky tumbler.

He hesitates when he sees her. Just for a beat. Then he comes forward and opens the door. Warm air, laced with cigar smoke and Nick's citrus cologne, wafts out.

They examine each other for long seconds. Then Lucy says, 'I'm not sure this was wise.'

Nick takes a sip of whisky. 'Probably not.'

When he steps back, she walks in. With the door closed, the tension between them intensifies. Rainwater drips from Lucy's clothes. 'I'll get you a towel,' he says. 'And a dry top.'

Nodding, she kicks off her soaked trainers. Then, seeing the puddles they're making on the hardwood floor, her socks. Nick returns and leads her to the living room.

It's an impressive space, conspicuously masculine. Logs crackle brightly on a circular stone-built firepit at its heart, sending smoke up a suspended copper chimney. A huge TV on one wall offers the only other source of light. Its screen is frozen partway through a boxing match. A black leather couch is arranged opposite. Cowhides and reindeer skins cover sections of the floor.

Lucy strips off her wet hoodie. She accepts the proffered towel and dries her hair. Nick goes to a drinks cabinet and pours her a cognac.

At the firepit, she holds out her hands to the flames. She's conscious, suddenly, of her damp vest and what it exposes. On her arms, her flesh puckers into goosebumps.

Nick brings over her drink. He sets it on the edge of the stone surround.

She stares at him. He stares back.

'Lucy,' he begins. 'I always—'

'Daniel doesn't know I'm here.'

He nods, eyes wandering over her bare skin. His throat bulges as he swallows. 'I hardly imagined he would.'

Another long silence as they appraise each other.

'It's been a while since I came to the house,' Lucy says. 'You've done a lot of work. It looks . . . amazing.'

Nick swells a little at that. He takes another sip of whisky. The ice cubes clink together in his glass. 'Some might say it needs softening. A feminine influence.'

Already, the heat from the firepit has dried Lucy's vest. She pulls on what Nick brought from upstairs—an old rugby jersey with his name printed across the back. Doubtless he'll get a kick from seeing her wear it.

Considering that, Lucy feels her heart thump harder. She tosses back the cognac in one gulp. 'Must've cost a small fortune.'

'Money well spent, now it's done.'

'Nice to be able to afford it.'

Nick measures her. Then he flashes his teeth. 'I'm starting to wonder why you came.'

'Why do you think I came?'

He takes her empty glass and retreats, returning with a refill. 'You know how I feel about you. You've known a long time. And we both know you'll get something from me that you'll never get from Daniel. When you look around this room, there's a part of you that imagines yourself here. A part of you that realizes you'd fit right in.'

Lucy's stomach tightens. She tries to control her breathing; aware of her chest rising and falling; of the growing flush of blood at her throat. 'I'm Daniel's wife.'

Nick hands her the refilled glass. She takes it, maintaining eye contact. 'Why do it, Nick? If you wanted out that badly, you could have sold to Daniel. We'd have found the money somehow. Nothing would've been destroyed. No jobs would've been lost. Everything you helped to build would have survived.'

'You couldn't have afforded what they offered. Hartland wanted us out of the way. They wanted Daniel neutralized. They were prepared to pay a premium to make that happen.' His mouth twitches. 'A huge premium, it turned out.'

'And that's all you have to say? There wouldn't have *been* a business without Daniel.' She gestures around the room. 'There wouldn't have been all this. It was his idea, his design work. He even funded the expansion. We have loans secured on our house we're still in the process of paying off.'

'Life's tough. Daniel knew what he was taking on.'

Lucy stares. She's not surprised by what she's hearing. She knows this attitude—knows how and why it develops. Fruitless appealing to Nick's

165

conscience. To him, life's a zero-sum game. What he wants, he'll take—better to be a winner than a loser because that's all there is. Despite her abhorrence of what he's done, she can, at least, recognize his motivation.

'I know you, Nick,' she says at last. 'You always plan six moves ahead. Whatever deal you did with Hartland, you'd have left yourself a way back in. You enjoy the game too much to cash in all your chips and walk away.'

Nick studies her. 'Are we negotiating, Luce? Is that what this is?'

She takes a swallow of cognac. 'You know we're negotiating.'

'I thought we might be.'

He finishes his whisky, savouring it before he swallows. Then his eyes crawl over her, languid. 'So what have you brought me to trade?'

2

Lucy gasps and the memory recedes. In the Drift Net's cramped office, she leans closer to the iMac's screen, moves her mouse, clicks. The email from Daniel opens.

>> Daniel (Not Work)   Over and Out   03 Mar

> You thought I didn't know but I do. And you might think you know me but you don't. You don't have the first clue. Nor does Nick.
>
> Do you have the slightest understanding of how it feels to be betrayed by both your wife and your best friend?
>
> People reap what they sow.

Lucy reads the message five times before she can breathe. The earlier rushing of blood fills her ears, a roar like the sea. Jake said Daniel broadcast his distress call at 12.37. When she looks at the timestamp, she sees this email was sent two minutes later. Two minutes in which she'd imagined Daniel hustling Billie and Fin into their immersion suits.

Daddy, no—

Lucy closes her eyes. When she concentrates, she can suppress her son's voice. Other times, like now, it boomerangs back.

You thought I didn't know but I do. And you might think you know me but you don't. You don't have the first clue. Nor does Nick.

Tacked to the wall is a photo of the *Lazy Susan*. Daniel crouches on the foredeck, his arms around Billie and Fin.

Ray-Bans hide his eyes.

Lucy controls her breathing: slow in, slow out. She knows he loves her. She *knows* it. But this email changes everything.

She hears commotion in the passage leading to the bar. Checking the door is still closed, she reads the message one last time. Footsteps now, outside. Lucy deletes the email, opens the trash, deletes everything there too.

'Luce?'

She leaps up. Blood rushes into her cheeks.

Tommo stands in the doorway. 'Didn't mean to startle you. But you might want to see this.'

3

A TV hangs from the wall behind the pool table. Every face in the Drift Net is turned towards it. Onscreen, the crag-faced detective is talking.

Abraham Rose.

It's clear he hates the cameras. Likewise, the microphones held towards his face. Gone is the gruff self-assurance from their car journey. Rose holds himself awkwardly and speaks haltingly. He relates yesterday's events and appeals for CCTV and dashcam footage. He confirms that the search-and-rescue operation has resumed. Then a reporter asks if Daniel Locke's going to be arrested.

Abraham Rose hesitates before answering. Lucy senses the atmosphere inside the Drift Net change—as if all the oxygen has escaped.

'At this time,' the detective says, 'our efforts are focused squarely on recovering Fin and Billie Locke.' He holds up his hands, signalling the end of the press conference.

Off-camera, a female reporter shouts, 'Did Daniel Locke kill his children for money or was there some other reason?'

Shoulders raised, Abraham walks back towards the police station. The live feed cuts to the studio.

Silence, from everyone inside the Drift Net.

Lucy feels like she's just been kicked in the gut. Slowly, painfully, conversation resumes. But it's quieter now, more self-conscious. She trades glances with Noemie, Tommo, Bee. Others—like Matt Guinness and Wayland Rawlings—deliberately avoid her eye.

Lucy sets her jaw. She feels a rush of anger that quickens her blood. But she can't afford to take this personally. Has to focus on the only thing that matters: Billie and Fin.

She thinks of the email she just deleted from her computer.

People reap what they sow.

'It's OK,' Noemie whispers, at her side.

On TV, they're talking about the weather again. A map of the UK appears, split by a giant band of low pressure.

'Lucy Locke?'

A woman stands at the bar. Strong face, auburn pixie cut, hard eyes that nonetheless radiate empathy. She flips open a wallet inscribed with the constabulary crest. 'I'm Sergeant Jesse Arnold. I've been assigned as your family liaison officer. I can't imagine how hard the last twenty-four hours must have been. But I'm here to guide you through whatever comes next and help in any way I can.'

'Why the delay?' Noemie asks.

'It's not ideal, and for that all I can say is sorry. Truth is, this storm's broken all records—stretched us to our limit. I know that won't make you feel any better, but there it is.' To Lucy, she adds, 'Is there somewhere we can talk?'

Lucy stares at her a while before answering. 'We'll use the back office.'

4

It's cramped, just the two of them—and awkward. There's only one chair and Lucy doesn't want to sit.

'I heard you sailed out there yesterday,' Arnold says. 'Right when the storm was at its worst. Brave as hell, a lot of people would say. Crazy, too. But I'm a mum. What else would you do?'

For a moment, overcome by exhaustion, Lucy can't decide if the question is rhetorical. But when she meets Arnold's eyes her tiredness falls away. Because there's something terrible lurking in the police officer's expression.

'They're not dead,' she says immediately. And hates the desperation in her voice.

'My colleagues said you were injured last night. A couple of broken ribs. Looks like you knocked your head, too. How're you feeling now? Any concussion?'

'They're not dead,' Lucy says again. 'Billie and Fin. They're not.'

'We've got hundreds of people out looking,' Arnold replies. 'Efforts might've been hampered yesterday, but turnout this morning's been huge. Not just coastguard and police but a combined community response.

'All the same, Daniel made his distress call yesterday lunchtime. In water that cold, without protection, survival time is three hours *maximum*. That's for an adult in calm seas. Not like conditions yesterday, where you'd need every ounce of energy just to stay afloat. Daniel was rescued after five hours and he couldn't have lasted much longer.

'It's the worst news in the world, Lucy. The worst thing that could possibly happen. I'm so, so sorry, but I think you're going to have to face the reality that we're unlikely, now, to recover Billie and Fin alive.'

Lucy shakes her head. Her earlier anger returns, a volcano threatening to erupt. How dare this police officer—this so-called *mother*—try to plant these thoughts? 'That's bullshit,' she spits. Twisting away, she grabs the flyers she just printed out.

'Lucy, I—'

'They're alive! Those immersion suits we bought are *Arctic-rated*. Here, take a look. Read the stats.'

'Lucy, listen to—'

'Daniel would've got Billie and Fin into their suits, OK? He'd have prioritized the children over himself. That's why he was found first. Don't you get it? Because he'd have been closest to the boat, the last one to leave. That sea was unbelievable yesterday. I was—'

'Lucy, last night our crime scene guys did a full—'

'—out there in the middle of it—'

'—inventory of the *Lazy Susan* and they discovered three unused immersion suits onboard.'

'But that doesn't . . . It doesn't . . .' Lucy stops, swallows, blinks. She breathes, resets. 'Look at the photo,' she continues, printouts trembling in her hand. 'We had one for each of us.'

'Lucy,' Sergeant Arnold says gently. 'Listen to me. That image is an exact match to the immersion suit Daniel was wearing and the three we found onboard. I'm so sorry. We don't believe there's any way that your children can have survived. The recovery operation will continue, but it's no longer an active rescue.'

Everything stops. Everything.

Then, without warning, the volcano erupts.

Lucy flings out her right hand, knocking the printer off the desk. She lifts the iMac, hurls it against the wall, grabs it when it bounces back, smashes it down once, twice, pitches it across the office. Upending a shelf, she sends box files crashing to the floor.

Her anger isn't done. Isn't even started. She turns on Arnold, panting for breath, teeth clenched from a knifing pain in her ribs.

Clear, now, that until she can speak to Daniel, she's in this alone.

She bends, hissing with the effort. Snatches up her crash helmet.

'Lucy, where are you—'

'Away from *here*!'

In the main bar conversation has died again. This time, she can't meet anyone's gaze. Only when she's outside does she realize she's sobbing. She climbs on the Triumph, slides the key into the ignition, kicks down on the starter.

170

The engine responds. A deep-throated roar. It's what she needs to hear.

Not words but action. Movement.

Billie and Fin stare at her from the windows.

People reap what they sow.

She has no Seago, no immersion suits, nothing left to sustain her except blind faith. That email has changed everything. But she knows she was right to delete it. Unsure of her destination, Lucy twists the throttle and peels away from the quay.

5

Blasting along the coastal road, leaning into the turns, Lucy retreats in time. It's night again, a week ago. She's standing barefoot beside Nick's firepit. Cognac burns in her throat as his eyes rove over her body.

'*So what have you brought me to trade?*'

She doesn't answer him directly. Instead, she carries her drink to the couch. Her feet leave a trail of damp prints, breadcrumbs for Nick to follow. And follow them he does—like a puppy, or a wolf cub, or a snake slithering after its prey.

On the couch, Lucy draws up one leg, balancing her drink on her knee. This close, she can smell more than just Nick's cologne. She can smell *him*—his barely contained restraint. He takes a slug of whisky. She matches him with a swallow of cognac.

'Where does Daniel think you are?'

'At the Drift Net. Covering a staff member who phoned in sick.'

A muscle in his jaw twitches. 'Saturday night. Late closing.'

'Very late.'

He smirks. 'Lots of time to negotiate.'

She smiles back. Feels like throwing up. But if there's a way out of this—and she *knows* there's a way out of this—it's through Nick.

Lucy swirls her cognac. He might play this game better than anyone, but she's no novice. Nick's lust for what he doesn't have is his weak spot. If there's information to be learned, an opportunity to save what Daniel's built, she'll find it.

Because Nick's treachery, Lucy now believes, far surpasses his sell-out to Hartland International. She spent last night studying the Locke-Povey Marine accounts. Money has gone missing from the business—in recent weeks, a huge amount. So far, she's been unable to trace it.

Perhaps there's a way to claw back Nick's shareholding from Hartland; perhaps there isn't. But Lucy is going to find that stolen cash. And although she won't give Nick what he wants in return, she'll dangle it.

He shifts closer, trailing a finger down her arm. Hard to work out if he's admiring his old rugby shirt or what lies beneath. 'You know, I always had a—' he begins, and then something explodes in the hall.

6

Lucy is first to react. Perhaps because she has more to lose. When she leaps up, she loses her grip on her glass. The sound of it shattering on the hardwood floor barely registers.

Nick's on his feet an instant later. He springs to the living-room door and throws it open. Lucy follows, heart thumping in her ears. It takes her a moment to work out what she's seeing. Because there seems to be a *tree* lodged inside the entrance hall. Around it lie shards of glass, fragments of black pottery and soil.

'Are you *kidding* me?' Nick roars.

But Lucy recognizes what's happened.

The tree is an ornamental boxwood. Earlier, she saw two of them flanking the front entrance. Someone just hurled this one through Nick Povey's glass door. When she lifts her eyes from the wreckage, she sees Daniel poised on the threshold.

A sound of dismay rolls from Lucy's throat. Nick follows the direction of her gaze. Cold wind twines into the house. Rain speckles the hallway floor.

Daniel says nothing. He simply stares. At Lucy's bare feet. At her towel-damp hair. At her unbuttoned rugby shirt bearing his best friend's name.

It doesn't just look bad. It looks catastrophic.

When she drops her head, she notices blood pulsing from her right foot. *Lots* of blood.

Lucy frowns, confused. Glancing behind her, she sees a line of scarlet footprints. They retreat to Nick's couch through slivers of daggered glass.

TWENTY-THREE

1

While Abraham waits for the assigned solicitor, he speaks to the CPS South West office in Exeter. A meeting is arranged for later that day. Daniel Locke's confession has changed everything, but there's still work to be done. The prosecutor's office fears an ambush at the court hearing. In the meantime, Locke can be held without charge for twenty-four hours—although no magistrate will raise a frown at an extension request.

Sitting at his desk, Abraham reviews what he's learned about Daniel Locke. Forty-two years old, born in Skentel, a marine engineer turned entrepreneur and joint owner of Locke-Povey Marine. With the exception of driving offences, of which there are several, the man has no adult convictions. Going further back, it's a different story.

Aged fourteen, he served six months in custody for a vicious attack on two boys at his hostel, carried out while they slept. Locke went about them with a cricket bat before returning to his own bed. The next morning, he refused to tell the arresting officers anything, only admitting guilt pre-trial in exchange for a lighter sentence. The violence, he claimed, was payback for slights both victims denied.

It isn't the only entry on Locke's record. A year earlier, he was the subject of a youth rehabilitation order, along with his friend, Nick Povey. Together, over a six-week period, they'd stolen alcohol from a string of Plymouth off-licences.

Abraham wonders if Lucy Locke knows all the details of Daniel Locke's past. He can't stop thinking about what her husband said in the hospital, about his wife deserving everything she gets. Nor his reaction when she arrived.

According to Lucy, they've been together nine years, married after two.

Only the worst kind of monster could live a decade with his partner before killing both her children. Yet in his thirty-year career, Abraham's witnessed plenty of comparable atrocities. God granted humanity free will, and humanity now lives with the consequences.

Or perhaps God had no hand in it at all.

Pain, without warning, radiates across his back. It's bad. The worst yet—as if razored wings beneath his skin are attempting to spread. He spins the cap on his pill bottle, swallows an OxyContin. For five minutes he concentrates on nothing but his breathing, his pain and his crumbling faith.

Did Daniel Locke intend to kill himself along with his kids? Was that the reason for his rage, back at the hospital? If so, why put on an immersion suit? It seems blind luck saved his life. Abraham wonders if he'll consider himself fortunate.

He looks at his computer screen. The faces of Billie and Fin stare back at him. Their scrutiny is terrible; their innocence cleaves his heart. He'll never have kids of his own, but if he did, he'd want two just like these.

'Lord God,' he whispers. '*Defend them from all dangers of soul and body; and grant that both they and I, drawing nearer to Thee, may be bound together by Thy love in the communion of Thy Holy Spirit, and in the fellowship of Thy saints.*'

On the desk, his phone starts ringing.

2

Same room. Same recording equipment. Different interviewee.

Opposite him sits Beth McKaylin. Years of manual work and summer sun have left their mark on McKaylin, but they've also tempered her. Beneath the flannel work shirt, her body is hard with muscle. She's recently stopped dying her hair, Abraham notices. Three inches of grey have sprouted from her auburn mass.

'You don't live in Skentel.'

McKaylin shakes her head. 'Not me. Prefer a simpler life. Got a static van at the Penny Moon, up by the old lighthouse. Own the place, I do.'

'Busy?'

'Peak season I live on four hours' sleep. Quieter now. Just the passing-throughs till Christmas.'

'You have help up there?'

'Casuals, kids mainly. Some from the women's shelter in Redlecker. Don't have a *man*.'

The emphasis is a gauntlet tossed down. Abraham decides to ignore it. 'You volunteer for the RNLI in Skentel?'

'Fifteen-year vet.'

'And you went on the shout in response to Daniel Locke's distress call?'

'Aye. If that's what it was.'

'Meaning?'

'Listen,' McKaylin says. 'When that request from the coastguard came in, I was at the boathouse within minutes of my pager going off. We headed straight out. Direction finder pinpointed a bearing for that broadcast, but when we found the *Lazy Susan* she wasn't even close. Don't tell me that's down to drift. After the Mayday, that boat moved away at speed before she was scuttled. Daniel Locke might've wanted rescuing, but he didn't want the same for his yacht. Nor for those kids.'

'Can you talk me through what happened when you found the yacht?'

'By the time we got alongside, she was so low in the water I figured it was hopeless. But we lugged a salvage pump onboard and managed to fix the leaks with a couple of Sta-Plugs.'

Abraham nods. He's seen the results first-hand. 'You were first onboard?'

'Nope. That was Donny—Donahue O'Hare. Old Man of the Sea, we call him. If you lived in Skentel, you'd know him well enough. Walks around town with three big Dobermans, never one of 'em on a lead. Obedient as hell, those dogs. Not so much as a sniff or a lick unless Donny gives 'em the nod. Anyway, he went first. I followed after with the pump.'

'Did you notice anything unusual on deck?'

'Other than the fact no one was on it? I didn't see nothing particular. But I'll tell you this—and you'll probably think I'm some kind of witch for saying it—but I felt a *shadow* fall over me on that boat. Never experienced nothing like it. Horrible feeling, right in the pit of my stomach. Something downright evil happened on that yacht. Something so bad the very memory of it was burned into the deck. We didn't even know about those kids at that point, but I can't deny what I felt.' She pauses, scratches an armpit. 'See? Like I said. Some kind of witch. Crazy talk.'

She doesn't sound crazy to Abraham. He knows more than most how evil has a foothold in this world. Yesterday, he'd sensed the devil stalking the halls of Headlands Junior School. Later, on the *Lazy Susan*, he'd felt exactly what Beth McKaylin is describing. He'd felt it last night, too, in Daniel Locke's hospital room. And again when he visited this morning. 'Who was first belowdecks? You or O'Hare?'

'Muggins here investigated while Donny set up the pump.'

'The hatch was unlocked?'

'Unlocked and wide open. That boat was a modern-day *Mary Celeste*. I didn't much fancy going down into the cabin. As I said, at the time I didn't even know about those kids. But that feeling, it was worse down there. Sort of thing I reckon might come over you if you visited one of them Polish death camps. 'Course, it was waist-deep in water at that point. You could see it coming up through the hull.'

'From the smashed seacocks.'

'Aye.'

'Did you notice anything else? Any signs of a struggle? Anything else at all that seemed . . . off?'

'Right then, I was more focused on plugging those leaks than having a good nose about. Afterwards, I took a closer look, but there was noth-ing—what's the word?—*tangible*. Just, like I say, that sense of something lingering.'

She fills her lungs, trapping the air in her chest before releasing it. Abraham glances at the logo stretched across her undershirt, then meets her eye.

Beth McKaylin tilts her head. Examines him. Blinks slowly, like a cat.

'Once we got the pump started and those plugs hammered in, it was pretty obvious she wouldn't sink. A person in the water takes priority, so our Tamar redeployed. Our coxswain didn't want to leave the *Lazy Susan* drifting, even so. Not with what was coming. The radio was still working so I stayed aboard. A Tamar from our flanking station towed me back to harbour.'

'So you weren't on the Skentel boat when Daniel Locke was found?'

She shakes her head. 'Moment I got done at the quay, I went right on up to St Peter's. Not been inside since I was a kid, but that *shadow*—I wanted it washed off me. Being in the church seemed about the best way. From there I went back to the boathouse. I saw your white-suit brigade looking over the *Lazy Susan* later on, but I'm guessing they came up blank. Seawater had flushed that yacht good and proper.'

Abraham purses his lips, non-committal. 'I'll need to draft this into a statement. Then I can read it back to you before you sign.'

'No problem. You looked at *her* yet?'

'I'm sorry?'

'Lucy Locke. Husband's one thing, but the wife—*she's* something else.'

Abraham stares at her. 'Go on.'

3

Beth McKaylin pulls a face. 'I'm talking out of school and I really shouldn't—about a Skentel native, too, which makes it doubly bad, but . . .'

She pauses. He knows not to interrupt. Loose tongues love to fill a silence.

'Something off about that couple, always thought it.' McKaylin puffs out her cheeks. 'And there, now I've said it. But if you ask me, *she's* the driving force—the one with the ideas, the *power*, in that relationship. I don't reckon there was a thing going around in Daniel Locke's head that Lucy Locke didn't know about. If she didn't like it, she'd get rid of it. And if it was still there, it's because she endorsed it.

'That place they have? Up on Mortis Point? Jesus. You know what "Mortis" means, don't you? You go back a few hundred years, it's where we used to hang people. Smugglers and thieves, rapists and murderers— they'd be carted up to the Point and hanged from a giant scaffold pointing out to sea. Not just those from Skentel but places all around. Buried them up there too, we did, or flung their corpses off the clifftop. You gotta ask how much bad karma you soak up, living at a spot like that.

'And Lucy Locke . . .' McKaylin licks her lips and scowls, as if she just tasted something rancid. 'Skentel businesswoman of the year. What's her story, eh? Nobody seems to know. Lived here till she was eighteen, shagged half the town before she left. Buggered off to London and turned up six years later with a kid. Lives the perfect life these days, by all accounts, but let me tell you: man, that chick has a *temper*. I've seen a side of her she tries to keep hidden. Ugly, it is. Frightening. I ain't sayin' she killed her kids. And I ain't sayin' she drove *him* to it, neither. What I *am* sayin', I don't quite know—I just got a feeling, is all. Like when I was down in that cabin.'

McKaylin grins humourlessly, rolls her eyes. 'I should probably watch my mouth.'

She's missing a couple of teeth, Abraham notices.

His tongue probes the corresponding molars in his own mouth. 'Let's get back to the statement.'

TWENTY-FOUR

1

Lucy parks outside the hospital and heads up to Lundy Ward. A receptionist tells her that Daniel's been released.

'Released where?'

'Just . . . well . . . released. I couldn't tell you what he did after.'

Back outside, she checks her mobile. This far inland, she has four bars of reception, but she's received no calls or text messages. When she calls Daniel, his phone goes straight to voicemail. 'It's me,' she says. 'I'm at the hospital. They said you've been released. I don't know if you still have your phone, but if you get this, please call me.'

Lucy's about to say more when she catches herself. It's likely Daniel's messages are being monitored. Hanging up, she climbs back on the bike. At the police station, five minutes later, she identifies herself to the desk sergeant and asks for DI Abraham Rose.

Lucy doesn't know what to tell him. She can't decide what to reveal. Her head's a wasp nest, buzzing and scratching. She finds a seat and eases down on to it. When she closes her eyes, she sees Billie and Fin; their images on the Drift Net's windows.

In her lap, her hands go round and round. She realizes she's rocking. Forces herself to stop. Then her mind wanders—and when she comes back to herself she's rocking even faster.

She's been there twenty minutes when Beth McKaylin walks past, head down in her phone. The buzzing in Lucy's head intensifies. If Beth's been talking, it doesn't spell good news. She glances around the waiting area. How many other Skentel residents have given statements? How many others have a story to tell?

She thinks of Billie's party, the night of the blood moon. Of what happened in the study, and days later at Nick's. Of everything the police will have dug up about her husband.

Of everything they might have dug up about her.

'Lucy?'

Abraham Rose is as imposing as she remembers. When she stands, he doesn't offer his hand.

'I'm sorry I had to keep you,' he says. 'Would you like to follow me?'

He leads her to a windowless room that smells strongly of disinfectant.

'You're speaking to Beth McKaylin?' she blurts, grimacing when she sees his expression. 'Sorry. I realize you probably can't talk about that. She was part of the crew that found the *Lazy Susan*. I guess it makes sense that you'd interview her.'

He watches her a while before answering. 'How're you holding up, Lucy?'

'A police officer came to the bar. Family liaison. Said there was no way Billie or Fin could have survived. But that's . . . It's not true.'

'I just got off the phone with Sergeant Arnold. I'm very sorry if she upset you. I realize it's an impossible situation. But I'm glad you're here. I was just about to call. I need to speak to you about Daniel.'

'I need to speak to *you* about Daniel. I just came from the hospital. He's not there. Have you . . .' She can't get her words, nor her breath. 'Is he here? If he is, I need to see him.'

'I'm afraid that's not possible, Lucy. Not right now, because—'

'So he *is* here?'

'Yes, but—'

'Please,' she says. '*Please* just listen to me. Everyone lets me speak, but no one actually listens. I need answers, from Daniel. He's my husband, they're our children. All this is . . . It's going round and round and I can't make any sense of it. What's he told you? What's he saying?'

Lucy pauses, scrutinizes what she just said. Her emotions are so out of control that she's speaking without engaging her brain. Right now, that's not just dangerous. It's lethal.

Abraham Rose leans forward, elbows resting on his knees. 'Lucy,' he says. His voice has changed; more solemn than it was. 'We interviewed Daniel under caution earlier this morning. It's very hard to tell you this, and it's going to be very hard for you to understand, but I'm afraid that during that interview Daniel confessed to the murders of Billie and Fin.'

She blinks. His words reverberate around her skull for a long time before they settle. Even then she has to replay them, try to extract some kind of meaning. Finally, she shakes her head. 'No, that's not right. It can't be.'

People reap what they sow.

Hand pressed to her side, she climbs to her feet. There's no room to pace about. She turns one way, then another. 'That's . . . It doesn't make any sense. Look, let me speak to him. Let me—'

'As I told you, we can't allow you to see him at this time. Following a meeting with the CPS, Daniel was charged with two counts of murder. There'll be a press conference in an hour, at which it'll be announced.'

Lucy's left leg gives out. She sinks to one knee. Abraham Rose reaches for her, but she waves him away.

'If you'd like,' he says, 'I can get Jesse to drive you home.'

Sergeant Jesse Arnold is the last person she wants to see. Lucy shakes her head, knocks loose that nest of wasps. She grabs on to the chair, tries to stand. 'He wouldn't have *confessed*.'

'Lucy—'

'He wouldn't have confessed because they're not dead. They're alive, both of them. I'm *telling* you.' She feels a spike of pain from her ribs. Thinks, for a moment, that she might be sick. 'What happens now?'

'Now that he's been charged, he'll be remanded in custody here until his court hearing—likely first thing Monday. After that he'll be taken to whichever prison has space. Exeter, probably, although Dartmoor's possible. There's a slim chance he'll be sent somewhere further away.

'Lucy, if you don't want Jesse Arnold, how about I find another officer to take you home? If you want a familiar face, I'd be happy to—'

'When *can* I see him?'

Abraham presses his palms together. 'That depends on the prison. It'll take a day or so for him to pop up on their system. Even then, Daniel will have to put you on his visitor list. If he does that—and it's entirely his choice—you'll be able to book a visit. Usually twenty-four to forty-eight hours in advance. Do you *want* to see him?'

'He's my husband. Of course I do.'

People reap what they sow.

She can't talk to the police. And she knows that Daniel won't. Which means, until they let her see him, she's Billie and Fin's only hope.

2

An hour later, she's back at home. Except Wild Ridge isn't a home right now. It's a museum. Walking through it, she feels like one of the artefacts. Everywhere she looks, she finds evidence of a family now lost.

In the living room, she finds Fin's Spider-Man slippers discarded among the houseplants. A cardigan of Billie's hangs over a chair.

Lucy goes to the window. Outside, the worst of the violence has abated. The sea looks much calmer than it did. No rain is falling. Even the wind has dropped. She sees fishing vessels and cruisers on the water, Skentel's inshore lifeboat coming back into harbour. How many of them are still looking? How many have turned their minds to other things?

Impossible that her children have survived this long in that sea. Which means, if they're alive—*which they are, they have to be*—they must have washed up on land.

Plenty of reasons the shore-based searchers might not have discovered them: horrific conditions, limited manpower, miles of wild and inaccessible coast. And yet, without immersion suits or some other protection, there's *still* little chance they could have survived this long.

So where does that leave her? Where can she invest her last hopes?

Upstairs, Billie's room is a cathedral of silence. Lucy forces herself across the threshold, breathes the ghost of her daughter's Jimmy Choo perfume. Billie's dressing table is a trove of bangles and bracelets, necklaces and make-up bottles, phone chargers, empty mugs and magazines. But there are no waymarkers. No hastily scribbled messages. No clues to what happened, or where she might have gone.

On the windowsill is a silver bracelet adorned with charms: tiny starfish, tiny surfboards, tiny shells. Billie bought it a few years ago in a Cornish boutique. Lucy still has Snig tied around her arm. Now, she fastens her daughter's bracelet around her wrist.

Fin's room is harder. Everything in it is so small. Small furniture, small belongings, small clothes. On his pillow, neatly folded, lie his dinosaur pyjamas. His Iron Man dressing gown hangs from the door.

Her son's desk is a precariously stacked testament to his interests: comics, Lego kits, a partially dismantled telephone, a partially built crystal radio set, the dried-up remains of old chemistry experiments, collections of shells, rocks and fossils. Sprouting from everything is a yellow forest of Post-it notes, complete with Fin's lopsided scrawl.

Remember to tell Miss Clay about tektonic plates on Monday.

Make sure to draw Bogwort for my book after school.

Ask Mummy if we have any Vikings in our family.

Find out when the next luner eclipse is and if I can stay up late this time.

Remind Daddy to think about a Playstayshun 5.

Suddenly, Lucy can't fill her lungs without her broken ribs skewering her. She sits on Fin's bed, trying to catch her breath. On a shelf of his bookcase stands a row of die-cast models: a Volvo XC90, a blue sailing sloop, a grey dinghy, a Tamar-class lifeboat, an AgustaWestland helicopter, a Sikorsky S-92 and a Triumph Rocket.

Lucy studies each model in turn. Then she pushes up from the bed. Teeth clenched against the pain, she barrels out of the room and thunders down the stairs.

3

Outside, she lifts the garage door and flicks on the overhead fluorescents. The space is cluttered, but not messy: carpentry tools, gardening equipment, boxes sorted for charity. At the back, protected by dust sheets, is everything Daniel used for the *Lazy Susan's* restoration, along with all their yachting apparel.

Lucy whips away a sheet, raising a fine haze of dust. She smells petrol and motor oil, wood varnish and timber. She pulls off more sheets. With each reveal her heart beats faster.

She takes out her mobile, dials Abraham Rose. When the detective doesn't answer, Lucy leaves a message. Behind her she hears the pop and hiss of shingle—a vehicle pulling on to the drive. She walks outside in time to see Noemie and Bee climbing from Tommo's car.

'Hon,' Noemie says, after an embrace. 'We just heard from Jake. Bee and I wanted you to get the news from friends rather than strangers. The shoreline searches are still going strong. Most of Skentel's out looking. They won't let up until every inch of coast's been covered. But—here's the thing—Jake says the coastguard's about to stand down the offshore search and rescue. It hasn't been announced to the media yet, but it's coming. They're saying that with the water temperature, the conditions and how long it's been since the Mayday, there's just no way that, well . . .'

Lucy nods. She doesn't need Noemie to spell it out.

'Dude, so we came up with an idea,' Bee says. 'Something to raise everyone's spirits when the news hits. You said you wanted to make Billie and Fin famous until they're found. We figured we'd hold a vigil, tonight, on Penleith Beach. There's a shit-ton of media in Skentel right now. I'm pretty sure the TV people would cover it. We just wanted to check with you first.'

'I think . . . I think it's a great idea.'

'There's something else,' Noemie adds. 'Again, best you hear it from us first. Couple of journalists out there are trying to dig up dirt. We've all been approached. Obviously, no one's saying anything, but we just wanted you to know.' She pauses, glances briefly at Bee. 'Have you heard anything more from the police? One of the hacks said Daniel's been released from hospital. Is he here?'

Lucy shakes her head. 'He's at the police station.'

'Is he . . . Have you seen him?'

'Not yet.'

'What are the police saying?'

We interviewed Daniel under caution earlier this morning. It's very hard to tell you this, and it's going to be very hard for you to understand, but I'm afraid that during that interview Daniel confessed to the murders of Billie and Fin.

Lucy straightens. She thinks about what she just discovered in the garage. The voicemail she just left on Abraham Rose's phone. 'You'd better come in.'

TWENTY-FIVE

1

Twenty minutes later Abraham's at his desk, looking at a long list of people to call back. For a while he reflects on his conversation with Lucy Locke. Surprising, given Daniel's confession, that she's so desperate to see him.

Tell her she deserves every fucking thing she gets.

Is Lucy really that clueless about her husband's animosity towards her? She was in the hospital when he freaked out on the bed. Is there a reason, other than the obvious, for her insistence on a meeting? Is she simply delusional?

Abraham thinks of Billie and Fin. He wonders what it was like, growing up in that house. He knows Billie Locke applied to Sea Shepherd, the marine conservation charity, for a crewing position. Other than her clear environmental passion, was there another reason she wanted to travel?

He recalls his conversation with Sergeant Jesse Arnold, Lucy Locke's FLO. Regrettable that the weather chaos delayed the pair's first contact. Scant chance, now, that any bond of trust will form between them.

Arnold had visited Lucy down at the quay. She'd explained that the possibility of finding Billie and Fin alive was now negligible. Angered, Lucy had insisted that her kids were in their immersion suits. Then Arnold revealed that the three remaining suits had been found onboard the yacht.

'At which point,' Arnold said, 'she just lost it. And I don't mean your regular flash-in-the-pan kind of losing it. This was full-on rage. *Sustained* rage, too. She smashed up her computer, took out a shelf with all her files, destroyed plenty of other stuff as well. But the look in her eyes was the thing. For a moment there, I genuinely thought she'd attack me.'

'It's understandable, though, don't you think?'

'In all honesty, I'm not sure. This felt like something different. I'm no wallflower, but I *really* didn't like being alone with her in that room.'

'What happened then?'

'She grabbed her crash helmet and bailed. It was all . . . I don't know, sir. It's hard to explain just how *intense* it was.'

Abraham recalls Lucy's behaviour at the hospital. How she'd burst screaming into Daniel's room on Lundy Ward. He thinks of their earlier conversation: how she'd still wanted to see her husband, despite learning of his double murder charge.

'He wouldn't have *confessed*,' she'd said.

Arnold isn't the only officer to have felt Lucy's wrath. PCs Noakes and Lamb—first responders at the harbour—interviewed her at the Drift Net. At the time, no one knew Daniel had taken Fin with him on the boat. Understandable, even so, that Lucy would be upset. She'd just learned her husband was missing. And yet Noakes and Lamb had still found her behaviour odd. Lucy reacted badly to being called Mrs Locke, demanding to be addressed by her first name, screaming it so loudly that half the bar fell silent.

He recalls something she said to him on their journey to Skentel: *I went away. For a while. Then I came back.*

Abraham checks the logbook, reviewing all the decisions made so far. Then he does something he shouldn't: he goes fishing. The Police National Computer holds no information on Lucy Locke so he asks Cooper to check ECRIS, the European Criminal Records Information System. Data on there should get ported to the PNC, but the system isn't infallible. Once that's done, he phones Patrick Beckett in the Criminal Finance team and asks him to widen his investigation.

Abraham turns back to his laptop. His hands hover over the keys. He tells himself not to do what he knows he's about to do. It'll only hurt. It always hurts. But he's already typing. And then her Facebook page is open on his screen.

No privacy settings, still. He can look at everything she posts without becoming her friend. Sometimes, he's dared to think it's deliberate—a window left open, through which she knows he'll be able to see. But of course that's ridiculous. So many decades have passed. Doubtful she even remembers his name.

Six months since he last checked in on her. In that time Sarah's made eight more posts. The latest is a selfie with her husband and two grown-up daughters. They're on a hill in the Pennines, rain-soaked and wind-blasted: *They've promised me roaring fire, shepherd's pie and red wine later. They'd better be telling the truth!!!!*

Abraham scrolls through her other posts: snapshots of a woman enjoying her blessings. *What a fool you are*, he thinks. *What a mess you made of your life.*

Ten minutes later, he holds his press conference. He tells the gathered journalists that following a confession, Daniel Locke has been charged with the murders of Billie and Fin. He fields a dozen or so questions, then heads to his car.

2

Bibi Trixibelle Carter is nothing like Abraham imagined on the phone. He expected an old woman in pearls and a dusty evening gown, possibly surrounded by cats. What he gets is wellies, a bramble-torn Barbour and a pack of baying dogs. Bibi herself is white-haired and ribbon-thin. Abraham can't guess her age. She could just as easily be seventy as one hundred.

Her house stands on the coastal road two miles from Skentel, no other buildings in sight. She's outside when he arrives, feeding her dogs lumps of carcass that look home-butchered. When Abraham slips through the gate, two spittle-flecked gundogs put their paws on his midriff and commence a busy sniffing of his crotch.

'Nero! Trajan! Leave the poor man alone,' Bibi shouts. She tosses a gruesome chunk of flesh at Abraham's feet. The animals fall on it noisily. 'Into the house with you,' she tells him. 'I'll make a pot of tea.'

Inside, the rooms looks like they haven't been decorated in fifty years: threadbare rugs, dog-scratched furniture and cracked plaster walls. Bibi makes space for him on a leather sofa piled with newspapers. She serves Earl Grey into the finest bone china. Then she stirs up the fire and retreats to a wingback chair. 'Remind me of your title.'

'Detective Inspector Abraham Rose.'

'Detective Inspector, that's good. And Abraham's a fine name.'

'Thank you. I'm sorry I was so brief on the phone. Perhaps you could tell me again exactly what you believe you saw.'

Bibi shakes her head. 'I'll tell you what I *saw*, Detective Inspector. Not what I *believe* I saw.' With that she puts down her cup. 'It was Friday morning, ten past eleven. I was taking Marjorie to Soundsett.'

'Marjorie?'

'Her anal glands needed expressing and it's not a job I relish.'

'Marjorie's a dog?'

'Well, she's not a parishioner. If you drove here via Skentel, you'll have passed the lay-by I told you about. That's where I saw them. A large grey Volvo—looked like it might be a four-by-four—and parked behind it a black car, much smaller.

'A girl was standing beside the Volvo, talking to the driver through the window. Blonde hair, black shorts. I remember thinking it was a very cold day for bare legs. There was someone on the other side of the Volvo wearing a grey top with the hood pulled down. When I passed by an hour later, the black car was there on its own, no one else around.'

'Forgive me,' Abraham says. 'That's a remarkable amount of detail.'

'You're a detective.'

'Yes.'

'I'm sure, therefore, you pay close attention to your surroundings, and that which happens around you.'

'Of course. But most people don't.'

'I,' says Bibi Trixibelle Carter, 'am not one of those people.'

Abraham nods, chastened. He takes a sip of tea. It's excellent, just as he expected.

'We've faced terrible problems with fly-tipping lately,' Bibi continues. 'I slowed right down because I wanted to see what they were doing. The one in grey ducked out of sight as I passed, but they didn't seem to be unloading anything and I could hardly get out and ask. I'm not a *busybody*. Instead I did what I always do and memorized part of the Volvo's registration plate: BLK.'

'BLK? You remember that?'

Bibi stares at him, her eyes narrowing. 'Bibi Likes Kibble.'

'I see. Did you recognize the make or model of the second car?'

'I didn't pay it as much attention. If they were fly-tipping, it made sense they'd be doing it from the Volvo. But I can tell you it was a hatchback. Not a Ford—possibly Japanese.'

'And it was definitely . . .' *Black*? Abraham almost asks, and stops himself. He clears his throat. 'This figure in grey, on the far side of the Volvo. What else can you tell me?'

'Not much more than I have. As I said, he ducked down as I passed.'

'You saw a face?'

'No. Like I told you—his hood was pulled down too low.'

'I'm just wondering why you're saying "he".'

Bibi blinks. She turns her head to the wall. Then her gaze returns to Abraham. 'You're quite right to challenge me. In hindsight, nothing I saw suggested it was a man.'

'It could have been a woman?'

'It could quite easily have been a woman.'

Abraham takes another sip of tea. He sits in silence, mulling what he's heard. *BLK* forms part of Daniel Locke's number plate. The timing also fits—Locke left the school at eleven and arrived in Skentel twenty minutes later.

Opening a folder, he withdraws a photograph and hands it over.

Bibi takes it, squints. 'This looks . . . Yes. This looks very much like the girl I saw talking to the driver. And actually, I do recall a mark on her leg that could easily have been a tattoo. Is this . . .'

'Billie Locke, yes.' Somewhere in the house a longcase clock is ticking, deep and sonorous. Beneath the mantelpiece, a log pops in the fire. 'The Volvo was pointing towards you as you drove by?'

'Away from Skentel. Towards Redlecker.'

'Just one more question: you're very precise with the time. Ten past eleven, you said.'

Bibi raises an eyebrow. 'That's a statement, not a question.'

'I'm trying to understand why you're so sure.'

'Because right after I drove past, I looked at the dashboard clock and remarked on the time to Marjorie.' Bibi taps her temple with a thin finger. 'And then I memorized it.'

Abraham nods. In Bibi Trixibelle Carter, in different circumstances, he thinks he might have found a friend. He finishes his tea and looks around. Above an overstuffed bookcase hangs a cross. In one corner, a set of dusty carvings forms a nativity scene not packed away since Christmas.

He feels at peace here. Less forsaken, less alone. Since his arrival, he's experienced absolutely no pain.

'Would you like another cup of tea, Detective Inspector Rose?'

Say yes.

Stay a while.

Talk to her about something. About anything.

'Abraham?'

He puts down his cup, dredging a smile from somewhere deep. 'I'm afraid I'm needed elsewhere.'

TWENTY-SIX

1

Early evening. Finally, a change in the weather.

The wind dies. The sea grows calmer than it's been in days. The last clouds sail east, revealing a black sky pricked with stars. Above Mortis Point, a gibbous moon offers its light. And down on the sands of Penleith Beach, Skentel gathers for two of its own.

Lucy arrives with Noemie at around eight. They park at the tail of a long row of vehicles and climb the backshore dune. Beneath them, Penleith's flat sand recedes gently towards the sea. The high tide has come and gone. Other than the boulders littering its southern flank, the beach looks like it did before the storm. Except, of course, for the crowd.

Lucy sees plenty of familiar faces: Jake Farrell is talking to his RNLI colleagues, Beth McKaylin among them. Wayland Rawlings from the hobby shop is in animated conversation with Ravinder Turkmish from the Bayleaf and Gordon and Jane Watson from the pharmacy. Matt Guinness, Lucy's old classmate, is standing with his mother and a few of her friends.

The gathering hasn't just attracted people from Skentel. Lucy also notices families from Fin's school who live much further away. Marjorie Knox, the head teacher, is addressing a group that includes Miss Clay, who teaches Fin. She sees Ed, looking like he's hardly slept, along with all Billie's friends from college, her theatre group and her various volunteer networks. Then there are those Lucy recognizes but doesn't know well, and an even larger number she doesn't recognize at all—people from Redlecker, perhaps, or further inland. Already, attendance is in the hundreds. And a steady stream of vehicles is still bouncing down the track from the coast road.

Bamboo tiki torches have been thrust into the sand, yellow flames throwing off smoke. Two guys are feeding a driftwood bonfire close to where a row of trestle tables has been set up; Bee and Tommo are hard at work behind them, serving tea and coffee from six giant urns. Many in the crowd are holding jam jars suspended from wire handles, tealights burning inside them. Some wear glowstick bracelets or necklaces. Others carry flashlights or penlight torches.

One sight closes Lucy's throat completely: the names of Billie and Fin, spelled out in huge letters on the sand from what must be hundreds, perhaps *thousands*, of candles flickering in glass containers. There's something magical about it; something ineffably powerful. Lucy can almost feel the heat rising from her children's names.

BILLIE   FIN

'You OK?' Noemie asks, and then curses. 'Sorry. Keep asking that. Bloody stupid question.'

'That press conference,' Lucy replies, studying the crowd. 'Everyone here must've seen it. By now, they all know Daniel's been charged with murder. It isn't true, because Billie and Fin are alive. But even though *I* know that, they don't—which means to most of them this is no longer a vigil, is it? It's a wake.'

'Oh, hon.' Noemie looks like she's holding back tears. 'We don't have to do this. We can turn around right now if you like. I can drive you back up to the house.'

'No, I'm OK.' From somewhere Lucy finds a smile. 'Look at all these people. You guys . . . This was *exactly* what we needed to do—get everyone together in one place and keep the focus on Billie and Fin. We just need to persuade them to keep looking, to have faith.' She rolls her shoulders. 'Let's go down.'

2

Minutes later, she's holding her own wire-handled jam jar as Luke Creese, the pastor from St Peter's, lights its tealight.

'Lucy,' he says, touching her arm. 'None of us can imagine what you're going through. I know you're not a regular at St Peter's, but I've heard so many stories about you and Daniel, Billie and Fin. I feel like I'm getting to know all four of you. One thing I can say with absolute conviction—there's a *world* of love for you in Skentel. A world of love for you here tonight. If there's anything I can do to support you—practically or spiritually—you only have to ask.'

Lucy nods. When her eyes begin to fill, she thrusts out her jaw.

Creese's face folds with empathy. 'On occasions like these, when people are gathered in solidarity, it sometimes helps if there's a structure—a focus, if you like. You might not want that, or you might already have something planned, but if you'd like me to say a few words, then by all means—the offer's there. It doesn't have to be a party political broadcast for God. I hope you don't think I'm speaking out of turn.'

'Does your God allow this?' Lucy asks. She searches Creese's face. 'I'm not . . . I genuinely want to know.'

The pastor looks out to sea before meeting her gaze. 'Yes, He does. And sometimes that's the most difficult thing to understand. God doesn't always offer us answers, Lucy. In this life, we may never really know why some things have happened. But God *always* offers us Himself. Whatever hardships we face, we can choose to go through them with God at our side or without Him.'

Lucy's hands form fists. She wants to get angry with Creese, but she sees his compassion. Knows his words came from the heart. Only moments ago, she was stressing the importance of faith. Suddenly, more than anything, she wants to believe in Creese's God.

'I think I'd like that,' she says finally. 'For you to say something, I mean. But the focus needs to be on Billie and Fin. On bringing them home.'

3

The moon slides across the sky, towing a flotilla of pale reflections across the sea. More vehicles arrive. More people climb over the dunes. More tealights and candles are added to Billie and Fin's names. Children gather seashells and create their own tributes.

Lucy finds herself supported in ways she'd never expected. But no one except the pastor mentions Daniel. Conversation is limited strictly to Billie and Fin. Stories are shared, anecdotes are told. Lucy hears tales of others thought lost to the sea and whose return was widely celebrated.

A PA system is erected on the sand. Creese's words, when he speaks, are pitch-perfect. Climbing on to a milk crate to address the crowd, he celebrates Billie and Fin, praises the community response and thanks those present for their search efforts. There's no hint of defeatism, no resigned inevitability. He ends with a simple prayer. To her surprise, Lucy finds herself bowing her head. When she looks up at its conclusion, Creese offers her the mic.

Taking it, Lucy surveys the candlelit faces arrayed before her. Only twenty-four hours ago, the thought of addressing such a crowd would have filled her with horror. Now, as she speaks, she finds herself strangely calm.

She echoes Creese's gratitude. Then she turns to her message. 'They're alive,' she says. 'I know they are. And I know, too, that some of you think that's impossible. The police didn't mention it in their press conference, but you'll hear soon that Billie and Fin's immersion suits were found on our yacht.'

A mutter of dismay passes through the crowd. Lucy tries to ignore it. 'But you'll also learn something else. As well as our life raft, we own a small dinghy: light grey, folding hull, detachable outboard motor. We hadn't used it in a few years, but when I checked our garage a few hours ago it wasn't there. The only place it could have been is back on the boat. But the police, when I asked, said they didn't find it.

'Daniel was seven miles offshore when that Mayday was broadcast. Billie knew how to operate the outboard, but in those conditions she wouldn't have been able to see land. If her navigation was slightly off, she and Fin could have made landfall literally anywhere along this stretch of coast. And if they weren't in the water for long periods, like we previously thought, their chances of survival are far higher.'

She pauses, making eye contact with all those standing close. 'The most important thing—the thing I urge you all to remember—is what I said earlier. I know, in my heart, that Billie and Fin are alive. I *know* it. So please believe in them. Please keep looking. Thank you.'

She switches off the mic. The sound of her voice is replaced with the hiss of surf, overlaid with the crackle and pop of the bonfire.

Then, from the midst of the crowd, a golden light rises. Lucy squints, unable, for a moment, to work out what she's seeing. Abruptly, another light floats up. Two become five become twenty and then fifty. Each light is a ball of fire suspended beneath a paper lantern. Those lanterns, as they rise, reveal themselves in a profusion of pastel colours. Watching them climb into the sky, Lucy feels lighter than air, as if with the merest breath of wind she could follow.

Black sky, dusted with stars. A hundred glowing lanterns floating into it. She watches them move south over Mortis Point. As they sail higher, they begin to drift apart, forming a lazy procession of colour. There's something ethereal about the spectacle. Something that seems to touch everyone watching.

Down on the beach, a breeze stirs the candles forming Billie and Fin's names. The flames flicker, but none of them go out.

TWENTY-SEVEN

1

At the Texaco in Barnstaple, Abraham buys cigarettes, smoking two on the drive to Skentel. He's got a bad feeling, getting worse—not just about Daniel and Lucy Locke, but about the whole case, and the reality of what happened to those kids.

Daniel Locke might have confessed, but he's armed himself since with a lawyer. If the confession is retracted, what then? Some of Abraham's higher-ups are already muttering about the wisdom of interviewing Locke so soon after his hospital release. If a retraction *is* coming, doubtless the man's questionable mental state will be the hook on which it'll be hung. While Abraham can prove the *Lazy Susan* was scuttled, he can't prove what happened onboard. And the boat, as a crime scene, is a literal washout.

Lucy Locke's phone call this afternoon muddies the water further. Now, suddenly, there's a missing dinghy—an obvious means of escape for Billie and Fin, but an even more obvious lifeline for any defence team trying to commute a murder charge. Lucy hasn't offered any evidence that the dinghy exists, but Abraham can't prove it doesn't. Maybe she's telling the truth. Maybe she isn't. There's no registration process for a boat that size.

Daniel Locke might rue his early confession. Events since, however, have started to swing in his favour. When Abraham recalls the man's attitude in the interview room and violent behaviour at the hospital, his hands tighten around the wheel.

I have a message. A message for that bitch. Tell her she deserves every fucking thing she gets.

Inexplicable, really. Because *that bitch* just offered Daniel Locke a life-line he'd be foolish not to grab with both hands.

North of Skentel, he follows the track down to Penleith Beach and parks at the end of a huge line of vehicles. From the top of the dune he sees those gathered for the vigil. A pastor from the local church is addressing them.

The man's words are designed for comfort, but Abraham finds them anodyne; Luke Creese, it seems, is the kind of New Testament preacher who retreats almost entirely from the God of Elijah and Isaiah.

Abraham doesn't close his eyes for the prayer. He keeps his gaze on Lucy Locke. He's surprised to see her bow her head, even more so when she clasps her hands together. Is it an act? Was she religious before?

The prayer ends. The priest hands the mic to Lucy. She surveys the crowd as if unsure what to say, but when she speaks her words come easily enough. She thanks everyone for their support. Then she tells the same story she told Abraham: the dinghy, missing from the garage; her belief that Billie and Fin used it to get ashore. Some in the crowd seem galvanized by the news. Others watch Lucy more warily.

Abraham can feel it: the tide of opinion, just like the weather of recent days, gradually starting to shift. The dinghy, real or imagined, won't change the main point in people's minds—Daniel Locke has already confessed.

Lucy stops speaking. A Chinese lantern rises from the crowd. Others float up to join it, a silent flotilla reaching heavenward. Abraham watches for a while. Then he returns his attention to Lucy, whose gaze has moved to the tealights illuminating her children's names. Moments later, her head lifts to the dune where Abraham is standing. He finds himself staring into her eyes. Those razored wings beneath his skin tense, threatening to split his flesh. He clenches his teeth against the pain.

Daniel Locke knows more than he's telling. Increasingly, it seems Lucy Locke knows something too. Pretty soon, Abraham will have to act. Not as an officer of the law, perhaps, but as a blunt instrument of God. He follows a higher authority. He—

'Samson,' says a voice.

He wheels around. Emma Douglas is standing beside him, lips tight around a cigarette. She surveys the crowd, breathing smoke into the night air. 'This dinghy. Is it bullshit?'

'I can't talk about the case.'

She drags on her cigarette. 'I'm hearing interesting things about the Lockes.'

'If you know something—'

'Relax, Samson. If it's relevant, you'll hear about it soon enough. She's pretty convincing—the mother. You think there's any chance what she said is true? That either of those kids could have survived?'

'There's always . . .' He stops, curses himself.

'Always what?'

'You were at the press conference. Daniel Locke confessed. We've charged him with their murders.'

'But what—you're having second thoughts?'

'Not at all. I—'

'You think they might be alive?'

'This conversation,' he says, 'is over.'

2

Driving back to the station, Abraham can't stop thinking about Lucy Locke. Her speech at the vigil was a perfect mix: agony, hope and rousing call to action. It didn't win over everyone, but she couldn't have performed better. When he recalls how her eyes sought him out at its conclusion, the blood in his stomach runs cold. Was it coincidence? Or had she known he was standing there all along?

He can't forget the reports he's received of Lucy's quick temper. He remembers how she burst into her husband's room on Lundy Ward. At the time, he'd thought her behaviour understandable. Now, he's not so sure.

There's a note waiting on his desk. It's a summary of what Cooper found on ECRIS. Abraham reads it once and then again, more carefully. While Lucy Locke's never been convicted of any offence domestically, that's not the case internationally.

3

Twenty minutes later, nursing a coffee from the machine, he's on a late-night call to Epifanio de Santos, a member of Portugal's Polícia Judiciária.

According to de Santos, Lucy arrived in Almería, Spain's south-eastern province, when Billie was five months old. Her destination was Alto Paraíso, an off-grid commune in the Tabernas Desert. There, she met a man called Zacarías Echevarria. It wasn't long before Lucy started sleeping with him.

Their relationship lasted eighteen months. Then, one night, Lucy helped herself to Echevarria's life savings, strapped Billie into his car and hit the road. On Portugal's west coast, she rented an apartment and found work in a beachside bar. Before long, she moved into the bar owner's home.

Back in Alto Paraíso, Echevarria was heartbroken. Not so much about his stolen money or car—he'd fallen for Lucy hard. It took him three months to track her down. Calling at her new home, he pleaded for a second chance. Lucy refused. When he persisted, she stabbed him three times with a chef's knife.

Echevarria survived but spent months in hospital. At trial, Lucy's defence team—hired at great expense by the bar owner—turned her into a victim. Echevarria, they maintained, was far from the mellow, pot-smoking hippie he portrayed. The man ruled Alto Paraíso like a feudal lord. Over time, his narcissism developed into a god complex. Initially, Lucy fell under his spell. When the mask slipped, she did the only sensible thing and fled. It was Echevarria, months later, who initiated the violence. Lucy was simply defending herself.

No matter that none of the commune residents corroborated her story. In the witness box, Lucy seduced the entire court. The jury cleared her of attempted murder. Although she was convicted on lesser assault charges, the judge—to the astonishment of law enforcement and local media—suspended her sentence. Lucy returned home with the bar owner who'd paid her legal fees. Two days later, she boarded a bus with Billie and wasn't seen again.

Overall, de Santos paints an unflattering picture: Lucy as a ruthless manipulator who used Billie to cast herself as a maiden in distress—a woman who started small but achieved greater affluence with each new conquest, leaving in her wake a trail of destruction and heartbreak.

Listening to de Santos talk, Abraham detects more than a whiff of misogyny, but the facts are clear enough: Lucy Locke has a criminal conviction for violence with a deadly weapon.

Nor can he refute the upward financial trajectory of her chosen partners. From commune vagrant, to bar owner, to lifeboat coxswain, to marine entrepreneur. Is there another rung on that ladder he hasn't discovered?

Abraham's still mulling it when, post-midnight, Patrick Beckett from the Criminal Finance Team appears at his desk.

4

They grab more coffee and Beckett lays it out. The Locke family's finances are a mess. The last three years' tax returns filed for Locke-Povey Marine show a decent profit, but that was before Daniel's business partner sold his stake. Speculation in the industry press is of a predatory buy-out intended to leave a husk. Many of Locke-Povey Marine's customers have already jumped ship. Most of the staff have been laid off.

That's calamitous for the Lockes. The house on Mortis Point isn't mortgaged, but there's a sizeable business loan secured against it, on which Daniel just defaulted. The couple are also paying off another large loan raised to develop the Drift Net.

But it's what Beckett's dug up on insurance that really stirs Abraham's interest. Daniel has a long-running life-insurance policy naming Lucy as the £500,000 beneficiary. More recently, Lucy took out a gold-plated family accident plan that pays out not just on the death or serious injury of Daniel or herself, but smaller amounts on the deaths of Billie and Fin. If Daniel had drowned with both children in that storm, Lucy would have gained an additional £120,000 on top of the half a million from Daniel's personal plan. Even more interesting—two months ago *Billie* Locke took out life insurance. The cover is for £200,000, with Lucy as sole beneficiary. There's no law against eighteen-year-old students owning life-insurance policies, but it's odd. Billie has no dependents, not even a declared income. In addition to the personal plans, the family yacht is insured for far more than it's worth.

'What do you make of it?' Abraham asks.

'Put it this way,' Beckett says. 'If the boat sank and all those on it never returned, Lucy Locke stood to gain over a million. Daniel Locke's survival—and the boat's recovery by the lifeboat crew—knocks that figure down substantially, but if we assume a coroner rules that Fin Locke died with his sister, the pay-out is still two hundred thousand from Billie's policy, plus a further twenty from the accident plan.'

'Both of which were arranged in the last few months.'

'Correct.'

'Fortunate timing,' Abraham says.

'Very.'

'Unless Daniel and Lucy are *both* convicted—at which point nothing pays out?'

'Also correct.'

'Keep digging,' Abraham tells him.

This is starting to feel like a ruthless game being played between husband and wife, the children used as collateral. He recalls Jesse Arnold, the assigned FLO, describing how Lucy Locke smashed her computer.

Blind rage? Or a deliberate ploy to destroy evidence?

TWENTY-EIGHT

1

Bee and Tommo drop Lucy home. She declines their offer to come inside; it's a relief to say goodnight and shut her front door. In the kitchen, she makes coffee and carries it outside. From the back lawn, she has a clear view of the ocean. Down on Penleith Beach, her children's names still flicker on the sand.

She *has* to get her head straight.

At the police station this morning, she'd noticed how differently Abraham Rose looked at her. Tonight, when she caught his eye at the vigil, the change was even more stark. Was that because of Daniel's confession? Or because of Beth McKaylin? It can't be much longer before someone decides to investigate Lucy. What will she do then? She needs the detective to take her message about the dinghy at face value. But its success—and her credibility—hinges on what he learns first.

You thought I didn't know but I do. And you might think you know me but you don't. You don't have the first clue. Nor does Nick.

She knows her husband's confession was a lie. Daniel didn't kill their children on that boat, nor anywhere else. Not just because he loves them and loves her, but because Billie and Fin are *alive*; she won't accept any alternative.

Do you have the slightest understanding of how it feels to be betrayed by both your wife and your best friend?

In the hours since reading those words, she's visited the hospital and the police station, talked to Sergeant Arnold and Abraham Rose, searched the house and the garage, attended the vigil and addressed the crowd. And through it all she's been thinking, watching, analysing; steadily formulating a plan.

Daniel overcame his poor start in life, teaching himself all the skills necessary to achieve his dream. But he didn't escape unscathed. His need for control, in every aspect of his life, is just one consequence of his trauma.

Another is a legacy of his inability, aged ten, to read or write.

Even now, Daniel has difficulty with spelling and grammar. Lucy's lost count of the times she's had to look over one of his business documents or proofread some of his marketing copy. Unlike every other email her husband ever sent her, the one she read a few hours ago contained not a single punctuation error or misspelled word.

Which means the possibility that Daniel wrote it is precisely zero.

2

At no point since this began has she believed him capable of harming their children. Even so, the unexploded bomb in her inbox was her first evidence of outside involvement. Of malicious intent.

The revelation that someone has deliberately targeted her family is almost too traumatic to face. But face it she must if she's to save Billie and Fin—and face it entirely alone.

No way could she have shared that email with the police. It wouldn't prove to Jesse Arnold or Abraham Rose what it proves to her; exactly the opposite. Hence her decision to erase it and later destroy the computer. Even if the email *hadn't* implicated Daniel, no way could she trust the authorities to handle this competently. Not after what happened in Portugal.

Nor can she confide in anyone she knows. Impossible—based on the email's content—that the culprit is a stranger. Which means everyone is a suspect. Even her closest friends.

From the kitchen, Lucy grabs her crash helmet. Minutes later she's in Skentel. Not the high street or quay but one of its wooded lanes. Just like before, she approaches the house on foot.

The front door is new. Opaque glass this time, so she can't see inside. There's no car in the drive or lights in the windows, but that doesn't mean she's safe. Keeping to the treeline, she circles around to the rear. The back lawn is contained by a natural border of trees. Other than a hooting owl, and something scratching around beneath a bird feeder hanging from the shed, she's alone.

Lucy creeps on to the deck. She crouches behind a covered barbecue. The living room's bifold door is a black wall, no curtains pulled against the glass. Nothing burns in the firepit beneath the copper flue. The wall-mounted TV is dark.

A fox screams, somewhere close. From the trees all around, birds take flight. Lucy turns her head, sees that the creature beneath the bird feeder has fled.

Her attention moves to the shed, gently illuminated by moonlight.

It's a windowless construction. From the look of it, brand new. The door is secured with a padlock.

Lucy steps off the decking and crosses the grass. At the shed door, she activates her torch. The lock is far better quality than the hasp and staple through which it's threaded. A few well-placed kicks should pop the screws loose.

Lucy slams her foot against the wood. The sound is horrendous. In the trees overhead, more birds take flight. She kicks the door a second time, a third. Already, the wood is splintering. Her fourth kick separates one side of the hasp. She slips her fingers under it and levers off the entire mechanism, padlock still attached. Then she yanks open the door.

'*Billie!*' she calls. '*Fin!*'

But one swab with her torch shows it's useless. Aside from a lawn-mower and a few basic tools, the shed's empty.

Lucy spots a hammer, picks it up. Her mind is racing again. She has to slow it down. Recrossing the lawn, she focuses on her breathing: slow in; slow out. Back on the decking, she approaches the bifold door. In a single smooth movement, she swings at the nearest pane. The glass shivers. The hammer flies from her hand.

Fingers tingling, Lucy retrieves it from the grass. She examines the pane more closely. With a tighter grip, she aims for a spot close to one corner.

This time there's no recoil, just a sharp sound of impact. Lucy continues to swing. Fracture lines appear. Glass chips start to fly. Soon, she's broken through to the interior pane. Once that's breached, the job becomes easier. A minute later, she's standing in Nick's darkened living room.

'Billie!' she yells. 'Fin! Are you here?'

Of everyone she knows, only Nick Povey would grope his best friend's wife. Only Nick Povey would attend the party of a family he'd just betrayed, or present Billie with an extravagant gift after destroying her stepfather's livelihood. Of everyone Lucy knows in Skentel, only Nick Povey was absent from tonight's vigil.

His behaviour, in recent weeks, has been more despicable than she thought him capable. That doesn't mean he's responsible for yesterday's events. But it does put him first on her list.

A door in the far wall leads to Nick's office. She checks there first—a desk, a chair, a few cabinets. Nowhere to hide Billie or Fin.

From the office she heads to the kitchen, where she discovers nothing incriminating. She looks inside the fridge, finds a pack of salami, a few beers. If Nick's keeping prisoners, he's not feeding them anything fresh.

Upstairs, she goes room to room, shouting her children's names. She checks cupboards, looks under beds. She holds herself still, listening for any quiet tapping, any signs whatsoever of life.

In Nick's bedroom, emerging from his walk-in closet, she hears the hiss of tyres on gravel and sees headlights sweep the frontage.

She's got thirty seconds before he's inside. Not even that if he's already spotted her torch. Shielding its beam, Lucy snatches three chunky watches from a side table. From a change tray she grabs a fold of cash, scattering coins across the carpet. Important this looks like a random break-in.

Outside, a car door slams. Footsteps crunch across the drive.

Lucy flees to the hall, and from there down the stairs. She reaches the living room just as the front door clatters open. Glass pops beneath her feet. She hears commotion behind her in the hall.

No time left for stealth. Lucy forces her way through the smashed pane, hissing as pain flares in her wrist. Moments later, she's sprinting through the trees.

3

Back at home she sits at the breakfast bar, carefully binding her wound. Cutting herself on the bifold door was careless, but she won't waste energy worrying about it. Better to focus on what comes next.

Closing her first-aid kit, she grabs a notepad.

People reap what they sow.

Angrily, Lucy bats away her tears. She knows that email didn't come from Daniel. Just like she knows her children aren't dead. On the ride down to Skentel, she'd convinced herself she'd find them at Nick's. She needs to recover fast. Force herself to reset.

Picking up a pen, Lucy starts to write down names: people she knows in Skentel, people who know Daniel. She adds everyone she saw at tonight's vigil; everyone who attended Billie's party. But the longer the list grows, the more hopeless she feels. She can think of no logical method of prioritizing the names. Every single inclusion feels absurd. No one in her close or extended circle is capable of stealing her children. And yet that answer doesn't fly. Because it doesn't save Billie and Fin.

She looks at the last name she wrote: Beth McKaylin, the lifeboat volunteer. Five weeks ago, at Headlands School, McKaylin's son took a dislike to Fin. The bullying started soon after. For a seven-year-old, Eliot McKaylin was unusually creative. One morning, Fin went to school and found that nobody in Magenta Class would talk to him. Worse, it seemed they couldn't even *see* him.

Lucy contacted Marjorie Knox, the head teacher. The woman reacted as if to a personal criticism. Days later, when Fin pushed Eliot over in the playground, Knox shrieked that it was no wonder the other children avoided him.

Changing tack, Lucy approached Beth McKaylin. Afterwards, she discovered where Eliot got his mean streak. Within hours of their confrontation, Beth was orchestrating her own campaign. This one targeted Lucy, although it wasn't as successful as her son's.

Or was it?

Ridiculous to think that an escalating playground feud led to yesterday's events. But *something* lies at the heart of this nightmare. McKaylin's a lifeboat veteran with plenty of knowledge of the sea. And her Penny Moon campsite, outside tourist season, is home to a population of itinerants who've caused numerous problems in the past. Might she have recruited one of them, just like her son recruited his classmates?

Lucy looks at the other names she's written down: ex-partners and lifelong friends such as Jake and Noemie Farrell, more recent friends like Bee Tavistock. It feels like a betrayal, this; the worst kind of faithlessness.

She sees Matt Guinness's name, thinks of his dirty hair and scrupulously clean nails. Friday lunchtime, Matt had greeted her on the quay, delighted to share the bad news. This morning, at the bottom of Smuggler's Tumble, he'd approached her in the car park: *'We'll find them kids, Luce, if it's any comfort. Whether it's today or next week, I just know they'll wash up.'*

Her eyes move to Wayland Rawlings, proprietor of the hobby shop on the quay. Rawlings is Skentel's resident eccentric, a pocket-book philosopher and long-term attendee of Lucy's midweek art class at the Drift Net. One night last year, he'd propositioned her as she locked up. A gentle rebuff had knocked their relationship back on track.

Lucy puts down her pen, knuckling away her fatigue. No need, of course, to limit her list of suspects to the recent past. She's lived in Skentel most of her life, but she spent a long time away, starting with her year in London and ending with what happened in Portugal.

One person she *can't* add to her list is Billie's biological father, because rightly or wrongly she doesn't know who he is. She'd wanted none of the candidate fathers as a permanent fixture in her life. Looking back, she can't even recall their names.

She does remember Lucian Terrell, the student who visited her in hospital after Billie's birth. She'd been awed by Lucian when she first met him. Despite a lack of attraction, she'd even slept with him once or twice—her oldest demon reacting to a few bones of praise thrown her way. Following Billie's birth, and before she left London for good, Lucian came into her life once again.

Perhaps she should have stayed, because her next relationship was with Zacarías Echevarria in Spain.

Lucy arrived with Billie at the Alto Paraíso commune purely by chance. After her car overheated in Almería's Tabernas Desert, two women stopped to offer assistance. When they couldn't fix Lucy's vehicle at the roadside, they towed her to the off-grid community where they lived.

Zacarías emerged from a trailer to greet them. Before Lucy knew it, afternoon had turned into evening, and a night's stay had turned into permanent residence.

Alto Paraíso wasn't a religious commune; she'd have had no patience for that. It was simply a respite from the world, a place focused on hard work, cooperation and humanist living. For the first time since leaving her great-aunt's house in Skentel, Lucy felt like she'd found home.

Zacarías was the glue that held the community together. An hour alone with him felt like a session with God's own therapist. In no time at all, he graduated from mentor to lover. As the months sailed by, Lucy realized that Alto Paraíso had a religion, after all; and that she was sleeping with it.

That year and the next, a steady stream of wanderers rolled into the camp. The demands on Zacarías's time increased; the queues outside his trailer lengthened. But as the commune grew, so did his hubris. Lucy began to suspect that their relationship wasn't as exclusive as she'd imagined. When she caught him in bed with two of the newest arrivals, she strapped Billie into his car and headed west.

Months later, in Portugal, Zacarías tracked her down. He pleaded for another chance. When Lucy refused, he used every trick of rhetoric to change her mind. When that failed too, he tried to take Billie. Lucy put herself between them. A physical fight ensued. Zacarías, screaming death threats, pursued Lucy to the kitchen, where she grabbed a knife and defended herself. In the criminal trial that followed, every word of her testimony had been true.

All these years later, would she recognize Zacarías if he passed her in the street? Possibly, but she couldn't guarantee it.

You might think you know me but you don't. You don't have the first clue. Nor does Nick.

Lucy closes her eyes and that's when the thought ambushes her, slipping into her mind before she can fight it off. It swells like a canker. And then it *bursts*, poison gushing from it in a tide.

What if that email *was* from Daniel?

What if she *doesn't* really know him?

She's always had a talent for self-deception. What if she's been engaged, all this time, in nothing but a monumental act of denial?

Lucy pushes away from the counter and staggers to the sink. She dry-heaves so hard and for so long that she feels blood vessels rupturing in her face. Turning on the cold-water tap, she sticks her head beneath the flow until she's soaked and shivering.

When she can take it no more she swills out her mouth. Then she turns off the water and tries to slow her heart. Gradually, her panic ebbs. She's allowed one moment of weakness. One moment of doubt.

Returning to the counter, she writes down Zacarías's name. Carrying her notepad to the study, she boots up Daniel's laptop.

Remember, years ago, that visiting production of Oedipus? *So many of us crammed inside that tiny theatre? You sat there enthralled, Lucy. I sat there bemused. Afterwards, over a glass of wine, you explained it. I don't think I ever saw your eyes shine so brightly, or you talk with such animation.*

You told me what all the great tragedies have in common: a hero destroyed by a tragic flaw. Hamartia, you called it. A defect of character leading to downfall.

That was somewhat harsh on Oedipus, I argued. His only failing seemed to be an ignorance of his parentage. But Oedipus's true flaw, you explained, was hubris: the belief he could escape a fate preordained by the gods.

I wonder, if I asked, how you'd define your own tragic flaw. Is it your faithlessness? Your infidelity? Your ability to self-deceive?

Funny, looking back, how you emerged from that theatre renewed. How your eyes shone and your cheeks glowed, despite everything you'd just witnessed. Katharsis, right there: an enema for the soul.

As we approach the third act of this tragedy written for your benefit, I can barely eat or sleep. Only a maniac would set these events in motion without once entertaining doubts. But I've committed us to this path. I have to see it through. Because only by taking away everything you ever valued can I hope to make you whole.

TWENTY-NINE

1

Lucy wakes, and something has changed. This morning there's no half-minute of solace. No period of confusion before reality rushes in. She opens her eyes and is instantly lucid. Hard to believe her body could feel worse than yesterday, and yet somehow it does. When she rolls over, pain tears through her right side. Her torso feels like it's been beaten with a baseball bat.

But it's only pain.

Receptors firing, nerves transmitting, brain decoding.

It doesn't mean anything.

Through the window, the pre-dawn sky is the colour of woodsmoke. She hears no wind beyond the glass, not even the crash of waves against the rocks of Mortis Point. Something has changed. But she doesn't know what.

Shivering, Lucy climbs off the bed. In the bathroom, she showers and brushes her teeth. Back in the bedroom, she's tying her running shoes when she hears commotion at the window. She turns in time to see a herring gull land on the ledge. It cocks its head, tapping its beak against the glass.

Lucy cringes, reminded of Friday lunchtime. The bird that appeared outside the study window heralded Bee's visit, news of the *Lazy Susan*'s discovery and every catastrophe since.

She yells, claps her hands. The herring gull flaps into the woodsmoke sky.

Knees cracking, Lucy stands. At the door she hesitates. Something *has* changed—something intangible in the feel of the world around her. When she breathes, even the air in her lungs seems different. Goosebumps flare out across her flesh.

Out in the hall she hears something shocking—a voice, unmistakeable in its cadence. Over it comes a silvery peal of laughter.

Her breath catches. She takes another step. To her left, a pair of casement windows looks down on the front drive. Directly opposite, the door to Billie's room stands ajar. Sounds of conversation drift out.

Lucy can't breathe at all now. She feels as if she's slid sideways into a different reality. As she passes the hallway windows, she sees movement beyond them—a herring gull, high above the peninsula, banking towards the house.

She recalls a story Daniel once told Fin, of a man-shaped creature called the Mobiginion, entirely composed of water. On moonless nights, the Mobiginion emerged from the sea, wandering the local streets until it chose a house. No door could stop it, no window or wall. Once inside, it inspected the sleeping inhabitants for a prize. Next morning, puddles of seawater would be found throughout. Within a few days, the chosen victim would be lost to the sea. A father would fall overboard from his fishing schooner. A freak wave would drag a child from the beach. Nothing could stop a Mobiginion from visiting, nor from claiming its victim once chosen. Fin had been so scared by the tale that Lucy had banned Daniel from retelling it.

She looks down, but the floorboards of the upper hall are dry. Two days ago, standing at the front door while talking to Bee, she'd glanced behind her to see a trail of wet footprints retreating to the study. In *that* reality, no Mobiginion existed. But in *this* one, which shares only the vaguest resemblance to the one she knows . . .

In this one, she hears a child's laughter.

2

Another step and she's at Billie's door.

Lucy pushes it open, sags against the frame. Quite how this is possible she doesn't know. There, on the bed, with a towel around her torso and wet hair snaking down her spine, lies Billie.

The girl's feet, toenails painted bright yellow, wave like fern fronds. Propped open on her pillow is a *National Geographic*. Billie rests her chin in her hands as she reads. Straddled across her backside is her brother.

Fin's wearing his *The Incredibles* costume: black-and-red one-piece, black eye mask, orange belt. 'His name's *Bog*wort, not *Dog*wort,' the boy says, bouncing up and down.

'You wrote a story about something called a *Bog*wort?' Billie asks.

'He's not a *thing*, he's an *old man*!' Fin shouts, bouncing even harder. 'With green skin and silver hair—'

'And purple prickles all over his back?'

'That's the *Gruffalo*! For *babies*! Bogwort's a *lot* scarier! He's got—'

'A poisonous wart at the end of his nose?'

Fin splutters for breath through his hysterics. Billie chuckles, glancing around at him. 'You're such a *nink*, Finny. But it sounds like a cool story.'

Finally, the boy recovers. 'Nin–COM–*POOP*!' he yells, riding even harder. 'Woo-*HOO*!'

'How?' Lucy whispers. The air rolling out of the bedroom is tinged with Billie's Jimmy Choo perfume. But there's another smell too: ocean salt and rotting seaweed.

Her children ignore her, or perhaps they don't hear her.

Lucy's hand moves to her bare wrist. Yesterday, she fastened Billie's silver bracelet around it. Did she take it off last night? Did it come loose as she slept? Snig, too, has disappeared. She remembers, vaguely, untying it.

'Billie,' she pleads. 'Fin.'

In response, the boy leans forwards and slaps his sister's shoulder.

'*Ow*, Nink! Leave off!'

As Lucy watches, a stain spreads out across Billie's towel. Fin's *The Incredibles* costume goes from dry to soaked through. He stops laughing. The blood drains from his face. 'I'm c–cold,' he stammers. 'Billie, what's happening? Billie, *please* . . .'

But the girl can't answer. Her eyes bulge. The arteries in her neck swell.

Then, an explosion of movement by the window—a herring gull landing on the frame. Lucy yells, diving into the room. With a cry, the gull flaps off. When she turns back to the bed, her children have disappeared.

She blinks, hears that other reality unzipping. The floor tilts and swings. When it rises up to meet her, the impact is stunning. Knees, chest, face. Her ribs feel like they've splintered into points. She tastes blood, hopes it's not from her lungs.

Somehow, she gets to her knees. Using the bed, she pulls herself up. The duvet, soaked a few moments ago, is now completely dry.

The Mobiginion, she thinks. And moans, dismayed at her own unravelling.

From the bed she moves to the door, from the door to the top of the stairs. Gripping the rail, she stumbles down the flight. Something has changed, but she doesn't know what. Herring gulls at the windows, another one circling—a warning of death soon to come.

It's a daft superstition. Just another story humans create to explain the world. Like God, like angels, like the Devil. All of it a sham—all of it a distraction from what's real.

Lucy reaches the bottom of the stairs. In the living room, she goes to the window. Overnight, a ghost mist has crept in from the sea. Down in Skentel, the buildings are pale shapes shrouded in white. The ramp of the RNLI boathouse descends into drifting smoke.

North of Mortis Point, Penleith Beach is similarly robed, but its flat expanse of sand isn't deserted. A few yards from where the surf is breaking, a collection of dark shapes have gathered. Lucy steps closer to the glass. Impossible to draw meaning from those half-glimpsed forms. Her stomach tightens as she watches them.

Snatching up her binoculars, she trains them on the beach. Deep inside that milky soup, part of the scene resolves. She sees a trio of grey figures clustered around a fourth.

Lucy's lungs empty. Her binoculars thump to the floor.

Out of the living room. Into the kitchen. Through the back door and along the house to the front drive. On to the Triumph, kick down the starter.

Rear tyre spitting shingle, she peels off the drive.

3

Wet road. Dead leaves. No grip. Lucy accelerates through the gears, wind scouring tears from her eyes. From the peninsula she pulls on to the coastal road with barely a glance for passing traffic.

Faster now. Wider tarmac, less debris. Lucy leans into the bends, pushing the bike harder. In her head, the slap of herring-gull wings, the tapping of beaks against glass.

Something has changed. Everything has changed.

She slows for the beach turning, wheels bumping down the track. At the bottom, she's off the Triumph before it's even stopped. Teeth clenched against the pain in her side, she scrambles up the backshore dune.

At the top, she's greeted by the same scene she saw from the house: indistinct figures wreathed in white. Lucy skids down the slope. She breaks into a loping run across the sand.

Dear God, I know I've never prayed and I know I've done bad things, plenty of them, but please, God, please, God, please . . .

In her ears, the rasp of her breathing. In her heart, a cracking, a rending. She loses a running shoe, keeps going. Trips over and crashes to her hands. Bites back a scream, tastes blood. Gets up. Limps on.

Ahead, the group begins to coalesce. She's sixty feet away now. Fifty.

Four figures in total. One, standing, is talking into a phone. Two others crouch over a fourth lying prone.

Lucy's strength goes. She stumbles the last few yards, falters.

The figure lying prone is a teenaged girl, clothes soaked from the sea. Her head is turned away but she has the same pale hair as Billie, cut into much the same style. The two leaning over her—female, middle-aged, red-faced with exertion—are taking turns to perform CPR.

Lucy moves around them so she can see the girl's face. With all her energy spent, she slumps down on the sand.

The woman performing compressions is Jane Watson from the pharmacy. Talking on the phone is her husband, Gordon. Lucy doesn't recognize the woman offering assistance.

Around them the mist settles thicker, cloaking everything but this small parcel of sand and the mercurial water that creeps up it each time a wave breaks.

Behind them, Mortis Point has disappeared. Penleith's backshore too.

Sound comes, though—bell-like in its clarity: the whisper of surf, the calls of the herring gulls, Jane Watson's breathing, the wail of a faraway siren.

Strange, how the sea has grown so tranquil—as if the enormity of the spectacle has affected it too. The gentle wash of water, in and out of the mist, replicates the rise and fall of lungs or gills, the basic mechanisms of life.

The girl is dead.

That's beyond doubt. Lucy doesn't know why the two women keep trying to revive her. That heart won't beat again. Those eyes won't see anything new.

She thinks of the story Daniel once told Fin, of the man-shaped Mobiginion that sometimes visits homes near the sea. She recalls the trail of wet footprints she saw on Friday, retreating to the study from the front door. And, a few weeks ago, the bloody impressions retreating through broken glass to Nick Povey's couch.

The siren grows louder. Jane Watson, still working on the dead girl, glances up and sees Lucy. She calls to her husband, still talking on the phone.

The dead girl's not Billie.

That, more than anything else, is the most difficult reality to grasp. Just now, as Lucy's energy abandoned her and she collapsed down on the sand, she thought her world had ended right here on this beach; that the dead girl, with sea-draggled hair so similar to Billie's in colour and style, *was* Billie.

And yet she isn't.

In a community of this size, it hardly seems possible that *two* families in twenty-four hours could be hit by tragedy. Yet that is what appears to have happened. And while Lucy has only sympathy for the mother of this poor child and the cataclysm she's about to experience, she won't spare her a drop if it means Billie can come home. The thought is ruthless to the point of inhumanity, but she won't deny it. To save her children, she'll sacrifice anything. Anyone.

One last whoop of the siren before it dies. An ambulance, probably, arriving behind the dunes. No need to rush. The diagnosis is clear.

Jane Watson wipes her brow and continues pumping. She starts shouting. 'Come on. Come *on!*'

Hard to know if she's appealing to the ambulance crew or the dead girl. Gordon Watson puts away his phone and walks over. He lays his hand on Lucy's shoulder, squeezes.

The dead girl's feet are bare. Her toenails are painted the same lemon shade favoured by Billie.

It's another disturbing coincidence. Another jarring detail. Lucy shivers—realizes for the first time how cold it is down here on the beach. If only she'd brought a coat, she could have used it to cover the dead girl. It wouldn't keep her warm, but it would be a gesture, at least. If Billie were lying here, she'd want someone else to do the same.

Two paramedics emerge from the mist, equipment jostling on their backs. Gordon sinks to his knees. He puts his arms around Lucy's shoulders and pulls her close. Together, they watch the paramedics drop their backpacks to the sand. One of them crouches beside Jane Watson and stills her attempts at revival. It really is very obvious that the girl isn't coming back.

'This doesn't make any sense,' Gordon croaks.

In all the years she's known him, he's never sounded so desolate. Jane Watson sags forwards and starts weeping.

Lucy forces herself to look again at the girl they were trying to save. It really *doesn't* make any sense. None of this does.

The dead girl's wearing Billie's favourite neon-green T-shirt; another strange thing. Under it is the same patterned bra Billie was wearing on Friday morning. On the girl's legs are the same black gym shorts cut to mid-thigh, bisecting an identical tattoo.

But it isn't Billie. It isn't.

Lucy hears her own breathing; like the roar inside a seashell.

'I'm so sorry,' Gordon says. And then he starts crying too. Lucy pushes away his arms, breaks free. On hands and knees she crawls forwards. A sound comes from her throat she doesn't understand.

The sea pushes cold water up the sand and calls it back. Around them the mist pulls close.

Lucy's hand reaches out. She thinks again of the mother—out there somewhere right now—and the wrecking ball about to swing through her life.

Ligature marks around the dead girl's ankles have turned the flesh dark grey. Did she drown while her feet were bound? That's certainly how it looks.

There's no God in this world, Lucy thinks. No omniscient creator. Only a deity of truly incalculable cruelty could allow suffering on a scale such as this.

Her hand descends. She touches lifeless skin. There's a soapy feel to it. A coldness so acute it flows up her arm. It isn't Billie, it isn't. Because Billie—like the storm of recent days—is a force of nature too powerful to be curtailed.

In death, she wonders, where does all the love go? What happens to dreams and hopes, to memories and joys? Impossible, suddenly, to believe they just end. There might not be a God, but that's not to say spirits don't endure.

Lucy crawls closer. As gently as she can, she pulls her daughter's head into her lap. She touches Billie's hair, strokes Billie's face, finds herself—for some strange reason—humming the same lullaby she sang back when she was breastfeeding.

This summer, for the first time in her life, the girl was to sail to the Faroe Islands. Now, and for ever more, she'll be able to travel wherever she wants.

PART II

THIRTY

1

In a lavatory cubicle inside Barnstaple police station, Abraham Rose shakes two white pills into his fist and crunches them down without water. Tilting his head, he tries to draw clean air into his lungs. He imagines his chest as an empty receptacle filling with life-giving oxygen. But the air inside the cubicle stinks of urine and disinfectant. Abraham can only manage half a breath before he's coughing up crap, thick and buttery and full of the stuff that's going to kill him.

For a while he leans against the partition, trying not to choke. The pain is bad, but he can handle it. The important thing is to keep it hidden. Wiping his mouth, he returns the pill box to his jacket.

He returned from the beach an hour ago. He won't forget the sight of Billie Locke on the sand, wind drying her salt-stiff clothes: captivating, even in death; astonishing in beauty and pathos and grace.

The post-mortem will happen next week. But Abraham saw the ligature marks on the girl's ankles. He knows, from his limited knowledge of pathology, that they weren't made after death. Billie was tied up before she was killed.

It's the ending they all expected but no one wanted. Hundreds of square miles of ocean searched, swathes of coastline too. A well-run volunteer programme, a huge local response. And all of it for nothing. Billie Locke returned to Skentel in the end, but she left her life with the sea.

I drowned them. I drowned them both. I tied them up and put them in the water. And when they were gone I jumped in after.

Those words replay in Abraham's head. Two minutes later he's in the interview room, sitting across the table from the man who uttered them.

2

Daniel Locke's been in custody twenty-four hours, but he looks like he's endured far longer. Gone is the robotic arrogance from yesterday. His face is a mess of red eyes and chapped lips. The rims of his nostrils are as wet as a dog's.

Abraham's seen this kind of transformation before but never quite so dramatic, nor so soon. Locke's demons, confined with their host in his cell, appear to be consuming him.

The man glances at his solicitor. His mouth stretches wide. Impossible to tell if he's leering or grimacing. 'Have you found him yet?' he asks. 'Have you found Fin?'

Abraham puts down his pen. He feels the urge to cough, stifles it. 'We haven't found your son, but we found your stepdaughter. Billie washed up this morning on Penleith Beach.' He waits for a reaction, a comment. Across the desk, Locke clasps his hands together, a vile parody of prayer. 'But you knew that might happen, didn't you? Tell me why you put her in the water, Daniel.'

For a moment, it seems like Locke's going to lunge across the table. Instead, he regains his self-control. 'I want to talk to my wife.'

'Do you? Or do you just want to torture her? "Tell her she deserves every fucking thing she gets." Do you still believe that?'

'I want to *talk* to her.'

'Twice now you've asked about Fin. Did you kill him the same way as Billie?'

The solicitor starts to protest. Locke waves away the interruption. 'How long are you going to hold me here?'

'Who did you kill first, Daniel?'

'Answer my question.'

'You're going to court first thing tomorrow morning. Then you're heading to prison until a trial date is set.'

'And then I can see her.'

'If she agrees. Let's talk about what happened on Friday.'

'Fuck this,' Daniel says. 'We're finished here.'

3

Monday afternoon, Abraham holds another press conference. In it, he explains that the body discovered on Penleith Beach was Billie Locke's. When asked about Fin, he confirms that the boy is still missing. They don't expect to find him alive.

Lucy Locke, he knows, is about to learn the fickle nature of public opinion. Three days ago, she was the tragic mother of two missing children. Since then, she's become the wife of a self-confessed child-killer. All too often, in cases like these, the partner attracts more vitriol than the perpetrator. The usual questions will be asked: How could she have lived with him all that time without understanding his true nature? How could she have entrusted her children into his care? On social media, in newspaper gossip columns, in bars and coffee shops and school playgrounds, details don't matter. Those who attack hardest are rewarded with the greatest exposure. Lucy Locke might be in hell right now, but just give this story a few more days to percolate.

The front page of this morning's *Sun—MONSTER JUMPED US AS WE SLEPT: pair breaks silence over brutal attack launched by tragic kids' dad*—is a warning of what's to come. The story features an interview with

Gethan Grierson and Adam Crowther, Daniel Locke's victims at the Glenthorne Hostel for Boys.

If Lucy Locke didn't know about her husband's past before, she knows about it by now. Increasingly, Abraham finds himself wondering what else she might know. Ten minutes later he's back in the interview room.

4

Bee Tavistock stares through him rather than at him, as if her focus is the wall behind his head.

'I want to thank you for coming in,' Abraham says. 'This is a difficult time. For everyone.'

Tavistock nods, listless. Her gaze drifts to the recording equipment. 'I was never in a police station before.'

'You're not in any trouble. But you can imagine, I hope, that we're trying desperately hard to figure out what happened. You work for Lucy Locke?'

'She's my friend.'

'How would you describe her?'

'Lucy's flame burns brightly,' she says. 'It warms everyone it touches. That's not some hippie shit I came up with because we're close. You ask anyone—they'll tell you the same thing.'

Abraham thinks of Zacarías Echevarria, from the commune in Spain's Tabernas Desert. Doubtful the man would agree. 'Can you walk me through your day on Friday?' he asks.

Tavistock rubs her bare arms. 'It started like any other. I arrived at the quay around four thirty a.m.'

'Why so early?'

'To survive in a place like Skentel, the Drift Net's got to be lots of different things to lots of different people. We open around five, depending on the tide. There's decent business to be had doing coffee and cooked breakfasts for the trawler boys.

'Harbour was busy Friday. Lot of crews going out early to fill their nets or collect their pots one last time before the storm hit. First I knew something was up was when a customer said a yacht had been found drifting. Then people started saying it was the *Lazy Susan*. I couldn't get Luce on the phone, so I hopped on my scooter and rode up to the house.'

'What time was this?'

'We were coming to the end of the lunch rush, so . . . around two, I guess.'

'Lucy was at home?'

'Uh-huh. Just stepped out of the shower. Most days she'd have been down at the Drift Net, making orders or helping out. But Friday she was doing her accounts up at the house.'

'How do you know that?'

'Because, like, there was paperwork scattered all over. Dude, is this relevant?'

'Probably not.' Abraham feels a cough coming from deep in his lungs. He breathes slowly, trying to suppress it. 'Prior to Friday, was Lucy worried about anything? Did she talk much about her relationship with Daniel? How things were going?'

'She talked about Billie and Fin. Lucy was so proud of them, so nurturing. A real mama bear.' Tavistock's throat bobs as she swallows. 'Sorry. I still can't believe they're gone. They were like my niece and nephew, those two.'

She blinks away tears. 'It's no secret things with Daniel's business were pretty dire. The money had them worried, but it never affected their relationship. They were the love story of Skentel. Kind of couple where you'd get burned by the sparks if you stood too close.'

Abraham nods. The cough is building again, a real chest-ripper. His lungs feel like they're filling with glue. He glances down at his notes and sees something that chills his blood: the inked motif that's haunted him in recent weeks, finally complete. There are his initials and date of birth. But the dome that previously protected them has grown vertical walls edged with moss. Abraham sees it for what it is: a gravestone, solid and stark.

There's no epitaph. Nothing to suggest he'll be missed.

'Let's take a break,' he croaks.

Bee Tavistock studies him like she's watching a condemned man.

5

An hour later, he's standing beside the Taw, smoking another cigarette. The river's running higher than he's ever seen it, dirty brown and cluttered with storm debris. He can't stop thinking about one of Bee Tavistock's throwaway comments: that when she went up to Mortis Point on Friday, Lucy had just stepped out of the shower.

Had she? Or was she drying off after a high-speed trip back to shore in the family dinghy? Wild thought: what if Lucy Locke was aboard the *Lazy Susan* prior to the distress call? What if this started as a plan for insurance money but morphed into something darker? What if Daniel agreed to go missing, not expecting to almost lose his life? Perhaps Lucy decided she'd be better off if her husband didn't come back. If so, that might explain his anger. But why confess to the murder of his kids? And how does Billie Locke's death fit? Was that another accident? Why bind her feet, in any case?

Abraham crushes out his cigarette. Right now, he's certain of only one thing: both Daniel Locke and Lucy Locke are lying to him. He doesn't know what they're hiding. But he does have an opportunity to find out.

Before that, though, he has an appointment he's anticipating with a good deal more relish.

6

The strains of a piano greet his arrival. Abraham recognizes the hymn: 'Abide With Me'. The playing is so beautiful that he waits outside the front door, head bowed, until it's over. Five minutes later he's sitting in Bibi Trixibelle Carter's living room, drinking another cup of her excellent Earl Grey.

'I saw you on television earlier,' Bibi says. 'That poor girl. It's devastating news. Too tragic for words. It must be a very harrowing thing to investigate.'

'We're fortunate that events like these are incredibly rare. But that does make them all the more upsetting when they occur.'

'Despite the awful circumstances, I will say it's nice to see you again,' Bibi tells him. 'I feared your last visit would be exactly that.'

Abraham nods, but his heart soars. How strange, the effect this old woman has on him. 'There's something I wanted you to see,' he says, opening a folder. 'You told me you saw two vehicles parked in that lay-by Friday morning. A grey Volvo and a smaller black car.'

From the folder he takes a colour printout. It's a still from the CCTV camera in Wayland Rawlings' quayside hobby shop. Yesterday, Abraham tasked his team to sift through all the available footage. He was looking, specifically, for sightings of black cars. The team found eight; but it's this one—Lucy Locke's Citroën C1—that interests him. 'Look at it a while before you answer,' he says. 'Was that the vehicle you saw on Friday morning?'

Bibi frowns, affronted. 'I don't need a *while*, Detective Inspector. I know I said a hatchback, but this is far too small. Before you ask if I'm sure, I'd stake my life on it—and believe me, I don't make such a wager lightly.'

It's good enough for Abraham. The figure in grey Bibi saw beside the Volvo could still be Lucy Locke, but he came here expecting to confirm it. He sips his tea and looks around the room. Just like his last visit, his pain has vanished. That aching heaviness in his chest has all but melted away.

To prolong the moment, Abraham reopens his folder. He retrieves seven more images of black cars, all harvested from the quayside CCTV. There's nothing to suggest a connection. He knows he's imposing on Bibi's time without justification, but he doesn't want to leave, not yet. 'How about any of these?'

Bibi takes the proffered images. 'Too big,' she says, dismissing two SUVs. 'Not this one, either—it's a saloon. Nor this Ford.'

Only three remain: a Lexus, a Toyota and a Vauxhall. 'This one has a surfboard and there was definitely no surfboard on the one I saw.' Bibi points to the Lexus. 'What's that little green window sticker?'

'It's too small to make out.'

'Hmm.' She examines the Toyota. 'Are those fluffy dice?'

'Looks like it.'

'I thought we left fluffy dice in the eighties.'

'Apparently not.'

'I did not enjoy the eighties,' Bibi says. 'The Space Shuttle and the Rubik's Cube were the high points. And that film, of course. The boy and the alien. I cried during the geranium scene.'

Abraham nods vaguely. If only he'd paid more attention to popular culture. Far too late, he's begun to understand its value in finding common ground.

Bibi tilts her head. 'Is there anything else I can do for you, Detective Inspector?'

Ask her.

Surprised by the thought, he looks around the room; at the trinkets on the sideboard; at Bibi's sewing box by her chair. He listens to the pop and crackle of the fire, smells the woodsmoke, thinks of the disease eating through his lungs. A wave of desolation hits him, so shattering he can barely raise his head.

Ask her.

'Abraham?'

He takes a deep breath. 'I heard you playing, earlier.'

She smiles. 'Fingers are still working, just about.'

'It's one of my favourite hymns.'

'Mine too. Henry Francis Lyte wrote the words, just weeks before he died. A prayer for God to remain close as death approached.'

'I didn't know that.'

'My father used to hum it when he was home from sea.'

Ask her.

He clears his throat. 'Do you think you might . . . I mean, I'd understand if you . . . I was wondering—'

'Would you like me to play it for you, Abraham?'

He's too embarrassed to speak, but he just about manages a nod.

So, Billie . . .

We'll talk about her when I see you. It wasn't meant to happen the way it did. Certainly not then. I was devastated at the time. Less so now.

In hindsight maybe it's a good thing. There's a tragic poetry to it this way. It does mark a turning point. Because you can't deny this any more, Lucy. Self-deception no longer works.

I saw a newspaper this morning. A day old, but I picked it up and read that feature on Gethan Grierson and Adam Crowther from the Glenthorne Hostel for Boys. I wonder how much they got paid.

It'll be emotional, I know, but I'm looking forward to our reunion. What happened with Billie was a tragedy that came far too early. But the third act will change everything.

THIRTY-ONE

1

Wednesday morning.

In her kitchen, Lucy sits at the breakfast bar beside a hamper wrapped in cellophane. Around her, lilies and white roses stand in vases or lie in unopened bouquets. Atlantic wind blows through a jagged hole in the windowpane. Broken glass lies scattered across the sill. Smaller fragments glitter on the drainer.

Five days ago, she watched her son eat breakfast in here as he talked to his sister. She remembers their banter and the question Fin asked:

'Did you know there's a storm coming, Billo?'

'Yup. I hear it's going to be a real monster. What they call a threat to life.'

Lucy bends double with the pain of it.

Best not to think, not to remember what was. Better, for now, to reduce herself to the basic functions necessary for life. Only when she hears the back door swing open does she raise her head.

When Noemie sees Lucy, her mouth forms an unhappy circle. She glances around, wrinkling her nose. 'Oh, hon.' Coming close, she enfolds Lucy into an embrace. 'Were you sick?'

'Just a little. I thought I . . . I thought I swilled it away.'

Noemie releases her and goes to the sink. She grimaces, flicks on a tap. 'Who sent the hamper?'

'Ed, Billie's boyfriend. Said he wanted to do something but didn't see the point of more flowers.'

'I guess he had a point. What happened to the window?'

'Herring gull. I threw a saucepan at it.'

'Uh-huh. Did you get it?'

'Wasn't fast enough.'

'Maybe next time.'

'Maybe.'

'Are you sure you're up to this today?'

'It's all arranged. If not today, it might not be for weeks.'

'There's no pressure, Luce.'

'I know. But I have to see him.'

Noemie nods. 'Listen, I don't want to make this any more daunting. But you should know there's a load of journalists outside. I tried to mow down a couple on the way in, but they move pretty fast when they're scared.'

'A bit like herring gulls.'

'Yeah. Or maybe vultures.'

'The police took away Daniel's laptop. Plus a load of his files. Billie's Chromebook, too.'

'You know what they were looking for?'

Lucy shrugs. 'Is this happening, Noemie? I mean, is it *really* happening? My mind feels like . . . like I'm losing my grip. Three days ago, at the beach, I was positive that girl wasn't Billie. Even now, when I try to reach out . . .' She pauses, shakes her head.

'If you lose yourself for a while, I'd say that's perfectly understandable. You don't need to analyse what's going on in your head. Right now, you've probably just got to roll with it. Throw saucepans at seagulls if it helps. Hell, I'll join you. This whole thing, it's like a tsunami—coming out of the blue and swamping everything. It's too big to think about all at once. Maybe, for a while, it's best to tune out.'

'That's what I keep telling myself,' Lucy says. 'Except I can't. I *need* to think. I have to figure out what happened. I can't just abandon them because it hurts.'

'And that's why you want to see Daniel?'

'Exactly.'

2

The journalists at the foot of the drive start yelling when Lucy emerges; she's so shocked by the white sky and cold breeze that their questions hardly register. Noemie makes no effort to avoid them as she swings her Renault on to the road. They scramble away so fast that a few of them fall over.

Pretty soon they're on the coast road. Not long after, they hit the inland route south. The devastation out here is shocking—swathes of forest flattened. On the radio, the presenter is talking about a hilltop stone circle east of Redlecker. Two 4,000-year-old megaliths have collapsed due to landslip caused by the storm. When the topic moves on to the Locke family and what might have happened out at sea, Noemie switches it off, but not before Lucy hears Daniel's name.

She closes her eyes and finds herself at the wheel of her old Suzuki. It's nine summers ago and the weather's hot enough to blister paintwork. Billie's in the back, shouting for a wee. They're heading home after a day of surfing at Sandymouth Bay. When Lucy spots a lay-by, she hauls the Suzuki over. Billie flings open the rear door, jumps down from her booster seat and darts through a gap between the brambles. Lucy climbs out, revelling in the feel of the late-afternoon sun.

They don't have the lay-by to themselves. Parked in front is a dusty Hilux pick-up, steam venting from it in white gouts. A forty-foot yacht sits on the vehicle's boat trailer, its mast unstopped for transit. A guy in Ray-Bans is staring at the truck, one hand trapped beneath his armpit.

Billie's still occupied in the bushes, so Lucy wanders over. 'I'm no mechanic,' she says, watching the steam. 'But I'd say that doesn't look good.'

'Well, I *am* a mechanic. Of sorts. Which makes this kind of embarrassing.'

'Are you OK?'

'I think I . . . I sort of burnt myself. It's fine. I'll be fine.'

'Did you try to remove the radiator cap?'

'That would've been the dumbest move ever.'

'Is that what you did?'

'Yes.'

He removes his Ray-Bans. Lucy's breath catches. His eyes are a deeper shade of cobalt than the ocean she just surfed. Even more startling is what she sees in them: anxiety, hope and good humour. She feels an unaccountable urge to put her arms around him.

It's a ridiculous notion. Lucy shakes herself free of it. 'Show me,' she says.

'It's just a slight burn.'

'So show me.'

Warily, he withdraws his hand from his armpit. Lucy recoils. 'I'll get my first-aid kit.' A minute later she's treating his wound while Billie performs cartwheels beside them. 'Do you have breakdown cover?'

'I've been meaning to get it.'

'So the plan is?'

'Wait for things to cool down.'

She grins. 'And if they don't?'

'An evening stroll back to Skentel.'

'Skentel's ten miles away.'

'Evening hike, then.'

Lucy glances behind her. 'We're going that way.'

'No need to rub it in.'

Her grin widens. 'I'd hate to leave a damsel in distress.'

'It's very chivalrous,' he replies. 'But I think I'll have to pass.'

He's far better-looking than she'd first realized. When Lucy finds herself considering that, she nearly heads back to her car. Instead, she tilts her head. 'It's the ego, huh? Won't let you get rescued by a young mother and her daughter.'

'Monster ego,' he replies. 'Quite revolting. I blame it for the lack of breakdown cover, too. Told me I could fix anything.' He smiles, revealing straight white teeth. 'Thanks for the offer. But I'd rather not leave the boat unless I have to. You're looking at the first gig of a new enterprise. Probably my last if somebody pinches it.'

Ten minutes later, Lucy's back on the road. Behind her Suzuki trundles the boat trailer. The guy with the blue eyes and white smile sits in the passenger seat.

'Daniel,' he says.

'Lucy. And this is Billie.'

'Nice to meet you both,' Daniel says. 'Particularly as you have a tow bar.'

'A lot more useful than shining armour.'

'Ah.' He nods sagely. 'Another damsel-in-distress reference. I'm guessing you're the knight.'

'That's right,' Lucy says. 'So you'd better tell me where the castle is, Goof, so we can see you safely home.'

'Goof?'

She glances at his hand.

His mouth twitches. 'You know the workshop behind Penleith Beach?'

'*That* place?'

'What about it?'

'It's virtually falling down.'

'Thanks. I just leased it.'

'Then I hope you didn't pay too much. It's the biggest eyesore in Skentel.'

'What about the tumble-down house on the Point?' Billie asks. 'That one's pretty bad.'

Daniel turns in his seat. 'I'm going to *buy* that tumble-down house one day.'

'Oh yeah? What for?'

'To live in, of course.'

They reach Skentel as the sun lights a fire in the western sky. Carefully, Lucy bumps down the track to Penleith Beach. At the bottom, she pulls up outside the workshop and they disconnect the trailer.

'I've got a barbecue inside,' Daniel says. 'Needs a clean, but it won't take long. How about I cook you both a couple of steaks as a thank-you?'

He lifts his bandaged hand. 'I mean, I get this isn't exactly a badge of competence, but I make a killer peppercorn sauce.'

'Can we, Mum?'

Lucy winces. It's been fun—if she's honest, it's been more than that—but this is definitely the end point. 'Sorry, missy. Mummy's out with Jake tonight. We've got to hand you over to the babysitter.'

'Gotcha,' Daniel says.

He grins, but he can't hide his disappointment. When Lucy's stomach tightens, she can't figure out if it's pleasure or guilt.

A week later she splits with Jake. A silly argument graduates into something larger, and eventually becomes an exit opportunity. It's horrible and it's sad and it's also inevitable—because for seven days straight she hasn't stopped thinking about Daniel Locke.

She hates herself for doing it. But Jake deserves someone who loves him completely and her recent preoccupation rules her out. More selfishly, she's twenty-eight years old with a nine-year-old daughter. Time and again, she's proved she doesn't need a man to survive this world. So it either has to be the full lightshow or nothing at all.

Two days after the split, she's taking Billie for that barbecue on Penleith Beach. A month later, Lucy's more in love with Daniel Locke than she'd ever thought possible. Not just the full lightshow but the accompanying orchestra and choir. It's scary and dangerous and she's never felt anything like it. For the first time since Billie's birth, her heart is equally divided. Two years after that, it divides in three.

Blink, and more time rattles by. And now she's standing outside Fin's room in their rented end terrace behind Skentel's main street. Daniel sits in a rocking chair beside the cot. To his chest he cradles Fin, a tiny scarlet mass. Their son's breaths grow weaker by the moment.

'What's his temperature now?' asks a voice in Lucy's ear.

'Forty degrees,' she says, gripping the phone tighter. 'Please, send an ambulance. Quick as you can.'

Blink, and five years zip past. Happier times now. Healthier ones, too, for their precious boy. They're in the water, all four of them, swimming beside the *Lazy Susan*, anchored just off Mortis Point. A splash, sunlight glimmering on grey, and suddenly they're no longer four but nine.

'*Mum!*' Billie shrieks.

But there's no fear in her daughter's voice, only joy. Around them, five bottlenose dolphins snail up and down. They click and they whistle and Billie laughs with glee; and Lucy sees, immediately, what her daughter will one day become—how her life will be shaped by her love of the sea.

'Dolph!' Fin shouts. 'Dolph! *Dolph!*'

His cetacean audience nods as if it understands.

Blink, and they're barbecuing again—Penleith Beach, that day from the photograph on Daniel's desk. Blink, and Lucy's making love to him as Atlantic wind blows through their bedroom windows and dries the sweat on their skin.

Blink, and it's a week ago. Daniel's standing at the breakfast bar, showing her something on his laptop. There's money missing from the business and a sizeable number of assets. Obvious enough who's the culprit, but so far there's no way of proving it. Worse, a handful of supplier invoices haven't been added to the system. There's not enough money left to honour them.

Blink, and she's standing in Nick Povey's hallway, staring at a boxwood tree hurled through his front door. Daniel stands in the wreckage. He doesn't say anything, just stares—at her bare feet, her towel-damp hair, her unbuttoned rugby shirt bearing his friend's name.

When Lucy drops her head, she notices blood pulsing from her right foot in time with her heart. Glancing behind her, she sees a line of scarlet footprints retreating through slivers of glass.

Daniel steps over the boxwood, passing Nick without a word. Gentle as snow, he lifts Lucy in his arms and carries her from the house.

Outside, rain crackles off their heads. Within seconds they're soaked. Daniel's Volvo is parked behind her Citroën. He opens the passenger door and lowers her on to the seat. From the boot he grabs a flashlight and first-aid kit. Kneeling in running water, he removes the shard of glass from her foot and carefully binds the wound.

'Like the first time we met,' Lucy says, crying.

'Consider the favour returned.'

Already, her guilt is a cold stone. Daniel's tenderness sharpens it. 'I'm so sorry. I'd never have—'

He shakes his head. 'I know why you went. What you were trying to do.'

They drive home. And Lucy knows they still *have* a home. Whether in this house or somewhere else.

Blink, and it's Friday lunchtime. Lucy's in the study, examining Daniel's balance sheet, working out how to save him and claw back whatever Nick stole. On the desk is a stack of correspondence that has sat there far too long. In it, she finds something that doesn't make sense: communications from two insurance companies about policies taken out in her name. She doesn't recognize them and when she phones, she doesn't recognize the account through which they've been paid.

Blink, and she's on *Huntsman's Daughter*, watching the helicopter winch Daniel from the sea. Blink, and she's crouching beside Billie on Penleith Beach, her daughter no longer a force of nature powered by an incredible beating heart but an empty vessel; cold flesh and grey skin and—

Blink, and she's back in the car with Noemie, throat creaking as she tries to suck down air. Too dangerous to keep thinking. Too painful to let her mind roam free. She counts road signs. Then she counts cars. They're in Okehampton, turning east. Thirty minutes later they're in Exeter. They park by the railway line and cross the bridge.

'I'll wait for you,' Noemie says.

Lucy can't speak.

Blink, and she's outside the prison's red-brick entrance. Blink, and she's stuffing her belongings into a clear plastic bag. Blink, and she's through security, into the visiting hall.

Blink, and there's Daniel, climbing to his feet.

THIRTY-TWO

1

Gone is the man Lucy thought she knew. Because what rises from the table is hardly a man at all. Daniel looks like a taxidermy project gone wrong, a waxwork figure left too long in the midday sun.

Around her, the visiting hall rotates like a fairground ride. All Lucy can hear is the thump of her pulse, the roar of her blood. She wants to scream; feels, if she does, she might not stop.

Somehow she starts moving again, one leaden foot in front of the other. And then she's at the table. For two days she carefully constructed a fantasy, deceiving herself that Billie and Fin were alive. So much truth she had to bury while building it, so many voices she had to ignore. And yet if she held her breath and didn't look too closely, the edifice managed to endure.

Sunday morning, on Penleith Beach, it all came crashing down. She wonders if there's anything left to be destroyed.

One step and Daniel's closed the gap between them. Lucy's so frightened of being touched that a tear spills down her cheek. His head moves close to hers, his lips angled towards her ear. She can smell him, can hear him breathing.

'They're watching,' he whispers. 'We don't have long.'

2

Suddenly it feels like there's a blockage in Lucy's throat, sealing it shut. She sinks on to a chair. Daniel sits opposite. He laces his fingers and rests his top lip on a knuckle.

'Who—' Lucy begins. She stops when he shakes his head.

The covering of his mouth is deliberate, she realizes. Whatever he's about to say, he doesn't want it overheard.

'You need to listen,' he tells her. 'And you can't interrupt before I'm done, because you need to hear all of it. What you do afterwards might just save Fin's life.'

Her mouth falls open. She's breathing again, huge lungfuls of air.

Lucy's about to speak when she remembers Daniel's warning not to interrupt. Glancing around the hall, she sees one of the prison officers watching, a couple of the other prisoners too. Turning back to the table, she parrots Daniel's pose.

'This is a nightmare,' he says. 'I thought, for a while, I'd wake up. Now I know I won't. That doesn't matter. What happens to me doesn't matter. It's all my fault, Lucy. I can't guarantee—'

He chokes. His face turns red. Somehow, he swallows down his emotion. 'I can't guarantee Fin's still alive, but there's a chance. If he is, you're the only one with any hope of finding him.'

The colours in the visiting hall grow so vivid they seem to glow.

I can't guarantee Fin's still alive, but there's a chance.

Lucy cradles that sentence like a live grenade.

'Friday morning Billie called me,' Daniel says. 'She said Fin had a dentist's appointment—that you were tied up at the Drift Net and needed me to help. She sounded weird on the phone but I didn't think too much of it. I collected him from school and we took the coastal road towards Redlecker. Couple of minutes later we spotted Billie in a lay-by, frantically flagging us down. I pulled over and that's when it happened.'

A tremor passes through him. 'Billie came up to my window. Then the door behind Fin opened and this . . . this *guy* gets in.'

Daniel lets out a breath. 'He pulls Fin's seatbelt taut and puts a knife against his throat. He's wearing gloves—those blue surgical ones. And he tells me to obey him fully or he'll cut Fin open.'

Lucy stares across the table. There's a buzzing in her head so loud it almost obscures Daniel's words.

'My own seatbelt was still fastened. However quick I'd been, Lucy, however fast I'd moved . . .' He looks off to the side. Then his eyes snap back to her face. 'Billie gets in and I ask her what's happening. I ask the *guy* what's happening. He tells me to turn around and head back towards Skentel—that if I comply, he won't hurt Fin. All the way there I think about crashing off the road. But although he's not wearing a seatbelt, he never takes his knife off Fin's throat. Next thing I know we're in the car park on Skentel's quay.'

A prison officer walks past. Daniel pauses until he's further away. 'The guy produces a bottle of Talisker and tells me to drink. When I refuse, he starts wondering aloud if the blood will reach the windscreen if he opens Fin up right there, and whether we'll all get hit by the splashback.

'That's when I start drinking. Once I get through a good half of it, he tells me to ready the *Lazy Susan* for launch. At that point, I thought it was all some bizarre robbery attempt. That it was best to do as he asked. I'm onboard the boat, pulling off sail covers, when I notice he's forced Billie and Fin out of the car. They come along the dock and climb into the cockpit. He takes them down to the cabin and makes me take us out of the harbour. And then I realize that up on deck I've got nothing—no weapon or radio—and already the whisky's kicking in. I thought about capsizing us, letting a wave hit us broadside. But nobody was wearing a life jacket, and you know what a weak swimmer Fin is. Once we reach open sea, the guy handcuffs me to a winch. Then he . . . he drags Fin and Billie up on deck and I see that they're both tethered.'

Daniel's pupils swell.

Lucy's hands tighten over her mouth.

'My phone was in my pocket. I hadn't dared use it until then. While the guy was occupied I managed to speed-dial your number. He noticed and came at me hard. I got in a few punches but I was still shackled—and the whisky had slowed me up a lot. What happened next . . .'

Daniel moans, a sound so low it's almost lost inside the visiting hall. 'Billie, she . . . He killed Billie, Luce. I was there and he killed her and I didn't stop it.'

A spasm of shaking hits him, then. A full minute passes before he regains control. He folds his arms, unfolds them. Starts to reach for her, snatches back his hands. 'This next part—it'll be difficult to hear. There's no good way of telling you, so I'm just going to say it and then you'll have to get out of here, try and do something about this.'

He stops again, this time to get his breath. Lucy's grateful for the silence. The world he's describing is so alien to the one she thought she inhabited that she needs a moment to reset.

Daniel puffs out his cheeks. 'This guy, he's the Devil. Satan, Lucifer, whichever name you want to use. He started talking, then. This awful reverential voice. He said he wanted to *help* you. That he intended to change you from the hateful creature you'd become into something beautiful.

'It didn't make sense, any of it. But he *knows* you, this guy. At least, he knows *of* you. He said he wanted you to experience a period of self-reflection. A sharp shock and a moral change of course. If I helped him achieve it, my reward would be Fin's life.'

Lucy unsticks her tongue, works up some saliva. 'I don't understand. What does he think I did?'

'I don't know, Luce. He brought out our dinghy, made me tell him how to assemble it. Once that was done, he got me to radio in a distress call. Then he started the engine and took us south. He said Fin's life was in my hands, that he'd wait three days and if I followed his instructions he'd let him go. He tossed me an immersion suit and told me to get into the water.

'I was pretty drunk by then. I didn't want to leave Fin. But that blade was back against his neck and I'd just seen—'

Daniel pauses, collects himself. 'Before I went over the side, the guy gave me final instructions. When I was rescued, I was to tell police I'd drowned Billie and Fin. And I had to pass on a message, very specific: *She deserves every fucking thing she gets.* He'd be watching, he said. He'd be listening. If I did as he asked, in three days he'd release Fin. But I *have* done as he asked. To the *letter.* And yet Fin's still missing.'

For a while they sit in silence. Horror has piled upon horror. It's too much to take in, and yet Lucy *has* to take it in, because if Fin's alive—

'The police told me the *Lazy Susan* was recovered,' Daniel says. 'What about the dinghy?'

She shakes her head. 'I told them about it. But by that point they'd already stood down the search.'

'I'm not getting out of here any time soon. After the things I've said, possibly never. Like it or not, this rests with you now. You have to find Fin. Bring him home.'

'I will.'

'This guy's ruthless, Lucy. You'll have to be ruthless too. Whatever it takes.'

'I can do that.'

Daniel glances around the visiting hall, at the various prison officers standing guard. 'The first thing you do, when you get home, is figure out some protection. Before you do anything else, you do that.' He pauses. 'I've been wondering if I should have told the truth. Perhaps I—'

'*No.*'

Lucy's reply is louder than she intended. She takes a breath, sits back in her seat. She knows how desperate he must be to even consider that; his distrust of the police is etched into his bones.

Daniel was six when he first ran away from his parents. At the police station where a member of the public took him, he'd believed his ordeal was over. Instead, officers drove him straight home. Despite the beating Daniel took as punishment, he escaped again two months later. A different police station, this time, but the same result.

Another year passed before neighbours, concerned about what they were hearing through the walls, made a complaint. Children's services attended. They found Daniel with injuries so severe he spent three weeks in hospital recovering.

His life didn't improve much in care. And then one morning, aged thirteen, he woke to police officers arresting him for assault. Two boys had been attacked overnight. A bloody cricket bat had been found under Daniel's bed.

No point protesting his innocence. He pleaded guilty for a shorter sentence and quietly served his time. Lucy's pretty sure Daniel shares her suspicions about the true culprit.

Her own experiences with the police are no more positive. When Zacarías Echevarria tracked her to Portugal after she fled the Spanish commune, she knew he intended to take her back. Only when she saw he'd rather leave her dead than return empty-handed did she grab a knife and defend herself.

The Portuguese police cared nothing for her version of events. At trial, the prosecution portrayed her as a violent and ruthless manipulator. Contrary to the allegations, she never stole any of his money. She did take his car, but he'd sold hers to fund repairs to his solar rig.

'I think you were right to keep quiet,' Lucy says. 'I'm not ready to put my trust in them, and I don't think you are either. The stakes are just too high. You were right earlier—this is on me now. I don't know what I'm going to do, but I'll figure it out, I swear it.'

'Everything this guy's done so far has been orchestrated, designed for maximum effect. Almost like he's directing some sick piece of theatre. We might not have heard from him since, but I don't think leaving the stage quietly is in the script.'

'You think he has something else planned?'

'I'd bet on it. Which means you'll have to figure out his next move and disrupt it before he acts.'

'What else can you tell me?' she asks. 'You didn't recognize him?'

'I'm pretty sure I've seen him around Skentel, but I couldn't say where. Clean-shaven, pale skin. Kind of forgettable face. Around my age, maybe a few years either way.'

'Did he have an accent? A particular way of speaking?'

'He . . . I remember he never raised his voice. That he never showed any emotion, even when . . . even when Billie went in the water. I don't know how much it'll help, but I remember a smell, from when we were in the car. Some kind of ointment. Something for skin, maybe. A medical smell, rather than cosmetic.' He grimaces. 'I'm sorry. It's not much.'

Lucy reflects on what she's heard. 'How was Fin when you last saw him?'

At the mention of their son, Daniel's eyes fill. 'He's going to be different after this, Luce. There's no getting away from it. But he's still going to be Fin. I know how much love you can give him. If anyone can guide him through this, it's you.'

She can. She will. But she has to find him first. 'Billie,' she says at last. 'Did she know? At the end? Did she know what was about to happen? Did she have a long time to be frightened?'

Daniel's jaw starts to shake. 'This isn't the time or place,' he says. 'But she was *so* brave, Lucy. I can't begin . . .'

He swallows. 'She was thinking of you. Right at the end. It was the last thing she said. "Tell Mum I love her."'

Lucy stares, can't speak. Daniel's words are a wrecking ball. She closes her eyes and an image comes back to her: dawn, three summers ago, down on Penleith Beach. A violet sky above a milk sea; no wind, no waves, just gulls and guillemots to break the silence; and, lying prone on the sand, the gleaming black mass of a pilot whale.

Lucy and Billie are there for their regular pre-dawn jog. Now, instead, they're caught up in something extraordinary. They approach the animal in silence, anxious not to cause more stress. Billie strips off her hoodie. She soaks it in seawater and carefully sponges the whale's flanks. Lucy digs out her phone and calls everyone she knows, urging them to bring buckets and towels—anything to keep the whale alive while the tide creeps back in.

Help takes time to appear. For a while it's just the three of them: Lucy, Billie, the whale.

'Will it die?' the girl asks.

'It might,' Lucy tells her. 'On land, a whale this size can get crushed by its own weight. All we can do is keep it hydrated and hope the tide comes in fast enough.'

'And pray?'

'If you'd like to.'

'Do you think that stuff works?'

'A lot of people do.'

'What about you?'

Lucy scrunches up her face. For fourteen years, she's danced around this subject. 'I've generally believed the best way of achieving something is to work hard for it.'

'And if it dies, what do you think happens then? Where do you think it goes?'

'If it dies, its body will break down. Tiny pieces of it will go on to make new animals, new life.'

'But what about its spirit?' Billie asks. She presses her cheek to the whale's skin. 'What about its soul?'

'I'm not sure whales have souls.'

'What about humans? Do you think *we* have a soul? Do you think a part of *us* carries on after we die?'

At the time, Lucy had favoured honesty. If only she'd lied. If only she'd told Billie something to offer comfort. 'I believe we have one life. One opportunity to make the best of ourselves we can.'

'So you don't think anything comes after? That there's a God? Or a heaven?'

'No,' Lucy had admitted. 'I don't.'

In Billie's last moments, did that conversation run through her head? Unforgivable if it did. Worse, Lucy's not even sure she still believes what she told her daughter. Because now, in the cruellest of ironies, she's start-ing to question her lack of faith. Billie removed from the *world* she can just about understand. But Billie gone completely—her entire essence extin-guished? Suddenly that's very hard to accept.

Arching her spine, Lucy snaps back to the present. Across the table, Daniel watches her with naked concern.

'Don't,' he says softly. 'I know what you're doing, and it doesn't help.'

'If I'd—'

'No. This isn't your fault. If anyone's to blame, it's me. I had a chance to stop it and I didn't. And now I'm stuck in here, asking you to take this on alone.'

'We had a good life.'

'We had a *fantastic* life. We gave *them* a fantastic life too.' A tear spills down his cheek. 'You remember the time we sailed them to Norway? That cod Billie caught? Nearly tore her arm off, but she landed it and we all stuffed ourselves silly. What about the trip to Nazaré? Fin making friends with the porpoise. It swam alongside us for days.'

She nods, clutches herself.

Daniel closes his eyes, opens them. 'All that matters now is Fin. And whether we can save him from this.'

'You matter,' she whispers. 'Please don't forget it. Are you safe in here? If the other prisoners think—'

'You don't need to worry. I've been in places like this before, remember? Just concentrate on finding Fin. Whatever it takes.'

'I love you,' she says.

'Go,' he tells her.

THIRTY-THREE

1

Back on Mortis Point. Home. Although it doesn't feel like that now.

In the bathroom, Lucy runs a shower and rinses the prison off her skin. Afterwards, dressing quickly, she still feels dirty.

Maybe it's not the prison. Maybe it's what she learned inside.

A photo of Fin stands on the dresser. 'I'll find you,' she tells him. She notices Snig at the foot of the bed and ties it around her arm. 'I don't know how, but I will. Because your life's not over, Fin. It's just beginning. And you're my beautiful boy.'

Downstairs, she tours the house, filling a backpack with everything she might need. From the study, duct tape, a retractable Stanley knife, a handheld GPS and a VHF radio. From the kitchen, a bottle of Evian, a packet of pineapple Yoyo Bears, a filleting knife and a carving knife. From the living room, her binoculars. From the wet room, a coil of rope, a flotation belt, two rocket flares and Fin's winter coat.

On the living-room wall hangs a 1908 Pattern cavalry sword, an heirloom passed down from Daniel's great-grandfather. Lucy stares at it a long while before dismissing it. But she does take the man's curve-bladed *kukri* from its display stand on a side table. Nepalese in origin, a thirteen-inch blade curves from its bone handle.

At the breakfast bar in the kitchen she closes her eyes, replaying part of her conversation with Daniel.

He knows you, this guy. At least, he knows of you.

Did he know Billie, too? Clearly, he used her to manipulate Daniel. Did she do it under duress? Or did he deceive her into helping him?

He knows you.

On the counter is her notepad with its list of constructed names. The last one she scrawled there, and by far the most convincing, belongs to Zacarías Echevarria. But on Saturday night, hunched over Daniel's laptop, Lucy had googled him. Zacarías died of a coronary at an Andalusian blackjack table six years ago. She can't think of a single past resident of the Alto Paraíso commune who might bear her ill will.

After Zacarías came Jesús Manzano, in the Portuguese beach town of Zambujeira do Mar. Lucy worked in Manzano's bar, eventually moving into an apartment adjoining his house. But again—despite the Portuguese prosecutor's allegations—they never embarked on a relationship. Manzano treated her like a daughter. When Lucy left town, she did so with his blessing. Years later, when she sailed to Portugal with Daniel and the kids, they visited Manzano for three glorious days.

He said he wanted you to experience a period of self-reflection. A sharp shock and a moral change of course.

Daniel's words describe a monster; a lunatic. But which name, of all those she's written down, might they describe?

It's hell, this. Worse than hell.

She stares hard at her notepad. And realizes, with a lurch, that she can hear music playing from somewhere else in the house.

2

Lucy tilts her head.

Definitely music. It's tinny and distant, like the theme from an old-school video game. From the rucksack she retrieves one of the knives and moves to the door. In the hall, the music's fractionally louder. It's not coming from the ground floor. She's halfway up the stairs when it stops.

Lucy pauses. One of the treads creaks beneath her. She edges closer to the wall, carefully continuing her ascent.

A breeze is blowing through the upper hall, legacy of her feud with the herring gulls. In all the destruction, she hasn't killed a single bird. But she's created multiple entry points into the house.

This guy, he's ruthless, Lucy. You'll have to be ruthless too.

She creeps up to the landing. Stops. Listens.

A door creaks. Billie's, possibly. Or was it Fin's?

Cold air against her face. Could wind have moved the door? Lucy turns her head, wary of someone rushing her from the master bedroom. Now, the bathroom door squeals. She watches it move two inches forward, another inch back. Definitely the wind.

But the next sound she hears isn't a door. It's the music again. And it's coming from Fin's room.

THIRTY-FOUR

Abraham's phone starts ringing as he's leaving Exeter prison. Once he learned Lucy Locke had booked a visit with her husband, he decided to observe their interaction. What he just saw concerns him greatly.

At the hospital, and later during questioning, Daniel Locke indicated an utter hatred of his wife. On Sunday, at the station, Lucy acted like someone in denial of the facts. Neither of them behaved like that today. Abraham couldn't hear their discussion but he witnessed their body language—and saw what looked like two people who loved each other, carefully planning their next move.

Crossing the road to his car, he recalls Beth McKaylin's comments about Lucy Locke.

She's the driving force—the one with the ideas, the power, in that relationship. I don't reckon there was a thing going around in Daniel Locke's head that she didn't know about. If she didn't like it, she'd get rid of it. And if it was still there, it's because she endorsed it.

The more Abraham discovers about Lucy, the more troubled he becomes. Friday lunchtime, while the *Lazy Susan* was drifting offshore,

254

Bee Tavistock had been expecting her boss at the Drift Net. Instead, she found Lucy at home, wet from the shower and working through a mass of paperwork. Or, just possibly, destroying incriminating documents after a high-speed dinghy ride back to land.

When he answers the phone, he hears Cooper's voice.

'We found the dinghy,' the DS tells him. 'Or at least one that matches Lucy's description. Search team discovered it south of Smuggler's Tumble. They just sent over photos. Looks like someone dragged it into the forest above the beach, slashed the air tubes and folded it up. Probably why the shoreline searchers missed it during their sweep. Other than the damage, it seems pretty well maintained. I can't imagine it isn't the one she mentioned. They've got the outboard, too. Not a spot of rust.'

'You've called out Mike Drummond's team?'

'On their way. Although I'm not sure what saltwater and two days' heavy rainfall will have left them. Where are you?'

Abraham reaches his car and slides behind the wheel. He shakes out an OxyContin and swallows it. 'Just leaving Exeter. I'll meet you there.'

Hanging up, he pulls out of the car park. He thinks of Fin Locke, the little storyteller; his curvy chimp ears and gap-toothed smile. If the boy's alive—and it's a *huge* if—he made it back to land in that dinghy.

Abraham recalls his journey with Lucy in the pool car back to Skentel. She'd been so *convincing*—so obviously concerned about her family.

There are six things the Lord hates, seven that are detestable to him: haughty eyes, a lying tongue, hands that shed innocent blood, a heart that devises wicked schemes, feet that are quick to rush into evil, a false witness who pours out lies and a person who stirs up conflict in the community . . .

Abraham had suspected that this started as an insurance fraud and developed into something darker. What he saw at the prison changes that. He knows he's missing something vital. He needs a leap—a connection between two disparate facts; something that will pull together the pieces of this disjointed picture.

Exhaustion washes over him, so heavy that he nearly veers off the road. Abraham grimaces. Leaning forward, he accelerates past the speed limit.

THIRTY-FIVE

1

Often, in her previous life, Lucy had been startled by one of Fin's electronic toys spontaneously reactivating. But she doesn't recognize this melody. As she draws closer to his room, she hears a rhythmic buzzing beneath the music.

Not a toy, she realizes, but a mobile phone.

Lucy's hand tightens on the knife. She arrives in the doorway and steps over the threshold. Fin's room looks just like it did when she last checked: his desk with its pile of half-completed projects; his telescope angled at the sky.

The music stops.

She glances around. So many places to hide a device. At the bookcase, she examines its contents: paperbacks, comics, the collection of die-cast models. Abruptly, the music starts up again.

Lucy turns to the bed. On Fin's pillow lie his neatly folded pyjamas. She pulls them away. And leaps back as if bitten.

There's the phone. A push-button Nokia she's never seen until now.

Malevolence pours off it like poison. The screen glows blue. On it, one word: *UNKNOWN*.

Lucy snatches it up. Her fingers feel numb, her whole arm. She connects the call and holds the phone to her ear.

A crackle of static. An electronic whine.

Her scalp contracts. She thinks of the voicemail from Friday afternoon: *Daddy, no—*

Goosebumps break out across her flesh. She hears a voice and suddenly her bones are like water. Her heart feels as if it'll erupt from her chest. Because she was expecting a demon and instead she hears an angel. '*Hi, Mummy. It's Fin.*'

2

The world is a fairground ride, rolling to a stop. Lucy says her son's name, then screams it. For a moment, her brain seizes. Then: 'Where are you? Tell me where you are, what you can—'

'*Mummy, you need to listen.*'

She puts out a hand to the bookcase. 'OK, I will. Just tell—'

'*I'm going to say something important.*'

Her abdomen feels like someone's plunged in a corkscrew.

'*You found the phone.*'

'Fin?'

He keeps talking. As if he hasn't heard her. '*You need to look for something else.*'

In a flash, Lucy understands. This isn't a live conversation with her boy. It's a broadcast, a recorded message.

The moment she realizes, it starts again.

'*Hi, Mummy. It's Fin.*'

Beat.

'*Mummy, you need to listen.*'

Beat.

'*I'm going to say something important.*'

Beat.

'*You found the phone.*'

Beat.

'*You need to look for something else.*'

Lucy turns, half expecting to find someone in the doorway. But the hall, beyond the bedroom, is empty.

'*Go downstairs, Mummy.*'

Teeth clenched, knife thrust before her, Lucy does as she's instructed.

'*Go to the living room.*'

She complies, sweeping it for intruders. No one lurks by the window. No one waits behind the door. She checks the shadows behind Daniel's houseplants, the blind spots behind the sagging Chesterfields. Wind twines through the broken windows, stirring the heavy drapes. She's alone.

Lucy's gaze moves to the artworks crowding the walls, a collection reflecting two decades of her changing taste. She examines the fireplace— its cast-iron mantel festooned with finials and pilasters.

Her gaze is pulled back to the art. As her eyes move over the paintings, her skin prickles and she shudders. She can't figure out what's wrong, and yet—

'*Mummy, on the bookcase are two books.*' Fin sounds like he's reading from a script. '*One is* The Painted Word. *The other is* The Unknown Masterpiece.'

She scans the shelves for them.

Fin says, '*Mummy, I*—'

The line goes dead.

Lucy rips the phone from her ear. The screen is blank, a smooth, blue oblong. She turns back to the bookcase. On the bottom shelf she finds the two titles Fin mentioned. Between them, the dust jacket of a third is no longer wrapping a book. Lucy puts down her knife and eases it out. When she opens the cover she finds, inside, a Samsung tablet computer.

THIRTY-SIX

Abraham reaches the search location south of Smuggler's Tumble via a steeply descending track. At its terminus lies a gravel car park used by forestry workers and water-sports enthusiasts. A crumbling concrete ramp offers a launching point for boat trailers. Even now, five days since the storm, slow-breaking Atlantic waves are punching hard against it.

He parks beside a BMW with three kayaks strapped to its roof. Already, uniformed officers have set up a cordon. The dinghy lies in tangled woodland twenty metres from the shore. Abraham takes out his phone and pulls up a satellite image of the site.

As the crow flies, they're only a handful of miles from Skentel, but this far south the coastal road is a bunched string, looping in and out of the bays. Friday lunchtime, a few hours before the storm broke, the shoreline here would have been deserted. No houses stand close by, nor any roadside businesses; Bibi Trixibelle Carter's home is far to the north, along with all the others his team doorstepped. Nor is there any ANPR.

So—no risk of prying eyes but also no fast route out; not unless a vehicle was left here in preparation.

Abraham scuffs his feet, kicking up blue gravel. His thoughts return to something that's been bothering him since Saturday; the black hatchback in the lay-by behind Daniel's Volvo. Bibi claimed it wasn't Lucy's Citroën and he's half inclined to believe her. So whose was it?

Earlier in the week, his team analysed the available CCTV footage and noted which black cars showed up. Back then, he was mainly interested in the Citroën. Little reason to tie any others to the one Bibi spotted on Friday. But Abraham doesn't like loose ends.

Three of those vehicles were small hatchbacks: a Vauxhall, a Lexus and a Toyota. The Vauxhall, registered to a Redlecker address, was snapped on the quay on Thursday afternoon, a surfboard strapped to its roof. Friday lunchtime, an ANPR camera captured it near Newquay, ruling it out. The Lexus is registered to a London address, but the Toyota is owned by Barbara Guinness, a seventy-two-year-old widow who lives in Skentel with her son. Twice, Abraham's crossed paths with Matt Guinness, a barman at the Goat Hotel and a highly visible member of the volunteer search team.

Craning his neck, Abraham scans the car park. His gaze returns to the BMW loaded with kayaks.

He frowns, examines it more closely. Something turns over in his gut. He thinks of Beth McKaylin, the lifeboat volunteer who piloted the Lockes' yacht back to harbour, and the black Lexus from the CCTV. Moments later he's back in his car, fishtailing up the track to the coastal road.

THIRTY-SEVEN

1

Lucy takes the Samsung tablet to one of the sofas, sits.

She wakes the device, sees the home screen, hisses with revulsion. The chosen wallpaper is an image of the *Lazy Susan* floating in Skentel's harbour.

The tablet's proprietary apps have been hidden. In their place is a solitary grey thumbnail. Under it, one word: *TRUTH.*

Lucy hovers her finger, taps.

The thumbnail expands to fill the screen. The clarity is sharp but not photo-sharp, a single frame of video. She recognizes the view: the bow of the *Lazy Susan* as seen from the cockpit.

The sea is oily dark. The sky is the colour of a bruise. Lucy knows, instinctively, that she's looking at a shot from Friday morning, just before the storm hit Skentel.

The clip begins to play. The yacht's bow rises and falls in the swell. Then the camera tilts and Lucy nearly loses her grip on the tablet, nearly slides from the sofa to her knees.

'No,' she mutters. 'That can't be.'

Because what she's looking at isn't possible—a distillation of all the world's cruelty into a single shocking image.

She recalls the question she asked Daniel at the prison: *Billie. Did she know? At the end? Did she know what was about to happen? Did she have a long time to be frightened?* Clear, now, the answer to those questions. Lucy can *feel* her heart being crushed.

Sunday morning on Penleith Beach, she'd prayed for the first time in her life, had pleaded with a deity she didn't think existed. But the girl at the water's edge had still turned out to be Billie. Lucy's appeals hadn't worked then and she knows they won't work now. And yet even though it's pointless she can't stop the words coming: *'Please God, please God, please don't let it be, please don't . . .'*

The clip continues to play. Lucy wants to close her eyes, hurl the tablet across the floor.

Instead, she leans closer. Stares at the spectacle unfolding onscreen.

The *Lazy Susan*'s stern is shaped like a sugar scoop. Three built-in swim steps descend from the cockpit to the water. For Lucy, they were always the boat's best feature. In summer she could sit on the bottom step and trail her feet in the sea. The kids could use them as a dive platform. They were an easy launch point for their dinghy.

As the camera swings round, the stern is fully revealed. On the bottom step, facing the bow, stand Lucy's children.

2

Billie's wearing the same clothes she was found in on Penleith Beach: black gym shorts, neon-green T-shirt. Her expression defies belief. There's fear, yes. But overlaying it is something much more extraordinary: dignity, courage, granite-hard resolve. Here is the girl who would have disrupted the annual *grindadráp* despite her horror. Here is the girl who has made Lucy proud every minute of her life.

Beside Billie stands Fin, grey shorts flapping around his legs. His chest rises and falls like a tiny set of bellows. When he looks up at his older sister, he seems to draw strength.

Lucy is praying again, can't stop. She isn't even forming complete words, now. Just sounds of abject misery.

Her children's ankles are bound.

That, of everything, is the hardest thing to see. Sunday morning, on Penleith Beach, Lucy had noticed the ligature marks on her daughter's flesh. Now she knows what caused them.

Beside Billie stand three roped-together oxygen tanks. A coiled line connects them to her bound feet. Fin's line attaches him to a trio of cast-iron weightlifting plates.

So far, the video has played in silence. Now, for the first time, Lucy hears sound—wind, water, the clang of a halyard, the creak of the *Lazy Susan*'s boom.

Behind Billie and Fin, the sea is steadily building its strength. The yacht heaves up through the water, rolls from side to side.

The camera lingers on Lucy's children a few seconds longer. Then it swings around. For the first time, she sees inside the cockpit. There, staring at her through the lens, is Daniel.

3

His wrist is cuffed to the *Lazy Susan*'s starboard winch. He looks *grey*, his skin the same shade as the sea. His eyes betray his emotions: terror, impotence, rage.

Lucy hears a voice, then: '*Choose.*'

Daniel stiffens. He glances towards the stern.

'*That's right,*' the voice continues. '*You get to save one of them. In a way, Daniel, you get to play God. I know it's difficult. Big decisions always are. If you choose to do nothing, they both go into the water.*'

The camera tracks left and pans around. Now, all three of her family are in shot. '*Imagine Lucy's pain if you remained silent, and because of you she lost them both.*'

Daniel's lungs are working as hard as Fin's. He jerks his tethered wrist, grimacing as the steel cuff bites flesh.

'*Choose. That's your only option. Tell me who to put in the water. Billie? Or your son.*'

Lucy's gripping the tablet so tightly her forearms start to shake. 'Oh fuck, Daniel,' she moans. 'Oh no, please.'

She doesn't want to know. Doesn't want to see this play out. And yet she can't look away, has to be there for her daughter's last moments, even if her daughter's already gone.

The screen goes black.

Lucy screams.

At first she thinks the batteries have failed, but when she presses the power button the home screen reappears. There's the *Lazy Susan*, sitting in Skentel's harbour. The grey thumbnail—*TRUTH*—has disappeared.

Lucy drops the tablet. Sinks from the sofa to the floor. She's breathing too fast—as if she's going into labour. Gritting her teeth, she tries to insert obscenities into the gaps between her breaths.

The curses come haltingly at first. Then faster, more aggressively. By degrees, she turns her wretchedness into rage. She crawls to the bookcase where she left the knife. Closes her fingers around it. For a moment, all she can think of is silencing the creature behind that voice. But first she has to save her son.

Lucy looks around the room, hardly recognizing what she sees. Once, she believed that items in this house gained value as they aged: the scarred furniture, the chipped crockery, the art on the walls.

No longer. The collected ephemera aren't just worthless but something far worse—a source of agony; a reminder of what was.

As her gaze moves over the framed paintings, that sense returns of something wrong. It's so outlandish she nearly dismisses it. Because *everything* is wrong. Her life—all their lives—has been comprehensively destroyed by whichever ghoul decided to target her.

Still, that feeling of wrongness persists. Lucy takes a steadying breath. She smells woodsmoke, damp soil, the fleshy scent of the succulents. She's never been one to doubt her gut. She's not going to start now.

Her vision has started to skip, the result of too much adrenalin. She blinks, shakes her head, tries to throw off the effects. The savagery of what she just witnessed is impossible to set aside. And yet if she's to stand any chance of saving Fin, that's exactly what she must do.

Lucy clenches her fists, screams again.

It helps. A little. Releases some of the pressure. Her gaze sweeps the wall. There are too many paintings for the space, but this room was never a gallery. Back in her old life, the haphazardly curated art made her happy.

You get to save one of them. In a way, Daniel, you get to play God. I know it's difficult. Big decisions always are. If you choose to do nothing, they both go into the water.

She recoils from those words as if they're barbed wire. And yet somewhere in her head a door opens. She's heard that voice before. And recently. She just can't place where. It's different to how she remembers. As if it's trying to disguise its true timbre.

Tell me who to put in the water. Billie? Or your son.

The answer is somewhere in her head. She just has to find it.

Lucy closes her eyes, opens them, scans the paintings.

And notices something odd.

Watching you these last few days has been more distressing than I ever imagined. You're a broken bird, still trying your best to sing, still telling yourself you can bring Fin home if only you're strong enough.

It's a false hope, Lucy. The only thing more tragic than the future I've dealt you is your presumption that it can be stopped, that I can be stopped. It adds a layer of cruelty I never intended.

It can't have been easy seeing the footage. Did you weep for Billie? Did you cry out for Daniel? Or did you scream at him for what he chose? Did you want to watch through to the end? Or are you glad I withheld her last moments?

We're approaching the denouement. I know it'll be devastating for us both. Never, at the outset, did I expect to be so emotionally invested. This tragedy was written entirely for your benefit. And yet in bearing witness, I'm finding my own salvation.

THIRTY-EIGHT

1

South of Skentel, the Penny Moon campsite stands atop a granite head-land that offers astonishing views of the sea. A Georgian-built lighthouse marks the site's northern border.

Abraham parks in an area reserved for new arrivals. Opposite, a single-storey building serves as office, toilet block and shop. A raisable barrier controls site access.

Inside, the front desk is unstaffed. There's a bell, which Abraham presses. Moments later, Beth McKaylin appears from a backroom.

'Oh,' she says, pulling up short. 'You.'

The woman is as well muscled and self-assured as he remembers. She's wearing hiking boots, denim shorts and a grubby vest beneath her plaid work shirt. Cocking a hip, she examines him. 'Well, it's off-season, so I can do you a good price. That is, unless there's something else you're after.'

2

Since Abraham's second visit to Bibi Trixibelle Carter, where he showed her the black hatchbacks captured by the quayside CCTV, something's been itching at him: the small green sticker visible on the Lexus's windscreen.

Earlier, at the dinghy recovery site, he parked next to a BMW loaded with kayaks. On its windscreen he found a matching green sticker. Close up, he could see the image printed on it: a black crescent moon poking through black clouds.

Immediately, he'd recalled his interview on Saturday with Beth McKaylin. Her undershirt had featured the same logo. Just now, he saw it on the flags flapping from the Penny Moon's poles.

Retreating behind the counter, McKaylin grabs a handful of vinyl stickers. 'I get a new batch printed every year,' she tells him. 'Green this season, purple the one just gone. It's how we identify guests. Means we can operate the barrier from here without having to traipse outside.'

'You keep a record of each guest's vehicle?'

'Make, model and registration number.'

'Can you—' Abraham begins. And then he groans, fingers splayed. Pain spreads out across his back, deep and sickening.

McKaylin tilts her head. 'You OK?'

Abraham can't speak. He leans against the counter, breath coming in bursts. This is bad. Really bad. He grinds his teeth, tastes blood, gradually rides out the wave. Finally, he says, 'Looking for a car.'

Initially, it's all he can manage. Somehow, he adds, 'Before you say "data protection—"'

'Data protection, my arse. What do you need? Other than an ambulance.'

Abraham can't speak again. There's a pad on the counter. He scrawls down the Lexus's registration number.

McKaylin tears off the top sheet. 'Seriously—you want me to call a doctor?'

He shakes his head, points.

Going behind the desk, she opens her ledger and searches through it. 'Oh, *this* guy. He's been here a while. Said he came here to paint.'

'Name?'

'Manning. Richard Manning.'

That's not the name on the Lexus's logbook. Through the window, Abraham counts two pitched tents and a single caravan. 'Where do I find him?'

'Not in any of those,' McKaylin says. 'I rented him that.'

Abraham follows the direction of her finger all the way to the sea cliff, and the Georgian-built lighthouse standing upon it.

THIRTY-NINE

1

Lucy has chosen every single painting that hangs on these walls. The collection represents a passion stretching back to adolescence, to a time before Billie and long before Daniel or Fin. In recent years it's spilled out of this room, marching into the hall, up the stairs, to other parts of this huge, old house. But the paintings in here have the longest history.

And she sees, now, that one of them is new.

It hangs on the wall furthest from the mullioned windows, near the bookcase where she found the Samsung tablet. It's a drab watercolour of Skentel's harbour—the kind of painting that clutters countless charity shops and gift shops.

As Lucy draws closer, she notices something that clearly wasn't part of the original work. The addition is tiny but cleverly done. Out beyond Skentel's breakwater floats the *Lazy Susan*. The bow is submerged, the stern angled up. Beside the boat float two abandoned lifejackets.

Lucy snatches the picture off the wall. She turns it over, half expecting to find a message scrawled on the back, some kind of instruction or taunt. But all she sees are the canvas's wooden battens.

And then she hears music.

In her pocket, the phone vibrates against her leg.

2

Not a call, this time, but a text message.

WANT TO SEE FIN? Y/N

Lucy blinks at the screen. Her brain has slowed down again. She forces more oxygen into her lungs and texts back: *Yes*.

Almost immediately, the phone buzzes with a response.

PREPARED TO MAKE A SACRIFICE? Y/N

Lucy texts *Yes*. She pauses, then types: *Tell me why*. She hits send, waits. Half a minute passes before the response arrives.

KATHARSIS.

I don't understand.

RENEWAL.

What does that mean?

A longer pause. Then:

YOU HURT PEOPLE.
YOU DON'T REALIZE IT, BUT YOU DO.

Lucy crumples a little as she reads that. Because it's proof, irrefutable, that this nightmare represents a very personal form of vengeance. She thinks of Billie, lying cold on Penleith Beach; Daniel, sitting broken in the prison visiting hall; Fin, reduced to a recorded voice on a throwaway mobile phone.

How did she invite this into their lives? What did she do?

The phone buzzes. More text, this time—a list of instructions. Lucy scrolls through them, her stomach hollowing out. She has no choice but to comply. Clear, now, that the intention from the start has been to destroy every pillar of her existence. Her only hope is to play along and pray she gets a chance to fight back. Crazy, even so, to obey these demands without question. She hunches over the phone, clicking the little plastic keys.

I want to speak to Fin. Not a recording this time. Before I do this, I want to know for sure he's still alive.

Lucy sends the message before she can reconsider. Then she exhales explosively. There's still far too much adrenalin flowing through her system. She zips the knife back into the rucksack, checks the phone: no reply.

She goes to the corner, retrieves the painting. Looks, again, at the image of their upturned boat. Examines the lighter patch on the wall left by the previous artwork to hang there.

Her fingers tingle. She studies the charity-shop painting again, then the wall. She's close. *So* close. The revelation hovers just out of reach.

Still no response to her demand. Did she go too far? To distract herself, she moves to the window and scans the water through her binoculars.

Katharsis, she thinks. An ancient Greek word for purification.

It transports her to the philosophy classes she took, back in her old life. Aristotle was the first to link katharsis to tragedy. He proposed that the experience of tragic events was purgative, purifying body and soul. But Aristotle's focus was the dramatic works of early theatre, not real life.

Lucy checks the phone. No message.

Where has she heard that voice before? Because she *has* heard it, even though it sounded different. Of that she's absolutely sure.

She looks at her watch. Just under two hours until sunset. Lucy trains her binoculars on Skentel.

Steadily, the town is recovering from Friday's storm. The telephone pole that came down has been re-erected. Men in fluorescent jackets are working on the buildings that lost their roofs. In the harbour, the yacht that was floating keel-up now sits along the quay.

Katharsis, she thinks.

And then the phone starts ringing.

FORTY

Lucy's praying again. Praying and fumbling with the phone. Her fingers don't work. The handset nearly slips from her hands. Praying turns to cursing turns to panic.

And then, somehow, the Nokia is at her ear and she's listening to static, an electronic squeal. Reception in Skentel has always been poor. She fears the connection's going to die.

'Mummy?'

The voice is a hammer blow.

'Fin?'

'Mummy, Billie went in the water. And Daddy went in too.'

Her little boy sounds broken, fundamentally changed. Gone is his melodramatic inflection, his theatrical way of speaking. In its place is a weariness that piles her heart with rocks. 'Fin,' she says. 'Oh, my sweet. Mummy's here, OK? I'm doing everything I can to come and get you. Are you hurt? Has he—'

'They died, Mummy. And then the man sank our Water Home.'

She closes her eyes. Fin hasn't just been mourning his sister. He's been mourning Daniel, too.

'Daddy's alive,' Lucy says. 'A helicopter saved him. He's alive and he's safe and he's going to be *so happy* to see you.'

A pause. 'Real?'

'For real, Fin. I swear.'

'Is he there?'

'Not right now. But you'll see him ever so soon. OK, darling?'

A pause. A sniffle. 'I lost Snig.'

'I found him.'

'You did?'

'I have him here. He was in the back of my car. You must have left him there before school.'

'That's good.' He swallows noisily. 'Mummy?'

'Yes, darling?'

'Please be quick.'

Lucy's pain is physical now. Her chest feels like it's inside a vice. 'Fin, I'll be as—'

The line goes dead.

She screams. The third time in an hour.

Movement beyond the broken window. She looks up to see three herring gulls land on the back lawn.

FORTY-ONE

1

In the office, Beth McKaylin turns from the lighthouse to Abraham. 'Is this connected to what happened on Friday? Billie Locke's death?'

'It could be, yes.'

She nods, pulling a key fob from a rack. 'I don't see his car. You want to take a look?'

The lighthouse climbs five storeys, a red-painted lantern room crowning its tapered white walls. They use a golf buggy to reach it. Outside, instead of a Lexus, Abraham sees a red Renault Clio so old its paint has started to lift.

McKaylin hammers on the lighthouse door. When there's no answer, she lets them both inside. An L-shaped kitchen opens on to a tastefully decorated dining area. Beyond it, a sofa and two reading chairs are arranged around a wood burner. The view through the west-facing windows is of cold Atlantic sea.

The place looks spotless. Vacated.

Upstairs, the beds in both rooms have been neatly made. In the master, a single packed suitcase is the only evidence of occupation. Abraham ignores it for now. 'Can we access the main tower?'

McKaylin leads him through a doorway set into a curved wall of bare brick.

It's a remarkable space, perfectly circular. Sanded boards and white-washed walls. A spiral staircase offers access to the upper floors. A west-facing window admits an oval of sky and sea.

In the centre of the room stands an artist's easel. Abraham saw the same type in Wayland Rawlings' hobby shop. Leaning against the wall are three large packages wrapped in grey polythene.

He coughs into his fist, bites down on his pain.

'You want to get that checked out,' McKaylin tells him. Uninvited, she picks up the largest package and places it on the easel. Then she offers him a penknife. 'Shall we?'

Abraham considers. Then he takes the knife and cuts off the wrapping. They both stand back.

'Holy shit.'

The painting is a chocolate-box rendering of Skentel. All the town's landmarks are represented, contemporary and historic. Abraham recognizes the lifeboat station, the Goat Hotel, the Norman church, the Drift Net and the hobby shop.

But where this image differs from the reality is the river of dark blood running down the high street and spilling into the harbour.

A foul smell seeps from the canvas. McKaylin says, 'I've got a horrible feeling that's real blood.'

2

Outside, Abraham goes to the Renault Clio and peers through the driver's window. The interior's a mess: cracked CD cases, carrier bags filled with rubbish, petrol receipts, bundled up T-shirts, empty Coke cans. Pulling on a latex glove, Abraham tries the door. When it pops open, he ducks in his head.

Whoever hid the dinghy south of Smuggler's Tumble needed an escape vehicle. It couldn't have been Daniel's Volvo, found abandoned on the quay. Nor could it have been the black hatchback Bibi spotted in the lay-by before and after her vet visit.

The Clio's interior smells of mildew and some kind of medical ointment. In the driver's footwell Abraham notices five blueish chips of gravel. They're strikingly similar to those covering the car park at the dinghy site.

It's not a slam dunk, by any measure. Not until Forensics take a look.

Pain radiates from his chest. Abraham ignores it. He needs to find Lucy Locke, and fast.

FORTY-TWO

1

Lucy doesn't bother with a crash helmet. After pocketing the Nokia and throwing on the rucksack, she climbs on the Triumph and kicks down on the starter. The bike sprays shingle as it turns on to the lane.

Her feeling, growing each moment, is that she's heading to her death. The prospect frightens her less than she'd imagined. If she can rescue Fin and prove Daniel's innocence, at least they'll have each other. As she cycles up through the gears, she marvels at her new-found composure.

Katharsis, she thinks. *Purification through tragedy.*

And then it hits her.

2

Lucy recalls the charity-shop artwork with its macabre addition. She sees the lighter patch on her living-room wall, legacy of the previous painting that hung there. Years ago, an art teacher told her to look for what she *couldn't* see, not just what she could. Now, recalling that paler patch, she recalls the artwork that created it.

The Triumph hits a slick of wet leaves, nearly slides out from under her. But Lucy can't afford caution, can't afford to slough off any speed. Leaning into another bend, she balances between past and present.

Over the years, as her tastes evolved, her art collection evolved too. She never held on to pieces that no longer gave her joy—with only two exceptions: any work she personally commissioned and any work created for her as a gift.

The missing painting, she remembers, is a portrait.

Not of how Lucy looks now, at thirty-seven. Nor how she looked at the time. Instead, the artist sought to capture her in old age.

The resulting depiction wasn't flattering. Possibly due to a lack of talent. Perhaps because the artist didn't understand how life shapes a face, or how old age means more than mere attrition.

Admittedly, some features were recognizably Lucy's. But the eyes expressed no humanity. The overall result had all the life of a cadaver.

Lucy's always believed that good art creates emotion—although not necessarily emotion that uplifts. Visual art can be as difficult to witness as dramatic tragedy. It can *depict* tragedy, can capture a dramatic moment and distil it.

But *that* painting was something different. Lucy's unease came not from the image itself but from what it might say about the artist and the artist's feelings about her. Was it painted as a message? A warning she ignored?

At the end of the lane, Lucy turns on to the coastal road and opens the throttle. On her right, the Atlantic keeps pace. She daren't take her eyes off the road but she can feel the ocean regardless, there like it's always been. It took away Billie. It brought Billie home. It might take Fin. It'll almost certainly take her.

Katharsis, she thinks. *Purification through tragedy.*

Her jaw pops as she clenches it.

Hard to believe what she's abandoning. Harder to countenance where this leads. Impossible to consider how it ends.

Here's the turning for Skentel. Once she's through the switchbacks, the town begins to reveal itself. Locals scramble to safety as she blasts through the high street. Without her crash helmet, she's easily recognizable. She sees startled faces, shocked looks.

Lucy passes the Goat Hotel, the Bayleaf, the tiny Norman church of St Peter's. She thinks of its pastor, Luke Creese, and his words to her at the vigil: *God doesn't always offer us answers, Lucy. In this life, we may never really know why some things have happened.*

She'll never understand why *this* happened. But she does know it has to end. And it *will* end, today. Although likely not the way she hopes.

Lucy can see the harbour now; the lifeboat station and breakwater wall. At least she doesn't have to look at the *Lazy Susan*—a marine police unit has towed it to another port.

On the quay, she passes Gordon and Jane Watson's pharmacy and the hobby shop owned by Wayland Rawlings. And then she's rolling to a stop outside the Drift Net.

Lucy grunts when she sees the windows. The supersized images of Billie and Fin are twin kicks to the gut. She gets off the bike and opens the front door.

Music is playing inside. A group of trawlermen stands around the pool table. Three other tables host solitary drinkers. A fourth punter leans against the bar.

This late in the day, Bee has been replaced by Tyler, who runs the evening shift. Lucy sees him chatting to the customer at the bar. Tyler's late thirties, an easy-going surfer. She's always liked him. A shame this is how he'll remember her.

Lucy fills her lungs. 'Everybody out!' she yells. 'Out of my bar *now!*'

3

The conversation dies. The music continues to play.

The Drift Net's customers stare at her as if she's insane. Emil Potts, skipper of the *Tandem Tackle*, lays down his pool cue and raises his hands.

'Easy, Luce,' he says. 'You're among friends here. I know how much you've been suffering.'

The empathy she sees in Emil's eyes is almost too much, but she doesn't have time for niceties. 'Get the fuck out, Emil. Tyler, you too. *NOW!*'

To emphasize her point, Lucy kicks over the trawlermen's drinks table. Then she snatches up the pool cue and rips open the door. 'I swear to God, if you haven't all left in the next ten seconds . . .'

'OK, we're going,' Emil says. 'Whatever you want, OK? Just . . . we'll get out of your hair.'

Tyler comes around the bar, ushering the other punters ahead of him. 'Luce, is there anything—'

'*Leave,*' she hisses, slamming and locking the door behind them. She flips the sign to closed. Then she drags a bench table across the entrance.

Just her, now, and the music.

The track on the stereo changes: 'A Change Is Gonna Come' by Sam Cooke. It's one of Daniel's favourite songs—one of hers, too. Through the windows she sees Tyler, Emil and the others peering in. Lucy angles her head, looking past them to the RNLI boathouse high above the quay. Lights are shining inside, like they do every day of the year.

Her gaze returns to the harbour, to the boats bobbing on the water. She knows it's the last time she'll get this view. She drinks it in for a few seconds. Then she goes to the windows and lowers the blinds.

She built this place the same way Daniel built Locke-Povey Marine, from what was once a dilapidated wreck. So much work has gone into it over the years, so much attention and love.

Lucy checks the Nokia. No new messages. Then she goes to her office.

Someone's cleared up since she was last here. Her smashed iMac has been removed. The spilled box files have been tidied away. She puts the Nokia on the desk and sits. On the wall is a photo of her family: that shot onboard the *Lazy Susan*. Daniel's cuddling the kids. Billie's smiling. Fin's bent double with laughter. Lucy can't remember what had tickled her son. Until his classmates made him invisible, he'd found most things in life hysterical.

Ignoring the Nokia, Lucy picks up the office phone. She checks the contact sheet on the wall and dials. The call is answered on the second ring.

'Hi,' she says. 'It's me.'

Silence on the line. Then: 'Are you OK?'

Lucy laughs. She reaches out and touches Fin's face. 'Not really. Listen, I don't have much time. I just wanted . . . I wanted to say sorry. I know I've caused you a lot of pain.'

More silence. Finally, Jake Farrell says, 'A long time ago, Lucy. Ancient history.'

'Maybe. But I still needed to say it.'

'Are you in trouble?' he asks. 'Is that why you're calling? Because if you are, you know I'll help.'

Lucy closes her eyes. She has no right to ask Jake anything; not after how badly she's treated him. 'I can't—'

'You can,' he says. 'More than anyone else, you can ask me. Billie wasn't my daughter, but I loved her like one. I still do.'

Listening to him speak, Lucy recalls *Huntsman's Daughter*'s cabin: the woollen pompom her daughter once made crowning a brass barometer on the bulkhead; the faint marks from the girl's colouring pencils still visible on Jake's chart table. Right now, the tiniest examples of Billie's impact on the world feel sacred.

'I don't believe Daniel's guilty,' Jake continues. 'If I'm right, and I think I am, you're going to need help with whatever it is you're facing.'

Is she manipulating him even now? Did she call Jake knowing he'd offer assistance, and knowing she'd accept? Opening her eyes, she begins to talk.

4

Afterwards, she carries the Nokia through to the bar. Ten minutes, now, since she left the house. Grabbing a tumbler, she fills it with sparkling water from the gun. She drinks until it's empty, checks the phone.

Nothing.

Lucy runs her fingers across the bar top, a single oak slab recovered from a naval sloop. She bought it at auction in Okehampton, driving it here on the bed of Daniel's truck. She sanded and varnished it herself, just like she sanded and varnished the floorboards beneath her feet.

Sam Cooke stops singing. Amy Winehouse replaces him: 'You Know I'm No Good'.

Lucy picks up her empty tumbler. This time she jams it under the Herradura Añejo. When the optic refills itself, she hits it for another measure.

She checks the Nokia again: nothing.

Lifting the glass to her lips, she downs the tequila in two large gulps. The phone buzzes. Lucy snatches it up.

I SAW

Her hand shakes as she types.

I did what you asked. I'll do what you ask now.

I KNOW.

Don't hurt him.

Please.

No response to that. Sixty seconds of pain before the phone buzzes once more. It's another list of instructions. Quickly, she reads through them.

Katharsis, she thinks. *Purification through tragedy.*

Or—in this case—purification through self-destruction.

When she lifts her rucksack from the floor, she hears the knives clink and scrape. There are sharper objects in the Drift Net's kitchen. Perhaps she should find herself one. Instead, she picks up the Nokia and starts to type.

Before I do it, I want proof. A photo of Fin.

A PHOTO PROVES NOTHING.

It'll prove you're where you say you are.

She puts down the phone. Just her and Amy Winehouse now. It feels like she's playing chess, with Fin as her last piece on the board.

The phone buzzes. A photo file, this time. Lucy opens it, fumbles the Nokia and nearly drops it. Her heart slams. If the phone breaks, any chance of saving Fin will be lost.

Gingerly, she turns the screen towards her.

Katharsis, she thinks. *Purification through tragedy.*

The tequila burns her stomach. Lucy thinks she's going to be sick.

The phone's screen resolution is terrible but the figure in the photo is unmistakeably her boy. He still has his glasses. She's grateful for that. But he's lost his trademark smile.

Lucy just wants to hold him. And if she can't do that, she wants to make sure someone else can. Opening the rucksack, she takes out the notepad and pen. The top sheet is her list of names—pointless, now she knows who's responsible. She rips it off, starts writing. When she's finished, she gets to work.

FORTY-THREE

As the Penny Moon campsite disappears from the rear-view mirror, Abraham speed-dials Barnstaple. He gets through to a female DS and barks out a list of instructions. 'I need a background check, too,' he adds. 'Everything you can find in fifteen minutes, no longer.'

'What's the name?'

Abraham tells her. Then he tosses the phone on to the passenger seat. He's already breaking the speed limit. It's a challenge just keeping the car on the road. Each bend reveals a new hazard: toppled trees or road signs, long patches of standing water.

In his head, a theory is forming. He doesn't like it much but he thinks it might be true. It *would* prove Daniel Locke's been lying to him—Lucy Locke, too. It wouldn't prove their involvement in Billie's drowning, nor Fin's disappearance. Quite the opposite.

Twice, as a child, Daniel escaped his violent home only to be returned there by the very police force charged with his protection. In Portugal, the Polícia Judiciária investigated Lucy for attempted murder before a jury ruled her innocent.

Little wonder, if the couple are in trouble, they haven't placed their trust in Abraham. Especially considering what's at stake.

Sweat beads on his forehead, rolls from his armpits. When he breathes, he catches his own reek—like raw chicken past its date. Rolling his tongue around his mouth, he tastes blood.

For the first time, Abraham admits he's frightened. Frightened of his disease. Frightened, not just of death itself, but the actual mechanics of dying.

He's seen it often enough. He's watched people in their last moments, has witnessed that look of existential panic swell and then seize; the body a stopped clock. Never has it failed to shock him. Always, in the past, he's consoled himself with the knowledge that the deceased has departed for somewhere new.

What if he's wrong? What if he's been wrong all this time?

Abraham chokes, coughs. A mist of pink droplets sprays the windscreen. He activates the wipers, but they don't clear the mess. Checking his speed, he realizes he's doing eighty.

Rain starts to fall. Slow, fat drops at first, as if the clouds are testing their strength. Through the side window he catches glimpses of sea. The water out there is oily dark, black skin stretched over liquid muscle. It reminds him of the weather front he saw on Friday—the shelf cloud racing in from the Atlantic. Contemplating it, a description of the End Times had rung in his head:

And there will be signs in sun and moon and stars, and on the earth distress of nations in perplexity because of the roaring of the sea and the waves, people fainting with fear and with foreboding of what is coming on the world.

He needs a cigarette.

Snagging a pack from the door pocket, he pulls out a smoke with his teeth. He lights it, takes a drag, sprays a lungful of blood and diseased gak over the steering wheel.

It's a disgusting habit. He wishes he'd never started.

A sign blips past: *SKENTEL 2 MILES.*

Abraham takes another drag. This one he manages to hold in his chest.

Perhaps he wouldn't be so afraid of death if he thought someone would remember him. He wonders if Bibi Trixibelle Carter will remember.

The road narrows, winding closer to the sea cliffs. Abraham looks north-west. He frowns, stubs out the cigarette. When his phone starts ringing, he snatches it up.

'I'm down by the shore,' Cooper says. 'You're not going to believe this, but—'

'I see it,' Abraham says. 'Have you called—'

'I've called everyone.'

'Good. I'm two minutes away.'

FORTY-FOUR

It's time.

Lucy grabs a baseball cap from behind the bar and screws it on to her head. Grabbing her rucksack, she takes one last look around.

The Drift Net.

So many memories.

Again, she touches the bar top's oak slab, feeling the grain and the varnish. Then she wrinkles her nose. It's just a piece of wood. This place is just a bar; a gallery; a music venue. Part of a life that no longer exists. Old news.

But there's one thing she can't leave behind.

When the Drift Net first opened, Billie was twelve years old. To celebrate its first night, she drew Lucy a picture of the venue. Billie's Drift Net is populated not with humans but with sea creatures. In it, pufferfish and manta rays nurse pints of seawater. At the pool table, two purple octopuses wield cues while a couple of great whites serve drinks behind the bar. Onstage, the band features a starfish on drums, two lobsters on guitar, a turtle playing keyboards and a singing seal. Sea urchins, clownfish and hermit crabs form the crowd.

Daniel framed the picture using driftwood gathered from Penleith Beach. Lucy hung it over the bar, where it's lived ever since.

Now, unhooking it, she stuffs it into her rucksack. Then she lets herself out through the fire exit.

The back alley is deserted—just a few commercial-waste bins and a stack of broken pallets. Halfway along it, a walkway between the Watsons' pharmacy and Wayland Rawlings' hobby shop leads back to the waterfront.

Lucy emerges into the midst of a growing crowd. Not just Tyler and Emil and the others she ejected from the Drift Net. Upwards of thirty people are standing on the quay, with more swarming on to it from the high street. Everyone is gazing up at Mortis Point.

The peninsula's granite cliffs rise hundreds of feet, forming a natural boundary between Skentel to the south and Penleith Beach to the north. Up there, above the coastal trees crowning the summit, a column of black smoke gushes into the sky.

Wild Ridge is burning with a savagery hard to comprehend. The flames aren't orange but a deep, sooty red. Already, half the building is alight. Fire twists from every window on its southern side.

Even though she expected to see it, Lucy can't tear her eyes away. The fire she started in the hallway has spread much faster than she'd anticipated. She thinks of everything inside—the scarred furniture, the chipped crockery, the art on the walls. She thinks of all the life lived inside those walls; all the laughter and music and love.

Oddly, it doesn't affect her too acutely. Perhaps she's too numb to express any more sorrow. Before others on the quay notice her presence, she finds Tyler and pulls him aside.

'I know you think I'm crazy,' she tells him, ignoring his startled look. 'Maybe the truth'll come out. Maybe it won't. But Daniel didn't drown Billie and Fin's not dead.'

'Luce, are you—'

'No time. Here, take this.' Into his hands she presses the letter she just wrote inside the Drift Net. 'This needs to go to Detective Inspector Abraham Rose. Big guy, craggy face. I'm sure he'll be down here soon.'

'I know him,' Tyler says. 'He was down a few days ago asking questions. Luce, you've—'

She shakes her head. 'I need one more thing. And please, Ty—Fin's life might depend on it. Don't say where I've gone, OK? If anyone asks, you didn't see.'

Lucy knows from his eyes that she can trust him. She kisses his cheek and jumps from the quay to the floating dock. When she clambers aboard Jake's yacht, she sees that the hatch is already unlocked. A key has been left in the ignition.

Lucy throws down her backpack and casts off the mooring lines. She flicks the ignition key to the left, heating the glow plugs. Then she twists it to the right.

Nothing on her first two attempts. On her third, the engine thrums beneath her. Engaging the throttle, Lucy spins the wheel. The boat responds, edging out from the dock. She glances back at the quay. The crowd is too engaged with the fire on Mortis Point to pay *Huntsman's Daughter* any attention. Fanned by the wind, those crimson flames reach higher. The entire roof is burning now. Greasy black smoke churns into the sky.

Once the bow has swung around, Lucy throttles up. Jake's yacht follows the breakwater wall, heading for open sea.

FORTY-FIVE

Abraham Rose rockets along the lane that winds over Mortis Point. The smoke from the house fire blows east towards him. Within moments it starts seeping into the car. He tastes it when he breathes, feels it scratching at his throat. When he rounds a bend, he can hardly believe what he's seeing.

Wild Ridge is a grand old house, Georgian in roots. Two centuries of modifications have added a hotchpotch of styles. A Victorian turret room wears a witch's-cap roof reminiscent of Carcassonne. An Arts and Crafts-style wing branches off along one side.

The building is an inferno. Smoke like boiling tar rolls thick overhead. When Abraham opens the car door, he feels the heat on his face. He hears timbers cracking, glass shattering, structures inside the house starting to collapse. As he watches, a portion of the roof falls in. A huge gout of flame licks out.

Doubtless Cooper will have raised the alarm, but Abraham can't hear sirens. The fire station in Bude is fifteen miles south; Barnstaple's is even further. On these roads, even if they blue-light it, they'll arrive just in time to stamp out ashes.

Abraham turns the car around and accelerates back down the lane. His flesh smells like dead poultry and his lungs are sprayed halfway across the windscreen. And yet he feels oddly invigorated. *Lucy Locke*, he thinks. *She's your task. She's why you're still alive. Whatever the truth of this, Lucy Locke needs your help.*

In his rear-view mirror he sees the entire south wall of Wild Ridge bow out and collapse, releasing a torrent of sparks and ash.

FORTY-SIX

1

Back to where it all began. Back to the sea.

Lucy points *Huntsman's Daughter* west. The water is restless but not violent, rising to gentle heights without breaking. She unties Snig from her arm and secures it to the wheel. Then, unzipping the rucksack, she takes out the filleting knife and slides it into her back pocket. Retrieving the flotation belt, Lucy clips it around her waist.

The Nokia vibrates against her leg. She checks the screen. No message this time, just numbers.

50.9407

-4.7734

With her binoculars, she scans the sea for other boats. A few trawlers are moving southwards. North-east, an oil tanker is crawling towards the Bristol Channel; beyond it, just visible, the shivery grey shape of a freighter. She sees no yachts or motor launches. The recent bad weather has chased all the weekend sailors back to port.

Lucy loops the binoculars around her neck. She switches on her GPS and plugs in the coordinates. While the device connects to available satellites, she glances past the stern to the inferno engulfing Wild Ridge.

Katharsis, she thinks. *Purification through tragedy.*

Already, she's a mile offshore. According to the GPS, her destination lies much further west. Lifting the binoculars, she searches the horizon. Nothing out there except ocean and sky.

No surprise. At her current position, the Earth's curvature limits her view. She's got at least another two miles before she'll learn if she's been deceived. At seven knots, that's just over fifteen minutes.

Lucy finds, suddenly, that she's crying. And that strangely, out here, it doesn't matter. The sea pays no attention to her tears. It doesn't react to her pain.

If she's going to die, at least she's on the water, breathing ocean air. She thinks of Daniel, imprisoned. How much worse to be there, utterly powerless. She closes her eyes, just for a moment, as an even more vivid image forms.

Fin.

Her boy.

Her star-gazing, card-sorting little bookworm. Her weaver of words, her teller of fine tales, her storyteller extraordinaire. How sharp, the pain of her love for him. How immense, the responsibility to bring him home.

Before his birth, she carried an image of what her son would be like. Fin confounded all her expectations—not physically robust, like she'd imagined, but contemplative and inquisitive, funny, insightful and astute. His fragility enhances rather than diminishes him, makes her love him all the more fiercely.

Less than a mile, now, until that spot in the ocean reveals itself.

Lucy recalls the video she watched: her children standing on the *Lazy Susan's* swim step; Daniel, cuffed to the winch. Thinking of that image weakens her, so she pushes it away. She needs cunning now, not grief or rage. She needs to empty her head of emotion—bury, particularly, any thoughts of vengeance. She's not here to end a life but to save one.

A herring gull cries out. Lucy spots it flanking the yacht. She gri-maces—wants to hurl her knife and cleave it from the sky. Instead, she lifts the binoculars. And sees, on the horizon, the pale shape of another boat.

2

It's her target.

Nothing else it can be. That's not the profile of a trawler or any other commercial vessel. It's the sleek outline of a yacht.

Strange, how much calmer the sea is this far from shore. The wind has dropped to a preternatural calm. Off the stern there's no sight of land—nothing but dimpled water and granite sky.

For the first time, Lucy realizes how cold she is, how stiff her fingers and muscles. She clenches her fists, stamps her feet, forces the blood to her extremities. Then she retrains her binoculars on the boat.

Closer now. She can make out a little more detail. Furled sails, a single white mast.

Her skin prickles.

Lucy retrieves the duct tape from her rucksack and uses the Stanley knife to cut several strips. She secures the carving knife and two rocket flares to a vertical board beside the wheel. Then she takes out the antique *kukri*. With more duct tape, she secures its leather scabbard to the boom and stuffs the Stanley knife into the front pocket of her shirt. Retrieving the Evian bottle, she takes a drink.

Closer, closer.

Details begin to emerge.

The other boat's a racing yacht. Larger than *Huntsman's Daughter*; smaller than the *Lazy Susan*; far more modern than either. She sees its name—the *Cetus*—and wonders if it's a taunt; Cetus was the monster sent by Poseidon to punish Andromeda's parents for their arrogance.

Movement, now, near the bow. Two figures, standing there. Lucy's heart is a boulder in her chest.

She reverses thrust, halting her forward momentum, and flicks the stick into neutral. Between the two boats, the sea rises and falls like the lungs of something sleeping. Ten yards away, the *Cetus* floats with its bow pointed towards *Huntsman's Daughter*.

A few feet from the pulpit, no grab rail to protect him, stands Fin. Her little storyteller. Her superlative human.

A sound comes out of Lucy, then. Half bellow, half lament. Because her son is alive, he's *alive*—and yet his survival has never been more in doubt.

The two yachts, like satellites attracted by gravity, begin a gentle orbit. Lucy hears the slap of water against the hulls, the rasp of breath in her throat. She feels the back-and-forth twisting of her gut.

Fin starts crying—a low and miserable sound. He bites his lip and frowns and she knows he's trying to be brave. 'Please, Mummy, please,' he moans. 'I want to go, I want to go home.'

Standing beside him, the only other person on deck, is Bee.

FORTY-SEVEN

Abraham accelerates up the lane leading off Mortis Point, Wild Ridge burning in his rear-view mirror like a solar flare. When he brakes at the junction for the coast road, he hears the wail of sirens. Two pumps, from the sound of it. Some distance away yet.

Turning off the lane, he hurtles down the coastal road towards Skentel. Instinct tells him it's the most likely place to find Lucy Locke. Below, through the hedgerows lining the route, he sees strobing blue lights heading north.

Abraham takes a left bend too fast, drifts over the centreline. He wrestles the wheel and corrects. The road straightens. Ahead are the two fire engines, racing towards him. Siren blaring, the first pump shoots past, an angry streak of red.

He brakes hard, waiting for the second pump to pass before he takes the Skentel turn-off. To his surprise, it sloughs off speed and swings in ahead of him.

Abraham cuts across the road after it. He hears the hiss of air brakes as the pump negotiates the switchbacks. At last it reaches Skentel's narrow high street and passes the first shops. Outside the Goat Hotel, its brake lights flare red. Abraham skids to a stop. He remembers what happened five days ago—the TV truck that got stuck in the same position.

Swearing, he flings open his door and climbs out. Blue light strobes off Skentel's whitewashed buildings. The sound from the siren is nauseating. When Abraham edges around the pump, he's greeted by a street jammed with people and cars. Just as he feared, smoke is rising from the quay.

'Out of the way!' he roars. 'Get these cars *moved*!'

Shocked faces pivot towards him. But the street's so crowded he can't fight his way through. Losing patience, he climbs on to the bonnet of a stationary Ford, using it as a springboard to jump to the vehicle in front. He hears angry shouts, ignores them, leaps to the roof of an Audi. From the Audi's bonnet he vaults on to a Vauxhall Corsa and from there into the flatbed of a Mitsubishi pick-up. In less than a minute, he's on the quay.

Thick smoke is rising from the Drift Net. Abraham shoulders his way through. He doesn't get far before someone snatches his arm. Wheeling around, furious, he recognizes the guy who grabbed him: Tyler Roedean, one of the Drift Net's managers.

'Got something for ya, man,' Tyler says, pressing a scrap of paper at him. 'Compliments of Lucy Locke.'

Abraham scans the handwritten sheet. When he glances at the bar, he sees the blinds have been pulled. 'She's gone?'

'I . . . uh . . .'

'Where?'

Tyler's eyes slide away. 'She just, like . . . vanished.'

Following his gaze to the floating dock, Abraham sees a single empty berth. He looks past it to the sea, but the breakwater wall blocks his view. Turning his head, he seeks out the lifeboat station. Then he runs to the caged switchback steps and climbs.

FORTY-EIGHT

Bee Tavistock is dressed in her signature style: black Doc Martens, black miniskirt, candy-cane tights. Lucy can read the T-shirt beneath her unbuttoned black cardigan: *STAY BACK: I'M ALLERGIC TO MORONS.*

Five years they've known each other—ever since Bee walked into the Drift Net and demanded a job. In anyone else, it would have seemed like arrogance. Bee had the charisma to pull it off.

Her make-up, today, is typically dramatic: false lashes, iridescent eye shadow, bubblegum-pink lipstick to match the bubblegum-pink hair.

A coiled line on deck connects a padlocked metal chain around Bee's waist to a trio of roped-together gas tanks. A separate line attaches Fin's ankle to a set of weightlifting plates.

Tears stream down Bee's face. 'I'm so sorry,' she moans. 'This is all my fault. He was kind to me. He was kind to me and I fell for it. I didn't know what he was.'

Lucy shakes her head. Bee isn't to blame for anything.

She sees movement from the stern—someone climbing out of the hatch—and knows who it's going to be before he appears.

Katharsis. Purification through tragedy.

Only a student of philosophy or art would choose the Greek spelling of that word. Lucy didn't make the connection when she read it on the text—not surprising, considering it was a nineteen-year delve into her past—but it must have nudged her subconscious. Because *something* had pulled her attention to that spot on the wall where one of her artworks had been replaced.

On to the deck of the *Cetus* climbs Tommo. He's wearing an oddly reverent expression. His leather jacket flaps open, revealing the legend on his T-shirt: *BADASS UNICORN*. In one hand, Tommo carries a six-foot metal boathook.

Lucy studies him, trying to reconcile the image with the person she knew at art college, but there's barely any resemblance. Little wonder she didn't twig when Bee introduced him at Billie's party. Nor any time this past week, while her brain was shot to pieces. Clear now, too, why Daniel had so much trouble identifying him; her husband hasn't visited the Drift Net in months. And the only other time his path could have crossed Tommo's for certain was at Billie's eighteenth, five weeks ago. That night, the house had been packed with guests. And Daniel had been distracted both by the implosion of his business and his fight with Nick.

Tommo hasn't aged well: body run to fat, soft belly hanging over his jeans. The once-hard angles of his face have entirely disappeared. Except for a patch of eczema on his throat, there's a greasy look to his skin.

This guy, he's the Devil. Satan, Lucifer, whichever name you want to use.

Daniel's words, back at the prison. Nothing hyperbolic about them. Tommo's puppy-dog persona disguises something monstrous.

Staring at him, Lucy casts her mind back. Tommo's not his name, of course—it's Lucian.

She fell into his sphere during her first week at the Slade School of Fine Art. She was eighteen, new to London, anxious to shrug off her provincial naivety, desperate to be accepted by her peers. Lucian was a mouth on a stick, an endlessly pontificating self-aggrandizer. He lived to shock, to subvert. He worshipped everything anathematic, went out of his way to offend. In Lucy's entire life, she hadn't met anyone like him. He was dangerous and exhilarating and *new*. Never was she physically attracted. And yet within a few days she was sleeping with him. Lucian's background, she soon learned, was one of unimaginable privilege. His budget, for a single month in London, approached her funds for a year.

Lucy made other friends that first month. Her social circle swelled. But no one else in her undergraduate crowd seemed as mesmerized by Lucian Terrell. She witnessed, admittedly, his interactions with their peers; his barely concealed contempt. On more than one occasion she, too, became the target of his scorn. And yet when Lucian wasn't mocking her new friends or attacking her for some opinion he considered bourgeois, he could be disarmingly charismatic. He'd make her feel like the most interesting person he'd met.

The semester progressed. The work of creation gathered pace. The students threw themselves into their art: sometimes haphazardly, always joyfully, increasingly obsessively. They experimented, they failed, they learned. And through the process they grew. Lucy found herself amazed by the quality of the work she saw developing around her. From everyone, that is, except Lucian.

The self-importance of his art made it juvenile. The harder it tried to shock, the more anodyne it became. Not that Lucy cared much by then. Within a few weeks she'd met someone new. And while she never cheated on Lucian, she dropped him like a stone. When the new relationship ended, Lucian came back to her with a gift, a portrait of her in old age. It was a freakishly horrible painting—everything bad about his art distilled into a single image. Worst of all—and much to her chagrin afterwards—she slept with him as a thank-you.

Following Billie's birth, Lucian once more sought her out. Supportive at first, his behaviour rapidly deteriorated. At that point Lucy gave up on London completely. She swapped her bedsit for a trailer in Spain's Tabernas Desert. And never thought of Lucian Terrell again.

'Strange,' Lucian says, walking along the side deck. 'Everything's been leading to this moment. And now it's here, I'm hesitant to face it.'

He stops between Bee and Fin. 'First off, let's bury Tommo, shall we?

Put him over the side, out of his misery. Honestly, Lucy, I cannot tell you how much I despised him.'

When he lays a hand on Bee's shoulder, she moans at his touch. 'This one liked him, though, didn't you? Although that, in itself, is an indictment.'

Lucy breathes steadily—in through her nose, out through her mouth— as if the slightest sharp movement could destabilize the *Cetus*. She tries not to look at Fin. Instead she listens, intently, to the water slapping the hulls of both boats. 'Lucian,' she says, 'I haven't seen you once in eighteen years and then—'

'She bought me this crazy T-shirt,' he says. '*BADASS UNICORN.* Gross, no? I mean, who *does* that?'

He blinks, and every trace of humanity drains from his expression. 'Let's get one thing straight,' he says. 'It *hasn't* been once in eighteen years.'

When you left London, I counted myself blessed. You'll never know how dif-ficult I found the months after you spilled that lizard from your belly. I loved you and yet I hated you. I wanted to help you and also punish you. The conflict was tearing me apart.

But the relief didn't last long. I couldn't sleep for asking myself why you'd left. Especially after all my support. No one else came to that hospital the day you gave birth. No one else offered to drive you home, or buy you food, or point out the manifold ways in which you'd ruined your life.

Despite the pain, I told myself to forgive you. And then I looked you up.

But you'd gone, Lucy. Vanished off the face of the Earth. I tracked you to a ferry port in northern France, but from there the trail went cold. Even the spe-cialist I hired couldn't smoke you out.

After six months passed, I stopped caring as much. A few more years and I gave up completely. There were other women by then. None of them had the dark Lucy magic, but at least they hadn't busted themselves open with a worm.

Then, last year, I was at a gallery opening in Mayfair. An underwhelming night, until I fell into conversation with an arts journo. She started gushing about this place she'd visited out west, which combined art and music and good food and drink.

I wanted to take her home so I nodded along and made nice noises, and before I could protest she whipped out her phone and googled it. And suddenly there

YOU were, the lead feature of a Sunday newspaper lifestyle piece this journo had written.

My God, Lucy. Most people knocking forty don't look anything like their teenage selves. But you did. There you were, standing on a driftwood stage in an emerald dress and cowboy boots. Older, yes, but wiser—and ten times more beautiful for it.

Staring at your picture, that dark Lucy magic hit me just as powerfully as before—as if the eighteen years since we'd parted were just a dream. I spent a week telling myself to forget you; to keep you in the past, where you belonged.

And then I packed a bag for Skentel.

I didn't intend to announce myself straight away. Instead, I booked into the Goat Hotel and watched from afar.

What a life you'd built for yourself, Lucy. Quite the unexpected turnaround: the arts venue on the quay; the sailing boat; the quirky old house on the hill. And what a dashing husband.

I could see, straight away, that you'd filled that town with dark magic. Walking its streets, I was intoxicated. Do you remember the day I walked into the Drift Net, Lucy? Because you didn't remember me.

Admittedly, I didn't tell you my name. After the stinging little death you'd just served up, why should I? Instead, I bought a drink like a good customer and tried to soak up the ambience. What awful art, though, hanging from those walls. Really, the very worst.

I had another drink and told myself to forgive you—just like I'd forgiven you seventeen years earlier. People grow, they change. Maybe I'd grown too much.

I decided to give you another chance, and I really wanted to help you with the art. I moved out of the Goat and rented the old lighthouse a few miles from town, where I could paint without distraction. And—can you believe it, Lucy?—I made the best art of my life.

Strange. I'd never liked the sea. But the air on this stretch of coast and the cries of those herring gulls—it just fills you up. I bought a boat and a captain's hat. And I painted and painted until I was done. Eight individual pieces that I knew were my best work. They were for YOU, Lucy, all of them. A helping hand from a loving friend.

The Drift Net's website had a submissions page. I wasn't ready to reveal myself so I sent in my images under a pseudonym. I left clues in each painting, even so. I thought them sufficiently oblique, but I knew you'd find them thrilling once I revealed myself. Of course, I didn't explain I was donating the paint-ings—that would have aroused your suspicions.

Your suspicions weren't aroused at all, were they, Lucy? Because back came your email: 'You have amazing talent but I'm afraid these aren't a good fit.'

After all those years, that was how we ended up: YOU, rejecting MY work. Rejecting <u>ME</u>.

Despite my initial anger, in a couple of days I'd recovered. I realized it might be a test. Perhaps you'd figured out the truth and were scared of seeing me again, of dredging up all those old feelings.

I should have burned the paintings and sloped back to London. Instead, I let the dark magic talk its talk. Chances come in threes, so I decided to give you a third.

That's when Tommo came into being. People talked to Tommo like they'd never talk to me. Maybe it was because they were looking down, rather than up.

I spent more time in Skentel, hung out at the Drift Net. When I heard about the party for Billie's eighteenth, I knew I had to go. I developed my relationship with Bee and suddenly there I was, up on Mortis Point. In your home, Lucy. With your friends and your husband and your brood. With <u>you</u>.

Really, I can't tell you how emotional I found it. Even more so when I dis-covered a painting of mine hanging on your wall.

Still, something wasn't quite right in that house—all smiles and laughter on the surface, but something more troubling lurking beneath. I plied Bee with alco-hol and watched you hard all evening. And then I saw the utterly grotesque Nicholas Povey follow you into your darkened study and purposely close the door.

I knew what was coming. I'd been on the receiving end. And now I was watching it unfold again. Worse, this time. Because you were <u>married</u>, Lucy, and you hadn't learned, and Povey was so incredibly vulgar.

I had to make absolutely sure. I waited a few minutes and, when you didn't come out, I grabbed Bee's hand and burst in.

I didn't catch you in the act, but <u>something</u> had been going on in that study—the guilt was etched on to your face. I could hardly bear to look at you. I dragged Bee out but you didn't follow. Instead, you locked the door.

Within a week, you were sneaking out at night to visit him. Cosy drinks in his living room. You have me to thank for Daniel turning up. I phoned him—said I was calling from the Drift Net, worried that you hadn't turned up. Sad, really, that he knew exactly where to find you. We both know what would have happened had he not arrived.

That night, like an epiphany, I realized what you needed: a kathartic event; a tragedy so epochal it would purify the hateful creature you'd become. I returned to the lighthouse and started work. And now here we are at the end of it: the final scene in The Redemption of Lucy Locke.

FORTY-NINE

Lucy listens to him speak, and knows she's talking to a lunatic. Worse—that there's no chance of dissuading him from whatever course he's set. She feels the knife in her back pocket, senses the other weapons she's secreted about the boat. But she's on *Huntsman's Daughter* and Lucian's on the *Cetus* and there's a gulf of deep ocean in between.

Might she have avoided this? At no point, now or then, was she ever aware of his search for her. In late autumn, she couldn't have foreseen that a newspaper feature would attract a monster. Nor does she recall Lucian's first visit to the Drift Net.

She does, now, remember the art: eight high-res images that appeared in her inbox one morning and raised the hairs on her skin. The first painting was a chocolate-box rendering of Skentel, a river of dark blood seeping down the high street. Another showed a woman chained to the rocks of Mortis Point. High above her, a crow-picked corpse swung inside a gibbet cage, while on Penleith Beach a crowd of modern-day locals pointed in delight. A third image, this one of the harbour, showed boats floating keel-up among pushchairs floating wheels-up.

She'd stared at those pictures for half a minute, growing cold. Then she'd sent her standard rejection and deleted them from her machine. Perhaps, if she hadn't been so preoccupied with Billie's Sea Shepherd adventure and the bullying at Fin's school, she might have seen the images for what they were: a warning, unequivocal, that calamity was about to strike.

Lucy feels the thump of her pulse at her temples.

There's too much water between the boats to reach her son. Whatever current was pushing them together is now pulling them apart.

'This was always a tragedy written entirely for your benefit,' Lucian says. 'But I never expected to be so affected. It's been hard, Lucy, watching your pain. At times, it's been unbearable.'

'Lucian—'

'No,' he says, his eyes welling up. 'Please don't make this any more difficult. We're at the denouement, Lucy. Tragedy grants us redemption. Through our suffering we are healed.'

Planting his foot in the small of Bee's back, Lucian shoves her forwards. She plummets from the boat, hits the water and immediately sinks beneath it. Before Lucy can scream at him to stop, Lucian does the same to Fin. One moment her boy is shivering up on deck. The next he's disappeared beneath the waves.

FIFTY

1

Abraham Rose climbs the caged switchback steps, taking them in pairs. As he rises above the stone breakwater, his view of the sea improves. He spots a couple of trawlers moving south, an oil tanker and a container ship heading north-east, but no motor launches or yachts. Wherever Lucy Locke went, she's beyond sight of land.

The wind changes. Smoke stings Abraham's eyes. He draws it into his lungs and coughs it out, appalled at the pain.

This close to Mortis Point's southern face, he can't see the house burning above him, but he sees the gushing black smoke. Below him, he recognizes the Drift Net's roof. The flames are coming from an alley that runs behind it, where a stack of wooden pallets is burning.

Why would Lucy start a fire *behind* the venue? Unless she's acting under duress and doing the bare minimum to comply? The house on Mortis Point can clearly be seen from the sea. The Drift Net, by contrast, is hidden by the breakwater wall.

Reaching the RNLI boathouse, he hauls open the door.

2

Except for the Tamar-class lifeboat angled on its cradle, the boat hall is deserted. Abraham sees the steel ramp descending to the water. Two metal walkways surround the boat, one on his level, another above it. 'Police!' he shouts. 'Who's in charge?'

A man appears on the overhead walkway. Wild grey hair, wild grey beard. 'I'm Donny,' he says, wiping his hands on a rag. 'Donahue O'Hare. What're you after, son?'

Abraham points down the ramp at the water. 'I need you to get me out there. *Right now.*'

O'Hare scratches his beard. 'What you need, and what I can deliver, might be two different things. You want to give me some context?'

'You know Lucy Locke?'

'Aye.'

'Have you looked out of the window in the last ten minutes?'

Frowning, O'Hare clangs around the walkway until he's right above Abraham's head. He's silent a moment and then he starts cursing. 'Son, you better get up here and explain.'

FIFTY-ONE

1

Two fizzing circles on the sea, the second far smaller than the first. As Lucy kicks off her boots and leaps on to the side deck, Lucian warns her to stop. She's about to dive into the water regardless when she spots his foot resting against the three weightlifting plates still on deck. It takes her scrambled brain a moment to process the implications.

The water between the two yachts foams afresh. Fin bobs to the surface, gasping and spluttering. Moments later, Bee emerges too.

Lucy knows how cold that water is, how quickly it strips away heat. But if she disobeys Lucian and dives in, he'll almost certainly kick over Fin's ballast. No way she can reach her son before those cast-iron plates yank him down.

Fin screams for her between breaths. Lucy's hands make fists, clenching and unclenching. Her son's cries are a torture. Hooks in her skin.

'Wait,' Lucian begs her. '*Please.* I've sacrificed so much to bring you to this moment. Please don't jeopardize everything now. This is what we've been building towards since the beginning. One choice that changes everything. An opportunity for redemption, if only you're brave enough to seize it. And I *know* you're brave enough, Lucy.'

If only she were closer. If only she had some way of reaching him. She might not be handcuffed, like Daniel, but he's rendered her just as powerless.

'You get to choose how this ends, don't you see?' he continues. 'And then you get to live with your choice. I just need a name: Bee or your darling boy. One life sacrificed for another. And—just like I told Daniel—if you choose neither, you lose both.'

His face creases, as if he's gripped by agonies of his own. 'I know it's brutal. But I also know how much you *need* this. There's beauty inside you, Lucy. But also such darkness. Take this last step and we'll purge it together. Renewal through suffering, just like the philosopher said.'

2

Lucy turns her head, searching sea and sky. She sees no boats, no helicopters, no signs of humanity. Her eyes pass over Lucian's yacht, studying it from bow to stern. There's nothing there to help her, nothing to offer any advantage.

'Tell me,' she says. 'Before we do this. Tell me how Billie died. You showed me some of it, but not all. If this ends here—today—at least tell me that.'

Lucian tilts his head, as if he's contemplating an artwork that resists all interpretation. 'Even now, at the end, you surprise me,' he says, a tear spilling down his cheek. 'You *genuinely* want to know.'

She doesn't, not at all. But she'll listen. If it keeps Fin and Bee alive a few minutes longer, she'll listen to anything.

The boats continue to drift. The more she keeps Lucian talking, the smaller her chance of intervening. But right now, she *has* no ability to intervene. 'Please,' she says again. 'Please, Lucian, just tell me. I'm her mum. I deserve to know.'

'OK,' he replies. 'If that's what you want. But I warn you: it'll be a difficult thing to hear.'

No way, of course, that I can tell you the truth. I doubt you'd find any comfort in it, but I simply can't take the risk. In this tragedy written for your benefit, no sanctuary can be given for hope. Only through suffering are we purified. Only through our complete undoing do we stand any chance of being saved.

You see, Billie was never meant to go into the water. Not that day, at least. The point of last Friday's tableau was to destroy just one facet of your life: any remaining trust you had in Daniel Locke.

Given the choice between saving his son or the lizard you spilled with his predecessor, it was hardly rocket science whom he'd pick. Once you saw the evidence, I knew you'd never forgive him. That's all I needed from Daniel: your daughter's name. I was never going to carry out my threat. If I'm honest, it was Daniel I intended to put over the side that day, the very moment he gave me his answer.

But how useless he was. How utterly ineffectual. Even when I threatened to drown them both, he just stood there gaping, as if a lightbulb had flicked off in his brain.

Billie should have been <u>here</u>, Lucy. With us right now. The real choice—between her life and Fin's—was meant to be yours: a decision that would lead to your undoing, and ultimately bring about your salvation.

Now, instead, you get to pick between your son and your friend. A far less punishing choice. And it's all your daughter's fault.

I don't know what kind of cosmic guilt you instilled in that girl, or what kind of inferiority complex she was hiding. But what happened on that boat last Friday was an abomination. It happened fast, too, like a finger-snap. And afterwards there was nothing anyone could do about it.

You see, it angered me that Daniel wouldn't choose. I'd gone to all that effort and he was refusing to play his part. His only task was to say Billie's name, but he couldn't even get that right. So I decided to apply some pressure. I told him his time was up, that I'd run out of patience. Then I made straight for those two kids as if I was about to drown them both. Daniel was screaming for me to stop, but STILL he wouldn't say your daughter's name, and then the craziest thing of all happened, because, without any warning, just as I was closing in on the pair of them, Billie shoved her own ballast overboard.

BATSHIT crazy.

I mean, I just stopped dead and watched. There was Billie's line, paying out faster and faster, and there she was, balanced on the edge of the swim step. She looked at her little brother and whispered something to him, and then she looked at Daniel and you know what she said? Her last words? 'Tell Mum I love her.'

And then splash. Down she went. Bubbles, ripples, nothing.

I've thought about it a lot since. If you want the truth, it scared the hell out of me. I couldn't sleep at all Friday night. Barely got much sleep Saturday. Every time I closed my eyes, I saw her face.

You know what I think? Now that I've had a chance to process it? I think Billie just gave up. She saw her cards, all laid out, and decided not to hang around. Really, it's the only explanation.

Of course, it altered the plan. But there were a few upsides. I hadn't intended for Billie to go in the water, so her legs weren't tightly bound. I suspect that's why the knots came loose and she washed up a few days later, giving the police their corpse.

But you don't need to know any of this, Lucy. What you need to <u>think</u> is that your husband made a devil's pact, and he chose his son over your daughter, and that the man you trusted over all others turned out to be a snake.

313

FIFTY-TWO

1

Lucian holds out his hand, palm up. 'What happened to the rain? It started promisingly enough. No wind, either. Even the sea's behaving itself—just this mill-pond calm.'

He pauses, shakes his head. 'I'm afraid there's nothing at all redemptive in what happened on the *Lazy Susan*. Daniel didn't need asking twice. I'd barely asked the question before he was shouting Billie's name. Anything to save his own son.'

The *Cetus* rocks in the water. Lucian sways back and forth. His foot scrapes the stack of weightlifting plates, nudging them closer to the edge. His eyes flick to them in an instant, then flick back to her.

Good.

Because that means he hasn't interrogated the boat's motion beneath his feet; hasn't paid attention to the slap of water against the hull; hasn't seen what Lucy's been waiting for: the briefest flash of movement from the stern.

2

Earlier, in the Drift Net, she'd known this would finish where it started, out at sea. At that point, she hadn't known if Lucian was still onshore. He'd certainly been close enough to Skentel to see the house fire on Mortis Point.

Accordingly, she'd agreed to Jake's suggestion on the phone: that when she climbed aboard *Huntsman's Daughter* at the quay, he'd already be inside the cabin.

During Lucian's speech, Lucy heard Jake slip over the side. And now there he is, the man she betrayed time and again, a crouched shape on the *Cetus*'s stern. Willing, even now, to put his life in danger and help her save her son.

But forty feet of yacht separates him from Lucian. And hardly a whisker separates Lucian from the two sets of ballast on deck.

'After that tragedy with Billie, Daniel became a lot more pliant,' Lucian continues. 'He didn't want to get in the water, but it didn't take much persuasion. I can't imagine *your* spirit breaking so easily. Of course, that's one reason we find ourselves where we are.'

From the cockpit, Jake climbs on to the port-side deck.

He's barefoot, dressed only in his old wetsuit. Seawater drips from his elbows, his hair. Moving slow and silent, he edges along the side deck, one hand braced against the coachroof.

'So,' Lucian says. 'Here we are at the fracture line. The point that separates the old Lucy Locke from the new. The moment where you have to trust everything you ever taught me about katharsis, about renewal. I just need a name. One life to sacrifice for another.'

Lucy can't breathe, sure that if she makes the slightest movement she'll alert Lucian to what's happening over his shoulder. She can't hear the seawater dripping from Jake's wetsuit, but she can imagine it far too easily.

Lucian's eyes narrow as he watches her. She needs to say something, keep him engaged. And yet her tongue is welded to the roof of her mouth.

Down in the water, Fin's eyes are larger than she's ever seen them. He spits seawater, sculls with his hands and tries to keep his face above the waves. Already, he's shivering uncontrollably.

When Lucy raises her eyes back to the yacht, she sees that Jake has edged forward another step. But he's still so far away. And then the unthinkable happens.

Lucian straightens, rolls his neck. His head tilts to the side, as if something invisible has put its lips to his ear and started to talk. He nods, almost imperceptibly. And then he turns and glances back along the boat.

Jake's still twenty feet away, the yacht's sloped coachroof between them. He's in a half-crouch, arms wide, fingers open in a wrestler's stance.

Disgusted, Lucian shakes his head. He reverses his grip on the boat-hook, pointing its spiked tip at Jake. 'Honestly, Lucy. After everything I've tried t—'

Jake vaults on to the coachroof and charges him.

Lucian's faster. He thrusts with his boathook. Its steel spike punches through Jake's wetsuit just below the sternum. Jake crashes backwards, snags a grab rail and just about saves himself from going over the side.

Lucian pivots, lips skinned back from his teeth. He places his foot against the trio of weightlifting plates and shoves. The ballast hits the water and instantly disappears. The coiled line settles on the surface, unspooling in rapidly decreasing circles.

Lucy screams. She launches herself off the deck, but she's so far from her son, and that line is unspooling even faster. She hasn't even hit the water before the last of it disappears. She sees Fin, her star-gazing, card-sorting little bookworm; her weaver of words, her teller of fine tales, her storyteller extraordinaire. And then he's gone.

3

Lucy plunges beneath the surface. The world dissolves into white. The sea is so cold that her first instinct is to gasp for breath. She takes a mouthful of water before she can seal her lips. Half a second later she bursts free, coughing and choking.

There's the *Cetus*, rising and falling. But no Fin—and now no Bee. She swims arm over arm towards the point she last saw her son. Already, a handful of seconds have passed since he went under.

Lucy takes a lungful of air, ducks her head below the water. She can't see anything. When she flings out her arms, blindly searching, she can't *feel* anything either. Breaking the surface, seawater stinging her eyes, she takes another breath, diving deeper this time, and reaches out in vain—because too many seconds have passed and there's nothing around her except cold. She needs to breathe. And then she's back above the water, taking another greedy gulp of air, her fourth since Fin went under.

Earlier, as she closed on Lucian's yacht, she checked the depth finder on *Huntsman's Daughter*'s display. Out here they're in eighty metres of water—more than forty fathoms of cold ocean. She twists around, unable to accept what just happened. First her daughter. Now her son.

Katharsis, she thinks. *Purification through tragedy.*

It can't be. It can't be.

Lucy casts about, takes her fifth breath. Hopeless now. Still, she refuses to believe it. Up on Lucian's yacht, she hears sounds of a struggle. She knows Jake's been wounded, knows Lucian won't show him any mercy, knows she's abandoned the man she once loved, yet again, to a fate he doesn't deserve, but there's nothing she can do about that, because *her boy has gone*, her beautiful boy, and her head is full of broken glass.

Even as she thinks it, the water boils a few feet away, a fizzing explosion of white. From the heart of it bursts Bee, heaving so desperately for air that her throat squeals with the effort.

She sinks beneath the surface, rises up, shoulders twisting as she kicks her feet to stay afloat. 'I've got him!' she shrieks. 'I can't *HOLD* him!'

Bee's arms are locked, but Fin is entirely beneath the water. Lucy swims hard towards her friend.

'I'm losing him!' Bee screams. 'Help me, I'm *losing* him!'

She's sinking again, too exhausted to keep herself afloat. Lucy scythes closer, but she's still so far away. And now the water's over Bee's mouth, her nose. If she tries to take a breath, she'll fill her lungs with the sea.

Abruptly, she sinks out of sight completely. Lucy takes a huge gulp of air—her ninth—and then she dives.

4

Silent cold.

The transition from sound to soundlessness is shocking, but the change from light to dark is worse. A few feet from the surface, the murk is so absent of definition it might as well be full dark. An ocean of water is beneath her and yet the claustrophobia is absolute.

She reaches out, touches Bee's shoulder. But her friend is battling so violently that Lucy's hand is knocked free.

An instant later she regains contact. Two hands this time—one on Bee's bicep, the other on her elbow. And then she's touching Fin. Lucy can feel her boy beginning to slip loose. She swims deeper, grabs his arm and snags a fistful of his top.

Bee loses her grip completely.

Fin sinks with an abruptness that catches Lucy off guard, nearly wrenching him loose of her grip. She kicks her legs hard but she's upside down in the water. The movement merely accelerates their descent.

If she lets go now, even for an instant, it's the last time she'll touch him in this life. And yet by holding him from above, she's merely following him into oblivion. Already, that vague grey smear has faded to black. They're sinking into a void that grows colder with every metre.

The urge to fight her way to the surface is overwhelming. But if she abandons Fin to this, there's no more life to live. Nine breaths she's already taken to his one. She feels him bucking, tiny thrashing moments—knows that he's drowning, that the process is almost complete. She folds her knees into her chest, curls her spine, nearly screams out her air at the agony from her broken ribs. Somehow, she wraps her legs around Fin's torso. Once he's secure, she releases his T-shirt and hugs him under his arms.

Pressure is building in her chest. Her ears fizz and pop. She straightens her arms, forcing herself lower, her legs no longer wrapped around Fin's torso but the weighted line beneath him. Locked on, she feels in her back pocket for the filleting knife.

It's gone.

Maybe it slipped out when she dived into the sea.

Fin is loose against her now. She knows his lungs have filled with water.

Down they sink.

A memory flares in Lucy's head. Back on *Huntsman's Daughter*, she'd cut strips of duct tape with the Stanley knife. Afterwards she'd tucked the blade into her top pocket.

In an instant, it's in her hand. She saws at the binding around Fin's ankle, but there's so much of it and her panic is so great—and her oxygen so depleted—that she can hardly operate. Another thought pushes through the chaos. Why cut through the multiple layers around his ankle when only a single length attaches him to the weights?

Her blade doesn't sever it on her first attempt, but two hard slices and she's through. Detached, their descent is arrested. Lucy abandons the knife, feels herself rolling in the water. She clutches Fin close. Can't work out which way is up or down.

Lucy kicks hard, propelling herself forwards, but a panicked part of her brain rebels, convinced she's plunging deeper. It tries to communicate a thought.

Last of her air now. She knows she's too far from the surface to reach it before she's forced to breathe.

Katharsis, she thinks. *Purification through tragedy.*

If she surrenders and takes a breath, her purification will be complete.

Instead she reaches out, not with her hands but with her mind. She seizes that earlier thought fragment and examines it.

The flotation belt.

Teeth clenched, Lucy feels for the activation cord and yanks it. Even this far below the surface she hears the CO_2 cartridge fire. She senses something burst loose from the belt, inflating like a car's airbag. It drags her sideways—except sideways, it seems, is actually up. Pain explodes along her right side, a thousand impaling spears. Lucy feels her head rolling. Knows she's about to pass out. Hugs her boy even tighter.

Within seconds, the darkness yields to a little light. How fast they're rising she can't tell. She's on molecules of oxygen now, fighting her diaphragm, fighting her lungs, fighting the instinct to breathe. At last she can fight no longer. The breath spools from her lips in a greedy gush of bubbles, seawater floods her mouth—

Fin, at the breakfast table, his bare legs swinging

—and suddenly the world returns in a paroxysm of sound and light. She's drawing down air, half a lungful, before she sinks beneath the ocean once more. But it's enough, just enough, and with a surge of fresh energy she launches herself back above the surface.

Every one of her senses is re-lit.

Water fizzes in her ears. Cold Atlantic air pushes against her face. There are the two yachts: the *Cetus* and *Huntsman's Daughter*. No help on the horizon. No help from above.

Fin—her boy, her little storyteller—is in her arms, but his head is still submerged. When she kicks her legs and raises him up, his eyes are fixed and unresponsive. Dead, yes, but she won't think about that yet.

One arm around her son, Lucy swims to *Huntsman's Daughter*. From the *Cetus*, she hears sounds of violence.

The pain from her broken ribs is extraordinary—deeper than before, more complex. When the inflating life jacket burst loose from the flotation belt and jerked her towards the surface, it felt like something catastrophic happened to her insides. Each new breath delivers a starburst of silver across her vision, a glittery firework that takes longer and longer to blink away.

At last, Lucy touches *Huntsman's Daughter*'s swim ladder and latches on. She lays Fin face-down in the water and positions her shoulder under his stomach. Then she grips the ladder in both hands, gets a foot on the bottom step and pulls herself up.

Another firework detonates behind her eyes. Another volley of spears pierces her side. She loses her grip, slips off the ladder, mashes her face against the bottom step. Blood, red and vivid, surges into the water. Her head sings like hammered iron.

Seawater stings her nose, her mouth. She feels shards of tooth on her tongue, spits them out, sees her boy starting to drift away. She hooks him, puts her shoulder under his waist and tries again.

This time, Lucy gets to the second step before her muscles give out. She strikes the ladder with her jaw, sinks beneath the sea, bursts free of it and spits blood and water and more broken tooth. She reels Fin back in. If she fails a third attempt, she knows she won't have the energy for a fourth.

When the next swell hits, she launches herself up, screaming with effort. It feels like something is haemorrhaging inside her torso, a pain even worse than childbirth. She blinks away silver, forces herself higher, clings on as a wave rocks the boat.

Up, another step. Another.

Fin is heavier than he's ever been, lungs full of water, clothes drenched from the sea. She flips him over, hears his head crack against a siding, watches him slither into the cockpit. Hanging from the ladder, pausing to get her breath, Lucy casts a look back at the *Cetus*.

Jake is slumped against the blood-slicked coachroof, hands pressed to his chest. Bee, her ballast still balanced on the side deck, is swimming towards the stern. Lucian has disappeared.

Lucy hauls herself over the transom and tumbles into the cockpit. She rolls on to her side, drags herself up, crawls towards her son. Fin's on his front, nose pressed to the deck. When she shoves down on his back with all her weight, seawater gushes from his mouth and nose.

Lucy flips him over, spits blood until her mouth is clear. One hand supporting Fin's neck, she tilts back his head. Then, pinching his nostrils, she begins CPR. A rescue breath, a pause as his lungs deflate. Another breath, three more. No signs of life from her boy.

She puts the heel of her palm against his breastbone and begins compressions. Two pumps each second for a count of thirty. She follows them with two more blasts of breath. Fin's mouth is cold against her lips. His chest inflates and sinks back.

Back to the pumping: *one, two, three, four, five* . . .

Before Fin was born, Lucy took an infant first-aid class in Redlecker. Over the years, because of his fragility, she's taken regular refreshers. Only once has she had to think about reviving him—back when they were still renting. They'd called an ambulance, waited half an hour for it, Fin's breaths growing weaker each minute.

. . . twenty-eight, twenty-nine, thirty.

Breathe. Pause. Breathe.

No response from her son.

One, two, three, four . . .

A wave of dizziness hits. Lucy closes her eyes and sees Daniel, hears his voice: *Like it or not, this rests with you now. You have to find Fin. Bring him home.*

She's failing. She's failing Daniel, she's failing Fin. Lucy hears an engine turn over, knows it belongs to the *Cetus*. When she opens her eyes, she sees Lucian at the wheel.

This guy, he's the Devil. Satan, Lucifer, whichever name you want to use.

Lucy can't refute Daniel's words.

And now that devil is escaping to wreak havoc another day.

On her way here, she'd prioritized Fin's life over vengeance for Billie's death. It seems, now, she won't deliver either.

In the cockpit, Lucian engages the throttle. Lucy sees what's about to happen. Even if Bee escapes the thrashing prop, her drag on the boat will pull her ballast into the water. That trio of metal gas tanks will pull her eighty metres to the sea floor. And yet Lucy can't help her friend because she has to work on her boy.

It's another betrayal. Another part of her humanity ripped away.

Katharsis, she thinks. *Purification through tragedy.*

Except this isn't a purification.

This is a corruption.

. . . twenty-nine, thirty.

Breathe. Relax. Breathe.

Her boy is lifeless. Lucy screams at the unfairness of it.

There *is* something she can do for Bee. And if she can't save her boy, she really should save her friend. The chance is slim but worth trying. She reaches for the carving knife duct-taped to the hull and tears it loose. Pulling herself up, she yells Bee's name. The woman twists in the water. Their eyes meet. Lucy tosses the knife. She doesn't even follow its trajectory before sinking back down beside Fin.

322

The *Cetus*'s engine winds up to full pitch.

Lucy returns the heels of her palms to her son's chest. Sweat and sea-water run down her face. There'll be a point when she can't continue, but she hasn't reached it yet.

One, two, three . . .

Impact, suddenly, against the boat. Lucy's thrown off her knees. She lands in a sprawl of limbs, shrieking with the sick raw fucking *agony* of it. *Huntsman's Daughter* rolls to starboard. It rocks back even faster, slam-ming Lucy against a cockpit locker.

Pain like white light. Followed by instant darkness. When she opens her eyes, she can't tell how long she's been out, but the yacht is still rolling beneath her. She grabs on to the locker, drags herself up. And sees Lucian crouched on the coachroof above her head, brandishing his boathook. Saliva shines on his teeth. 'Lucy,' he hisses. 'This *definitely* wasn't in the script.'

FIFTY-THREE

Strapped into his seat, Abraham Rose feels the Tamar-class lifeboat detach from its cradle and accelerate down the slipway, hitting the water with no loss of speed. Donahue O'Hare throttles up the twin diesel engines. The boat surges past the breakwater towards open sea.

He's one of seven aboard: coxswain, navigator, engineer; other roles he hasn't figured out. Through the starboard windows, he sees a crew member raising a communications pole from its stowed position.

Abraham holds his mobile phone and a VHF radio. In the last five minutes, communicating with the coastguard and his team back in Barnstaple, he's marshalled every available asset: NPAS helicopter support from Exeter, a coastguard helicopter from St Athan, additional RNLI resources from Appledore and Padstow. All marine traffic has been alerted.

Forty minutes before Abraham reached Skentel's quay, Jake Farrell, Lucy Locke's ex, was on duty at the lifeboat station. According to

O'Hare, Farrell received a phone call and immediately left his post. No one's seen him since, but his yacht, *Huntsman's Daughter*, is missing from its usual berth.

Just now, the DS in Barnstaple called back with the information Abraham had requested. As he'd suspected, the red Renault Clio parked outside the lighthouse belongs to Bee Tavistock. One of her distinctive T-shirts had been bundled up on the Clio's back seat.

The DS also ran a PNC check on the black Lexus's owner: Lucian Edward Terrell, thirty-seven years old, resident of an exclusive address in London's Belgravia.

Terrell's source of income isn't clear, but he has a long history with the police. Five times he's been arrested on suspicion of stalking or harassment. Three of those arrests led to charges. Two cases were retired by the CPS before they reached court. The third—the only time Terrell appeared as a defendant—was thrown out by the judge following interventions by the defence team. Since then, no further cases have been brought.

An internet search reveals that Terrell is a National Council member for Arts Council England and a trustee of several other institutions. According to his biog, he studied at the Slade School in London around the same time as Lucy Locke. Abraham recognizes the man from the Drift Net and the vigil on Penleith Beach.

In the note she left him at the quay, Lucy alleges what Abraham had started to piece together—that Lucian Terrell is pursuing a vendetta.

CCTV footage from Friday morning showed Fin Locke being driven to the quay, but the Volvo's privacy glass obscured the rear seat. If Billie was in the back, was Terrell sitting beside her?

That would make the black car in the lay-by Terrell's Lexus. If he returned to shore in the dinghy, perhaps he used Bee Tavistock's red Clio to drive away. It might explain why Tavistock used an electric scooter to visit Lucy on Friday morning.

Were the life-insurance policies a ploy to implicate the Lockes? Simple enough for Terrell to make the applications. Almost as simple to set up a bank account in Lucy's name. Slightly more difficult to intercept any paperwork before it reached the house. In her note, Lucy maintains she recently found exactly that.

One thing he wants to know more than anything: Did Lucian Terrell return to shore alone, or did he bring Fin Locke with him?

God, I praise you for your compassionate heart. Give me the relentlessness of the good shepherd who goes after wandering sheep and never gives up. Show me my task and help me fulfil it.

Abraham scours the sea for a sign.

FIFTY-FOUR

Lucy stands in the cockpit, legs braced, as Lucian watches her from the coachroof.

She can't afford this. Doesn't have time for it. Her chances of reviving Fin wither each second she delays. Already, she's missed a thirty-count of compressions. She's the only one in the world who can bring him back. And instead of *trying*, she's facing a monster.

The knowledge is barbed wire in her blood, a million scratching insects inside her skull. She has to end this, now, or by her inactivity face the consequences.

Lucy steps forward. She unsheathes the antique *kukri* taped to the boom. Lucian backs up a touch. His expression hardens.

Grimacing, her insides shifting like a drum filled with broken parts, Lucy climbs on to the side deck and from there to the coachroof. Her *kukri* is more lethal than his boathook, but its reach is far shorter. With the mast and boom between them, Lucian will keep her at range all day if she lets him.

She lunges with the knife. Lucian deflects it easily. Before she can recover, he reverses his grip on the boathook and strikes the side of her head. The blow isn't hard enough to drop her, but it fills her ears with white noise.

Lucy swings wildly, missing Lucian by a yard and severing the boom brake with her blade. She swings again, slicing through more of the yacht's lines. In return, she receives a jab above her left breast just hard enough to puncture skin. He's toying with her, she realizes, his intention not to wound but to delay.

She rolls over the boom and charges. Lucian thrusts out with the boathook, harder this time, a genuine attempt to cause injury. She bats away the shaft and, before he can readjust, she's on him, her shoulder slamming his chest, the flat of her blade bouncing off his arm. It's not the result she intended but he staggers back, unbalanced, grabbing the mast for support.

Lucy swings again, a backhand tennis move, puts all her energy into it. The blade shears the air, scything towards Lucian's face. He jerks away his head just in time. Before her blade has even completed its arc, she sees him drawing back the boathook, his intention to bury the spike in her gut. The *kukri* slams into the mast with a hollow clang. The shock of the impact explodes up Lucy's arm. The weapon skitters across the coachroof, coming to a rest on the forward hatch.

'Oh, you *bitch*!' Lucian screams, staggering back.

She gasps for breath, tries to work out what just happened.

There's a bloody streak on the mast. When she looks at Lucian's hand, she sees dark blood welling from the stumps of two fingers.

Furious, he thrusts out his boathook. She sidesteps, grabs it in both hands, shoves back. Lucian catches his foot on a deck moulding and body-slams the hatch. Blood, bright and shocking, flicks across the deck.

He reaches out, snags the *kukri* in his good hand and climbs to his feet, putting the mast between them. Now *she's* the one with the inferior weapon.

'Boy's cold and dead,' Lucian says. 'You should have trusted me. All this effort—and now you lose *everyone*.'

She advances, shaking his words from her head, moving around the mast. He's on the starboard side now, backing towards the stern. No longer is there any barrier between him and Fin. A few more steps and he'll reach the cockpit.

She jabs with the boathook. Just a feint, but Lucian falls for it, swinging with the *kukri* to fend her off. Before he recovers, she thrusts out a second time. The steel tip sinks into his cheek, rips loose. Lucian screams again. Blood spills down his shirt. He drops his weapon, raising his good hand to his face just as she cracks him with the boathook, connecting above his ear. He goes down hard, spitting and choking. Lucy leans over him and delivers two vertical punches, breaking his nose.

Lucian's face is a wreck. A blood bubble swells and bursts on his lips. Livid, he grabs a tangle of her hair. Dragging her close, he bares his teeth. Lucy slaps him away but he's too strong. Those teeth graze her cheek, snapping like a turtle's. She reaches past him for the *kukri*, first with her right hand and then with her left. All she can find is a loose line hanging from the unfettered boom.

Lucian reels her in until they're cheek to cheek. She feels his blood pulsing over her, instinctively turns her head. It's a mistake.

Monstrous pain, suddenly, in her left ear. Lucian rears back, spits out a chunk of it. She feels her own blood running, a warm flood. Before he can bite her a second time, she loops the severed line around his neck. Lucian releases her hair and scratches at her face. He spits a mouthful of blood into her eyes. Lucy grimaces, half blinded. She loops the rope twice more around his neck, staggers off him.

In her head: Billie, lying dead on Penleith Beach. Daniel, sitting broken inside the prison hall. Fin, cold and unresponsive in the cockpit.

Her boy. Her beautiful boy.

Screaming with agony, summoning every shred of aggression she has left, Lucy leans into the boom. She straightens her legs, pushes with her hands, drives out the boom from the deck.

Lucian is dragged backwards, bloodied hands scrabbling at the line around his throat. His heels scissor against the coachroof but he can't stop his momentum. His calves bump over the grab rail.

Without a brake to inhibit it, the boom bows out across the water. Lucian hangs from it by his neck, his feet kicking and splashing.

His face darkens. His attempts to free himself grow more frenzied.

He smears blood from his severed fingers across the rope above his head. His feet dance with more vigour. He spasms and he twitches. And then he stills.

Lucy half steps, half falls into the cockpit. She pulls one of the rocket flares from the vertical board where she fastened it. Knocking off the retainer cap, she fishes out the firing cord and fires into the sky. Then she drops down beside her star-gazing, card-sorting little bookworm; her weaver of words, her teller of fine tales, her storyteller extraordinaire.

Lucy reaches out, touches him.

Fin is colder than the ocean, his eyes fixed on something she can't see. *Katharsis*, she thinks. *Purification through tragedy.*

She struggles to take a breath. Her strength has evaporated, along with the last remnants of her hope. Lucy bends over her son regardless. She puts her hands on his chest and pumps.

One, two, three . . .

No thought, no emotion. Just a mechanical process, an up-and-down movement, a piston that doesn't know when to quit.

. . . twenty-eight, twenty-nine, thirty.

Lean forward, lips over mouth. *Breathe.*

Nothing.

She rocks back on her heels. Looks up at the sky.

An image returns to her: Penleith Beach on Sunday evening, her children's names spelled out in candlelight on the sand. And Luke Creese, the pastor from St Peter's, trying to offer her comfort.

'*Does your God allow this?*' she'd asked him.

'*Yes, He does. And sometimes that's the most difficult thing to understand. God doesn't always offer us answers, Lucy. In this life, we may never really know why some things have happened. But God always offers us Himself. Whatever hardships we face, we can choose to go through them with God at our side or without Him.*'

Such bullshit, she thinks.

Such empty comfort.

Opening her eyes, she snarls at the sky. 'Don't take him.'

Lucy pauses, tries again. 'Please—don't take him. He's got too much potential. Too much *life*. He needs to be here, with me. I need to see him grow.'

But Billie had brimmed with potential too, had overflowed with life and love. Even though she knows it's useless, Lucy bends back over her boy. With two hands braced on his chest, she continues to pump.

FIFTY-FIVE

The prayer has barely left Abraham's lips when he spots it: a white light arcing up from the sea, south-west of their position.

'There,' he rasps, coughing blood into his fist.

Moments later, the light reaches its peak and bursts into a red flare.

'I see it!' the coxswain shouts. The lifeboat heels over and throttles up to full power.

Abraham's seat pogoes on its mount, absorbing some of the shock. 'Listen up,' he says, raising his voice above the roar. 'I don't want *any*one putting themselves in danger. If that's *Huntsman's Daughter*, I'm first onboard. No one joins me without my say-so.'

A couple of the crew exchange looks. Then the navigator glances up from his radar display and lifts his binoculars. 'Got something,' he says. 'Two forty-one degrees.'

Abraham strains his eyes. All he sees is ocean and sky. He feels the boat marginally change course. When someone hands him binoculars he pans them across the horizon. And then he sees it: the shivery white outline of a yacht.

The Tamar bumps closer, eating up the waves. That faint shape resolves. Abraham realizes he's looking not at one yacht, but two.

The pain in his chest is a serpent constricting his lungs. He wants to take out his pills and toss a couple down his throat, but his seat is shifting so violently he's worried he'll choke.

'Two yachts, side by side,' the navigator says. 'Looks like one of them hit the other. Can't see anyone onboard either but . . . yeah . . . second boat's *Huntsman's Daughter*. And it looks like . . . it looks . . .'

The man's words trail off. Abraham knows why. He's staring at the same thing.

FIFTY-SIX

One, two, three . . .

Lucy hears engines now. The slap of a hull against flat sea. And, just about distinguishable, the distant chop of rotor blades. When she looks up, she can't locate the helicopter, but she does see Skentel's offshore lifeboat, thundering across the water.

They're too late.

They're far too late.

She's not sure if she has the fortitude to face what comes next. Doesn't think she can look at another human being again. Perhaps she should find something heavy, climb into the water and sink beneath the surface.

Because however hard she massages Fin's heart, however much air she breathes into him, she can tell that he's gone.

. . . twenty-eight, twenty-nine, thirty.

Breathe.

Breathe.

Nothing.

Dropping her hands to her thighs, she stares at her little boy; at his

334

cold face, his lost expression. A face that made her laugh, made her cry, that stirred in her a depth of feeling she hadn't believed possible.

Katharsis.

Purification through tragedy.

Lucy doesn't feel purified. She feels bereft.

Everything beautiful atrophies—or is torn down and destroyed before its time. A month ago, she had a life: a husband and two extraordinary children; a surfeit of love and laughter. At the time, it hadn't seemed perfect. Only now does she realize how close it came.

Luck blessed her. And now luck has taken everything: a magazine article in a Sunday supplement leading to a monster hunting her down.

The Tamar-class boat is far closer. When she turns, she sees a coast-guard helicopter growing in the southern sky.

Lucy raises herself off her haunches, bends over her son. Places her hands on his chest.

One . . . two . . . three . . .

But her strength has gone, her hope. Her star-gazing, card-sorting little bookworm has departed. A cruelty to keep trying to drag him back.

. . . four . . .

. . . five . . .

The lifeboat throttles down as it pulls up alongside *Huntsman's Daughter*. The yacht rocks violently in the wash. Lucy grabs a cleat and steadies herself. The helicopter is louder, closer, its turbine a steady whistle.

Someone lands on the deck, up towards the bow. Moments later a man kneels beside her. Lucy ignores him, keeps working on Fin. She's not ready to stop, not quite. She needs another minute before she can accept what's happened. '*Fifteen . . . sixteen . . .*'

The man beside her is Detective Inspector Abraham Rose. Crag-faced, ill-looking, solemn. Never has she seen such empathy. He places two enormous hands over her own and, with a gentleness belying his size, guides them away from Fin's chest.

FIFTY-SEVEN

1

The boy.

Ignoring the dead man hanging from the boom, Abraham leaps on to *Huntsman's Daughter* and climbs into the cockpit. There's Lucy Locke, ragged as a stray, soaked and shivering and desolate. And there, lying in front of her, is the reason why.

Abraham recognizes Fin in an instant. But gone is the little entertainer he saw on Lucy's phone. In his place is just a shell.

The sight is so tragic—so profoundly shocking—that he sinks down beside the mother. All he can think about is the boy with the bow tie. Fin Gordon Locke: weaver of words; teller of fine tales; storyteller extraordinaire.

'Once, there was a hunchbacked old man called Bogwort. Bogwort was very grumpy, because he believed everyone thought he was ugly, even though they didn't. What was so, so sad is that he could have had lots of friends if he hadn't made people nervous of him, and frightened of him too.

'But I don't want you to worry too much about that, because this isn't going to be one of those sad stories at all but one to cheer you up, cos you'll see that

336

actually in the end some nice things happened to Bogwort. Because he deserved it. And that's what people get if they're good.'

Beside him, Lucy Locke keeps counting, announcing each compression through teeth clenched against her loss.

Fin Locke didn't live long enough to learn life's toughest lessons. Perhaps that's a blessing. Because nice things, Abraham knows, *don't* happen to people because they deserve it. Sometimes—in fact, quite often—bad things happen, terrible things. Things just like this.

Silent, he puts his hands over Lucy's.

A few days ago, when he sought to comfort her, she flinched from his touch. She doesn't flinch now. Instead, her head bows. She sobs, once, a broken sound.

Abraham lifts Lucy's hands from her son's chest.

Closing his eyes, he recalls the anecdote a doctor once told him, about a cold and lifeless sailor pulled from the sea: *You're not dead until you're warm and dead.* That sailor went thirty minutes without a pulse before the medical team shocked him back to life. The cold water had chilled his blood, protecting his brain from fatal damage.

Putting his hands on Fin's chest, he begins to pump.

He knows he'll have to be brutal. Lucy's compressions, when he arrived, were far too delicate to do any good. Possibly because she'd run out of strength. Possibly because, unlike him, she's not one of God's blunt-edged tools.

Abraham shoves down on the boy's breastbone, compressing the chest a full five centimetres, cringing when he hears the crack of bone but not slowing.

He meets Lucy's saucer eyes. 'We'll do it together. You and me, side by side. When I finish the count, you breathe.'

She nods. He nods.

'Twenty-eight, twenty-nine, *thirty.*'

Lucy leans over, blows twice into Fin's lungs. The boy's chest inflates and sinks down.

Abraham continues to pump.

That anecdote about the sailor wasn't the only one the doctor shared. There was also the Spanish woman half frozen in a snowstorm, revived after six hours with a stopped heart. But that situation was completely different to this one. Abraham doesn't know how long Fin was in the water. Or how cold his blood.

'She asked me,' Lucy says. 'Before she died, Billie asked me what came next. I told her nothing did. She was looking for comfort and I didn't give it.'

'Twenty-eight, twenty-nine, *thirty*.'

Lucy bends to Fin's mouth, gives him two more breaths. When there's no response, Abraham carries on pumping.

'What kind of mother does that?' she asks. 'Daniel says she talked about me before the end. What if she remembered what I said?'

'Twenty-eight, twenty-nine, *thirty*.'

Abraham watches Lucy fill her son's lungs with air. He wants to offer her comfort but he can think of no words. And then he doesn't have to, because Fin Locke's hand twitches.

2

Lucy groans as if a plug has been pulled. She leans over her boy, her ear close to his lips. Abraham's eyes are on those fingers. It could have been a random muscle movement, could have been the yacht shifting beneath them.

With shocking suddenness, Fin's chest inflates. Life, rushing back. He gags, starts choking. 'Turn him over,' Abraham says. 'Get him on his side.'

The boy convulses, draws up his knees, half vomits and half coughs seawater. He takes another wheezing breath, blinks and screws up his face.

Abraham rolls his shoulders. He stands, staggers back, gives mother and son a little space. Lucy Locke's world, right now, extends to a radius of two feet—he belongs far outside it.

He tries to imagine what she's feeling, but he has no frame of reference. He won't complain. He's God's blunt-edged tool, formed at speed from the roughest clay to hand. Inelegant, uncivilized. Crudely and occasionally effective.

He's wrong about Lucy Locke, though. Her world extends a little further than he thought. Because she turns, just for a moment, and meets Abraham's gaze. Then she goes back to tending her son. It's enough. It's more than enough. He smiles at her, even though she can't see.

EPILOGUE

Penleith Beach. Summer.

In the flamingo light of dawn, the sea sucks tangerine crescents from the sand.

This early in the morning, Penleith Beach is entirely unspoilt. No tourists, no music, just the calls of gulls and guillemots as they wheel above the water.

To the south, the black rock of Mortis Point thrusts deep into the sea. Atop it, Lucy sees no evidence of her old home; the blackened wreckage has been entirely demolished and removed. She won't mourn it, won't allow herself to become maudlin over what was lost. She *can* see the bright yellow excavators that will continue their work in a few hours, preparing the foundations of their new home.

Crazy to think they could live up there again. And yet it's exactly what they plan to do.

Lucy has Abraham Rose to thank for that; one more thing on a long list. When she'd explained, back on land, that she'd torched the house to save Fin, he'd scowled at her and shook his head.

'*You* didn't burn it down, Lucy. I never want to hear you say that again.

In fact, I don't want you even *talking* about the fire, to anyone. It's too traumatic and you simply can't remember. That animal you euthanized started the blaze. You just wait a few weeks—I guarantee that's what the investigation will conclude. Certainly to the satisfaction of your insurance company. Do you understand me?'

She'd understood his look, certainly. A few weeks later, his words proved accurate.

Initially, the prospect of rebuilding their lives in Skentel had seemed unthinkable. How could she even countenance it after everything that had happened? Better to take Daniel and Fin and go somewhere far away.

But that would have handed Lucian Terrell a small victory, and there's no way in the world she could have allowed that. She'll live each day in defiance.

Everything he tried to destroy, Lucy will build back up. She'll pour so much love into Daniel and Fin that they'll glow like lanterns. She'll help her boy become the greatest, happiest and kindest human he can be. She'll rehabilitate her husband, too, from the horrors he experienced. Lucy knows the child growing in her belly, which so far remains her secret, will help.

The agony of Billie's passing won't fade, but she'll use that pain for good works. She'll strengthen the girl's legacy. And she won't stop.

Fortunately, she has an entire tribe—people whose lives Billie touched—who've vowed to help.

She talks of her daughter every day, to anyone prepared to listen, however stunning the pain. She tells stories about Billie to strangers and to those who knew the girl well. She writes down every anecdote, every tiny memory. She'll ensure the girl remains a blazing sun, radiating heat, for many decades to come. And she'll ensure Fin feels the presence of his older sister throughout his childhood and beyond.

She watches her son now, as he walks barefoot into the water. There's hardly any surf, just a soft lapping of the sea. Fin's wearing black shorts, a white shirt, his favourite velvet bow tie. He chose the outfit himself. At his insistence, the bow tie is extra-specially secure.

When he's up to his knees in water, he unscrews the urn he's been hugging and tilts it. Billie slides out as ash.

It's hard to watch. Lucy feels her chest quivering, her legs and her fingertips, too. Those soft grey grains—all that remains physically of her daughter—darken as they sink. Gradually, the ocean draws Billie from the shore. Fin upends the urn, shakes out the last ash. Then he reseals the lid.

Lucy hears him talking, but she doesn't catch the words. It's a private conversation between brother and sister. She wonders if Billie is listening.

At her side, Daniel pulls her close. She looks up, finds his eyes, wraps her arm around his waist. Fin wades from the water. He passes Daniel the empty urn and takes Lucy's hand. Already, father and son are stronger than they were. By the time she's finished, they'll be bulletproof.

They watch the sea for a while, all three of them, as Billie is carried away. Lucy closes her eyes, sending out a thought to follow Fin's words. Once she's done, she turns her family around.

Along the backshore, spread out across the dunes, is what seems like every resident of Skentel and its neighbouring communities all along this stretch of coast. She seeks out Jake Farrell, standing with his cane. The debt she owes him can never be repaid, but it's something else to work on. Because every day, in Billie's memory, she'll do good works.

Accompanying Jake are Noemie and Bee. Lucy sees Gordon and Jane Watson from the pharmacy, Wayland Rawlings from the hobby shop, Craig Clements and Alec Paul and Donahue O'Hare from the lifeboat station. Luke Creese has attended from St Peter's. Bill Shetland the harbour master stands beside Sean Rowland, the coastguard station officer. And then there's Ed, and all Billie's friends. Too many to name. Almost too many to count.

An entire tribe.

The only face she doesn't find belongs to Abraham Rose. The crag-faced detective died in the spring, taking his own life in advance of the cancer he believed was eating him. According to the note he left, he'd been too frightened to seek treatment or even confirm a diagnosis. The post-mortem found a serious but treatable lung condition—Abraham Rose was cancer-free.

Lucy went to the funeral. In the months since, she's learned as much about the man as she can. She's already pledged to make one person eternal. She's pretty sure she can manage two.

A whole life of good works awaits. At times the pain will be unbearable. But there's beauty in the world, a surfeit of it. Lucy can't wait to get started.

ACKNOWLEDGEMENTS

My huge thanks go to Frankie Gray, my editor at Transworld, who did lots of heavy lifting on this one. I'm also deeply indebted to Friederike Ney at Rowohlt in Germany.

Detective Inspector Dee Fielding provided advice, once again, on police procedure, for which I'm truly grateful. All mistakes or procedural shortcuts are, of course, my own stupid fault.

I owe massive thanks to Coxswain Lewis Creese at RNLI Angle, for patiently explaining the protocols of sea search and rescue, as well as the technical details of various lifeboats including the offshore Tamar-class, which he operates. Lewis even provided interior photographs when I couldn't visit in person due to Covid restrictions. Luke and Jacob, your dad is a true hero.

Coxswain Martin Cox at RNLI Appledore offered similarly invaluable help, including insights into sea conditions and weather patterns close to the location of my fictional town. Martin also operates the all-weather Tamar-class lifeboat, of which I'm now a self-confessed fanboy.

There can be few things more frightening than encountering

difficulties at sea. In 2019 alone, RNLI volunteer lifeboat crews in the UK and Ireland aided 9,379 people. Shore-based RNLI lifeguards aided a further 29,334. Together, they saved 374 people who would otherwise have been lost.

Since its inception, over 600 RNLI volunteers have sacrificed their lives in service. We owe them, and those currently serving, our immense gratitude.

More information about the charity, including ways to donate, can be found at www.rnli.org.

ABOUT THE AUTHOR

Sam Lloyd grew up in Hampshire, where he learned his love of storytelling. These days he lives in Surrey with his wife, three young sons and a dog that likes to howl. His debut thriller, *The Memory Wood*, was published to huge critical acclaim in 2020. *The Rising Tide* is his second thriller.